Standing on the Edge of Life

Stuart Lee

ISBN: 9798333397270

To my boys – for without you, there would be no life

Prologue

Martin was standing on the precipice of his own life. He'd visualised this scene hundreds of times in his head, fantasised about it even. But now, where he was, quite literally standing on the edge and waiting for his body to make the next move, Martin was motionless and empty. The visions he'd had didn't quite match this experience. It had been so easy in his head. Strategic, process driven and planned – just like his whole life had been in the time leading up to this moment.

The plan had been simple. He could've walked it, but he would drive his car over to the old National Trust car park. Reverse into the space at the foot of the oak tree. Pay the parking fee (I'm still respectful to others, if not myself, he thought), lock the car, make the 375-yard walk over to the clearing, clamber through the damaged fence and casually drop down into the gorge below.

Easy, thought Martin.

But now that the gaping gorge was staring right back at him, Martin was unsure. His unnaturally empty head and stone stiff body was not responding to the task he had meticulously planned for the days, weeks and months that had led up to now.

Was there more to life than Martin had led himself to believe? Was this really the dignified end to a life that could be so full of joy and happiness? Of prosperity? Of kindness and opportunity? Martin didn't really possess any of those words in his vocabulary, or at least he didn't think so. He'd convinced himself so much of his lack of worth and his complete sense of nothingness to others. He felt like a face in the crowd that could quite easily melt away like some pathetic snowman in the sun which would then just absorb himself into the earth, never to return. Nobody would notice. Nobody would care. And certainly, nobody would miss Martin.

This shameful existence he had branded himself with was about to end.

Chapter 1

3 weeks previous

'If I win the lottery, I tell you what – I'd be on the first fucking flight out of here,' announced George. Martin would tend to disagree with that. He hated flying and didn't really like foreign food.

'This country is full of tossers and the weather is absolute shite,' he continued. 'When are people going to realise that if you keep voting for pricks, you'll eventually to turn into one. And I ain't gonna be around for that to happen mate, no way.'

George had been Martin's best friend since their school days. They were a funny pair in some ways. Martin, the intelligent and hard-working pupil who his classmates would describe as slightly 'different,' but completely harmless. George however, was the icon of everything that any teenage boy would've wanted to be. Handsome, confident, clever (but lazy with it) and dangerously popular with both male and female counterparts. The reason these two actually became friends is because Martin saved George's life, (although the former used to argue that sounded very dramatic). During a Year 8 science class, George was showing off to a group of girls (or whoever he could impress) and inadvertently swallowed a pen lid as he rocked away on an old creaking stool in science lab 93B.

As classmates roared at the hilarity of George tumbling down, the joy was quickly replaced with horror as he cracked his head upon the floor and was now choking in distress.

As George's designated lab partner at the time, Martin had been diligently getting on with work and was used to ignoring the class cameos that George provided during third period Chemistry. But now that he saw a colleague in peril, he acted quickly and methodically by dislodging the pen lid from George's throat by using the Heinrich manoeuvre that he'd seen practised on Blue Peter a couple of years ago. But for a small pool of blood and disgusting saliva, George was fine, if not a little shocked at his own actions. In this moment he felt eternally indebted to Martin and quite often described the event as a 'life saving moment.'

'Do you remember that day when you saved my life? That dozy cow Mrs Biggs wasn't gonna do anything about it. I'm glad you were around,' said George.

Martin always felt embarrassed when George brought up this memory from the past. He wasn't heroic in any way shape or form, he thought.

'Yeah, but I only did what I had to do, how could I possibly let the most popular lad in school choke on a pen lid?' replied Martin.

'Speaking of Mrs Biggs, I saw her daughter the other week. She's still fit mind you.'

This was very typical of George. To change the conversation and talk about girls or football or anything else he knew he was good with, or at.

'Who, Carla Biggs? Is she still with Robbie whats-his-name?' asked Martin, who in truth wasn't really that interested.

'Nah, they broke up ages ago when he went off and shagged some Geordie bird in Benidorm,' George replied. He seemed to know the ins and outs of everything. Whether true or not, he always had some kind of theory or the answer to most questions.

Martin looked into his drink and swilled the bottom of his pint looking disinterested. 'You okay, Mart?' asked George.

'Yeah, just tired,' Martin replied. This was a lie.

Well, it was somewhat true, as Martin had not slept well for weeks (for various reasons) but it was not the full reason for his lack of contribution to the evening. Martin was severely depressed. He was unhappy in his own skin. He hated himself, but he also lacked the courage to admit that. It had been another lousy Christmas, he was estranged from his parents and the only person he saw outside of work these days was George, and that wasn't very often either.

'Let me get you another one mate, my round,' offered George.

'Uh... Yeah. Yeah alright. Cheers G,' said Martin, who was slightly lifted by the fact that after all these years, George still wanted to spend time with him.

George disappeared with the pint glasses clutched in his hands and gave Martin a friendly squeeze on the shoulder. George was one of those men who could sense unease in people and would always do something to provide comfort or show encouragement in the best way he could. Just in this small act, it showed Martin that he cared about his friend, but wasn't necessarily willing to sit down and talk about it. That would just be darn right uncomfortable for the pair of them. But at least Martin knew he cared. Maybe George would miss him if he was gone?

The pub was busy that night, for a Wednesday anyway. There must've been a party or a wake or something that had spilled over into evening. The Hilltop Arms (or, 'The Hilly') was that type of pub that would morph itself into any occasion – a real centre for the community. Family do's, pub quizzes, local tennis club Christmas drinks, Friday night piss-ups, whatever. Martin looked at the smartly dressed group across the room. It looked like a wake with all the black ties and sombre dress code. He wondered how many people would turn up at his funeral if he were to have one, let alone the wake in the local boozer. The reality is, he would never be able to know the answer to that question and the thought deeply consumed him while he waited for George to return to the table. He could surmise at the very least though.

'They've run out of that fruity IPA you like Mart, so I got you a pint of bitter. Is that alright?' George said, as if appearing from nowhere, which snapped Martin from his daydream.

'Yeah, thanks mate, that's fine,' Martin replied, but he couldn't care less really. He wasn't a big drinker by any means, but he could certainly handle the booze better than his friend could. Maybe alcohol was the way out? He thought darkly to himself for a moment. These intrusive thoughts were getting more common. No, he had the plan in place already and pushed down the additional musings inside himself and returned to the room again.

'So, anyway. Some dickhead Tory turns up at my house the other day and starts giving me the bullshit about voting for that muppet McClair. Did you know he once got done for sniffing coke in Parliament?' George said.

Martin wasn't paying much attention but nodded along to George's anecdote, which turned out he politely took the leaflet from the local Conservative campaigner on his doorstep and pretended to wipe his arse with it before handing it back to her. George loved opportunities like that. Anything to gain a reaction or create a bit of controversy.

'So then I shut the door in her face… you should've seen the look she gave me. It was fucking fantastic.'

Martin sipped his pint and wished he had the confidence to do something as daring as that. He'd always wondered what life would be like for him if he made some kind of big statement, or simply started just being a bit more of a George. The biggest statement of all that he could make was equally terrifying as well as it was intriguing. The thought of carrying out his plan was really growing on him day by day.

'Christ Mart, you must be tired tonight, you've hardly said a word!' George had snapped Martin out of his daze again.

'I know mate yeah, it's been a bit of a full on week already. Got this nightmare client up in Hereford who is being a right pain in the ass about planning,' lied Martin.

The truth is, Martin did have a client up in Hereford, but the client was no trouble at all. In fact, Mr and Mrs Longmore were quite the opposite and had been very impressed with Martin's work in getting their eco-barn conversion drawings completed. But Martin didn't want to lose face and admit his troubles, let alone draw any attention to himself that he'd done a good job – it just simply wasn't his style.

By day, Martin was an architect, having studied Architecture at Cardiff University and coming out with first class honours. George had gone to 'the other' University in Cardiff to do sports marketing or something like that. He was a recruitment consultant now, which he was very good at – being the handsome and charming individual that he was.

'Ah mate, tell me about it. I'd have the best job in the world if it wasn't for clients. Absolute pain in the ass all the time and taking fucking liberties of me,' George said.

Thankfully the conversation turned to George's work and Martin didn't really have to contribute much from here on in until he was surprised that he'd finished his drink and felt ready to leave. George was clearly thinking the same as he motioned for his coat.

'Right mucker,' said George. 'I will love you and leave you now. Let me know how you get on tomorrow with those old codgers. If you're around next week give me a shout and perhaps we'll grab a lunchtime pint or something.'

'Yeah, okay – thanks mate. Cheers for the drink, I'll catch you in a bit,' replied Martin. He wondered whether he'd be around at lunchtime next week, let alone at all.

George got up and gave Martin a wink with a thumbs up and made his way to the door. Martin just wished that sometimes he could open up about his internal struggles. He desperately wanted to burst the banks of his mind and flood anyone who would listen with his insecurities, letting loose a genuine voice for his self-loathing internal monologue. It was exhausting really, trying to conceal hatred for oneself. He often wondered how he had got here, but always struggled to pinpoint any particular moment in time that may have been a trigger. But none of that mattered now anyway. He'd made up his mind of how to release himself from the mental trauma.

'Martin?'

He was snapped out of his daze for at least the third time that evening. 'Yes?' he replied.

'How are you? It's Ruth… remember? From Uni?' said the tall, attractive girl now standing over him at the table. 'Are you leaving?' she said.

'Oh um, yes… I mean, no? I don't know. I mean, I was going to, but, yes. How are you?' Martin stumbled over his reply and instantly blushed.

'Well, I'm sticking around for another hour or so, most of that lot are pissed,' she said, pointing over to the smartly dressed group of men propping up the bar, who were the party that Martin assumed were at a wake.

'Okay, sure. Can I get you a drink?' Martin asked. 'Yeah, I'll have a glass of red please,' replied Ruth.

Martin nodded as he got up to go towards the bar and inadvertently banged his knee against the table.

'Oh, sorry, ow. Be right back,' he said, blushing further. Ruth smirked. This was why he hated himself he thought. Why am I so awkward? Why can't I just be normal? He was panicking now too because he didn't drink or know anything about red wine and he was too embarrassed to ask Ruth what it was she wanted in particular. Shit, he thought. Yet another reason. Why don't I just ask her? He wrestled with the internal monologue all the way to the bar, all the while during the wait and even at the point of ordering.

'Can I have a pint of bitter and umm, a... glass of red please?' he was hoping the request was generic enough that the barman would simply just abide, which he was grateful for when no further questions were asked. Martin made a note to himself. Get to know wines or other drinks potential dates might like. Not that Ruth was a date. He hated himself for thinking that. 'That was a little bit presumptuous wasn't it mate!' he said to himself internally. Oh God no, I didn't mean it like that, I meant for the next time. 'Next time? What next time? You've not had a date or a proper girlfriend in 6 years! When is there going to be a next time!.' He was right. It was very likely that there wasn't going to be a next time.

Martin would quite regularly beat himself up like this. It was no surprise when the barman caught him off guard staring blindly across the counter.

'£12.60 please mate,' he said.

Martin was still fighting his internal demon, but silently handed over his card for payment.

'Want the receipt?' said the barman, tearing off the small bit of paper and motioning towards Martin, as equally dead eyed and non-committal to this exchange as he was.

'No, thanks,' replied Martin and the barman disappeared to serve another customer without even a nod.

Ruth was looking at her phone when Martin returned with the drinks. She was probably texting her boyfriend, he thought. 'Here ya go, hope that's alright?' he said, putting the drink down next to her.

'Great, thanks,' replied Ruth, setting her phone down and resting her elbows on table with her chin resting on the top of her hands. Martin assumed she had had plenty to drink already if the rest of her party were anything to go by.

'What brings you back here anyway?' asked Martin.

'Well, my cousin sadly passed recently. He got himself into one hell of a state apparently. After his divorce, things kind of spiralled and next thing, his mate finds him hanging from the rafters in the garage. Really sad,' explained Ruth. She was never uncomfortable in declaring details and was generally one of those people who would chat to whoever would listen. Martin looked deep in thought for a moment. A million questions circled his brain but every single one felt as inappropriate as the next, especially to someone who had just lost a family member. He withheld any thoughts he had for now and just stared blankly across at Ruth for what felt like an uncomfortable amount of time.

'So… it's been a while hasn't it?' she changed the conversation, sensing the awkwardness. 'Yeah… I guess like, 12 or 13 years?'

Martin knew exactly how long, it was the kind of information he didn't forget.

'So what have you been doing with yourself? Do you still live locally?' He knew the answer to these questions already because otherwise he would've seen her. Oh and Facebook of course. Everyone has a snoop on Facebook these days.

'I stayed in Cardiff for a bit after Uni and did a bit of bar work,' said Ruth, 'But after a year or so I moved up to Nottingham for a job, which is where I met my boyfriend.'

Martin's heart sank. He didn't know why, because he hadn't seen Ruth for over a decade and had only seen her now for around ten minutes, so why was he disappointed that she had a boyfriend? It wasn't as if he was competing or anything. He hated himself for thinking that.

'...but me and him aren't together anymore,' continued Ruth. 'Which is why I moved back down here for a bit to sort myself out. After furlough, I was laid off permanently so was just – sponging around – his words, not mine.'

Martin felt a renewed sense of hope. He'd always got on well with Ruth and they clearly had some common ground because of their University days.

'Oh, I'm sorry to hear that,' he replied, 'are you looking to work in architecture again, or is it time for big change? I could see what's going at my firm if you like.'

'Well, we'll see how things go I guess. My ex is still being a right knobhead about the flat we bought together so I've got a bit to sort out up in Notts, but as soon as that's done, I'd like to move back around here.'

Martin didn't really want to pry on why Ruth and her now ex-boyfriend had gone their separate ways, but he was somewhat buoyed by the fact that this was the case. The pair talked about their University days for an hour or so and Martin was at ease for the first time in a while, talking comfortably and getting a laugh or two out of Ruth. He could be quite charming sometimes. Being George's friend must've had some kind of impact on him in that respect.

In the background, a glass smashed to the floor and the group of smartly dressed men appeared to be creating some sort of commotion. There was a lot of 'woah, woah woahs,' and 'easy Mike, steady now,' as 'Mike' gently let his legs buckle underneath him and fell to the floor while in the clutches of his fellow drunkards.

'Oh God, it's Uncle Mike. He was pissed hours ago,' said Ruth, 'I'm surprised he even lasted this long. I'd better go and see.'

Bloody Uncle Mike, thought Martin. Ruining a good bit of chat, the tosser. Ruth scurried over to the scene of drunk men and talked to them for a moment before returning to Martin.

'I think they're going to make a move now,' she said, collecting her things. 'I'm meant to be staying at my Uncle's and he's in no fit state to find his own way home.'

'Yeah, sure no problem,' replied Martin. 'Do you need a hand or anything?'

'I think we'll be ok. Auntie Val is just going to get the car so we'll manage. Thanks anyway.'

Martin was moving uncomfortably in his seat, or at least he felt like he was. He was itching to ask Ruth the golden question, it felt like the right thing to do in the moment.

'Howaboutmeetingupsometimesoon?' the words raced out his mouth at phenomenal speed, and were hardly audible. In fact, he wasn't even sure why the words had escaped his being.

'Sure, I don't know when I'll be around but you've got my Facebook, right?' Martin knew damn sure that he did.

'Yeah, I think so. We'll stay in touch.'

Ruth walked away and mouthed a 'goodbye' before rolling her eyes ironically as if to say 'he's always bloody like this,' while she and another man hoisted the bedraggled Uncle Mike out through the pub door. Martin sat motionless for a moment before getting his coat on and leaving too.

In a way, he didn't know why he had asked her. It wasn't like he was planning for the future right now. But perhaps it was just a spur of the moment kind of thing, it had felt like the done thing to do.

'Oh well,' he thought. 'I'll probably never see her ever again.'

Chapter 2

For the most part, Martin had enjoyed life. Or so he thought. He'd never really thought about whether he was actually enjoying life or not, he was just simply living it. Go to school, do exams, get to uni, get a degree, get a job, meet someone (hopefully), get married, have kids, etc etc. Except, Martin had got around 50% through what he thought the generic and socially acceptable life plan should be, but he now felt like he was floundering horribly. In truth, he wasn't, but his mind had allowed him to believe that where he was right now, was not where he should be. Helena was always telling him to plan. Plan, plan, plan. She always seemed to have a plan, but Martin didn't really act like he wanted to be a part of it. He wanted his own plans, his own destiny, but he just couldn't vocalise that so just carried on with the status quo – which was always somebody else's plan for life, whether Helena's or society's.

The break-up with her had been untidy, if nothing else. He resented her for that. Why couldn't things just have been okay? Martin had been bumbling along with the outline life plan for a long period and he was broadly happy with the relationship. It seemed like he and Helena were close to the next step.

He'd never really thought about proposing, but in the days that lead up to Helena's 30th, Martin thought he would take the risk and do something unbelievably romantic to surprise her. A ring. But not just any ring, a diamond one. The ones that get presented and are usually followed by a simple 'yes' by the recipient. Sadly for Martin though, he didn't even get the chance to present his showpiece gift that he'd managed to conceal in the days prior. Perhaps he hadn't seen the signs? Not just on the night of her thirtieth birthday, but in the weeks and months leading up to it. It was an impulsive thing to do on his part, he hadn't planned it per se. Perhaps he was just too preoccupied and nervous with just simply doing it that he didn't notice the offish nature that Helena had about her? The fact that she spent most of the evening ogling at her phone, or that she was quite happy to skip the dessert. Or even get home as quickly as possible, These were all red flags that Martin had failed to heed.

Surely Martin should've noticed all this by the time the pair arrived home though? A silent taxi journey through town and up to the doorstep of number 19 Meadvale Rise. But no. Far from it in fact. Approximately 37 minutes after arriving home from the birthday meal, Helena was leaving in her Fiat 500 with a rucksack and a ringless finger. Martin would later protest, but on this particular night, he was silent and nowhere near capable of protestation.

He was crushed.

Chapter 3

11 years previous

It was 5.07am. The bag drop queue at London Stanstead was full of excitable 'lads' and hen party going 40-somethings clad in very little apart from fancy dress. A bemused elderly couple were buried in the melee and staring straight ahead, not talking, unsmiling and praying they make it in one piece to their timeshare by 3 o' clock that afternoon.

Martin was in one of the excitable lad groups. Not a vocal member by any means, but physically he was there, if not mentally. He didn't really fit the mould of the group and was only there by association with George. It was indeed George who got him the invite because their other friend Ollie Sayers had managed to write-off his Dad's Ford Mondeo and therefore couldn't afford the annual European piss-up trip. It was Corfu where they were headed, the Greek island that Martin had frequented with his parents when he was growing up. However, the destination on the island this time was the party resort of Kavos. Once a small and sleepy fishing village on the south coast of Corfu, it had gradually been taken over – mainly by British boozers – all of whom were hell bent on two things: drink as much as humanly possible and shag anything that moved.

Martin felt nervous and was probably showing it. Dead pan, pale and motionless. Much like the elderly couple, he was facing straight ahead, undeterred by the noise around him. In truth, he'd have probably preferred to be staying in the timeshare with Mr and Mrs Walters for the next fortnight. Oh Christ. A fortnight! Who books a fucking fortnight with the intention of getting pissed every night? He thought to himself.

'Passport please,' said the lady at the check-in desk.

Martin was surprised that he'd just been gently carried along with the group and now found himself suddenly at the front. 'Oh, erm... yeah, yes,' he replied, handing over his passport.

She looked at him while checking the details of his flight.

'Bag on the scales please,' she said, as Martin hoisted his bag up onto the conveyor.

He was worried at this point that he may have over-packed in his panic about not wearing the same outfit twice during the holiday. Why did he beat himself up over this? He'd spent at least 4 hours last night checking and re-checking that there were enough different combinations of clothes to see him through. God forbid that anyone saw him wearing the same thing twice! He knew this was stupid and hated himself for it. None of the other lads seemed at all bothered. Not least the group of barely eighteen year-olds behind him who were wearing shiny gold hot pants and sleeveless vests with the words 'young, dumb and full of cum' emblazoned on the back. What a repulsive thought that was. And yet, Martin thought, they will still end up getting with more girls than he would even dare speak to. Why was there not a place for someone like him? Did women not like the sensitive approach? Or were they only hell bent on getting fucked by all the brainless morons also heading to this ghastly resort?

'Thank you, Sir,' the lady behind the check-in desk said, in a tone that suggested she had already said it more than once while Martin had been stood there, seemingly miles away from reality at that moment.

'Oh, yes. Thanks,' and he wandered off to join his group now heading to security.

The boisterous nature of the departure lounge at the airport was not one that Martin favoured.

'Here ya go, Mart. Get that down ya,' said George, who excitedly handed a frothy pint of lager over the table. 6.13am and he was drinking the worlds worst pint in what felt like the worlds worst place. Why hadn't he plucked up the courage to say 'no thanks, I don't want one' or 'no' in the first place to actually going on the holiday he quite clearly detested more than himself right now. In a way, he wanted to reward George some loyalty and show that he could be like some of his other mates. Was that even what Martin wanted? He wasn't actually sure, but he was confused in his mind about what he saw himself as, let alone what he wanted to be.

'Thanks mate,' replied Martin, as George shot him a wink and turned back to the group. Martin was sat on the periphery at a high table, which was equally sticky as it was uncomfortable. He gazed across the airport bar. If he didn't know any better he would've said it was 8.30pm in the Hilly on a Friday night. Alas, it was now 6.30am on a Tuesday morning and he had made absolutely zero progress with the dreadful pint of lager that stared back at him. There was probably more life in the lager than there was inside him right now, even though it looked completely devoid of taste, flavour and verve. Only 45 minutes until boarding he thought. If he could nurse this for another 40 then at least he wouldn't have to get another one in, as the group knew he was steady, if not the quickest of drinkers.

With boarding safely negotiated, they were finally on the plane and Martin was pleased he could have a bit of respite from the group.

Incidentally, he had been bundled into an aisle seat with the older couple from the bag drop for company. At least he could look forward to some nice quiet time to himself during the flight, which would be 4 hours or so.

Within minutes though, this vision had been dashed, as a group of screeching 'hens' made their way towards his row. And then more, then more. He and Mr and Mrs Walters were now engulfed by pink cowboy hats, logoed sashes and generally a lot of noise.

'Hey, lads look!' called a voice from down the plane. 'Mart has hit the jackpot here mind!' It was Dean Parsons who had reared his head up like an excited little meerkat from at least ten rows further down when he saw the women taking their seats in and around him. With that, the other seven lads in Martin's holiday group (including George) poked their heads up with a huge chorus of 'wheeeeeeeeeeeeey, GO ON MART!' while they motioned and mouthed obscenities at him. Obviously, this drew some attention from the girls who turned to look at him and he instantly turned bright red. The main reason being, that it genuinely looked like he was sat with his parents. A sad and pathetic 24-year-old going on holiday with his elderly parents, while every other twenty-something was there having a great time with friends. Oh God, they would actually think that wouldn't they? That he'd gone away with his friends but that his parents had to come with him because they wanted to keep an eye on their precious son. Fuck sake, thought Martin. Why me, why again? His only choice was to sit there and bear it.

Martin hated flying as it was, so was grateful when the captain declared that it was time to get seated and ensure that passengers had their belts on. It had been a bumpy flight to say the least. Not just the turbulence, but the constant noise and shaking of his seat from the occupants behind. The most pleasure he'd enjoyed on this trip so far was the seatbelt light coming on, so that now 'Jen's hens' could no longer treat the plane like it was a school bus from the 90's. They'd been giggling ferociously and shooting opportunistic looks at various groups of lads for the last 3 hours. Martin wouldn't have been surprised if one of them was blowing out bubblegum or trying to steal out for a cheeky cigarette in the toilets. In a way, he wished one of them would do that because that would see off the lot of them, including him.

Chapter 4

Morale was still high between George and his friends, but less so Martin, as he felt like he was being metaphorically dragged through hell. After an hour or so on a swelteringly hot coach, they arrived at the resort. It was hot, dusty, dirty and loud. Oh, how Martin wished he had exchanged details with Mr and Mrs Walters on the flight right now.

Thankfully, Martin was roomed with George, so at least he'd be able to talk to him one on one at some point during the trip and not feel like he was totally alone. After settling into their rooms, it was decided they would meet up in the hotel bar at 5.00pm. This was going to be one hell of a long night Martin thought, surely things don't usually kick off in these resorts until at least midnight? Be that as it may, highly fuelled on testosterone and copious amounts of sugary cocktails, 5.00pm soon became 10.00pm and it was time to venture into town. Night had drawn in and the streets were lit up with a mix of tacky glowing signage and gobby bar reps trying to get people into their bars. It had actually been quite fun for the few hours at the hotel, just having a few casual drinks and laughs with George and the rest of them. Martin had even loosened up a bit as a result. But now, this was different. What was happening now, was pressure. It was outside the comfort blanket of a group of friends and into the wild. He immediately began to hate every single moment from there on in and withdrew whatever good nature had been built up a few hours ago.

'Right. In here lads. I've sorted a free shot each and half price drinks for an hour. So get stuck in!' announced George, who it seemed that his negotiating skills covered beyond the usual realms of recruitment for various construction roles. To be fair to George, he'd done alright though. The atmosphere was okay, it wasn't too busy and although the music was not to his taste, Martin could at least enjoy half price drinks and get himself back in the mood at least.

But by about 1.47am Martin was done. He was absolutely dog tired from being up so early and although the amount of alcohol he had consumed was considerable, he'd got to a point where it just wasn't worth it anymore. He decided to call it a night and went over to George to tell him he'd be heading back so that he could leave a key out. Not that George would really have noticed. He was a picture of pure lad fantasy right now. Surrounded by drunk girls with his T-shirt tied to his belt loops, he had alcopops in both hands, a neon style Hawaiian garland round his neck and novelty sunglasses resting on his head. There may have even been a whistle in his mouth. Martin decided not to bother him, so found one of the other lads, Cameron Stacey, who was eating the face off of another girl in the corner. The pair of them looked as if they would disappear into each other throats if this carried on much longer.

'Cam. Cam... Cam!' shouted Martin.

'Oh, alright Mart,' replied Cameron with a hazy, yet content look of success on his face. 'I'm off Cam, can you tell George I'll leave a key out for him,' said Martin.

'No probs mate,' he replied, while slowly launching himself in for another round of tongue twister.

Whether George would ever get the message, Martin would highly doubt. Nevertheless, he made his way out of the nightclub and back onto the strip. The night was still buzzing and the low drone of bass lines thumped out from every bar and club he walked past. Groups of girls and boys stumbled around, laughing and bantering – having a good time. Martin walked through the crowds, both hands in pockets, expressionless. He must've looked like a dying flower amongst a garden of burgeoning plants compared to all the other twenty-somethings that were spilling out from all angles around him. By his own standards, he'd had a good time tonight, he thought to himself. But he just couldn't let himself go. That extra 20 or 30% of himself that was holding back, that wasn't relaxing and that was always conscious of saying the wrong thing or looking the wrong way. The 'wrong' was a barometer of Martin's own design. What he felt would be 'wrong' to transmit from himself or show to others. He hated the constant wrestling in his mind of what this should be, which is why in reality what he usually ended up portraying is that he was uptight, serious or just simply disinterested. The actual reality was that he was probably all these things, but most of all, he was miserable and hated himself, inside and out.

Martin wasn't hungry but thought it was probably best to try and eat something, so he plumped for a KFC. He was wary of foreign food and at least KFC was a global brand that he could only assume had some sort of framework for their food retailing. After all, wasn't the colonel's secret recipe under lock and key? He hoped they had managed to locate the key in order to bring it out this far into the world, he thought to himself.

Inevitably there was a queue, but Martin was in no rush so was happy to wait. Revellers were spilling out from the counter, laden with greasy bags and boxes of chicken and chips. It was like filthy animals getting their feed at the trough, getting their fill and returning to their mucky habitats.

Most were too inebriated to fathom their surroundings, stumbling around like idiotic robots programmed to act like a hideous mess. Martin was due to become one of these shortly, but at least he had a certain element of control over his body. Unlike the 20-stone lad who was so unsteady on his feet that he snapped his flip flop, slipped forwards and went tumbling into a pile of stacked chairs, causing security to rush over nearly as quick as the rate of processed chicken was being cooked just metres away. In the midst of the commotion, another row was breaking out between a group of girls and a couple of lads. Martin couldn't fully fathom what it was about, but clearly these lads had upset one, if not all the girls that were crowded together by something that had been said. They probably rejected him, thought Martin. The atmosphere was becoming slightly more tense as the volume of the argument rose further. Everyone was now aware of what was going on and starting to accept that it definitely wasn't okay.

'Ey, ey, ey, ey, ey!,' called a man from behind the counter, 'Out! You! Go! Out!' The calls were ignored and it seemed like whoever these lads were they couldn't give a monkeys about whether someone manning a counter of fried chicken was telling them to get out. For reasons completely unbeknown to himself, it was Martin who spoke up next. Whether he'd found some confidence from somewhere or just genuinely didn't like what he was seeing, he found the courage to say,

'Come on lads, leave it.'

No matter how brave it was in the moment, he knew how weak and pathetic it sounded. These lads were in a rage now. They looked mean, they looked wired and they probably weren't strangers to the odd scrap. Fuck sake, thought Martin, as soon as the last word escaped his lips.

'What did you say? Fockin' Romeo ova ere,' replied the first lad in a thick scouse accent. 'Think youra tough man d'ya?' he continued, now sidling over to Martin.

Oh for fuck's sake Martin thought to himself, why didn't he just keep his mouth shut. He felt hot with self-consciousness and anxiety had overwhelmed his body. The bravery of around five seconds previous had disappeared in a flash. He was now face to face with an angry, drunk and unreasonable twenty-something who had clearly been looking for trouble. His eyes must've lit up when Martin chimed in. Fucking hell, fresh meat – an easy target, primed for a good hiding. All the guy needed was an excuse, no matter how insignificant. With security still having their hands full with the fallen oaf in the corner, Martin was pretty exposed right now. Whether anyone would jump to his aid, he thought unlikely.

'Come on then pal, what didya say? Too fockin' scared now are we?' he bounded upon Martin and shoved him against the wall. Heads were turning now as a new commotion was happening. The fat lad with broken flip flop still lay stricken, but he would get a reprieve. Not that he had really done much wrong apart from fall over, but the security guards attention was now on the angsty lad who had Martin pinned up and cornered. By the time they got to him, Martin was already falling to the floor having taken a headbutt square on the nose. Fucking hell that hurt. He was temporarily not there, almost in a trance. But when he came to, the lads were gone. They'd possibly scarpered, or better still, were getting a hiding from the Greek authorities. Martin looked up through hazy eyes.

'Are you okay?' said the girl looking down at him. His nose hurt like hell, but thankfully he didn't think it was broken or bleeding too much.

'Um... yeah, I, uh... guess so?' replied Martin. 'Can I get you anything?' the girl asked again.

'I could do with some... um, ice if that's... if that's okay? Thanks,' said Martin, who was still a little bit bewildered. He'd only come in for a two-piece meal and a diet coke and next minute he's lying flat out on the cold greasy tiles of KFC in Kavos. It was only the first night of fourteen! What an escalation.

'Here you go,' said the girl, returning moments later with a bag of ice for Martin to administer to his war wound. 'I'm Helena, by the way. Sorry about those guys. They've been hassling us all week to be honest. It's about time someone said something.'

'No problem... sorry I couldn't... do more. I guess.'

Helena smiled. She had kind eyes, thought Martin. Though he wasn't 100% sure what or who he was looking at in all honesty. He slowly got to his feet as Helena pulled out a chair for him to sit on. The drama was over, revellers were back to queuing for their food. Apart from the odd comment and look, Martin wasn't getting much attention, which he was happy about. The last thing he wanted was attention, he hated the spotlight being on him no matter what the occasion. Thankfully, seeing someone with a bleeding nose at 2.00am in KFC wasn't actually that surprising. For most in fact, it seemed totally normal.

'I think you ought to get that looked at by the way, um... what's your name, sorry?' asked Helena.

'Oh, yes sorry... it's Martin. And yes, perhaps I should. Although I'd rather not be going to a hospital here. Look at the state of this place,' he replied.

'It's okay, there's a medical centre next door,' said Helena. She was right, of course. A medical centre was literally the next door down from KFC. What a place, thought Martin.

Within 30 minutes or so, Martin was checked and on his way into the night again. A few paper stitches and some cotton wool to help curtail the blood. As suspected, it wasn't broken or fractured and he could only think his luck must've come in to have avoided that. The night was dying down now as the time neared 3.00am. He wanted to thank Helena for all her support and accompanying him to the medical centre but he didn't want to seem creepy or anything. She'd already been harassed enough by the sounds of things and would likely just reject any advance, no matter how polite. He wrestled with this for a moment while they walked in the general direction of his hotel.

'So, where are you staying?' he asked.

'Oh, just up here at the Lefkimi. Don't judge. It was a last-minute thing. I wouldn't have chosen somewhere so close to all the nightlife but, hey. That's what a last-minute booking is all about, right?' explained Helena.

Martin nodded in agreement.

'We're at the Olympion Village. It's actually alright for this place to be honest,' he admitted. They walked on a little bit further in silence, almost waiting for each other to speak again.

'This is me,' said Helena, as they arrived outside her hotel. 'Thanks for your help tonight,' said Martin, 'I really appreciate it.'

'You're welcome. It wasn't like anyone else was going to,' she said with a wry smile.

Martin smiled back. Perhaps he was overthinking this next bit – he usually was overthinking – but he really wanted to see what Helena was doing tomorrow. He had taken quite nicely to her over the course of the last two hours. But would she think he was just after one thing? Wasn't everyone in this hell hole after one thing? Unless it was to fight of course, in which he had absolutely no interest in being involved in something like that again. He had no problem in opening his mouth earlier to protect Helena and her friends so why not just go for it and see what she was up to tomorrow?

'I uh, umm… better be off now,' he said, 'thanks again Helena.'

'Look after yourself Martin. Good night,' and she leaned up to give him a small kiss on the cheek. Before Martin could react, she was gone.

Chapter 5

When Martin arrived back at the room that night he found George already in bed. Well, to say in bed would be stretching it slightly. George was laid face down on the bed, with the only article of clothing still on his body being his right sock. How he had got there, God only knew. Today wasn't really going to be a day for much movement, thought Martin. It was already 12.30pm and he had little to show for it apart from a sore nose and a dry throat. All he could think about was Helena and what he should've said to her. Why hadn't he just plucked up the courage to ask if she wanted to meet? Or at a minimum, find out when and where she was flying home? He put his head in his hands, angry at himself for not acting on impulse in the moment. Ironically, the moment he did act on impulse during the night, he ended up getting a headbutt to the face. He regretted that. Fucking hell, he thought. Why me? Just learn from this Martin, for Christ's sake. He was beating himself up again for, well, not a lot really. But his self-loathing monologue was one that was hard to keep under wraps, especially when he knew a lot of what happened could've been avoided had he approached things differently.

George rolled over, opening one eye very slightly and painfully.

'Ohhhhhhh Jesus,' he moaned, then said something unintelligible which was muffled into the pillow. 'Morning mate,' said Martin,

'Good night?'

George rolled over and just blew out his cheeks while staring at the ceiling with his left hand on his forehead.

'It's like a fucking oven in here mate. How the hell did you sleep?' he asked.

'Well, I haven't really. Look at the state of me, I got headbutted last night,' replied Martin.

This seemed to galvanise George, who rolled over to face Martin, albeit slowly at first through squinted eyes, only to bolt himself into life when he saw the damage to Martin's face.

'Fucking hell mate! What happened?' he said, examining his friend.

He was looking at a bruised and bloodied Martin sat across from him looking forlorn, but also with a small sense of pride in his eyes. This sort of scenario was really uncommon for Martin. The first real experience of being subject to something truly 'laddy.' George was seemingly quite impressed and Martin was probably proud that he'd managed to impress him.

'So what happened? How did you get in a scrap? Did he come off worse?' George said wryly.

Martin explained to him the situation and events that had unfolded in KFC. This seemed to win praise from George again and a smile was back on Martin's face as he revelled in the storytelling. It was true, Martin was finally the subject of something laddy and impressive. His face hurt like hell, but hey, it was worth it for a moment at least.

'Right, so what are we doing about this then? Where can we find these little twats then?' announced George.

'No, G. We don't need to do that. Let karma take care of it mate. Idiots like that get what's coming to them in the end,' replied Martin.

'Well. If I see them, I'll give them a right hiding,' said George, with all the bravado you'd expect from a man whose confidence was never in short supply.

It was now nearly 2.00pm and as Martin had thought to himself earlier, he had very little to show for today.

'Milsom has text me. He's down at the pool chatting up some Scottish birds,' said George excitedly. It seemed the adrenaline was still rushing through his veins from his night out, or he was still on some kind of high from hearing about Martin's antics. Or perhaps it was more that when there was a chance to impress girls, George was always ready and raring to go, no matter what state of physical condition he was in.

Ten minutes later, both Martin and George were joining their rest of their friends by the pool.

'Please don't make a fuss about the fight last night mate,' said Martin as they walked down the path towards the pool.

'No, of course, don't worry mate – just let them ask questions and tell them what happened,' replied George. For all his bravado and storytelling, George was considerate and sensitive. He knew his role as a friend, especially with Martin, who he knew was delicate and that he wouldn't want the spotlight to be on him in a big group of lads. But some things are inevitable and sometimes avoidable. Despite George's best efforts, it was clear that the only thing that anyone wanted to talk about was Martin's bruised face.

'Fuck me, Mart you get hit by a bus?' said Robbie Milsom, his face incredulous as George's was only an hour or so ago. The rest of the group sat up from their loungers and started to inspect Martin's face with intrigue, asking questions about what happened.

'Well, not much really to be honest. Hate to disappoint you all,' started Martin, 'All I did was tell these scumbags to stop being abusive to a group of girls.'

'Yeah, so was it worth it? Did you get the ride, or what?' said Ollie Thomas in his usual crass and disrespectful way.

'Ollie, all I did was stand up against what I thought was wrong,' said Martin.

'Yeah, but you must've been trying to get a shag Mart. Why else would you have said something?' Ollie was pressing him for the answer he want to hear, but it really wasn't Martin's agenda to be defending a group of girls for sex.

'Well, I wasn't and I didn't,' he said back.

'Ahh well, fair play Mart. Very honourable of you,' and Ollie returned back to bantering the rest of the group like Martin wasn't even there. George gave him an encouraging nod, as if to say, 'well done for handling that maturely.' Martin returned the nod and laid out his towel on the nearest lounger.

He wasn't a huge fan of lying out in the sun for hours on end. But right now, he was happy just to relax for a bit and not be the focus of attention after his ordeal. Perhaps he would even try and catch-up on some sleep that had been lost. He was pretty drained right now, both mentally and physically. What last night had done to his mental health, he didn't truly know in this moment.

But it would later affect him in the way that events had unfolded. The alcohol in his system probably wasn't helping either. That and the amount of sugar in all the drinks had given him a certain type of anxiety and twitchiness that he didn't like. He was very reluctant to let this be known too – it was a kind of sickness that was overwhelming him right now, not to mention the heat of the sun that was beating down on him. He wrestled with the internal pain in an attempt to mask the physical that he was feeling right now. Both were sheer hell. What was he doing here? Why was he still led on this lounger? He probably looked ridiculous right now, he thought.

But in reality, nobody was taking the slightest bit of notice and he'd hardly moved an inch either. He felt like his insides were writhing and coiling, almost like something was taking grip of his body from the inside out, but still he lay motionless and devoid of emotion from the outside. If the inside of his body were to reveal itself right now it would show a heaving pulse and a slow tightening of every moving and beating part. What Martin was having was a panic attack. This overwhelming feeling of not being able to move, to not feel himself on the outside but be writhing within, must've been what it felt like. He began to grip the sides of lounger, his sweaty hands slipping against the warm plastic, but he held on hoping that by grabbing on to something might help this pass.

His heart now felt like it was racing at a ridiculous pace, thumping inside his rib cage, trying to free itself. All the while, he was desperately conscious of the fact he didn't want to be noticed by anyone and until he finally summoned the strength to release himself from the lounger, he stumbled as best as he could out of sight.

He was confused and dizzy, feeling his heavy head overwhelm the rest of his body as he staggered towards a pathway behind the hedgerow at the other end of the pool. In this moment, he felt blind. His vision was fuzzy and his head felt like it might topple off at any moment. After 10 or so yards further, he collapsed onto the thick spiky grass letting himself flop with the weight of his head now supported by floor. Apart from the anguished breathing, he made no sound, just glad to be out of sight and away from it all for a moment. He held onto his chest and began to take control of his breathing again. He felt cold, but he was searing with heat to the touch and wet through from sweat.

As Martin slowly regained some kind of composure, he just lay with eyes closed, like some defeated soldier in a battle. He felt as if he was losing this battle – a long hard battle with himself that never ended.

Chapter 6

In the subsequent years after the Kavos holiday, Martin was able to take at least some solace from the experience he had of his first (and probably only ever) 'lads' holiday. Returning home and feeling excited about seeing Helena again was a big positive. He'd finally managed to pluck up the courage to go down to her hotel ask for her number. It wasn't exactly plain sailing, but he'd done it – though it did come with a boat load of anxiety and misery in the run up to it, with some avoidable, some not. He was more than ready to throw himself off the balcony into the pool one night after what had happened in the day, not as an act of bravado or chivalry, but more in regret of his actions.

Martin had, to put it flippantly, gone a bit mad. He'd locked himself away in the apartment for a few days, which was reasonably sensible given the fact he'd been taken a pretty blunt trauma to the face, had a panic attack and that drinking was probably not the best thing to be doing with all the painkillers he was taking. But rest and relaxation was not exactly Martin's ally on this occasion. A baking hot room on a loud and jumpy hotel complex with only his thoughts and feelings for company and in addition, an internal monologue for light conversation. It was a toxic mix for his already fragile mind. He hated the situation, and he hated himself even more for getting into it.

Now would be a good time to just pack up and get on the next flight home, but he didn't have the balls to do that. He didn't really have the money for it either, let alone the courage to go and tell everyone else what he was feeling like. He let two days pass without really going outside his room, with only George being an infrequent visitor where he probably spent at least 95% of the time unconscious in the bed next to him. Martin felt low and unwanted. It wasn't as if any of the lads were offering to do anything for him, help him or chat to him. They were obviously too busy with trying to sweet talk the young women who had also landed on this abomination of a resort. Martin understood this, but it did little for his self- esteem. He was feeling lower than he had ever done so in his life. Which is where his thoughts began to take over.

However, it was by the third day that Martin felt it was probably time to venture out and get some fresh air. Although being the height of summer in the middle of a party town, the word 'fresh' was probably not and never will be applicable. He went down to the pool to join George and Cameron who were getting along well with the group of Scottish girls who were also staying at the Olympian village.

'Here he is! The holiday hibernator!' announced George, as Martin sat himself down on the side of the pool. 'How're you feeling mate?'

'Not bad, thanks,' replied Martin, who did appreciate the acknowledgement, but in truth he felt isolated, subdued and probably a tinge homesick. He could never say any of this out loud though. Imagine admitting to his friends in a pathetic little voice he thought, 'guys, I'm homesick.' He even hated the thought about doing it, visualising the roars of laughter it would probably get if he plucked up the courage to do it. In reality, this wouldn't be the case of course.

He had an incredibly understanding friend in George, and he was the leader of the group – so any sensitivity from him would no doubt rub off on the rest of the group. But still, Martin's mind wasn't working to this brief. He only saw himself as sad and weak.

'Get yourself in the pool mate. Have a dip and just relax,' said George. It was easy for him to say, thought Martin. He was very self-conscious of his pasty white complexion and skinny frame. The thought of removing his shirt in front of a group of girls was simply terrifying. The rest of the lads were okay, they had athletic frames that had been honed in the gym in readiness for the football or rugby pitch – not gangly legs and bony shoulders like his own. Even though he was under absolutely no pressure to get in the pool or reveal his body, he could feel anxiety rising in himself. Why did he care? Did anyone else even care? Why should he care that they cared? It was a real muddle for Martin as he wrestled with the idea of something as simple as getting in the pool or not. It did look inviting, even though he'd self-styled himself as a crap swimmer in the past. But hey, it was only 1.5m at its deepest and he was just over 6ft so it was not as if he'd be drowning anytime soon or indeed have to be swimming lengths of the pool all of a sudden. After what seemed like an eternity to make a decision, Martin got up, removed his t-shirt and lowered himself into the pool. It felt good, like a weight had been removed from his body and an itchiness was no longer consuming his skin. He slowly dropped himself lower so that the water covered his body and head, taking in the cool water over his shoulders and torso, providing relief to his fragile body. He held his breath and let himself float just beneath the surface, enjoying the freshness around his skin and felt a wave of relief over himself. He could stay here, he thought. Bury himself in the water and be concealed from the hubbub around him, because all of sudden his world was silent, it was calm, and he felt in control. It was almost a feeling of complete freedom and exultation, a removal from the outside world and into his own. The low thud of a bassline from the poolside PA system was almost inaudible, the soft throbbing was almost relaxing to him in this moment. He had not a care in the world, he was concealed from view, he was free…

Martin surfaced slowly and drew breath, the thrill of being under water had enlivened him somewhat. He pulled himself to the side of the pool and leant himself up against it. Finally, he felt content in this world, his own world and yearned for this feeling to stay. With his back against the pool wall he closed his eyes, finding himself in a relaxed state. He could ignore the noise around him, he was channelling some inner peace for once. There was no internal monologue or chipping away at his own character.

His moment of peace wasn't going to last too much longer though. Being a swimming pool in a hot country means there was always going to be noise or disturbances, but Martin expected it least of all to come from a child. What was a 6-year old doing here anyway? Whose parents would bring them to this place, so full of young adults with only one, if not two things on their minds. Drink and sex.

'Ally, don't do that,' Martin could hear the call of a soft Scottish accent coming from a parent across pool. 'Ally' had jumped into the pool right next to where George and his harem of women were situated and were potentially splashed a little bit. The child giggled and swam away, just as George gave the Mum of the child and reassuring wave that suggested, 'Ah don't worry, he's only having fun.' The boy had been doing it all afternoon by the looks of it and hadn't really bothered anyone, clearly enjoying the game of getting a reaction from the revellers who were dotted around the pool. Martin observed his movements and hoped he wasn't next to be splashed. For once, he was feeling quite relaxed and didn't want anyone or anything to ruin his moment of serenity, no matter how bizarre the circumstances may have felt.

However, the boy wasn't finished with his game. Clearly, he felt it was quite acceptable to continue, having had no such reprimand from his mother and was now fixated on another target in the pool. Martin. It was only a matter of time, thought Martin, who had been observing the boy's actions for the last few minutes. He was excitedly running around and jumping into the pool at will, with most ignoring him or to a lesser extent humouring him with a clap or thumbs up.

But Martin wasn't in the mood for a cursory clap or encouraging thumbs up, he just wanted some peace rather than entertain a child. The boy climbed out of the pool and sat on the side just away from Martin with his legs dangling in. He began to kick excitedly, creating a splash. It hadn't reached Martin yet, but the boy gawped gleefully at him to show that he was enjoying the impending game that he thought Martin might reciprocate. He flashed Martin a huge toothless grin in delight. Martin just looked back at him unamused and then looked away again, trying to ignore him. Undeterred, the boy shuffled himself closer and continuing his splashing game, laughing excitedly and making side glances at Martin to see if he was getting annoyed or not. The truth is, he was, but he wasn't showing it yet. The boy ('Ally'), was starting to push his luck though. He was up onto his feet again to fix his goggles into place and followed this up with another gleeful bomb into the pool. The splash this time was more considerable and closer to Martin.

He didn't want this, he wanted peace and quiet. How much longer he would tolerate it, he wasn't sure. Two more 'bombs' followed in quick succession and Martin could feel himself boiling inside, almost itching to let fly a verbal tirade on the child. But he couldn't, could he? The kid was only six, maybe seven at a push. But my God, there was something so irritating and annoying about little kids. If they weren't screaming on a flight, they were messing up a display in the shops or worse still, splashing water at adults who clearly weren't in the mood for fun and games. The boy climbed out of the pool again and resumed his position ready to bomb again. He looked at Martin and grinned, as if to say, 'shall I go again?'

This time, Martin returned the interaction with what he would later describe as completely and utterly out of character. He had absolutely no idea what had come over him in this moment, but for some explicable reason Martin pointed at the child and said,

'If you dive in one more time and splash me, I swear to God that I will knock some more of those fucking teeth out.'

Christ.

It was almost as if the whole pool was listening. George and his new women friends looked down on him shocked as to what had just come out of his mouth.

Fucking hell, where had that come from?

Martin went red with pure embarrassment. He hoped to God the boys parents hadn't heard – on the contrary, the boy seemed undeterred. But Martin was now glowing with white hot shame. The Scottish girls clearly had a surge in national pride of their own and shouted something over to him which for the most part, he didn't really hear. Everything was fuzzy again, muted and blurry. He couldn't even move, still shocked by what had come out of his mouth. Martin knew himself as a very placid and patient character, but a combination of stresses had led to this random outburst. He mustered the inclination to get out the pool and walk back to the apartment, grabbing a quick glance at George who was still open mouthed in disbelief. Martin was convinced he had mouthed a sorry towards his friends general direction but truth be told, he wasn't even sure if a noise had come out. He squelched his way back to the room to wallow in disgrace at his complete lack of judgement and self-loathing. He wished for the Earth to form some kind of vortex so he could disappear inside it and never return.

Chapter 7

Present day

The prep was done, the plan was made. Not long from now he'd be putting it into action. What it would feel like, he had no idea. He was focused on seeing things through now that he'd put this much thought into it. Right now he didn't feel nervous. If anything he felt steadfast in his approach to the act. It felt right, it felt like redemption. It felt like the right kind of statement to make and see if anyone actually cared. Ironically, he'd never know the reality, but the thought of this was a comfort to him. He was sick and tired of the embarrassments, the self-loathing, the humiliation and the bad luck that seemed to seek him out. He had no real relationships to speak of. His Mum had disappeared from view after the incidents at Christmas, his Dad seemed pretty happy-go-lucky on his own anyway, and George, well, it wasn't like he needed Martin to be hanging round him forever bringing down the mood. Work would find someone else. Senior Architects were everywhere, it wasn't like he was indispensable. This was the general thought process anyway.

With the day chosen, the location sorted and the planning to simply disappear into insignificance like he had always hoped to after every faux pas, Martin was finally ready to say goodbye.

Chapter 8

23 years previous

Growing up in the suburban bliss of a commuter town had its benefits. The safety and security of quiet roads, good schools and somewhere to park while doing the big shop at Tescos. This was a world that Martin had grown up in. He really didn't have much view of the world beyond a 20-mile radius of the town he grew up in until he went to University. The town he called home was a real safety blanket. It was the sort of place where proud parents paraded their children around in estate vehicles and mollycoddled their kids existence by buying them everything they ever wanted, but didn't need.

Martin's parents house was absolutely spotless. So much so that if you walked into the kitchen, you'd scarcely believe that anyone lived there. Even the toaster and the kettle were stowed away in cupboards when not in use, for fear that a drip or crumb may sully the immaculate work surfaces. This is generally how Martin grew up, a cosseted only child in a purely sanitised existence. He never knew any different at the time. In his own head, he was just like any other child of his age, going out to play, being called back in for dinner at 5.30pm and settling down to watch TV with parents for the evening. But it was this clinical lifestyle his parents were leading and living for him, namely his Mother.

Clearly they only wanted what was best for him, protect him and ensure that he succeeded at school. But unbeknownst to him until now, these memories that Martin looked back on suggested he had what others might have considered a seemingly unhealthy upbringing. He could look back at the past and calculate some of the emotions he felt as a child, like feeling guarded or restrained. He'd grown up scared and worried about the simplest things, unable to let himself loose or simply just go with the flow. Everything was analysed and risk assessed. He loathed his parents for this now he knew this piece. It was an uncomfortable psyche for him, as he felt a wasted youth and upbringing having been taken away from him.

But Martin's parents weren't bad people by any means. Far from it in fact. His Mum worked in a Christian school and his dad an IT Manager in a manufacturing company. Mum ruled the roost, it was her gig around the house. Even though she was a kindly sort, small and mouse like in appearance you could say, she still had a strict way about her with very old fashioned values. Dad was just happy to be led by this. He wasn't fussed by the drama of relationship politics. Looking back, Martin could see that his Dad just drifted through life. Wake up, work, eat dinner then go to bed. And then do this on repeat for 40-odd years. At a time when it was kind of taboo for men to speak out and say what they feel, he wondered whether Dad would've ever liked to have said anything about what he was thinking and tell his son how he really felt about his life. But he didn't of course. He was more than happy to sit in the conservatory on the pristine wicker furniture (plastic covers still on the seating) and read his Sunday paper back to back. This was probably the clearest memory that Martin had of his home life. Mum busily finding things to clean around the house and Dad just sat there, seemingly unperturbed with life.

Sundays were Martin's nemesis. When he was younger, he would accompany his Mum to Church and attend the Sunday school. The older he became, the less he would go, but the Sunday afternoon ritual that followed of Nan and Grandad coming over for lunch was one that he grew up with well into his mid-teens. A bland roast dinner followed by some stodgy pudding and then settling down in front of the television to watch Songs of Praise. Attendance was compulsory, and with Martin being an only child, he played by the rules, sitting on the floor while the adults occupied the sofa spaces and drank tea. Mum would be holding most of the conversation with Nan firing back answers at will, while Grandad snored away unapologetically in the armchair. Dad would usually sit motionless and nod along at intervals offering the odd, 'oh aye,' and 'yeah, we did,' to accompany his wife's anecdotes. Martin saw a lot of himself in his Dad. Placid, subservient, non-committal. He didn't blame Dad for inheriting any of these traits, but he certainly wasn't thanking him. In many ways, he wished that he and his Dad could've had more of a relationship when he was younger. But it always seemed to be the three of them, with Mum the ringleader. She didn't rule in a nasty way by any means, but she was tough, stubborn and knew what levers to pull with her husband, as well as her son.

However, there was one occasion that Martin and his Dad were 'let loose' so to speak – it was to be a time where they bonded the most and his memories of the weekend in question were probably up there with the best in his childhood. It was late May bank holiday weekend and Martin's local junior football team had decided to 'tour' Devon for the weekend. They had arranged a fixture, as well as accommodation at a static caravan site where the parents all chipped in for a decent BBQ and copious amounts of booze. Martin and the rest of his 13-year-old teammates were free to roam the site, full up on hot dogs and high on fizzy drinks and sweets. First and foremost, Martin was by no means the star member of this football team, far from it. He was a steady defender largely making up the numbers (and getting a game due to being the only left footer), but he loved it. Looking up to his friend George (the captain, the star player) and playing alongside a number of other school mates, Martin could feel part of something. He could have a belonging, no matter how insignificant it might have looked on paper – but it meant a lot to him in those formative years. So on this weekend in question, 15 sets of families from the Wilverton Athletic Juniors U-13 side headed to North Devon for an end of season celebration. All bar one person. Martin's Mum.

Martin's Mum was not generally one to socialise outside of her comfort zone. She had a tight circle of acquaintances from Church and a couple of old school friends who still lived locally, but generally, she wasn't interested in socialising with the other football mums, let alone drink and go 'on holiday' with them. Looking back, Martin could see that the excuse for her not coming was completely feeble. Their pet rabbit, Liquorice, needed to be 'taken to the vet' on Saturday morning, which meant Martin's Mum pulled out of the trip at the last minute. He never even started with the thought she was looking for a good excuse not to go, he just thought the rabbit probably needed an injection or something. But desperate not to miss out, Martin and his dad would still go, leaving Mum, rabbit, and any sense of boundary at home. The boys were off the leash, at last. And they loved it.

While Mum stayed home and tended to what appeared to be a perfectly healthy pet rabbit, Martin and his Dad headed off to Devon. The football match on Saturday morning had gone well, with Wilverton beating their Devonian counterparts by four goals to two. Martin was given man of the match for his performance, the first time he'd had such an acknowledgement, and the feel good factor around him for the weekend had clearly shown in his performance. There was a good spirit about the game too, which was followed by an afternoon on the beach jumping in the sea and an evening on the caravan site where the great British weather held and delivered a beautiful balmy night. It probably didn't get much better than this for a kid of 13. Charging about with your mates, having free rein on what was essentially a holiday and occasionally checking in with your drunk parents who were encouraging a real sense of fun. It wasn't until around midnight that things had to start dying down.

Martin wished this day would never end, his happiness at an all-time high. A round of karaoke had begun earlier in the evening for 'Dad and lad duets' with the music blaring out the back of Ben Allen's Dad's Renault Espace. Martin and his Dad did a rendition of 'Up the junction' by Squeeze, which went down very well indeed with kids and parents alike. Martin felt appreciated and proud. The song had always been one of his Dad's favourites and Martin knew the words off by heart due to the amount of times he had heard it in the car. He saw his Dad in a completely different light that night. Free spirited, happy, relaxed, and of course helped along the way by the fact he was pissed. He was engaging fully with the other Dads, like they were genuine friends, getting involved in the banter, playing cards or whatever game it was they has dreamed up into right up until the small hours. When he looked back, he hoped this was a true reflection of the man his father was – someone who knew how to have a good time, someone who was engaging, funny and likeable. These were all traits Martin wanted to model himself on, and he clearly had it in him somewhere he thought. There were certainly glimpses of that, but his inner monologue set the tone for most of his physical actions, and sadly this would do quite the opposite. He would withdraw, seem irritable and struggle with people warming to him.

This weekend however, would be a watershed moment for him and his family. He didn't know it at the time, but things were about to reach a crescendo, and the happiness he had felt in the Devon sunshine was about to be replaced with something far more sinister and painful.

Chapter 9

When Martin got home from school, he thought it was just like any other Wednesday afternoon. The first sign that things were not like an average school day was the fact that his Dad's Toyota Corolla was parked on the drive. Dad didn't usually get home until around 5.30pm, so to see him back at 3.30pm must mean something out of the ordinary was going on. Perhaps he was ill and came home early from work?

Martin let himself into the kitchen through the back door and walked into the dining room where he could sense a presence. Both Mum and Dad were sat at the table not talking. Something bad had happened here, he could sense it.

'Can you sit down for a moment, Martin? Your Mum and I would like to talk to you please,' said his Dad slowly and gravely. Martin proceeded to pull out a chair and took a seat at the table. His body was moving very slowly and carefully, though he couldn't feel much in his arms and legs. He had gone numb with fear and apprehension.

'Your Father has something to say to you,' his Mum said pointedly. And she glared at Martin's Dad, not reducing her irate stare for what seemed like an eternity. There was a gap before he spoke again. A cold, painful silence while he waited for inevitable bad news.

'Your Mum and I have decided to get a divorce,' Martin's Dad started. There was another moments pause while this sunk in. The words seemed to hit the floor with a resounding thump and the silence that followed was almost gruelling. Martin was struggling to compute what was happening. He had heard the word 'divorce' before, but he didn't think that this sort of thing actually happened to anyone, certainly not him and his family. He had no idea how to feel right now, an emptiness had engulfed him, he was even more numb than thirty seconds previous somehow.

'Tell him why then Alan,' said Martin's Mum, breaking the silence.

Martin's Dad looked irritably at his wife, wearing an expression of defeat on his face. Martin could tell that his Dad didn't want to say why. He wondered what the reason would be. He wasn't old enough to understand adult relationships, his view of the world was that kids his age just simply had parents who were together. Unless one of them died, he would always just have a Mum and Dad who lived together, through thick and thin. Right now, his parents were in the thick of it so to speak and he didn't like where this was heading.

'I've been having an affair,' his Dad said finally. 'What this means Martin, is that myself and your Mum will not be living together anymore. I will be moving out of this house.'

Martin didn't really know what an affair was, but it didn't sound like a good thing. In the years that followed he would begin to understand the reality of what was being said to him on that Wednesday afternoon around the dining room table, but today, all that he needed to know was that Mum and Dad were no more and that his life was about to change completely.

Martin's Mum began to leave the room, clearly trying to hold back her emotions. She disappeared upstairs out of sight without a word, leaving Martin alone with his Dad.

'I'm so sorry Mart, I really am,' and he put his head in his hands to seemingly hide his guilt. Martin was still unable to say anything, he just stared blankly into the room, at nothing in particular. He could feel his eyes glaze over and go out of focus while trying to collect his thoughts. He felt so empty, like there was no emotion in him. He had nothing to say, with the thoughts in his head simply whirring and spinning, completely lacking the ability to stop and focus on what should've been some pretty important questions.

'I… I don't know what to say,' he finally stammered. Martin left the room in silence, leaving his Dad to reflect alone. He went upstairs to his bedroom and sat on the end of his bed as the darkness of the evening gradually fell like a blanket over him. All he could do was sit there and try to compute what this actually meant for him, right now and in the future. Was it his fault that his parents were this way? Or was it his parents fault that he was this way? There was no logical answer to any question right now. He wondered how other teenagers like him would react to the news he had just heard. He began to bemoan his luck, his life and the situation that had just occurred. Even at the age of 14, Martin was already beginning to hate himself. The learning behaviours were setting in and this was his way of learning about himself – to hate every act in his existence, no matter whether it had been his fault or not. He was beginning to develop a knack for turning situations into negative experiences of his own creation. In reality, there was absolutely no culpability on his part that his parents were divorcing, he was just simply a product of their marriage, an innocent party in what he was now learning wasn't a solid family dynamic, but a broken situation that he was very much caught in the middle of.

There was a soft knock at the door. It was his Mum.

'Martin, would you like anything to eat?' she said, peering around the door. She looked sombre and devoid of energy, but still carried a sense of purpose and clearly had some pent up aggression that needed filtering somewhere.

'No thank you,' came his reply. He didn't even look up from his blank stare. Everything in his world right now was empty. The sanitised house they lived in seemed even more devoid of life than usual, there was nothing. He hated the thought of having to go downstairs and eat a meal under the watchful eye of his Mum – he was assuming Dad had left – and didn't feel hungry anyway, or indeed in the mood for listening to his Mum saying what a shithouse his Dad was. Not that he was defending his Dad in any way at all, but the very thought of even communicating right now was dreadful. He was avoiding the situation at a cost to his own wellbeing, but this felt comfortable and the only way he felt he could deal with it.

'Okay. Just let me know if you want anything,' came the reply from his Mum.

Although his Mum had shown compassion and consideration by checking on him, he didn't feel particularly loved in that moment. He didn't have the arm round him that was so desperately needed. He didn't have the space to let out any emotion, to talk, to question, to cry even. For Martin, this was a huge moment in his life where his habit would become one of filling up the proverbial bottle and tightening the lid until nothing could escape. It was safe this way, for now at least. Little did he know that this trauma could have such a bearing on the pathway his life would take, a pathway that would slowly but recklessly meander and ultimately turn into a slippery slope of self-loathing and destruction.

Chapter 10

1 year previous

Martin's phone vibrated on the side of his desk. It was George.

'Spare ticket for Cheltenham races if you want it mate? Gold Cup day this Friday'

It was probably the last thing Martin felt he needed at the moment. Drinking and betting while he felt so low – it could go either way – though in reality, there was no pressure to do either of course. It had been just over three weeks since the split from Helena and he was generally not in a great place from where things had ended up. He was staying at his Mum's house trying to reflect on what went wrong and getting deeper into his own head.

However, much like the Kavos holiday, it was sometimes just too hard to say no to George. He thought about it over the next couple of hours at work. He knew it would be a somewhat 'laddy' affair, with pissed up twenty-somethings pretending that they're gentleman for the day, but in reality they were just smartly dressed thugs pissing on each others shoes and sniffing lines in the toilets. He tapped out a message in response, which actually surprised himself.

'Yeah go on then'

This was the somewhat reluctant yet agreeable reply that Martin gave. He knew deep down that some time with his friend might be the best thing for him, even though he knew the day came with the additional baggage of big crowds and pissed up knobheads. The betting thing was very much secondary to all this, he hadn't really ever given this much thought. It could be fun, of course. He had been intrigued by a small gamble now and again, but nothing serious. With George saying that the ticket was already paid for, all he needed to do really was turn up. He knew he wouldn't be drinking too much as it wasn't really his thing, so in which case he could stick to just betting on some horses, watch the racing and put his personal problems behind him for the day.

*

When Friday came, he still felt apprehensive about the whole experience, but would've never admitted it to anyone, or God forbid pull out. He hated the thought of losing face in front of George and his friends. Besides, it was too late by the time Mum's partner Gary had dropped him outside Gloucester station ready to take the short train ride to Cheltenham. The platform was packed with race goers and a sign of things to come about the sort of clientele he would have to mix with that day. He looked up and down the platform at the groups of lads around him, of which there were plenty. Most of the male contingent were wearing three piece plaid suits trying to look sophisticated. They had cheap looking aviators dangling from their pockets and suede tassel loafers with no socks, all drinking sweet cider from the can and generally being loud. Martin himself wasn't exactly 'dressed up' per se, but he did look reasonably smart at least. Although now, looking at himself in isolation amongst the swathes of dodgy suits and naked ankles, the crew neck wool jumper and smart trousers made him look like he was on his way to school. He didn't know whether to feel embarrassed by the way he looked or relieved that he didn't look like everyone else.

He boarded the next train and did the best he could to keep himself to himself before meeting George at Cheltenham Spa. That was his safety blanket for the day, his friend.

On arrival at the station he filed out with the crowds and met George in the car park before boarding a bus that would take them to the racecourse. It felt like he was having post traumatic stress disorder from the coach journey across Corfu during the holiday from hell in Kavos.

'All set for today then mate?' asked George, taking a seat next to him on the top deck.

'Yeah all good,' he replied, 'You reckon £100 is okay?' Martin said.

'Fine mate, fine. You can bet as much or as little as you like. My old man used to say, 'only bet what you can afford to lose,' and I think that's a pretty good place to start. So yeah… a hundred is fine I reckon.'

Martin nodded in agreement. He could probably afford financially to lose a bit more, but that wasn't really his style. He'd lost enough in the last few weeks which included a relationship, a beautiful home that he had been told to move out of and generally a lifestyle that had become comfortable. Perhaps it had become too comfortable? Maybe that was it. This thought and a whole host of others had plagued him over the last few weeks. The reckless thing to do right now was to bet beyond his means and chase the losses that might help numb that pain. But Martin's mindset was one of sorrow and reflection, the one thing that was clear being he didn't fancy losing too much more than he already had done.

The bus rolled into the racecourse and he, George and hundreds of others swarmed across the car park through the security turnstiles and into the complex. It was a crisp day, cold enough for a jacket but pleasant enough for sunglasses. Inside the course, Martin observed that there were plenty more cheap suits and loafers, together with flatcaps and wax jackets that suggested 'horsey' or that the individual in question had some kind of affiliation with the countryside. In reality they probably lived in a 2-bed semi on the fringes of Dudley town centre and spent the majority of their days laying out cones on the motorway. Martin knew he had a cynical mind at the moment, it was slightly poison, he had to admit.

He queued at the bar with George and ordered himself a diet coke. He couldn't stomach alcohol at the best of times and certainly not at just past 11.00am.

The place was buzzing. There was positivity all around, with people enjoying themselves, drinking and chatting excitedly. It was probably the best part of the day as nobody had got too pissed or causing trouble – that would no doubt come later of course. Indeed, Martin felt slightly out of place. He didn't feel that excited to be there, stood on the periphery with his diet coke. He'd be glad when the racing started as at least it would give him something to focus on. He felt a bit sick with anxiety, it was like the masses of people had started to close in on him. He knew he didn't belong there today in that environment, with these people and his mental state. But walking away from it all would be worse, he'd convinced himself of that. He tapped George on the shoulder.

'I'm just gonna go and find a race card and sort my bets I think mate. It's a bit loud round here,' he admitted. 'No worries mate,' responded George with a wink.

Martin knew that George wasn't his minder, but he would've appreciated his friend to join him. Equally, he didn't want to be a burden on his friend as he could see that he was having a good time. Martin made his way over to the desk and purchased a race card.

He then found a quieter spot in the auditorium looking down on everyone else while reading through the various races, including the biggest race of the week, The Cheltenham Gold Cup. He made marks against the horses he thought looked promising, reading about form, conditions and the trainers. Martin was doing things in his usual methodical and meticulous way, which kept him occupied for a little while at least.

He looked down on the crowds below. There was a part of him that yearned for the characteristics and personality to fit in and be more sociable, especially with George and his friends – many of whom were veterans of the Kavos holiday. Cam, Briggsy, Tommo and Milsom, to name a few. Perhaps this was one of the reasons why Helena didn't want to be with him any longer? Was he simply not enough for her? Would she feel more at home with an outgoing, outspoken type of lad like the ones who had filled this event today? He felt very alone momentarily with only his thoughts for company, which were riddled with danger. He needed an outlet, a focus. There wasn't much to occupy him apart from work these days and that finished between 5.00pm and 6.00pm everyday so the remaining five hours before he slept had become a struggle as he didn't want to sit with his Mum and watch soaps on TV. Gary was a nice enough bloke, but they had very little in common. He stared blankly over at the crowds of people, each face blurring into the next. He was wondering what his life would become and whether this feeling inside of inadequacy right now would ever get any worse.

*

It was approximately 3.15pm and surprisingly, a smile had appeared on Martin's face. How? Winning. He'd won the first three out of four bets he had placed and even had a return from the one he didn't win outright because of an each-way finish. The £100 he'd arrived with had turned into nearly £600 and George was buzzing around him excitedly with the rest of the group in tow asking for tips and wondering where this lucky streak had come from.

'Fuck me, Mart! How have you managed this?' George exclaimed. Martin looked slightly bashful, but also proud.

'Mate. I really don't know. Beginners luck?' He said, flippantly. He knew he'd been due some good fortune as it seemed like he'd been down on his luck for a little while now. Maybe this was the turnaround and boost he needed? It felt good to be winning.

'Who have you got in the Gold Cup?' asked George, 'I haven't won a penny all day!' He laughed.

'I've got Desert Stinger at 7/1. Seemed to have an okay record over the fences and the trainer is in good form,' said Martin, 'Although I would concede that it's usually one of the favourites who come away with this race.'

'Seriously, how the fuck do you know all this!' Laughed George. 'I dunno, I just read it. Retained the information,' he said.

It seemed so obvious to Martin that this would be the way to do it. Betting, that was. Do some prep, read the background and make an informed judgement. George and his mates were either just backing favourites or choosing the names or colours they liked. They might get lucky once in a while, but not today anyway. It was Martin's turn.

'Well I've gone for the fave. Alabama Sitcom is nailed on,' George said. Martin gave a knowing look and raised his eyebrows.

'Thanks for coming today by the way mate. I know it's not really your cup of tea all this,' said George, nodding over to a group of lads who were singing Neil Diamond's Sweet Caroline at the top of their voices for the umpteenth time that day.

'Yeah, I think I needed to get out and do something. Can't dwell on things forever can I?' he replied.

Though in reality, he probably was and would continue to dwell on the hurt of his relationship split and the baggage that accompanied it, today was a small glimmer of hope on the otherwise bleak horizon.

The 3.30pm race was nearing its conclusion and the pair watched intently as the horses came around the final bend towards home with two fences to jump. The commentary over the tannoy could barely be heard over the ferocious atmosphere which seemed to be willing on the favourite in what was the biggest and most lucrative race of the festival.

'And now Alabama Sitcom makes his move, he's got two lengths to make up on the leader Nordic Warrior who looks like he's fading now, with Desert Stinger just falling back slightly now too…'

'Here we go then!' said George excitedly.

'Maybe my luck has run out,' Martin said, resigned, 'Might get a place though.' The crowd roared louder.

'And it's Alabama Sitcom now out in front… the favourite for Gold Cup glory, coming down the hill with two to jump… and he's cleared the first…'

'Fuck me, the bookies will have taken a hammering here. I reckon everyone has backed him,' said George, who like everyone else could start tasting victory from this particular race.

'So Alabama Sitcom, leading Nordic Warrior by three lengths and Desert Stinger just little further back in third…'

The race was moments from finishing now and probably a foregone conclusion as the leader and favourite Alabama Sitcom would shortly pass by them, providing he was able to negotiate the final fence in front of him. A frenzy of shouts and cheers was being whipped up with the increasingly excitable commentator on the tannoy taking his voice to within an inch of its limits without even summoning breath.

'Just one fence stands between Alabama Sitcom and Gold Cup glory for the second successive year, he's now seven lengths from Nordic Warrior as he approaches the final jump…'

And then, a collective gasp of cries and screams as the race favourite stuttered his way towards the fence, took off unconvincingly and unseated his rider on the other side. All time seemed to stand still.

'…AND HE'S FALLEN! ALABAMA SITCOM HAS GONE!'

The tannoy screamed like a news bulletin amidst a chorus of shocked jeers from unhappy punters. 'Holy shit!' cried George, 'He was fucking nailed on!'

Martin knew he now had a chance. It was like a betting Lord above was shining on him today, because his horse, seemingly out of the race a moment ago was now making strides to win it…

'So Nordic Warrior leads now! He approaches the fence and though a slight fumble, he clings on, but here comes Desert Stinger who launches perfectly into the jump and lands with momentum! He's neck and neck with Nordic Warrior now, here comes Desert Stinger, he's taken the lead! It's Desert Stinger out in front, he's here for Gold Cup glory, Nordic Warrior has nothing left, so Desert Stinger now, pulling three lengths clear… he's going to take the Gold Cup in the most unlikeliest

of circumstances! It's Desert Stinger across the line… and WINS!'

And with that, it was over in a flash. It was a pulsating two minutes or so. George turned to smile wryly at Martin. 'You lucky fucker!' George chuckled, 'How have you managed another one!'

'I really have no idea,' he laughed to himself.

'How much have you won now?' He said excitedly.

'Well, he was actually in a double with the race before, so that's…' he did some quick maths on his phone. 'That's about £245, on top of the £600 I won earlier. I think I'm done now to be fair,' he smiled.

'Fuck that are you done! We're buying a lottery ticket later and you're picking the numbers!' laughed George.

Martin had to admit, it did feel good. His winning streak had erased the subdued feelings he'd had at the start of the day. He felt invincible. This betting thing wasn't half bad. Maybe his luck was finally in for good? Perhaps just one last bet and he'd be done though. To be nearly £850 up on the day was amazing, he'd only bet with what he could afford so with him being sensible, perhaps he could spare the money he'd come with or at least half of that original hundred on the last race.

*

'Come on then Mart, get a round in for the lads!' Said Briggsy.

They were back in the auditorium where the crowds had now thinned considerably now the racing had finished.

'Yeah go on Mart, you've cleaned up today, give the poor bastards some money back!' laughed George.

'Alright, alright,' said Martin, laughing it off, 'You lot still on the Guinness?'

'Guinness' all round fella,' said George, 'You not gonna have one?' he asked.

'Nah, I'm alright. I don't really fancy it,' Martin replied.

'Fair enough mate, fair enough.'

Martin walked over to the bar which was only a few paces away from where the group were stood. He'd even had a place in the final race of the day, albeit third, but at least he'd covered the bet he had placed. This meant he had no qualms about getting a round in. It had been a good day all in all and there was a smile on his face for the first time in a long time.

'Hiya... can I have five pints of Guinness and an orange juice with lemonade please,' he asked the bar maid.

The pints of Guinness were already made up in readiness and she handed them over the counter to him, along with the orange juice and lemonade.

Martin didn't hear what the round had cost but at least there was some evidence of change coming back to him from the fifty pounds note he had handed over. He didn't want to know exactly how much it had cost, but hey, he'd won well today and it was nice to treat the group.

'Thank you,' said Martin, and he began ferrying the drinks back over to the group, which was greeted with a chorus of 'Cheers Mart!' and 'thanks moneybags.'

Now it was quieter, he was starting to feel like he belonged a bit more. He was joining in with the occasional bit of banter and felt more at ease. However, what was about to happen would take him and everyone else by complete surprise.

Around the perimeter of the auditorium were a number a curtains leading to exits, which were used by staff and security. One minute, Martin was there sipping his orange juice and lemonade, while in the next he was being bundled behind a curtain by a security guard. Nobody noticed at first, it had happened that quick.

'What the fu...!' exclaimed Martin spilling his drink across the floor and was then quickly being ushered down the corridor and told to sit down.

'The police will be here in a moment to question you,' said the burly security guard who had grabbed him from beside his friends.

'The police? What? Why?' Asked Martin, incredulously.

'Just stay there, they'll handle any questions,' said another man. He was the more smartly dressed of the two, like he was some kind of security or operations manager or something. Not someone who got into the rough and tumble of peace keeping unless he had to.

Martin was shaking with fear. What had he done wrong? Was it the money he'd won? Had he taken something that wasn't his? It was all very unnerving for him as he sat there alone waiting for the aforementioned police officer.

Moments later an officer made his way down the corridor and spoke with what Martin assumed was the security manager.

'Yep, use that office there, that's fine. We've got the CCTV running now,' he said to the police officer. The CCTV? What the hell was he talking about?

'Come this way please, Sir,' the police officer motioned to Martin. The security manager followed behind and thanked the burly one before letting him get back to the main auditorium.

'Take a seat,' said the officer.

It was all very official, it was almost like he was in custody, which in a way he was, but he had absolutely no idea why. Martin sat down, trembling.

'We have reason to believe that a man matching your description has just carried out an assault on a bar assistant here,' the security manager started.

Martin stared back, wide eyed, incredulously.

'Assault?' Are… are you serious?' he asked, bewildered.

'The victim has identified you as the individual who assaulted her while ordering drinks at the bar just now,' the security manager continued.

'I… I haven't had a drop of alcohol all day… what is this?' asked Martin, who was becoming increasingly more flustered. He could feel a Kavos style panic attack manifesting itself in his body.

'She is confirming this for us on a CCTV recording,' the security manager added. 'What CCTV? Can I see it? Can I at least identify myself?' asked Martin, panicking.

'I'm afraid not,' was the drab response.

The Police Officer just sat there, looking bored. Maybe he could see how farcical this was too.

'This must be mistaken identity, I swear to you I haven't assaulted anyone and would never dream of doing so,' said Martin. He felt a huge wave of emotions take over his body. He felt hot, sick and numb. It was like pins and needles had taken over his body.

The security manager looked at the police officer. The latter gave the sort of look that suggested, 'I mean, look at him, this ain't the guy we should be talking to.'

'Even so. We're treating this with the utmost seriousness,' the bored Police Officer said.

Martin just sat there, incredulously. It was ridiculous, how had this even happened? It felt like just when he'd had a little bit of luck, the world shot something back at him and bowled him over just for being him. The winnings from earlier were insignificant. If they had the 'evidence' that was being discussed, he was banged to rights. But how? He hadn't done anything.

Just then, the burly security guard walked in again, this time followed by George. Martin looked up, promisingly. 'I believe this is your friend?' the guard said gruffly.

'It is, yes,' answered Martin.

George addressed the police officer, he was probably a bit pissed as well as angry but he was managing to come across respectful enough.

'Excuse me officer, my friend has a right to see the CCTV footage he has been claimed to be in here... and you know that's lawful,' he said, almost pointedly like a some kind of fake lawyer. In reality, George actually had no idea if it was lawful or not but he was an excellent blagger.

The Police Officer looked across at the manager.

'Yes, okay. He should see the video, I think that's fair,' he said.

'Very well,' said the manager reluctantly, 'come with me.'

They all followed him out of the room, back past the burly security guard, and along the corridor. They came out into the auditorium where groups of people were still gathered. George and Martin's friends looked over in bewilderment as the officer and the security manager led them across the floor to the other side. George gave the group a nod as if to say, 'it's okay, everything under control,' Martin however, just looked shaken, embarrassed and completely fraught.

They entered the small control room where another person from the security team was operating the screens.

'Excuse me Dennis, can we get another look at camera four in the auditorium please,' said the security manager. He sounded annoyed. The kind of annoyed where he knew that in any moment now he was going to find out they had taken in the wrong man. He had the look of someone with complete self-importance. The kind of person who never likes to be wrong, especially in front of Police Officers, who indeed hate nothing more than time wasting and ultimately, getting the wrong man.

Dennis ran the tapes back to the moment in question. What the group saw was hardly an assault – it was actually quite unclear, but the clearest thing of all was that it was indeed, not Martin.

'Right, the guy there has got a suit jacket on,' exclaimed George, pointing at the screen. It was hard to argue that point, because stood next to them in a jet black duffel coat was Martin. The security manager looked over at Martin. It looked like he wanted to say something petty like, 'yeah but you must've changed into your coat then.'

But of course, there was no comeback. The surveillance was crystal clear. The security manager walked out in a strop without a word, leaving Martin, George, the Police Officer and Dennis in the room, with the latter looking bemused.

'Is there anything else you need?' said Dennis, innocently.

'I think that will be all, thank you Dennis,' answered George, proudly.

'Right lads, just do us a favour and disappear now. I know you've caused no trouble here, he's got on his high horse about something, no pun intended, and wanted to make a sting in front of the coppers,' said the Police Officer. 'I'm sorry about the inconvenience caused this evening.'

Martin looked relieved, although he still hadn't said anything.

'No probs Sarge,' said George, probably riding his luck slightly now. They did as promised and walked out into the cold night air.

'What the fuck was all that about?' Said George, 'talk about a cock-up!'

But Martin still didn't answer, all he could think about now was how his luck may have turned today, despite the hiccup just now, and his thoughts were consumed by a new emotion. Winning.

Chapter 11

Present day

Sat at his desk he was finding it hard to hold back the tears. His very insides were hurting and aching, like they were swollen inside him waiting to burst. But all the while, his outward demeanour suggested placidity and calmness. Nobody would've ever guessed or sensed the internal torment that Martin was dealing with right now.

Twice he had walked out to the work canteen to see if he could release some emotion in the form of tears, but to no avail. He felt like his insides were jostling around, bouncing off of one another like a mean spirit had taken hold of his lungs and stomach. He didn't know how else to control it apart from give himself pain, but torturing himself physically from the outside was not the answer, and he knew it. He couldn't wait to leave his desk, get in the car and drive home. He could hide there. Get straight into bed and close the world away, then do it all over again tomorrow. He wasn't hungry, he had lost his appetite weeks ago since getting into what was now some kind of monotonous and depressive syndrome. He didn't know how to express it, he was irritated with himself, avoiding others and simply felt as low as he had ever done in his entire life.

What concerned him most was whether he was able to get any lower, and if he did, then what were the consequences of that? He already had the inkling of answer. He knew the way out, it just depended on whether he was brave enough to go through with it. In many ways, his mindset was just to disappear, become swallowed up whole by some invisible monster who could then spit him out somewhere else, away from where he was, into a parallel universe where his head was fixed and he could feel close to whatever normality was. But these thoughts were the stuff of fantasy. There was no magic bullet here or indeed a magic monster to take him in its clutches. If he wanted to keep living his life, then he would have to make changes – he would have to accept the pain and torment he dealt himself on a daily basis – and at the very least, find a coping mechanism for it, or worse still, tell someone about the dark and distressing thoughts he was having. The latter still felt like a bridge too far for Martin. He didn't like the idea of talking about himself, or admitting to the kind of pain he was suffering inside. Seeing Ruth the other evening had lifted his spirits slightly, and he still had George as a friend, but he felt weak and pathetic at the very thought of expressing his innermost torments.

'Hello Mart, you making a cuppa?'

It was Steve Crossley, one of the partners at Williamson Crossley Peters, the architects firm that Martin worked at. He had unintentionally taken Martin by surprise, given that he was in his own little world for a moment there with his back to the door and unaware of anyone behind him. He wondered how much Steve had witnessed before saying something, because Martin was pretty certain he had been on the verge of a panic attack as he let go of the edge of sink that he had been gripping tightly whilst trying to control his breathing.

'Oh, hiya Steve. Nnn… no, no thanks. I mean, no, no I'm not, sorry,' he was stumbling over his words, hating the fact that he may have been caught in the act of having some kind of breakdown or something.

'Not to worry, can I just squeeze in there?' said Steve, motioning towards the sink so he could wash his mug. 'Oh, yeah… sure, sorry,' said Martin, awkwardly removing himself from beside the sink.

'Are you ok Mart? You look like you might have seen a ghost? Or worse still that house builder from Yeardley and Sons!' Steve said, cheerfully.

'Oh, ha ha, no… I'm okay, thanks Steve, just a bit tired,' replied Martin and lowered his head, walking out towards the corridor.

'Good work on the Hereford job by the way Mart, really good,' Steve called over his shoulder to Martin as he walked out of the room.

'Umm, yeah, thanks… cheers,' he called back, disappearing down the corridor into the toilet.

The toilet was more of a safe haven, he thought to himself. At the worst, he could get away with saying he had tummy troubles. This would buy him at least 20 minutes if he needed it. He locked himself away in the cubicle and put his head in his hands. He was shaking again. Not through feeling cold, on the contrary, the heating was on in the building and that gave it the feeling of being in something close to a blast furnace sometimes. He sat for a while trying to compose his breathing while thinking about his next move. If he saw Steve again, he would probably think there was something up. At best, he could pass it off as just having a poo. But then, he didn't want people to know he was having a poo, even though he wasn't, but disappearing from your desk to the toilets for a prolonged period of time can only mean one thing, right? He weighed up what was worse in his head. His colleagues thinking he was having a shit or that he was mentally unstable right now? It seemed like an odd choice to be weighing up, but amazingly neither option seemed very attractive to him right now. He was scared of losing face in the office and if they knew he'd been having a poo, there would be a bit of banter for sure. Banter he didn't really like or pay heed to. In fact, he had been a very economical 'pooer' at work, either getting his business done in next to no time or escaping to the local Pret on his lunch hour.

He pretended to look at himself in an imaginary mirror for the moment. What the fuck was he so worried about? He despised the constant weighing up in his head about whether or not he would be bantered for having what was essentially a fake poo at work or fronting up to his colleagues to say he was really struggling with his mental wellbeing. There was only one winner here and it wasn't the latter. He'd just have to hope nobody said anything, and if they did just discreetly say he ate something dodgy. Yes, that was it. Dodgy food was always a good way out, he could shut it down quickly and get around any questions this way. It wasn't the best tactic by any means, but it would explain a lot if questioned, he thought to himself.

Two minutes later he was back at his desk and nobody had batted an eyelid. Tom was still trying to flirt across the desk with the Portuguese intern Gabriella, Susannah had her headphones in and Craig was on the phone to someone or other. Why did he have to get himself in such a state about the reaction he may or may not get by returning to his desk from the toilet? All this was just one big problem in his head that just so happened to be a bi-product of another big problem, the biggest problem of all in fact. His anxieties, self-loathing, hatred and constant feeling of failure. It was like he was embarrassed and self-conscious of his presence even though nobody could see him. The pressure he put on himself was unfair, but he couldn't shake it. It was ingrained now, never to leave. And it felt like the only way it would leave was if he didn't to exist. And if he wasn't to exist, then he'd have to do something pretty damn dramatic to make that happen, which of course he had considered many a time.

He limped through the rest of day, barely uttering a word to his colleagues – headphones on and eyes fixed firmly on the screen. He wasn't even listening to anything. It was more a protection from others who may invite him to engage. Martin just simply didn't want that, where in reality, human engagement and emotion were the most vital thing he needed for his wellbeing – certainly the state he'd worked himself into right now. His upbringing had a lot to do with this, the avoidant and emotionless experience of that fateful day his parents sat him round the dining room table. And then the hours on end he spent in his bedroom staring into blank space.

It's where it started, it must've been. Dad leaving and Mum living in anger, quietly frustrated, yearning for revenge. It wasn't healthy at all for a teenage boy experiencing his own changes as a human being, developing into a young man. At fourteen, he was still a minor, confused and naïve. He needed role models and communication. He needed love, affection and affirmation. How he came out of secondary school with straight A's was incredible really. Though the academia was something for Martin to focus on fully, and it was his one release from the torment of home life that came with the toxicity between his parents. He wanted to go back, to say something to his parents, knowing now what he didn't back then. He blamed them, he hated them. But most of all, he felt sorry for them that they had him as their son.

Chapter 12

Though Martin was glad another working day was over, what faced him back at his flat was hardly uplifting. There was nothing he wanted to eat, nothing he wanted to do. The fridge was empty anyway and he hated going to the supermarket. Bumping into people he didn't want to talk to and feeling like he had to spend the whole experience trying to avoid or make eye contact with people he used to know from school. He was becoming disorganised with this type of thing too. Food shopping and meal planning had been the first to go. His whole life had been calculated and process driven by academic success. Complete one challenge and onto the next one, whether it was revising to pass exams or preparing the ideal pitch for a new client. Right now, there were no challenges left for Martin – he felt as if he was living a very unfulfilling life. And if there were any challenges out there for him, he didn't have the energy or the fight for them.

What had happened to the motivated young man seeking a job at a top architects firm? What had happened to the same man who got himself a relationship, a future with someone and nearly a proposal that could've confirmed that? The same boy who lived through a broken home at a critical time in his own development and found the ability to pass exams, get into university, sustain friends and make a success of himself? He had mustered the confidence and the motivation to do all those things in the past, so where was this life he was seemingly doing so well at before, but now failing miserably and losing the very will of it. Martin was exhausted. He had nothing left to give, not even for his own pride. Every setback nowadays was ten times worse than the last. They hurt, and the pain seemed to pile on more pain that already sat festering there from the time before. It was mental torment, but the anguish was physical and he was starting to see it in his face and body. He looked thin and pale. His face had lost its relative fullness.

His eyes sagged with despondency and his cheekbones had become pronounced, making him look gaunt.

Just like last night and the night before, he loaded up his laptop. He typed in the familiar web address, or at least one of them that was recognised by his browser. Which one tonight, he thought to himself?

betmaestro.com.

Gambling wasn't something Martin had ever really got into. However, since his big wins at the Cheltenham Festival earlier in the year it had ignited some sort of passion within him to chase a prize. Before this, sometimes he had done football accumulators and alike, but genuine gambling was becoming his thing. It was a release for him, where he could come alive again. He could focus on something, get the buzz from winning and enjoy the rewards, so long as he actually won. The money he'd earned when Helena bought him out had just been sitting in an account. Now it was fuelling Martin's new habit of playing glitzy Vegas style games, late night online bingo and football matches happening in some far off land, in countries that he'd barely heard of.

To begin with, Martin's betting diary looked something like this:

Monday: Roulette and Blackjack. Just dabbling. Won £100 initially, but overall, £50 down.
Tuesday: More roulette. Lucky Stars Bingo. £17 up.
Wednesday: Back to Blackjack. A selection of football results from the Saudi league. £42 up.
And so on.

That had been the first week proper that Martin had opened the gateways to online gambling. What started off as a little bug which gave him a buzz, had turned into a nasty and addictive virus, which had taken hold of his psyche and was threatening to rule his life. Initially, it was a pretty innocuous toe dip into this other world. But now it had become an incredibly serious problem for him. Alongside his other anxieties, it had added more angst, more fear and a constant worry about the depth of trouble he now found himself in financially. In his head, for a while at least, it was 'free' money that he was throwing away. The settlement from Helena and their house that he should be using in future for a deposit on a new place, was instead being used to bet and gamble. And he was now stuck in a rented flat, draining all the resources he had because he simply couldn't muster any motivation to move on and build a new life somewhere for himself. So, just over five weeks from the initial foray into the gambling world, Martin's betting diary looked like this:

Monday: Roulette. Bingo. Saudi Football. Tennis in Malaysia. Bit of blackjack. Stateside Horse Racing. More Roulette. Overall: £29,781 down.
Tuesday: Instant win games. Blackjack. Questionable football accumulators for games in Kazakhstan and Qatar. Back and forth with hours

of Roulette waiting for zero to come in. Overall: £44,019 down.

This final loss was the tip of the iceberg. He had lost what would be to the average person an eye watering sum of money. And tonight, he intended to use his final reserves of cash to try and win some, if not all of it back. For the first time in a while, he had a plan. However, the viability of this plan was questionable at best. Some quick, if not detailed research into the Saudi Football league had told him one thing. There was a front runner. A team called Al-Hilal. They had just stretched their unbeaten run to 15 games and sat top of the table 9-points clear of the rest. They were playing against lowly Al-Khaleej, on a dreadful run, with 1-point to show from their last 7 games. An absolute shoo-in. Combine this in a double bet with another match, say, something from the Andorran Primera Division and he would at least be able to make a dent in his losses if these both came in, because given the odds, they were bound to. He threw in a game from the Albanian Superliga for good measure too. He was desperate to up the odds at this stage and there was no seeing past the might of KF Tirana getting a home win against JF Erzeni. Three football matches at 6/1 in a treble.

At these odds, for all the results to land, he could make himself a cool £10,805.21. However, in order for this to happen he would have to make his biggest stake yet and use all but the last of his cash reserves from the Helena fallout. £1,500 deposited. £1,500 bet.

As the games were all kicking off in different parts of the world, he'd be made to sweat on the last one coming in. But that was the Saudi game, so no problems there. He just had to hope that the first two came in then he'd be home and dry.

This wasn't any good for Martin's anxiety and he'd even put himself in this position, heaping the misery upon himself for the next six hours. He would be tense, he knew that. There was a lot of money at stake. But the button had been pressed, with the bet now placed and his fate in the hands of a combined total of sixty-six men running around kicking what was essentially a round bag of leather filled with wind on a rectangular piece of grass in various corners of the world.

How ridiculous this was, he thought to himself. The reality of this had already set in as soon as he did it. This was big, this was the last straw, a dumb impulsive move to win back some of his losses in the blink of an eye. But this initial blink would be followed by at least 270 minutes of football over the course of six hours. He would be up until midnight to check on his last result. He could probably watch it somewhere on the internet, and though the desire was there to do so, he simply felt like he couldn't. It would be like watching a horror movie from behind the sofa. His eyes covered, cowering away, too afraid to watch what could become a ghastly experience. He reassured himself some more, trying to take his mind off it. Perhaps he'd take a walk this evening while it was all unfolding. Why sit here and let the whole thing happen just staring at a screen? He couldn't do anything about it, so he may as well try and get out of his own head and out of the house for a while.

It was a pleasant evening, the kind where summer is turning into Autumn, so ideal for a walk really. There would be plenty of people out and about thought Martin, so he took his headphones and sunglasses just in case he saw anyone he knew. He really didn't want to chat to anyone, should he bump into a colleague or someone he'd known from yesteryear, so he blocked himself off from the rest of the world. Even further still, he wore a baseball cap to truly cover himself and hide. This was almost a symbol for his embarrassment about himself and his situation. He'd rather hide and pretend he didn't exist, and while still living in physically, this was the best way to do it without being completely invisible. It was a relatively short walk over to the woods that flanked the gorge. It was an absolutely beautiful place to live and it was clear that Martin didn't appreciate this enough. The rays from the sun were beaming softly through the trees creating an almost mystical and enchanting passage through the woods. It was reassuringly calm, which was one thing he needed right now. He'd chosen to listen to a mental health podcast from some doctor, accepting of the fact that he needed a strategy to get out of his current mindset and start to sort himself out. But in truth, if you had asked him what the content of the episode was, not even an hour after his walk, he wouldn't have been able to tell. It was almost like the words were being spoken in a different language, they weren't really landing with him, they were just there for company in a way. In truth, Martin was kidding himself that he would be able concentrate on a podcast during the time where he had the last of his money riding on obscure football matches. He was trying not to think about how much he hated this situation right now and just look at the path in front of him while he walked. But as he walked, it was like Martin was submerged in a different realm, as the whole world around him went out of focus, and a fuzzy din had covered his vision. He was naturally slowing down, or so it felt, and he couldn't even remember walking the last 200 yards, let alone the rest of the day. He spotted a bench in the near distance and limped towards it so he could compose himself again.

It was a relief to be sat down, it had felt like some kind of motion sickness or migraine as he was walking. He knew that it was panic causing his body to shut down. The sheer panic and realisation of his current plight taking hold on his senses and causing his mind and sight to fog. It was a painful feeling, and purely self-inflicted on this occasion. He hated himself for that, which only added to the misery he had already heaped upon himself. He removed his sunglasses and put his head in his hands with the intention of weeping, but nothing came out.

Just then, he heard voices coming along the path. A middle-aged couple were walking their golden retriever. He quickly composed himself and put his sunglasses on. The dog bounded happily along and came to sniff at Martin.

'Sorry! Oh sorry! Maisie! Maisie! Come back,' called the woman from along the path. But it was okay, Martin didn't mind this type of dog. He always really wanted one, but Mum would've never sanctioned it in her palace of suburban bliss. 'Too many bits on the floor' she would say. Not like it really mattered Martin thought, you have the fucking vacuum out every five minutes anyway.

'It's alright,' said Martin softly as the owners came closer. He gave the dog a stroke and a neck rub. He felt calm with the interaction with the dog, but it was off again before he knew it.

'Sorry about that,' said the owner again, 'What a lovely evening!'

'Oh, yes, no not at all, lovely dog. And yes, really lovely,' Martin replied somewhat awkwardly. 'Cheers, see ya,' he added, smiling nervously.

The couple both gave reassuring nods and cheerfully continued on with their walk. For a moment he was taken out of a depressive zone, he had to act quickly to cover what he was feeling so that the couple wouldn't judge him, or worse still ask how he was, and it seemed to have worked momentarily.

But there were more pressing matters at hand. Full time was approaching in the Andorran Primera Division in the game between UE Santa Coloma and UE Sant Julia. Thankfully, Coloma were romping to a 3-0 victory without any hitches. First one in the bag and a small crumb of relief for Martin to cling to. One down, two to go he thought. Headphones back in, Martin continued his walk through the woods, urging himself to appreciate the natural beauty of the environment he was in. The hues of yellow and pink from the sun creeping through breaks in the trees and the stillness of nature, earthy greens and browns created an enchanted mix of woodland bliss. It was a nice place to be, he should come here more he thought.

Walking along the track, he'd found some composure until a buzz in his pocket had suddenly sent a shot up his spine and a thump in his chest. He'd decided to setup notifications for the next match (which is where things might get quite interesting) and had hoped that KF Tirana, a record 26-time winner of the Albanian National League were holding up their end of the bargain. And they were, almost instantly. A 4th minute own goal had put them ahead and hopefully on course for a routine victory. Of course, he had 86 more minutes of this one to endure first, but the signs were positive. Martin was starting to feel that buzz of winning again. A feeling of relief and gentle satisfaction, that for once, he felt like he was getting something right. The ten grand or so that he could win would go a fair way to getting out of the financial deficit he'd got himself into. He'd only be a few grand short of the original deposit he had put in with Helena on the house. He'd have taken a pretty hefty hit on the equity he'd earned, but still, this was good. He started to plan how he could make up the rest, perhaps with a few 'foreigners' on weekends where he could do freelance architectural drawings for private clients. The debt shortfall would be gone in no time he thought, nothing to worry about. He would quit gambling, delete the apps – he pictured himself handing himself in at a local bookies like a criminal would at a police station.

'It was me, I did it, I promise I won't do it again, so please don't punish me,' would be the leading line to a somewhat bemused cashier. Of course, he wouldn't actually do this, but the fact he could visualise that the end might be in sight after weeks of addictive nights on betting apps and the instant win games gave him some kind of comfort as he made for the pathway back to the entrance for the woods. Dr Ranjit Subrava was still offering some calm wellbeing advice through his headphones, interviewing some leading business bod about their mental health experiences, but in reality Martin wasn't listening. The talking was just a background noise really, as he began to let himself get more and more optimistic about the results that could improve his financial situation and set him on some kind of pathway towards something of a rehabilitation.

Letting himself into the door of his flat, he felt a lot better than the hour previous when he let himself out. Though he was still tense, at least he felt like there was some kind of control coming back and that the panic was reducing. 'Everything will be okay,' he told himself over and over in his head. He poured himself a glass of water and stood back against the worktop to take some deep breaths. This was going well, so far. He reassured himself with the news that FK Tirana had reached half-time in their game still 1-0 up. The buzz was real, the excitement was building, but he still had a sense of unease creeping into his body – which was only natural, he thought. Focus on the positive, focus on the positive. The Saudi's will be okay and that will be that. He had already written the script and it contained a happy ending, the ending and the outcome he wanted. His phone buzzed on the opposite counter. A goal, surely? His body went stock still, heart beating fast with hairs standing up on his neck in excitement. Or was it fear? He didn't know. He rushed to the opposite counter to collect his phone, FK Tirana 2, JF Erzeni 0.

'YES!' he shouted, finally letting out some of the emotion. He covered his mouth with nervous laughter, a mix of excited energy and anxiety all piled into one.

'This is happening, this is on!' he told himself encouragingly. Only

25 minutes left for the game to end and FK Tirana were now very much on course for victory. He checked the cash-out value on betmaestro. It was standing at £2,658. Not bad, but not nearly enough to get him out of trouble. In theory, he could double his money and go again by cashing out. And by this he meant cashing out and going back to the same bet that his current bet was riding on with the Saudi game, a sure thing. He could make even more money, potentially. This was a crucial time right now, time for a cool head and measured decision. Perhaps he should wait until the final whistle in Tirana and reassess… Surely they would see out the rest of this game and the rewards might be even greater by that point?

He decided to let it run, when suddenly, his phone buzzed again. Goal for Erzeni, 72 minutes. Shit. Cash-out value had decreased slightly, so he'd probably have to stick with the original plan to get his rewards. Fuck, this was horrible. It had been plain sailing until a minute ago, but now he was studying the tiny football pitch graphic on his phone, watching the stats and intermittent ball movements, trying to discern if what was happening was what he wanted to happen. If Erzeni were to score again, he'd quite literally be financially fucked. There would be no shot at the big money with the Saudi game. He wouldn't even get to that. He focused on the negatives of this, thinking about the final lump of cash he'd stand to lose and what he would do next. Panic was starting to set in again, apprehension was rising. His body was tense, the excited buzz he had felt earlier was fading and the reality of losing was looming over him like a monstrous beast who was quite keen on swallowing him up whole. Shit. Erzeni looked like they had won a free-kick in a dangerous position just outside the penalty box. 84 minutes on the clock… surely not. 'Please, no,' he said to himself quietly. It was then that the picture on the screen in front of him froze ominously.

GOAL.

The graphic pulsated on the screen like some cruel mocking joke. Number 17 for Erzeni had smashed in a free-kick with barely 5 minutes left to level up the scores at 2-2.

'Fucking fuck fuck FUCK!' bellowed Martin. The 'fucks' getting louder the more they were repeated. Cash-out gone. Money gone. £1,500 down the drain, but it felt like more given the chance he had not 20 minutes ago to even double his money. Gambling was a cruel game, he knew that. But this, this was emotional torture. He was so close only moments ago to

getting the second of three bets confirmed, going into the last game with everything to win it would seem. He sank to the floor with his back to the kitchen cupboards, staring at his phone in disbelief. His heart beat fast and his stomach felt sick. He'd blown it, again. The light was now fading around him with the sun finally setting and he felt as gloomy as the room he was slumped in. He placed his phone carefully on the floor beside him, head in hands. His pathetic plan at redemption had failed. How had it come to this?

Two minutes later, 'buzzzzz,' went his phone again.

Chapter 13

The shouts and screams coming from flat 18A could've probably been heard from at least a mile away. Martin's neighbours might be wondering what all the commotion was about, was he happy? Was he sad? Should they call the authorities?

Turns out that the buzz on his phone was good news, at least for Martin, who was celebrating a late winning goal for Tirana to secure a last gasp 3-2 victory. He was still in the game. Shit, that was close. He had looked into the abyss for a moment and didn't like what he saw. Hopefully now he could compose himself slightly and look forward to the end of the next game and secure the ten thousand pounds he so desperately needed. But he certainly didn't want to go through that again. Should he cut his losses and cash out? He'd at least doubled his money. Would this at least help him live to fight another day? He didn't really want to fight, he just needed to win this time and then it could all be over. That was his plan, that was his strategy. He got himself into the mindset of carrying on and stuck with his original decision. It would be too late in an hour anyway as the game was going to kick off. The doubt was still lingering ever so slightly though. Cash out and go to blackjack? Stick it on roulette? At least the results would be instant. No, he thought. We're sticking to this now. The odds were in his favour, he'd come this far so why bother quitting on it now.

The rewards were great, but the pain could be excruciating.

After pacing the kitchen for about 10 minutes, Martin decided to make himself some toast. He hadn't eaten dinner because of his lack of appetite, but thought he should probably eat something, despite the anxiousness in his midriff telling him it was a bad idea. With buttered toast and tea in hand, Martin went through to the lounge where it would be a little bit more comfortable to sit and wait for the last result to come in. It had to come in, it simply had to. His phone buzzed again, but this time a message from George:

How's it going mate? Do you fancy that pint up the hilly sometime this week?

It felt nice to be wanted, and in truth he'd been largely non-committal to George's offer of a drink when he'd suggested it the other week. He felt preoccupied now so would text George in the morning perhaps. Right now he felt like his focus should be solely on the matter in hand, despite not being able to do anything about it. He nibbled at the toast that he didn't really want, but convinced himself enough in the end to finish it. 10 minutes until kick-off. He studied some stats on his phone to try and reassure himself about the game ahead.

Al-Hilal were Saudi national champions for a record 25 times, the most decorated team in the country. Their top scorer was a Brazilian recruit from the European leagues who arrived for big money, albeit controversially. He'd netted 24 goals already this season and was taking the league by storm. Martin looked him up. Yep, he was playing this evening. That was good news. All seemed well on this front, so he checked their opponents.

Al-Khaleej weren't exactly covering themselves in glory right now. Their usual goalkeeper had fallen out with the manager (he wasn't playing) and their only real goalscorer this season seemed to be a central defender who had scored three penalties. This was all looking very promising thought Martin and he felt comforted by what he had read. Now all he had to do was wait. He flicked on the TV for some background companionship and opened up his laptop so that he could see what was happening in the game, some 4,000 miles away.

The sheer weight of what he was doing was laying heavy on him. This was what gambling was though. Not just a simple transaction to try and gain more than you have, it was much more than that. And it was so much more when you didn't really have anything to transact with. He thought about the amount of online betting adverts he had seen, they were everywhere. On the back of buses, on the TV, on his phone, even on the footballers themselves. They had glorified the narrative around it and only now had started to add in what seemed like a caveat to say, 'when the fun stops, stop.' Well, it had never been that much fun to Martin. An initial buzz from the Cheltenham winnings had just simply escalated into something more sinister and desperate, a simple release from his monotonous existence. But there was good news coming from the laptop screen in front of him, because 13 minutes into the game between Al-Hilal and Al-Khaleej, the favourites were doing their bit in Martin's big money escape. 1-0 to Al-Hilal. Relief, unbridled joy and gratefulness that he just might not fuck this thing up. This was it. Surely the might of Al-Hilal would just be able to plunder in a few more and make it safe? This evening had been nothing short of an emotional rollercoaster, it had been hideous. Now he was tired, but he had to hang on until the final whistle. Because as long as he was awake, he could at least have some kind of control over what was happening, even though he had absolutely zero power over the actual result that was being played out in the middle east. He checked the cash-out again. It was standing at just under £4,000. Not to be sniffed at thought Martin, but still not really what he had come for tonight. He had made that decision earlier and was determined to stick to it.

He'd lost himself momentarily as his phone buzzed to update him on the half-time score. Still 1-0 to the good and cash-out value continuing to rise. It was tempting, so so tempting. But all the same this game was being billed, and currently being played out for that matter, as an incredibly one-sided affair. The current odds on Al-Khaleej even scoring were at 20/1, let alone even winning the bloody game. Martin's money seemed all but safe.

He relaxed into his sofa, waiting for the second half to begin. His heavy eyes were drooping slowly and he had no real control over it. He'd let himself succumb to the peace, having exhausted himself with worry and anxiety over the course of the evening. His body was running on empty, not even the adrenaline from earlier could keep him awake. For Martin, falling asleep right now could have potentially catastrophic repercussions. Because as long as he was awake, he could, (within reason) do something about the situation and intervene if things got a bit hairy towards the 90th minute and cash out on the bet, taking a very minimal hit on the full bounty. He knew how these things worked and at the end of the day it just wasn't worth the risk, so that's what he would do. Let it run for as long as his nerve would hold.

Martin watched as Al-Hilal's Brazilian superstar crashed a lethal right-footed shot into the top corner and celebrated jubilantly, his team 2-0 to the good. He copied the player in kissing the floor in celebration (probably something to do with religion he thought), but right now, you are my God, Sir. I love you Mr Brazil Striker! And then Martin rose to his feet and presented the player with a trophy that he had bought with the bet winnings, smiling for the cameras and letting confetti rain down on the scene while the rest of the team celebrated behind. It was a glorious moment, the game had finished in an instant, it was all over and it was a huge relief. He would thank each and every Al-Hilal player in a moment, he thought. But first he needed to find his phone. Where was his phone? Perhaps he dropped it somewhere on the pitch while he was celebrating.

It let out another loud buzz next to him. What the hell was happening?

Martin woke up, confused and disorientated scratching around for his phone. The laptop had died of power. Seriously, where the fuck was he right now? He blundered off the sofa and scooped up his phone from the floor in a discombobulated panic. Hang on. It was over wasn't it? Fuck. No, he'd fallen asleep and had been woken by what was now the most dramatic ending to this football match that anybody could've foreseen not 45 minutes earlier. The notifications Martin was now staring down dumbfounded at were as follows:

86' Penalty awarded – Al-Khaleej
86' Red card (no. 13) – Al-Hilal
88' Goal! (no. 5) – Al-Khaleej

Oh shit. Oh shit, shit, shit. What on earth was happening right now? Martin was still half asleep and unable to come to terms with what he was witnessing. What stirred him from his trance was looking down at the betting app and reading the words 'Cash-out unavailable' in a banner underneath his bet. His world was getting smaller, closing in on him. This was it, there was no way back, he'd lost it all. He'd fallen at the final hurdle. The Al-Hilal goalkeeper had inexplicably conceded a late penalty and got himself sent off in the process. Then, the trusty penalty taker of Al-Khaleej crashed in an equaliser to make the game all square at 1-1. Full-time.

And with that, Martin's money disappeared with no chance of getting it back.

He stared in disbelief at the screen in front of him, unsure what to do next. He felt hot, sick and tired. Then his stomach lurched violently and while covering his mouth and running towards to bathroom, he vomited a mixture of toast and bile into the toilet just in time.

Then the tears came. The tears he was pushing for earlier today were certainly very real now as he leant himself up against the cold and discomforting porcelain. He had never felt so alone, so destructive and so helpless. This time, it was all of his own making too, which piled on the shame and misery more. He wept quietly before brushing his teeth and getting into bed, a broken man.

This latest setback had to be the end of it all, didn't it?

Chapter 14

'Buzzzzz,' went Martin's phone. It was 10.47am on Thursday morning, he should've been in work. He looked at the screen. Four missed calls and a voicemail. He dialled into the voicemail and listened to the message that was waiting for him.

> *'Hi Mart, it's Steve here… noticed you hadn't come in this morning and just wondered whether everything was okay? I also noticed you were, uh, a little bit under the weather yesterday so just checking in… Anyway mate, it's no issue, but uh, please give us a call as soon as you can. Thanks, bye.'*

Anyone waking up past their alarm and being nearly three hours late for work would be completely panicked right now, making immediate efforts to rush out the door as soon as possible. But Martin just lay there, wrapped in his duvet of depression. Steve was right, he was under the weather, but he could never let him know the extent of the shitstorm he was actually in the middle of. He appreciated the call, Steve was a good guy. He probably should text back or something, because he really didn't have the energy to speak to anyone. Last night had completely drained him both mentally and physically with the emotional rollercoaster of the betting result and the flip flop of the winning/ not winning scenarios he had experienced on more than one occasion. He tapped out a message to Steve and hoped that there would be no further questions.

'Morning Steve, I'm so sorry, I've just woken up as I hardly slept last night. I think it must be a fever as well as some kind of bug. I will take today sick and let you know how I feel about work tomorrow later or at the latest by the morning. Thanks, Mart'

Message sent. That would do, nobody would argue with that sort of thing in this day and age. The Covid-19 pandemic had changed everyone's perspective on illness. All of a sudden, everyone had turned into a huge germophobe. Sure, nobody wanted to be ill, but a snotty nose was hardly life threatening. Door handles would be sanitised, office deep cleans performed and the protagonist in question would have their ailment analysed and scrutinised until everyone had had their chance to say whether or not they were feeling the similar sort of 'symptoms.' 'Oh, and do a test while you're at it, because you never know,' someone would say (usually Sandra in accounts, she was the office busy body). All this meant that Martin was okay to be in bed this morning and hide behind the façade of a post covid era, which suited him absolutely fine.

A message flashed through, from Steve.

'Thanks for letting me know Mart. Hope you're doing ok. Speak soon. S'

Okay, good. No more dialogue. That's what Martin wanted. He'd probably bought himself two days of sick as a result, then the weekend, so by the time he returned to work next week the questions about his 'sickness' would have disappeared. Of course, plenty of questions still remained over the actual sickness Martin was feeling. Mental sickness. His mental health was clearly not good and he was struggling to articulate it, and worse still, even open up and talk about it, let alone truly admit it to himself. In fact, talking about it at all wasn't even on his radar. He was being far too stubborn in trying to dream up his own reckless strategies to try and free himself from this misery but suffering alone had become a torment and a constant battle. He rolled over, burying himself in the bed again, hiding. What the hell had happened last night? Results aside, he could've nearly saved himself had he not fallen asleep. He hated himself for that.

It was this thought that could haunt him forever and now it would never change. It was consigned to history as the single most stupid thing he had ever done in his life and there was a growing list to add to which he also hated himself for.

Regret. That's all it could be summed up as. But why me? Why, why, why? He was tormenting himself, analysing his behaviours and digging beneath the surface into some of the deepest and darkest places in his mind, over thinking scenarios and running back the tapes over and over like some cruel cinema viewing. This wasn't doing him any good, but he didn't know any other way.

Although he looked up and respected his best friend George, it was hard not to be jealous. He had it all really, and he was never getting into stupid scrapes or high-risk situations. If he was, he was handling them very well, thought Martin. He had zero confidence in his own ability right now to handle any situation with his self-esteem at an all-time low – and that was saying something. He really should message George back, while he thought about it.

'Hey mate, sorry. Mad few days and now I'm in my sick bed haha. Work told me to stay away as they think I've got Covid. Catch-up next week.'

It was a half-truth in essence, he wasn't at work and he was in bed. But nobody was telling him to stay away and he definitely didn't have covid. In many ways, it was something much, much worse and far more terminal.

'No worries pal. Take it steady.'

That was the almost instantaneous response from George. He wondered whether deep down George knew a little bit more than he was letting on. Martin could tell that he sensed something the other week at The Hilly – the night they met and when he had bumped into Ruth. Shit, Ruth. He was meant to look her up and see what she was up to now. But not like he had a chance with her, he thought to himself. Was she really going to be interested in a depressive 35-year-old singleton living in a rented flat who had recently flushed his entire future down the proverbial toilet? He decided that he couldn't be bothered to look her up right now, it would depress him too much to see her lovely smiling face looking back at him through the screen. So basically, today would be a complete write-off. He would stay in bed and try and pass the time thinking up a strategy of how not to completely fuck things up from here on in, but he didn't feel too optimistic about it. He would rather something far more low maintenance for his mind and to lie there and wallow in some self-pity, or better still, disappear from view entirely.

*

It was now the dead of night in Martin's flat. He'd surfaced slowly and found himself at the front door in his trainers and dressing gown. He carefully turned the lock and walked outside, ignoring the fact he hadn't even closed his front door, then made for the exit from his block. He crossed the road and joined the little lane that would ultimately bring him out at the entrance to the woods. Though it was at least a 200 metre walk or so, he glided along the lane and was out the other end before he knew it. His body was weightless, he felt indestructible. Strangely enough, he was retracing his steps from the previous night, but this time there were no headphones, no irritating podcasts, no smiling dog walkers and especially no beautiful pinky-golden sunset glimmering through the trees. It was just him and the sleeping world, floating through time in the pitch black woods. Although weirdly, it wasn't completely dark because he could see everything despite the lack of natural light. It was all in focus and like the daytime, but just dark. There was no overspill from the city here, the only light would come from the moon, and although he couldn't see it, it must have been there. He thought it was strange how everything was in complete focus, but he wasn't questioning it any further right now. He seemed focused on only one thing.

He had noticed on his walk last night that the path through the woods flanked the side of the gorge, and it hadn't occurred to him before that the woods were that close to the edge of what would be at least a 250ft drop to the bottom. He continued walking until he found the spot. The fence had been tampered with at some point, or an animal had slowly been chipping away at what was now a big enough hole for a grown man to fit through. There were the remnants of a sign on the fence that had been removed or ripped off. It probably would've said, 'DANGER – CLIFF EDGE' but he wasn't the slightest bit scared. He stooped down onto the dusty track and crawled underneath the hole in the fence and through the hedge. There was seemingly no feeling in his body, he couldn't even feel the brush of the brambles or the dried dirt on his palms as he navigated his way through. His mind was only thinking about one thing, getting to the vantage point, his spot. It was a vantage point he knew, he could see it in his mind, but he'd never been there. In fact, he couldn't work out why, but he was just so determined to get to this location, acting both stealthily and very deliberately to reach it. Now standing on the other side of the fence, it was just how he visualised it. The gaping hole into the abyss staring right back at him. The moon was now visible up above, bathing the humungous gorge below in an eerie and milky blue light. He took a deep breath and held his arms out, gently leaning forward like a serenely falling tree and then let his toes release their grip, and with it, himself from the edge.

Martin jolted violently in his bed. Fuck. He was covered in sweat and breathing deeply, trying to catch it back after what was in retrospect, a pulsating last 15 minutes. Maybe it actually was a fever? Maybe he'd been hallucinating? The experience he had just now in his dream felt so real, so calculated. It was scary, but also slightly reassuring, even a bit exciting. His mind had taken him on a journey to what could be the end, showing him how simple it could be to release himself from this life and disappear for good. This is what he thought he was trying to be told anyway.

He put his head back on the pillow and stared at the blank ceiling. Christ, he thought. It was 3.00pm in the afternoon, he must've dropped off. What had just happened? Did he just make all that up? It wasn't as if he'd ever given that path or that fence or that hedge a second thought when he'd seen it before. His mind was filling in the blanks, creating a narrative for Martin and finding a way for him to try and release itself. It was like some dark beast had taken control of his mind, showing him a new and sinister passageway to another world. He'd flirted with the idea before, as in, he'd had thoughts, but nothing too serious. When he turned on his self-loathing mode and truly hated himself, the yearning for disappearance was most prevalent, but he'd never dreamt so vividly of it before. It was almost like his mind was split, a fight or flight type of scenario. The fight was quite clearly to battle with his demons, get help, find a road to recovery and gradually turn the corner out of this depression. The flight however, was to act impulsively, to do something with complete reckless abandon. To channel the feelings of shame, guilt and hate into fuel for an engine that would drive him quickly away.

There was a realisation now. He had woken up to the fact that this was happening in his head and he wasn't sure right now about which side was going to win.

Chapter 15

6 years previous

'Do you believe in fate?' asked Helena, inquisitively. She asked a lot of questions, did Helena. Martin didn't mind, he sometimes quite appreciated the attention, and she seemed happy doing the quizzing while he just simply had to answer, so it seemed like a balance they were both pleased with.

'Umm… yeah, I guess so. I mean, I don't believe that the future can be predicted or anything like that. Like, nothing has happened until it's happened… if you see what I mean. But everything that is happening, happens for a reason,' was Martin's somewhat convoluted reply.

'No, I understand what you mean,' she said with a smile. 'It's just interesting, isn't it. How we ended up together. Imagine if you hadn't walked into KFC that night in Kavos, or you hadn't said whatever it was you said to those boys!' she giggled at the last bit.

'Hey, I saved you from those twats!' Martin bounced back.

'Yeah, what was it? "Cheers Romeo",' she said in a mock Liverpudlian accent.

'Well, you're still here aren't you? Romeo must have something about him at least,' he said with a grin. He could be quite witty sometimes, when he felt like it.

This was very typical of the early days between Martin and Helena. They'd found each other in relatively bizarre circumstances and they seemed to run along just fine. It was Martin who did the hard work (in the end), he finally plucked up the courage to march himself down to her hotel and ask after her. In reality, it was George who marched quite an apprehensive Martin down the hill to her hotel (but that wasn't what he told Helena). Their first hour of courtship was spent in a sports bar playing pool. The time that followed until they were to leave the resort was spent by the pool at Helena's hotel. Martin was far too embarrassed to show his face around the pool at his own hotel for any length of time at all. They drank cocktails, ate KFC, and in the end, it actually turned out to be an okay second week of the holiday for Martin despite the absolutely disastrous start it had got off to.

When they'd returned home, they would text and call most evenings – a true long distance love story. Although, it wasn't too long a distance. Helena was only up the motorway in Worcestershire, so Martin would drive up and see her most weekends. This was the most wanted Martin had ever felt in his entire life. He was happy, he was content and even his old insecurities – those that had plagued his teenage years and early twenties – seemed to be gone when he was with her.

Helena was his antidote. She had put him on a level, cared for him, loved him, even. They shared similar interests, or rather, Martin had realised he liked certain things after giving them a go for the first time, such as hiking and paddle boarding.

They'd packed up Martin's Peugeot 206 for the weekend and were heading for North Wales to have an adventurous weekend. Helena had always wanted to climb Snowdon and do all these action type activities in the caves and quarries. The forecast looked okay, so they would be going for a hike first thing the following morning. This was the first time they'd been away together in the eight months they'd known each other. It was all very new to Martin. A girlfriend. Trips away with a partner. New and exhilarating experiences. He was excited as well as nervous. They pulled into the B&B just as the light was fading and checked-in to their room before going downstairs to get something to eat.

The B&B had a restaurant and pub, which was slightly tired and old-fashioned, but it was just fine for their needs over the weekend.

They entered the pub through an internal door that joined to the rooms and walked into what a typical Friday night would look like in countless pubs up and down the country. Locals propped up against the bar, couples coming in for a quick drink after walking their dogs and the odd group of work colleagues drinking after a long monotonous week doing whatever it is they did round here. Suddenly he felt quite apprehensive, like all eyes were on him. He was conscious of himself, he felt very English. He almost didn't even want to speak. Helena just bounded over to the bar where a sign said, 'Food must be ordered at the bar, please note your table number.' She wasn't short on confidence, or didn't care who thought what. But why was he so nervous all of a sudden? He didn't particularly like unfamiliar surroundings or faces, it gave him anxiety. Even Helena's confidence on this occasion was something he didn't feel like he could hide behind.

'Hello, hi! Is that table over there taken? We'd like to order some food if that's alright,' said Helena.

'Yeah sure, here's a couple of menus just pop back up here when you're ready,' replied the smiling barman.

'Great! Thanks,' said Helena. Martin nodded to the man behind the bar, still not opening his mouth.

The couple waded through the bar area and found their table

where he and Helena sat down with their menus.

'This is cosey!' said Helena cheerfully.

Martin nodded back, still looking around and over his shoulder in what seemed like a display of apprehension. To the rest of the pub he probably looked like some undercover pub critic, but one that wasn't very good at hiding the fact he was undercover, when in fact he wasn't undercover at all.

'Are you okay?' asked Helena, reaching over the table to touch Martin's arm.

'Yeah, yeah, fine. I'm alright,' he replied, thinking that if he actually admitted that he was nervous about being here he'd be ridiculed. He would've liked somewhere quieter to be honest, not in the throngs of what was essentially a glorified gastro pub, not a restaurant. It was a homely place, but very typical of the kind of pub that had shoehorned food into their offering and probably used to be a standard village boozer. Dark wooden furniture, muted crimson, green and cream Jacobean patterned carpets. The kind of ones that had swirly and ornate features, but were also very well trodden to the point that they were black and mostly sticky. These sorts of environments were quickly disappearing from the pub scene, but right here was like a time warp from pubs that he'd been to with his parents on the way home from day trips in the 90's.

'Right, what are you having then? I'm starving!' announced Helena.

'Hmm, I'm not loads hungry but probably go for the burger maybe?' He didn't sound sure, it was almost like he was asking for her approval.

'Well I'm having fish and chips I reckon. That guy over there just had his brought out and it looked good to be fair,' said Helena, peering over again at the table that had just been served their food.

'Are you okay ordering while I go to the toilet?' she continued.

Bugger, thought Martin. Why hadn't he thought of that to get himself out of ordering. It wasn't as if he wanted to get away with paying or anything, he assumed that would be after the meal. He just simply lacked confidence with interaction and having to speak in new environments. There was also pressure. Pressure? What fucking pressure though, he thought to himself. 6oz beef burger and chips (no mayo) and a portion of fish and chips. Hardly fucking pressure was it? He was grappling with this as Helena motioned to get up and go to the toilet.

'Helloooo, Earth to Martin!' she joked, waving ironically across his eyeline.

'Oh yeah, sorry. Miles away,' he replied. 'I'll go up there now. Do you want a drink?'

'Oooooh yes please, white wine spritzer would be lovely thanks!' she said happily.

Martin didn't fully know what a spritzer was, but he wasn't about to ask anyone.

'Yep, no worries,' he said, and went off to the bar to get the order in.

Martin gingerly waded his way up towards the bar. It felt like the world was closing in on him, like all eyes were judging his very presence in the pub and questioning why on earth he was going to the bar. Of course, it was something he had again cooked up in his head. He just felt anxious in this sort of situation, like there was an added pressure that he put upon his already apprehensive nature. He squeezed his way nervously between two groups of people sitting around the bar and waited at the counter. He was choosing not to make eye contact with anyone around him, God forbid that they might look at him, or worse still say, 'hello.'

'What can I get for you mate?' said the barman. He seemed pleasant enough, not scary or anything.

'Umm yeah, can we… can we get some food ordered please? Oh and some, uh… some drinks please,' came Martin's reply.

'Of course, is it table 23?'

'Oh, um yeah. Yeah it is,'

'Okay, what can I get you?'

'Can I have the 6oz beef burger, but no mayo in the bun, and uh, the fish and chips, with uh, a white wine spritzer?' The last bit was almost asked as a question, like he wasn't sure what he was asking for. 'Oh, and uh…,' Martin scanned the ales and drinks available on tap, '…a pint of the IPA please?'

'Yep, sure anything else?' enquired the barman, jotting down the order happily. 'Um, no. No thanks,' replied Martin.

He stood waiting at the bar awkwardly for a moment, not knowing what to do next. There was no hard and fast rule for the next bit. As in, should he stand there and wait for the drinks to be poured and then take them back to his table, or simply walk off and expect them to be brought over? The latter would seem more likely given they had a food order, but equally he didn't want to assume this and wander off ignorantly.

He was feeling very self-conscious just standing there, not understanding what to do next. Why didn't he ask? Was everyone looking at him? Was he embarrassing himself by not knowing what the general procedure was? The barman was off up and down the bar collecting orders and preparing drinks. Were they Martin's? Should he wait? What a ridiculous thing to be getting flustered about. But the longer he stood there the worse it got. There were others waiting to be served now and he was just standing there in the way, having made his.

A few minutes passed (it seemed longer), where the barman caught his eye and called over to him.

'I'll get those drinks brought over mate, you can sit down if you like.' As helpful as this critical bit of information was, Martin felt it had come much too late. Even in this small act he felt like an idiot. He blamed himself for what could've been a situation that was so easily avoided with the slightest bit of communication. Martin blushed.

'Oh, right. Yeah, sure. Yeah. Thanks,' he stumbled over the reply.

He waded his way back to the table where Helena was already seated, feeling embarrassment at the fact he had just been effectively stood in no mans land for the best part of five minutes. You twat, Martin. Done it again he thought, as he took his seat.

Grappling with these sort of situations was very much at the heart of Martin's troubles. The internal barriers he afforded himself in social situations quite often left him in a silent flounder – with the moment at the bar just now being testament to that. It was hard to work out why. He didn't have the answers and maybe he never would, but the one constant in any situation such as this was obvious. The dislike and regret he allowed himself to bathe in after any incident had occurred. It lingered too, because it only added to the discourse of his internal monologue for the next time it happened. In fact, the sheer anxiety of similar situations wasn't acting as a reminder for next time, it was adding layers of unhappiness and withdrawal from wanting to put himself there in the first place. Poor Martin was stuck in a never ending battle with himself, no matter what the situation.

'All good with the order?' said Helena, smiling.

'Yep, he's bringing over the drinks in a mo,' replied Martin.

Part of him thought that Helena probably realised that he didn't like those sorts of encounters. Going into a crowded pub, rubbing shoulders with the locals and ordering something from a menu. She was his shield normally. For most people, this would be the most straightforward and mundane task that they could do in their sleep. But not for Martin. Maybe this was Helena's way of training him? Building up his confidence in those sort of situations so that she would end up having a confident and assertive boyfriend? Perhaps. Though, perhaps not. He was probably over thinking it now, and all because of an order for a burger and some fish and fucking chips. Good God, this was hard work, he thought to himself.

'...and then that's probably the point where those paths fork and you can take either way down from there,' explained Helena. She must've been talking for a little while he assumed, and he had found himself nodding along throughout the explanation of what he thought was probably something to do with their hike up Snowdon tomorrow.

'How does that sound, would you prefer the same way up and down?' she continued.

'Oh, um, yeah... I don't mind to be honest. Shall we just see what the weather is doing tomorrow? We might be wet through by that point,' he was already worrying about feeling wet, cold and tired – if that was to be the case.

'Yeah okay, that's true,' she smiled.

Martin was surprised she had agreed without protestation, because she had a habit of having the last word, even if it wasn't in a confrontational way, just a way of making her point and filling space. It was sweet really, about how engaged she got in everything, but it did surprise him when she didn't add anything.

'Oooooh thank you!' said Helena excitedly as a waitress came across with the drinks. 'Are you having food too?' the waitress asked.

'Oh, yes... I think we've ordered actually. At the bar?' Helena said, looking across puzzled at Martin. He thought that this made him look stupid. He was confused for a moment, because he had made the order and this looked like he was being undermined, as well as causing Helena to question him for a second.

'Yeah, I ordered a moment ago, all good thanks,' Martin added in.

'Oh okay, great. We'll have that along shortly for you,' the waitress replied. She turned on her heels and scurried off back towards the bar with a smile.

'I thought for a moment you'd just been stood up there the whole time and not said anything!' joked Helena.

Well, it wasn't that far from the truth, Martin thought to himself. He was still quiet in his seat and not adding much to evening, with the odd uncomfortable look across his shoulder every now and then. It was almost like he felt exposed in this situation, too far out of his comfort zone. There was noise, movement and bustling about past their table (and everyone else's for that matter). But it was a busy pub on a Friday night, this was just simply how it was. Martin didn't like that though. He preferred a more reserved location, in a familiar location close to home. The Hilly would get busy of course, but that was home turf. Nothing to worry about there. He quickly reminded himself of the pep talk he'd had before he left. It went something along the lines of this:

Try and embrace new experiences. Don't be scared of new stuff.
Don't look bored in front of Helena.
Be confident.
Try to smile more.
Try and engage with others.
Don't be afraid of doing something you wouldn't normally do.
Don't embarrass yourself.

It was a harsh assessment in reality. Lot's of don't's rather than do's. But this was the mindset of Martin. He was putting more emphasis on what he shouldn't do rather than what he should do. Okay, so he was encouraging himself to 'try' more things this weekend but they seemed insignificant parties with the other points for close company. Only time would tell as to whether he'd be able to look back on the weekend and feel like any of them were achieved. He had the rest of this evening to negotiate first, and the immediate feedback he had for himself was that he was struggling with most points that had surfaced during this mornings mirror pep talk. Perhaps next time he wouldn't stare at himself in the mirror while doing it, that was just odd really. The vision of this was lingering and it was embarrassing to even think about.

The food had arrived and at least this meant he was a step closer to going to bed.

'That's great, thank you!' Beamed Helena. Who promptly got her phone out to record the moment for her Instagram, or whatever it was that she posted to online. It wasn't something Martin was particularly interested in, or rather, had any gumption to do anything like that.

'Doesn't that look good? Amy will be jealous. She LOVES fish and chips!' she continued enthusiastically.

Amy was her best friend, basically a sister to Helena. Which sometimes made it feel like Martin was in a relationship with both of them, the amount he heard about her. 'Amy said this, Amy did that, Amy thinks you shouldn't do such and such… blah blah blah' thought Martin cynically.

'What's yours like?' asked Helena.

'Oh, yeah, well… It looks good?' said Martin, who hadn't even had a bite yet so was confused as to how he'd know whether it was any good or not. But he had to concede that it looked pretty good, which is of course the affirmation that Helena wanted. He'd learnt that as long as his answers to her questions didn't rock the boat – i.e., by saying anything negative – then she'd hardly even notice what he'd said. It wasn't quite the same as the relationship his parents had once had, but it wasn't dissimilar.

Martin's Dad had been generally pretty quiet. He would keep himself to himself and just lived for the status quo. Until of course he confessed about his affair with that woman who was a supply contact he had at work. It had all gone tits up then. Martin had mused on more than one occasion about the fact that this must've been the most his Dad had ever revealed to his Mum, by way of even having a conversation. In many ways, he couldn't even picture them having a normal conversation at the best of times. It was a terrible thing to have done in reality. But his Dad telling that to his Mum actually appeared quite brave, given their relationship. Martin wouldn't have fancied anyone's chances against Mum in that scenario, to feel her waging wrath. His actions were not brave in a chivalrous sense by any means – the circumstances should certainly not allow for that. But seeing as his Dad was generally quite fallible and with his Mum being the opposite, it was brave, yes. Martin thought cynically about this again, because bravery can generally be interchanged with stupidity in most circumstances. It just depended on whether the individual was stupid enough in the first place, which in this instance, it would appear so.

Martin felt stupid in other ways. Ways that he wasn't sure whether he could even do anything about either. His draining internal monologue and the lack of conviction he seemed to have in certain situations would generally just be put down to personal quirks he thought that he had. There was no malice in that, it wasn't even conscious. He just had to live with it. But the longer things went on, the more they were rearing up on him and with more sinister implications. They were affecting his decision making, disarming him. They were sending him into a spiral of defeatism and constant lambasting of the way he was.

Tonight, though fairly modest on that scale, was just another example of the torture he seemed to deal himself for doing something seemingly 'stupid.' He couldn't wait to finish his meal and just go to bed. He was genuinely tired from the drive and visibly uncomfortable with the situation still, shifting in his seat as he nibbled away at his food. Helena was having a lovely time, excitedly asking questions (which she generally then answered herself) and looking around the making observations saying things like, 'Oooh I wonder what she's been up to?' and 'Do they actually speak Welsh in Wales?' or 'I don't think I like the look of that man's beard.'

It was their first trip away, the first of many perhaps. He didn't want this to be a sign of things to come. Which to him right now was a picture of his parents, but from a different generation. With the same relationship politics in place, he could visualise a mirror being held out in front of them, showing them the future. Now he was the subservient husband sat in the conservatory on pristine wicker furniture reading the Sunday papers without the strength or initiative to be the person he wanted to be. He could change this, it didn't have to be like that. This moment could be the starting point, a change for the better perhaps? Maybe tomorrow he thought. Because in this particular moment, all he wanted was to get in bed and away from the table.

Chapter 16

Martin had to admit, Snowdon was pretty breathtaking. They'd reached the summit after a brisk hike (Helena was setting the pace while chattering away) and he felt good having had a bit of exercise with the fresh North Welsh breeze biting gently at his cheeks. The anxiety of last night had gone. He had almost forgotten about the negativity he felt around his relationship with Helena, questioning everything and comparing what he had to his parents. He was right last night – today was a new day. And today was off to a much better start. He had no feelings of fear or anxiety. He was engaging with Helena and he had enjoyed the hike thus far.

In many ways, he had weathered the evening at the pub, then kept quiet about it when they went to bed. Helena didn't question it, she was almost oblivious to it. If she wasn't, she was doing a damn good impression of someone who was.

The evening had finished without a word really. Well, from Martin anyway. The pub had died down by the time it had come to settle up. And the meal was charged to the room, so they went off to bed with Helena leading the way up the beaten staircase with Martin dutifully following behind, wearily and steadily. He was wondering to himself as they mounted the staircase last night whether this was a sign of what today's hike might bring – slow and heavy strides that felt tired with every plant of a footstep on a summit. But thankfully, and to Martin's surprise, it was quite the opposite. There was almost a spring in his step, with a newly found enthusiasm for the outdoors. It reminded him of fonder times on school trips that were had on The Malverns or The Quantocks. Those were good days, he thought to himself. The nostalgia set in and he visualised a scene from Year 7 residential camp where they had been left to their own devices in the woods for free time. Nature really was the healer he needed sometimes, he just didn't really know it.

'Dad said on a clear day you can see Ireland from up here!' said Helena excitedly at the top. There wasn't too much chance of that today, though it was clear for a considerable distance, the mist was visible over the Irish sea as they looked towards the West.

'God, it really is beautiful up here,' she continued, 'We need to do more stuff like this,' and she cuddled in close to Martin to show how content she was with the activity they were doing, but also with him. Martin took her into his arms, though slightly awkward at first as there was a few groups of hikers around, some doing charitable walks and suchlike. He didn't like an audience when showing affection, but in this moment he could probably let it be. He felt loved, he felt wanted. It was a truly wonderful feeling as far as he was concerned, despite his initial self-consciousness. He looked down on Helena and kissed her on the head gently. She looked up at him and through smiling eyes he could almost tell her inner most feelings towards him at that moment. It was a beautiful and tender moment, possibly the closest they'd ever been with each other in public. The hubbub around them was silenced as far as they were concerned. There were no voices or noise in this moment, this wonderful embrace of affection was like a snapshot in time. They were paused in the beauty of the landscape, with the wild and rugged peaks playing the perfect backdrop to this pure and tender moment they shared.

For Martin, it was everything he had ever wanted. To be loved and wanted. For someone to show sensitivity and care, which could then enable him to become something more than his usual placid and serious self. Helena looked up at him again and spoke softly and quietly, which was not common for her.

'Are you ready to go back down?' she said with a searching smile.

'Yeah, let's go,' replied Martin and he met Helena's lips softly with his own.

The walk down was a breeze, literally. Martin could've cartwheeled down he was so happy. The couple held hands as they sauntered freely along the miners path, laughing and joking more like giddy teenagers than adults as they made their way back to the car. It was like they had made a genuine connection at the top of the mountain. The romance of the beautiful landscape and the sense of triumph by achieving something together was all baked into their soaring affection for each other – Martin wasn't sure if Helena had ever had this feeling before, but for him this was definitely new. And as a result he felt like his heart might burst. What a difference to last night, he thought to himself. Their first real test as a couple, going away together and being with each other 24/7 for at least 3 days. It was only the first full day, and he was already revelling in the experience. Nothing could pull him away from this high, absolutely nothing. Or so he thought.

'Hels?' called a voice from a few metres away, 'Hello stranger!'

Helena turned round in surprise. Who on earth could she know here, right in the heart of a North Wales car park next to Mount Snowdon. Martin's face dropped when he turned, not that he knew the individual in question at all, but because he certainly recognised him. He recognised him from various Facebook photos that dated back to 2008 or something like that. The uni years. Helena's uni years. It was her ex-boyfriend, Nick. Though Nick was obviously a few years older than the pictures that Martin had seen, it was still obviously him who was now making his way over to what was now his girlfriend. And the man in question was beaming from ear to ear.

'Nick! Nicky-naks! Hey! How are you?' said Helena excitedly.

'Wow, yeah I'm good thanks!' replied Nick, going in for a huge hug with her. 'What are the chances eh?' Yeah. What are the fucking chances, eh Nick. Fan-fucking-tastic. Thanks mate, thought Martin.

'What brings you here then, bit of hiking in God's country I see!' as he turned to study Martin for a moment, without even a hint of recognition for the role he clearly had as Helena's boyfriend.

'Well yeah, we just fancied a weekend away and I wanted to get this one here on a hike so I thought, why not?' said Helena, shooting Martin a smiling glance. Martin was accepting his role as 'this one here' – he hadn't yet been given a name or introduction. It was almost like he was a bit of a secret and was better left unidentified.

'Ah, well good for you guys,' replied Nick, still not offering an introduction of himself to Martin.

It was actually a little bit awkward. Perhaps it was Martin who should introduce himself? What was the etiquette here? It wasn't a situation Martin had ever been particularly comfortable in – making introductions – especially to those who were ex-boyfriends. He sensed Helena's embarrassment. Almost like she'd been caught out with someone she didn't want to be seen with. This is how it felt to Martin anyway.

The misty rain was setting in now and the three of them stood in what was a pretty busy little car park and the weather could've served as the perfect excuse to get going. Martin was tired, the adrenaline from the moment they'd shared at the top of the mountain had somewhat disappeared. It was like the balloon of joy and opportunity had deflated in his stomach, a huge gut wrenching pop that changed his mood in an instant. He felt like a spare part all of a sudden, like he'd been invited along to make up the numbers. A genuine third wheel in his own relationship as he watched two former lovebirds make light conversation and reminisce about past experiences. His happy smiling girlfriend, the same one in the hours previous who he had caressed tenderly atop the mountain, was now repelling him like some sort of repulsive magnet that was resisting his presence. And on the opposite pole, she had was forming the perfect attraction to this other magnet, called Nick.

They were still chatting as all this ran through Martin's head. About God knows what, he didn't know. His awkwardness was palpable. This was just what Helena was like though. A truly lovely girl, of course, but when she started chatting there really was no stopping her. He may as well not have been there. It wasn't as if she was rude either, it was just a complete lack of awareness on her part, the lack of awareness to even acknowledge Martin. He could even tell that Nick was probably a bit awkward about this too, occasionally making eyes at Martin wondering if he should introduce himself or wondering whether Martin would do the same, or indeed if Helena would be able to realise either option and do it herself. A key issue here was that Martin was not one for this type of small talk and false introductions.

'So, yeah, we're heading over to the caves tomorrow. And maybe gonna do that zip wire thing in the quarry too if we get time,' continued Helena.

'Oh, really?' exclaimed Nick, 'A few pals and I were going to do that tomorrow too!'

Well this was just perfect thought Martin. Go on then Helena, just go ahead and fucking invite him along with us. Oh, in fact how about we come and pick you up from wherever the fuck it is you're from or staying? What an absolute shitshow. His weekend had been ruined thanks to this chance encounter.

'Cool, we might see you there then Nicky! Mightn't we Marty?' Helena had finally acknowledged his presence, and just short of saying they'd meet him there. Hopefully that wouldn't be discussed and he and Helena could chat about that later on.

'Umm yeah, sure. Should, uh… should be good,' replied Martin tentatively.

'Well you guys, good to see you – and nice to meet you Marky – good to catch-up Hels,' said Nick, moving away with a friendly grin.

Marky? Fucking Marky? Who the fuck is Marky? Martin didn't correct him, and nor did Helena. It was far too awkward by this point. He'd just have to live with the fact that 'Nicky' the all conquering alpha male of this unlucky meeting, had completely and utterly pied him, then to add insult to injury, got his name wrong.

The journey back to the B&B was a quiet one. Martin knew that Helena had finally come to the realisation of embarrassment, but she wasn't going to admit it. This was clearly one of those situations that they both hoped things would blow over. But sadly, 'alpha Nicky' would be back on the scene tomorrow with a bit of bad luck. How could they ignore that? The tension was clearly rising and the atmosphere was getting increasingly fraught. Martin was feeling very uncomfortable but chose to keep his mouth shut. He didn't want conflict and he certainly didn't want an argument. His mantra in this relationship was very much about keeping the peace – especially given the fact that it was their first weekend away as a couple. He concentrated on the roads, with the occasional question (that he already knew the answers to), 'it's right here, isn't it?' And that was about as much as he could muster to cut the awkwardness in two. Of course, true to form and in typical Martin fashion – he absolutely hated himself for this.

Chapter 17

Back at the B&B, Martin and Helena simply eased back to their normal relationship status quo. Not one word was uttered about the encounter with Nick or what tomorrow would hold, if they did happen to see him and his friends that was. Martin felt disappointed that he hadn't raised the point around not being introduced properly. It felt awkward, he had felt unwanted in that moment, or so he thought – but he could also sympathise with the fact that perhaps it was a little bit awkward for Helena to be standing in front of an old flame – who was clearly quite different to himself – and making introductions. But it was just common courtesy, surely? He wished there was something he could've said to stand up for himself, to give their relationship some worth and show her he wasn't happy with her attitude towards him. But was it because she was just so blissfully unaware of her surroundings? Was it just normal for her to go one hundred miles an hour and start talking? It was innocent on her part, he had concluded that. She wasn't a malicious type in any way. But she needed to know, though sadly, he would never find the strength to say.

'What do you fancy for breakfast Marty? Another big day ahead!' said Helena, in typical cheery fashion.

Martin didn't feel a whole lot better than he did before going to bed last night, he was still disappointed. This manifested itself as grumpiness, which he was able to easily pass off as tiredness, given their exploits yesterday. He still couldn't believe the dip his mood had taken, it was upsetting him. He couldn't let on though, the moment had passed, surely? He'd hoped that with today being a new day he could wake up with a positive mindset about the activities ahead which would be exciting for them to do as a couple. But the lingering point was that it may not be just them. He was dreading seeing Nick again. The thought had cast a depressive and jealous shadow over him. But what did he have to worry about, really? He was in a relationship with Helena, she was here with him and there was absolutely no chance she would just walk out on him to be with an ex-partner after a chance encounter in a car park. But this was the quandary he'd cooked up in his head. It was hard to shift. He hadn't had any kind of relationship before, nothing long term, nothing serious. This was the first time of feeling jealous and apprehensive about an outside influence whilst he had been with Helena. He was sowing his own seeds of doubt, thinking the worst, imagining Helena and Nick getting overly familiar and flirting their way back into some kind of relationship and one that he was completely powerless to resist. How could he? Look at Nick. A big, tall rugby player (probably). No more or no less handsome than himself, but slightly more charismatic and personable. Sure, he was no George (very few were) but in the short time Martin had been in his presence he had observed that Nick seemed to have that certain type of charm that girls bought into. It was something he lambasted himself for, his lack of confidence and charisma. But what was he worrying for? He had Helena. He didn't need to be any of those things on his personality wishlist. It was simply something he couldn't shift as a preoccupation.

'I think I'll go for the eggs. They looked decent yesterday,' he replied, finally.

'Oooooh nice!' Helena called back from the bathroom. She started a chorus of 'how d'ya like, your eggs in the morning' and danced her way towards him with a huge grin, expectantly waiting for Martin's reply of, 'I like mine with a kiss…,' which was a bit they had seen done before, Helena's parents having regularly joked with each other in this fashion on the mornings that Martin woke up in their house.

It was a nice place to be, he liked Helena's parents. They were so different to his own, always joking, singing and laughing. He enjoyed seeing it, and his younger self was probably yearning for it.

'Ummm, I think scrambled?' Martin replied, half-heartedly.

'Oh Marty! You're supposed to sing it back to me, silly!' Helena jokingly scorned.

Singing wasn't necessarily something in Martin's wheelhouse. He wasn't one for impromptu duets, certainly not this morning either.

'Are you okay, Marty? Did you sleep alright? Do you not want to go to the caves today?' Helena fired these questions at him without missing a beat. It was like one question would follow the other, had there been a chance for Martin to answer in between. This was just the way she processed things, it was how her mind worked, quickly and relentless.

'Umm, yeah, yeah. I'm good. Just think I need some breakfast and a coffee,' he replied.

'Oh, a coffee? You don't usually have coffee first. Do you prefer coffee first thing in the morning? Get your shoes on then, let's go downstairs!'

Sometimes the questions she asked were almost rhetorical, they didn't even need an answer. Or rather, she wouldn't be bothered if he had answered or not. She was just thinking out loud really, processing quickly like a computer, but also logging and jotting down her thoughts in a verbal way, like a giant whiteboard of all her thoughts written out into every inch of breathing space between them. Before he knew it, she was opening the door. Keen as ever.

'Come on slow coach!' she joked.

'I'm coming, hang on,' Martin replied.

He was being slow, methodical. He sometimes thought this annoyed her and was misconstrued as dawdling. But this was just simply his way, calculated and less impulsive – not as dynamic or rigid as Helena was. He could feel her frustration, but she was being good natured about it. After all, it wasn't even 8.00am. It's not as if they were about to miss the breakfast being served.

They creaked down the staircase into the restaurant area with Helena's excited monologue about the day ahead carrying them all the way to their table by the window. It did look like a great day outside already, a really crisp morning with the golden sun breaking through the trees. There was much to feel optimistic about today. Away together amongst the beautiful mountains and countryside, this was a couples getaway that only few could have dreamed of.

'So I was thinking we could do the caves one first,' said Helena, reaching into her pocket and extracting the leaflet she had been harbouring. 'It looks like it might be easier for us to do it that way round,' she went on.

It probably didn't make a jot of difference what they did first, he thought. It was just that she wanted to do that first, but didn't want to come across as bossy or too demanding. This annoyed him sometimes, why couldn't she just say? Perhaps he was being cynical though. He did like some of this quality about her though. He felt safe and secure knowing that she was on top of everything, had a plan, had a process. He could easily work with that for the times where he found it difficult to make decisions quickly or effectively.

'Yeah, okay sure. I don't really mind,' Martin offered passively, but not like it really mattered.

'Great! Well we'll have our breakfast then brush our teeth and we can get going before 9 o'clock then,' she replied.

What was the bloody rush by the way? Could he just not sit in peace for a moment after they'd finished their breakfast and just relax with a coffee? Was that too much to ask? Clearly, yes. Because as soon as Martin had finished his last mouthful of toast, Helena was chomping at the bit to leave the table.

'Have you finished your drink?' she pressed.

'Well, nearly, yes. I might just finish what's in that pot though?' he offered, weakly.

'You don't need another one, do you?' Helena asked, confused.

'Well… I uhhh don't need one, but I wouldn't mind it, yeah,' he replied, with a tiny bit of strength appearing in his response for once.

'Oh well hurry up then, I'm bored! We can get going early then can't we!' she said excitedly.

And although it was said in a way that was potentially light-hearted and jokey, the sentiment of those words was genuine. She was done with what she was doing (or in this instance, eating), so therefore he had to be done. That's exactly what this was. Why would anyone ever take so much time over a second cup of coffee? It just didn't make sense to her. All the points on her list had been ticked off and she couldn't understand why there wasn't any forward movement on completion of her days process. Wake up. Get dressed. Pack rucksack. Have breakfast. Brush teeth. Leave. Process was always driving her narrative, every minute of every day, with this weekend starting to pull it into sharp focus for Martin of what life might be like living with Helena. Perhaps he wasn't reacting to what happened yesterday afternoon he may have felt a bit different about things right now. But the fact that he had a problem all of a sudden started to create irks and rankles in his mind with her approach to certain things.

He sat drinking his coffee, not painfully slow by any means, but slower than he would. Why couldn't they just sit and chat for a bit? Chill out, enjoy some rest time. This wasn't on her agenda, because the die was already cast on her motivations for a particular task (or in this case, the day) and it was her way, or no way. Martin was probably pushing his luck with the speed in which he drank his coffee. He could tell it was winding up Helena somewhat, but she busied herself on her phone for a bit, probably texting Amy about something or other. What Martin really struggled with is that these sorts of stand offs were totally innocent. There wasn't any malice in what she wanted to do, or in fact, the speed she wanted to do it, it just wasn't a pace Martin was comfortable with. He stupidly kept his mouth shut and slowly sulked his way through the coffee, which in truth wasn't even worth the extra cup.

Chapter 18

They promptly left the B&B at just before 9.00am. He could tell Helena was delighted about this. Ahead of schedule, all plans aligning to the process. Martin felt sick. He could still taste the bitter coffee in his mouth which had mixed with his toothpaste creating a sour, sanitised flavour that lingered around his gums, not exactly helping his queasiness. He couldn't pinpoint why though – it was probably a mixture of things. In no particular order, it was likely that it was some, if not all of the following:

Anxiety caused by trying a new experience (which could potentially be scary and/ or nerve wracking)
Bumping into Nick again and enduring Helena's chit chat with him
The worry that perhaps his eggs were undercooked
The fact that he hadn't slept great because of another guest in the B&B snoring next door
His fear of heights and tight spaces
Getting lost on the way there and risking a bollocking from Helena

Thankfully, they didn't get lost on the way there and there was no sign of Nick in the car park when they arrived. Martin stepped out of the car and felt a gentle breeze lap over his tired eyes and hot forehead. It was a light relief after the drive that snaked around the mountains to their destination (Helena insisted she was cold so he wasn't allowed the windows open or air conditioning on). He took a deep breath and gently closed his eyes. He was trying to control the burning anxiety that had built inside him and was still steadily rising. He had no strategy apart from just to breath through it. This seemed like the only way he could control anything in his body. Helena was getting something out the boot so he was hidden from view for a moment while he composed himself.

He snapped back to reality as a car pulled in next to his own. A man got out of the drivers seat. Oh for fuck sake. Surely not? It was fucking Nick wasn't it. Typical, we've only been here two fucking minutes. Thankfully, it wasn't the aforementioned Nick. Relief washed over Martin for a moment as the driver looked over to him, probably wondering why he was staring at him in some kind of daze right now.

'Morning!' said the driver happily, although slightly confused as to why there was a man standing stock still next to his car. He headed over to the entrance, his attire suggested that he was probably an employee going to work. He looked the type. Pretty rugged and outdoorsy, athletic and jolly.

'Hello, hi,' Martin responded, albeit an uncomfortable amount of time after he had been greeted himself.

'Who was that?' said Helena inquisitively, appearing at his side.

'Dunno. Some bloke. Think he works here,' responded Martin.

'Oh, okay,' she said, not really caring now that the information wasn't that interesting. 'Shall we go in?'

'Yeah lets, uh… lets do it,' he sounded apprehensive. It wasn't so easy to turn it on and off. Sometimes you could just hide or disappear to a bathroom if you were having a funny five minutes. Or feign an injury in PE because you didn't want to get battered in rugby by the big lads. He had been known to do this. Martin wasn't exactly the kind of guy who threw himself into challenges if he didn't feel comfortable. He would concoct a soup of emotions in his mind, picking the key ingredients for what would look like failure. Not only would he be at the heart of making this unhappy soup, he would happily sit down and eat it during the aftermath of whatever situation he'd gotten out of, slurping on the emotions of regret and shame.

This was different now they were down in the caverns, ready to get going. He was right in the thick of something now and it was fight, or a pretty serious flight. That would mean making a huge scene in front of the other groups of people, including a stag do of blokes fresh off of their minibus. Could he fight whatever demons that were circling his mind right now? Or would he simply take off and run from the impending experience? He'd read about the caverns online. Sure, it looked like a lot of fun if he was in the right mindset, but his apprehensions and anxieties were telling him there might be an element of risk involved, not to mention some experiences of navigating heights and gaping drops – albeit safely on a harness. He could feel his legs twitching already at the thought of it.

They'd queued up, lingered around a bit and had the safety briefing. It was now or never for whether he was going to duck out. Helena was clearly excited about what was to come, smiling happily and engaging, agreeing with looks and nods with another woman in the group. Martin stood there sallow faced and nervous. If you were at sea, you'd focus on the horizon to let the sickness pass – focusing on a fixed point to steady your head and vision. But there wasn't exactly that luxury underground, here in the caverns of Snowdonia. Just the artificial light of pinks, purples and greens making the scene look like some mystical nightclub. But far removed from a typical nightclub with the heavy bass thumping through the darkness, the thump was in his head and his mind. He felt hot and nauseous, but he rallied enough to get going once the group was ready to head off. His mind was fuzzy and vision quite blurry, not that his vision was going to be perfect in these surroundings anyway. It almost felt like there was a lack of din around him, muffling of the noise that had dulled all his senses. Helena was looking back at him smiling, saying something that was barely audible to him. He gave her a semi encouraging smile that masked his true feeling. This was hell. He might even collapse in a moment, he thought. This was very real now, he'd have to do it. There was probably no going back. Just like in Kavos that time, he was starting to stumble and breath heavily – getting hotter with a rising of panic in his body, sweat pouring from every crevice in his body. Martin stumbled slightly and the force bumped him into Helena in front, he was for a moment akin to a clumsy robot who had lost the power of its programming, stumbling over his feet and bumping into all around him. He fell forward suddenly, reaching out at a railing but his sweaty palms missed as his chest thumped against the hard metal, sending him downwards and ending up in a heap on the floor.

Everything went black.

'Martin? Marty? Are you okay? Say something? Hello?'

It was Helena standing over him when he came to. He had quite clearly blacked out for a moment, losing his senses completely. The anxiety had become too much and he had fainted.

The scene was still blurry, but Martin was gradually coming round. He was incredibly dazed and really confused, his face milky white.

He blinked a few times as he came round. There were faces gawping at him from all angles showing their concern. This was the absolute worst. The worst of all the worst situations for Martin, all eyes upon him having just something ridiculously embarrassing.

'I'm… I'm okay. I think,' he responded finally.

'Oh Marty, are you sure? You don't look great. Not great at all,' said Helena, looking down on him with grave concern. 'Can you get up?'

'Yeah, I uh, give me a minute,' he responded slowly.

'Hi mate, my name is Alex – I work here,' said Alex, who it was apparent worked at the caverns and some sort of authority and/ or first aid training. 'We're gonna get you up slowly and take you back up to the top, okay? Your girlfriend said you hit the railings pretty hard so I don't think it's a good idea if you carry on,' he continued.

Despite feeling like absolute shit right now, this was one hell of a relief for Martin. His overwhelming emotions of fear, shame and anxiety were nearly trumped in that moment.

'Oh right, okay, yeah,' Martin replied meekly.

'Let's get him up to the café and make sure he gets a bit of sugar and water in him. He looks completely drained the poor fella,' said Alex to Helena.

She looked genuinely concerned right now, looking down at him knelt at his side. She was wonderfully caring when she wanted to be. This moment had brought that into sharp focus. She did truly care for him and was clearly shaken by this episode. Martin was slowly helped to his feet, firstly by Alex and supported by Helena. He was unsteady on his feet at first but he felt well enough to walk back. Thankfully, the group they were meant to be with in the caves pursuit had dispersed and were well under way by now.

'Thanks,' said Martin weakly to what was his new best friend and saviour, Alex. 'I think he'll be okay now,' said Helena, taking control.

It wasn't until after that Martin reflected on this part of the slow climb back up to daylight. He absolutely wasn't okay and though Helena was only looking out for him and was showing some care and genuine concern, she had basically answered the question for him about his own welfare. He really wasn't feeling great and would've happily had the help of a trained first aider and staff member to escort him back upstairs. But no. He obviously wasn't in the right frame of mind, or in a good physical state to be making decisions, but my God this had irked him for some reason.

'We'll just get you up there and sat down Marty, you'll be okay,' said Helena softly.

Martin nodded slowly with his eyes closed as they gingerly made their way up towards the exit. His stomach felt like it was sloshing around, much more than butterflies and the usual anxieties. There was sharp pain now and some movement. He gulped back some saliva as his throat went dry. He was chewing his cheeks trying to get moisture into his mouth, forcing down whatever was there lurking in his midriff. He knew what was coming, the sweats were coming on again. His head was pounding like mad too.

'Can we just… just stand here a second, I'm feeling a bit… you know,' he said to Helena. 'Yeah, of course. Take your time,' she said in return, rubbing his back gently.

He didn't want to admit what the feeling was. The 'you know' feeling of both dizziness and nausea. He composed himself and took some deep breaths, slowly and carefully.

'It's okay Marty, take your time. You had a nasty fall back there. Any idea what it could be?' asked Helena.

Fucking hell. Give me a fucking minute will you, I'm dying here, thought Martin. He really wasn't up for the questioning, but hey, that was to be expected.

'I'm… I'm okay. I'll be alright,' and he slowly turned to Helena, or so it felt slowly in retrospect, but it probably happened in a flash as his stomach lurched violently and he projectile vomited all over her.

Oh shit.

Yes, this was shit. The mother of all oh shits in fact. He'd just thrown up his breakfast over his girlfriend. There was absolutely nothing worse than this right now. But, oh wait. Yes there was. Not another wave of vomit, oh no, but coming along the corridor at that exact moment was Nick and his three 'buddies' that he said he'd be coming down the caves with. Helena had yelped the moment Martin's vomit had flown towards her and she was now standing open mouthed covered in remnants of crap coffee, eggs and bits of brown toast. This wasn't a good look for anyone, that goes without saying. But it was most definitely not a good look with your ex-boyfriend bounding straight towards you with a group of his jock mates, firstly smiling, then slowly turning their expressions into shock at the chaos that had just unfolded moments earlier. Helena's clothes were dripping with Martin's breakfast, and he, Martin, was standing there opened mouthed and heavy eyed, unable to fathom what had just happened.

For a moment, Martin felt a lot better to get rid of the sharp splitting feeling in his stomach. But only for a moment, because an emotion far worse was washing over him right now. It was one of pure shame and the deepest self-loathing he had ever felt in his entire life.

Chapter 19

Back at the B&B, the mood was typically sombre. Martin was laid up in bed feeling sorry for himself while Helena flicked through the limited selection of television channels and endlessly scrolled up and down her phone. He was unimaginably sorry for what had happened earlier and he'd done his best to show her that. At least she wasn't resenting him for it, the action of him being sick on her. He felt that any resentment she was feeling was born out of the fact that perhaps he should've said he wasn't feeling well before they went in.

As it turned out, Martin spent the rest of the morning sat in the café sipping water and nibbling at a plain digestive biscuit. He sat there in self-pity for at least 2 hours while Helena completed a circuit of the caves with, yes, Nick and his 'buddies.' This was even more of a punch in the stomach to Martin, as it was clearly something he didn't really feel comfortable about at all. But what could he do? Helena was very convincing, as well as persuasive and charming. It had been negotiated that she would quickly get her spare clothes from the car and meet them back where Martin had chundered his guts up on her not ten minutes previous.

How could he have possibly denied her? She was brazen enough to 'ask' for his permission as they all stood there, with Martin still reeling and dazed from his vomiting episode. He nodded and said yes, of course she could still do the caverns. Four pairs of eyes were staring back at him, including his own girlfriends, hopeful and now invigorated that she was getting a chance to do what she had carefully planned during this trip away. Was it worth reading anything into this? The fact that she was gladly ditching her current boyfriend to disappear down a cave with her ex one? It was in hindsight, pretty alarming. But at the time, it made sense for all parties. Martin couldn't really care less during the moment, so he happily agreed to the arrangement and said he'd meet her back in the café in a couple of hours or so. He just wanted to disappear from the embarrassment that he was being faced with. Helena, stood there covered in his sick and a group of lads probably trying not to laugh like schoolchildren would, staring in disbelief and anticipation. Poor Martin, it was a horrendous situation to be in. Feeling ill, tired, deflated and now, rejected.

During the two hours he had to himself he was able to try and make sense of his thoughts. He was confused and delirious, but also angry. He couldn't wait for this weekend to be over now, he'd had enough. Today was meant to be full of hope, with another experience together being ticked off. The next step on a journey into the future, where inevitably there would be more opportunities to do this sort of thing. To enjoy the company of one another, sharing experiences, growing their relationship and consummating their future together as a couple.

But today, this was not to be. It felt like a huge backward step, further away from the mountain top moment that he could ever have dreamt of. Because the stark reality was that his girlfriend was beneath the earth, navigating the caverns of North Wales with her ex-boyfriend and his twatty little mates. Fuck sake. Some serious self-reflection was required here and at the very least, a conversation with Helena.

'Are you okay Marty?' asked Helena.

At least she was showing some concern. In fact, she had been incredibly genial and forgiving towards him after returning from the caves. Martin figured that this was because she got what she had wanted – to an extent anyway – and loved him enough to forgive him and move on. She was a loving, caring type, he knew that. But my God, the world didn't stop for Helena. If she wanted something, she was going to get it. If that meant gaslighting him a little bit to cajole him into a decision or action, then so be it.

'Yeah, I'm not too bad. Sorry again that we've got to sit in here tonight,' he replied meekly.

'That's okay. It's not your fault! Just one of those things. At least it hasn't happened again since. Do you think it was the eggs? Or was it the fear? How will you know?' She fired three questions at him again without missing a beat.

'Ummm, well… I dunno. I guess a combo of things,' said Martin. 'I felt much better after a sleep and some water. It was just like a wave that hit me at the time. I don't know, I'm sorry.'

He had spent the afternoon laid up in bed too, whilst Helena took a walk into the small town near to where they were staying.

'I bought these for Amy,' she said, changing the subject and holding up a pair of gold earrings. 'Aren't they cute? I think she'll like wearing these at Nat's birthday in a couple of weeks.'

Martin didn't even have to agree with the question he'd been asked. It was almost like Helena would ask questions and not necessarily need answers. Anything but affirmation would be greeted with a stare or an instant challenge. For example, if he said, 'they look shit' or something derogatory then that wouldn't be great, but nine times out of ten, she really didn't care whether he said anything at all.

Oh, and Nat's birthday. Natalie. Her other close friend from when they were growing up in Worcester. It wasn't like it was a big birthday (29) but he was being dragged along even though he wasn't that keen. It would be the typical drinks in a bar, Martin standing round awkwardly while Helena bustled about with her friends, not really caring what he was doing just as long as he was there, that was the main thing. He was never going to be the kind of person to just mingle and hit it off with the other blokes or lads. It just wasn't his personality. What Martin needed was to have some kind of pre-established relationship with someone rather than being chucked in the deep end and having to fend for himself.

There was one occasion he ended up speaking to Grandparents of one of Helena's friends and spent a good while chatting with them about the Cotswolds, which wasn't too far from where he grew up. He remembered Helena saying afterwards, or in some group situations somewhere, 'You had a nice night didn't you? Speaking with the old people?' And then turned back to her friends before he could answer, continuing 'He likes talking about things like that.'

Martin had lost himself in these thoughts for a while, half sleepy and half dreading the party in a couple of weeks. He could bail? Perhaps not. Imagine the ruckus. Maybe just see how things were nearer the time. He couldn't lie, she'd be all over it like a rash. The amount of questioning he'd have to go under just wasn't worth it. He hoped that maybe he'd black out and feint again. It was a bit of a harrowing thought to be honest. His head still hurt from the sickness and dehydration, although he was feeling better now, just slightly disorientated. He turned the pillow over and laid his head to rest before slowly closing his eyes. He didn't think Helena really noticed, she was still absorbed in her phone.

*

He woke in the pitch black. It must've been the dead of night. He checked his phone to see that it was indeed, 2.07am. He had fallen into a deep sleep and had woken slightly groggy, unsure of his surroundings. It was ridiculously dark up here in the mountains. The lack of light pollution from a town or city and no streetlights made for what should've been an undisturbed nights sleep. Helena was fast asleep on the other side of the bed, she rarely stirred during the night, it's just that she was a very early riser. Lie-ins weren't really her thing either.

Martin had the urge to get out of bed, so he stepped into the small en-suite and used the toilet without managing to creak the floor or make too much noise. He was walking back towards the bed when he stopped. He suddenly had the urge to do something stupid. Something wreckless even. He didn't know what yet, but the only thing that made sense right now was to either break something or hurt himself. Why? He didn't know. His mind was taking control perhaps in a hallucinogenic sense, with the stress of the day catching up with him and seeping into his relaxed self. He'd slept almost 6 hours and was like a dead weight, waking up in the exact position he remembered settling in. But now, he was awake.

Everything was in sharp focus and there was a sudden urge for something. In a way, he wanted revenge. But not revenge over anyone else, Martin was the type who wouldn't hurt a soul. There was not a bad bone in his body. The revenge he wanted was over himself. He wanted to teach his mind a lesson for letting it be the downfall of him today. It was his stupid mind that had put him in this mess today, telling him he couldn't do something. Telling him to suspect something between Helena and Nick. Telling him he wasn't good enough anymore. Telling him he didn't deserve this weekend away with a lovely, funny and engaging girl.

Fuck it. He grabbed a hoodie, slipped into his trainers and stealthily left the room without a trace.

Chapter 20

Martin quietly descended the stairs and found himself in the reception area of the B&B. There was the usual display of glossy tourist leaflets, a token house plant that had grown out of control and a single lamp that was dimly lighting the otherwise darkened space. He approached the front door and tried the handle. It was locked. Of course it was locked. He looked round the vicinity and to his surprise he saw a large key hanging from a hook about half a metre away from the lock itself. A large wooden keyring attached to it displayed a handwritten note 'MAIN DOOR.' Well, that was easy. He unhooked the key from its position and tried it in the lock. A low click proved that the key was in fact for this door and he carefully and quietly pressed down on the large brass handle to exit into the porch. There were spare brollies, firewood and a few pairs of wellington boots stowed here. Thankfully he wouldn't need those, the night was clear and dry, if not slightly windy. Martin closed the door slowly behind him and placed the key inside one of the boots for safe keeping.

So what now? This had all been very impulsive back in the bedroom, to get up, walk into the night and do himself some mischief – if that really was what he was planning. He wasn't really sure what he wanted to do, but his head was still boiling with disappointment and shame. Shame in his actions, his choices and the situations he seemed to constantly get himself into. He walked across the car park and along a pathway which led to a small lane between some fencing that he had noticed when they had arrived two days previous. He was curious where it went, so he followed it down far enough before reaching a stile that crossed a dry-stone wall. It was dark, but his vision was impressively clear. He thought how amazing it was that the moon could be so bright and actually be his main source of light here in the dead of night. The B&B was a good 500 yards behind him now, with just a glimmer of amber light visible through the bushes that flanked the lane. He mounted the stile and arrived on the other side to a beautifully still lake. It seemed to have been carved out of the landscape, leaving something of a small shingle beach to the right where the water met land.

He still didn't really know where he was going or what he was doing right now, but he was drawn towards the tranquillity of the water, finding a flat rock to sit down on at the waters edge. He let out a breath, then filled his lungs back up with fresh air. He inhaled deeply, taking control for a moment of what was before, quite a reckless attitude that he had in mind. The lake had stopped him in his tracks. He hadn't expected to find something so tranquil and beautiful. The shimmering water was like a sheet of inky blue silk, glistening in the moonlight and gently lapping around in the calm breeze. This was real, he thought to himself. A real world, where his feet were on the ground. He was alive right now, he was real, he was something. He knew this because he could feel. He could feel the breeze on his face, the crunch of the stones beneath his feet and the scene around him that drew in his gaze and absorbed him with its beauty.

He wasn't here for this, or at least, he hadn't come for this. His senses had initially guided him here to act recklessly, to decompress and to let off anger in a way he didn't quite yet know how that could be done. Showing emotions wasn't exactly Martin's forte. He found it hard to express himself, relying on others to perhaps point out what it was they thought he was feeling. Helena was a great example of this. Maybe that's why he was drawn to her? She did a lot of the talking so he didn't have to. Sometimes that was fine, that suited him. But over time he felt like it was stifling him. He knew he had a choice as to whether he really cared about this or not. Was it petty? He wasn't sure. Was it frustrating? Yes, at times. But did he love Helena? Yes, absolutely. He welcomed the security of being with her and the tenderness she was able to express both physically and verbally. But that didn't explain anything right now. He was blaming himself for not being any of those things. He would punish himself a lot for that, with the lead up until now being sat here at the waters edge, in the dead of night in the heart of North Wales, a typically great example.

He stood up slowly, gazing forward at the water like it was inviting him in. He was drawn towards its serenity and wondered what it might feel like to wake himself by going in. He was standing on the edge, knowing it would be cold, but this idea didn't seem to bother him too much as he approached the water, slowly but surely getting closer. His trainers were now getting wet, as well as his ankles as the water lapped around them. He carried on walking into the water, hardly breaking its surface by wading slowly further through it until it was around his waist. He kept control of his breathing, seemingly focused on something that was out there in the dark, yet to be discovered.

He could feel the cold water from his clothes which were now sticking to his body. This was the intent, to be cleansed, to refresh. Like an exorcism of his thoughts and actions being washed away in the lake. He plunged his whole body forward, head first into the darkness and held his breath, floating face down on the skin of the water now completely weightless and without control as he let the water carry him. He had never been the most buoyant of swimmers, but perhaps this was down to his lack of coordination and the fact he spent most of the time in the water thrashing around and trying to get his gangly frame to function in some kind of technically able way. Right now this was different, his mind and body were focused, he was relaxed, he had let go of something which had enabled him to float serenely if just for a few minutes at least. But to Martin, this felt like an eternity. He wasn't scared, he felt in control here. It was a cleansing exercise to which he felt was necessary for mind, body and soul. A soul that felt tortured, full of shame and regret.

He finally pulled his head out of the water for breath. He'd managed to hold it for nearly two minutes straight. He was gasping for air all of sudden, feeling the adrenaline rush around his body like electricity. He waded his way back to the shore and knelt down on the shingle, finally catching his breath. Did he feel better? Perhaps. The overriding emotion he had was almost one of pride. He had proved something to himself in that moment, however bizarre the circumstances might have been. But it didn't matter. He was completely alone, nobody could see him. There was no shame or embarrassment providing anyone ever knew what he was doing. The wet clothes might be a giveaway, but he'd work something out. This was something that he had done for himself and he had enjoyed the thrill. His objective had been to get revenge on himself, to punish in some way – but this 'cleansing' that he had undertaken seemed to have appeased him for now. It was bordering on slightly sinister, yes. But his actions and motivations weren't to fully let go of himself or shut down, it was just simply to feel something again and take back control. He got to his feet and started squelching towards the stile.

Yeah, this might take a bit of explaining, he thought to himself. He was sopping wet and now started to shiver. He picked up the pace as he mounted the stile and then broke into a run as he fixed his gaze ahead and made for the B&B.

He was back at the porch in no time, but completely soaked through. He removed his hoodie and wrung it out, before taking off his shoes and leaving them next to where the wellies were stowed. He collected the key and entered the property quietly before locking the front door and returning the key to its position on the hook. His shorts were still dripping as he made his way back up the creaking stairs. There would be no trace of the wet by morning, he was sure that this age old carpet had seen worse over the years. The next part of whatever this 'episode' he was in was to negotiate his way into the room while Helena was sleeping. His plan was to try and not wake her and get himself into the bathroom for a shower. By this point if she woke up then he could pass off the shower as something he needed to refresh himself. Ironically, that was partly the reason he submerged himself in the lake, but a shower in a B&B en-suite seems far less daring, where would've been the risk in that?

He approached the door increasingly quietly and turned the handle to let himself in. A very faint creak could be heard but perhaps not enough to stir anyone from a sleep. He gently closed the door behind him and made his way towards the bathroom. Once in, he would be able to breathe a sigh of relief. The only downfall to this 5-minute masterplan was the fact he had a pile of wet clothes with him. Fuck it. Worry about that in a minute, he thought. He managed to negotiate the bedroom okay and it seemed Helena was still fast asleep still as there was no noise or movement from the bed. Through the darkness and silence, he was able to manoeuvre around the tight room with relative success, only brushing the corner of the bed with his leg as he approached the doorway for the bathroom. Once in, he slowly and carefully clicked the door shut and started to undress. He thought it was better to get undressed first and then switch the light on, as this would definitely make a noise and drive the fan into action. Off came his bed shorts and together with his hoodie he rolled them up into a spare towel. He could unravel this later while Helena was getting ready in the morning, at least they would be out of view and not invite any questions as to why they were so wet. Having safely done this in the dark, he pulled the cord for the light switch and the room filled with light and noise. He was out of the woods now, for sure. The shower went on and he dived into the cubicle. Safety.

He felt the warm water hit his body and lowered his head against the wall so his forehead was resting against it. It was a moment of reflection for him. What had he been doing for the last hour or so? Where had it even come from, the disposition to get up out of bed in the middle of the night, in a completely alien location and submerge himself in a cold lake? It sounded ridiculous as he reflected on the words in his head. He knew there was something slightly more sinister about his actions but he didn't want to admit it to himself. It was like the narrative in his head was just ignoring the huge elephant in the room. He had flirted with the idea of disappearance tonight, no question about it. Whether he was consciously thinking about taking his own life, or just to 'disappear' into some kind of abyss, the lines were still blurry. The problem was, if you were going to disappear properly, then there was only really one outcome. Disappear temporarily under the cover of darkness, yes, he'd achieved that. Disappear indefinitely? Well, that was a completely different outcome that there was no coming back from. He hadn't fully formed these emotions in his mind yet and he wasn't sure if he was even capable of doing so.

He opened his eyes and looked to his left sensing movement suddenly.

Stood in the doorway with a somewhat sleepy, but confused look on her face, was Helena.

Chapter 21

'Martin?' she asked. 'What are you doing?'

Pretty fucking obvious, he thought to himself. Having a fucking shower. 'I'm having a shower,' he replied calmly.

'Yes, I can see that,' she said with a wrinkled frown, 'I'm more interested in the reason as to why you are having a shower at four 'o clock in the morning.'

He switched the shower off and climbed out of the cubicle, reaching for a towel. His pile of wet clothes lay rolled up in the other towel which was a heap on the floor over towards the corner of the small en-suite. Fortunately, Helena hadn't noticed this yet.

'I just needed to freshen up a bit. I've been in bed for ages and my head was starting to feel heavy. I thought a shower might help,' Martin replied.

'Okay. Well… has it helped?' she was still confused even though Martin had delivered a completely acceptable answer to her question.

'Yeah. I feel better now, but still tired.'

'Well, yes. Me too, I'm not usually up at 4.00am,' She was starting to sound a little bit touchy.

Well you're usually up at the crack of fucking dawn, thought Martin to himself.

'I'm all good. You can go back to bed. I'll come back in once I'm dry. I just had to get my head off the pillow for a bit. I've been there since about two in the afternoon.'

'Okay. As long as you're alright,' she said, turning round. Martin could sense a touch of suspicion in her demeanour. Maybe she had woken up sooner than he'd realised? Perhaps she knew he'd been out of the room? He froze at the thought of this. Oh shit. Maybe she did know something. 'Here we go again' he started saying to himself in his head. He was over analysing something he didn't even know to be true yet. And with it, he was immediately carrying a huge bag of worry that he might come under more questioning where he would have to tell her about what he'd really been doing. No doubt she wouldn't believe of word of it. It did sound pretty unbelievable. Not that he was the type, by any means, but she may suspect he went out to meet someone. Someone he had met in the café during the time that she was down in the caverns? God that sounded more ridiculous than submerging himself in a lake for crying out loud. His mind was working in overdrive again, wondering what his next move should be. He could easily just say he went out for fresh air and a storm blew in that soaked him to the bone, surely that would be fine? There was an element of truth to that too, so it wouldn't be a difficult storyline to go with. He would of course now have to wait until later in the morning to see what was next as he climbed back into bed next to Helena who was already dozing peacefully. He was betting that these next few hours weren't going to be peaceful for him, let alone the car journey home later that day.

Surprisingly, when Martin stirred at around 7.30am, he was starting to feel much better. Helena was already sat up in bed scrolling through her phone and texting.

'How are you feeling?' she asked, looking over at him.

'Yeah, I'm alright,' he said, through a yawn. 'Might be able to stomach some toast I reckon.'

'Ahh good. I'm glad you're feeling better. Perhaps that sleep and a shower did some good!' she added.

He didn't respond to this for fear it may have invited some more questions, so he just lay back with his head on the pillow for a moment in contemplation, doing his best to appear placated.

'Right, I'm going to shower and then we can get packed,' she said, almost bursting into life and throwing the covers off her immediately. 'I was hoping I would be back home for around 2.00pm,' she continued from within the bathroom, engaging the shower into life.

'Okay, yeah,' Martin called back. Not that he really had any choice in the matter. If he was feeling better, then he may have protested slightly and suggested that they find somewhere to have lunch, but generally he was usually pretty content at going along with whatever plans and timescales she had set out.

He then suddenly remembered the pile of wet clothes rolled up in the towel that was left in the corner of the bathroom. Oh bugger. It was just like Helena to notice this sort of thing as she busied herself getting dressed and doing a whip round of the room whilst getting dressed. Low and behold, two minutes later, Helena appeared in the doorway of the bathroom while brushing her teeth with a question for Martin.

'Marty, why is there a pile of your clothes wrapped up in a towel?' she asked, albeit innocently rather than inquisitively.

Oh shit. It was like the blood had drained from his face, he hadn't expected this to happen and was going to try and control the situation before she found it. Think. Think think think.

'Oh... uh, well. It's a bit embarrassing I suppose,' he started to confess. 'I was getting really sweaty in the night and a bit smelly so, I, uh... put them in the shower before I got in.'

Jesus. This was ridiculous. Helena looked puzzled.

'Oh right. Well I'm not surprised really Marty,' she said with an ironic giggle, 'you had your hoodie on in bed, no wonder you were hot!'

'Yeah… well, uh, I only put it on because I was cold. Maybe I, uh… have a fever or something,' he quickly added.

'Perhaps yeah,' she responded. 'Are you going to be okay to drive home?'

'I'll be fine,' he said, getting out of bed and brushing past her into the bathroom with a relieved smile.

It would seem like he had just about got through that first line of questioning, but he knew there would be more. The story was plausible, yes. But was it a little bit out of character? Certainly. Martin wasn't known for this type of behaviour. He'd have hated the thought of putting his clothes in a shower cubicle and having to deal with whatever followed. If he was questioned again he'd have to pass it off as hallucinating or something. He certainly didn't enjoy the beginnings of this elaborate lie that was forming. But what else could he do? He had spun the web now. So in order to save himself, he had to catch any question in its intricacies and wrap them up in more strands of webbing to diffuse their threat. It seemed the only way.

Breakfast wasn't a problem. Martin was able to eat a few slices of toast and some apple juice before the couple cleared their plates and made their way back to reception to check out. They were standing at reception chatting with the owner when Martin noticed something out the corner of his eye. His trainers. The door to the porch was open so they were pretty much in clear view. Would Helena have the nous to recognise his trainers as they left? Perhaps it wasn't a risk worth taking, given the questions that would follow and the fact he had a three-hour journey home with her to navigate. Oh Christ, this was a conundrum. What should he do? He thought carefully for a moment. Helena was still chatting away about what they (she) had been up to yesterday so this had bought some time for him to think.

'I'm just going to take this all out to the car,' he said lugging a bag over his shoulder and picking up Helena's case.

'Okay, thank you!' she replied, courteously.

The B&B owner smiled in his direction.

'He's a good one isn't he. Well trained I see!' she said to Helena.

'Oh yes, indeed! Just need him to get cooking for me now!' she responded with a laugh.

Martin raised his eyebrows with a half-smile. He wasn't bothered about the comment, he was focusing on a way to grab his wet trainers on the way out without Helena noticing.

He turned to exit the porch focusing completely on the task in hand. What he hadn't noticed was the cast iron boot remover that was holding the door open. He kicked his left foot into it as he walked and lost his footing. He bumped over, taking down all the bags with him landing in a heap on the flagstone floor, smack bang next to his sopping wet trainers. This couldn't have gone any worse.

Helena and the B&B owner rushed out to his aid.

'I'm fine, I'm fine,' he said, getting to his feet.

'Oh he's been a bit poorly you see,' explained Helena, helping him to his feet. 'Had a few funny turns yesterday and overnight,' it was like she was referring to a child who couldn't talk, telling the B&B owner about his plight.

'Not to worry, not to worry,' she replied. 'Must be something in the air up here!' she joked.

'A bit dizzy from the mountains, eh Marty!' said Helena.

He felt mocked. Once again he was steeped in a deep shame that something else he had tried had been a right royal cock-up. Nonetheless, he took the opportunity to collect his shoes and gathered them up with his holdall.

'Ahh, yes. I was wondering whose trainers they were,' said the B&B owner. 'Saw them there this morning when I opened up, sopping wet they are!'

She had obviously noticed him grab them. Well, that was his cover blown then. He just had to hope and pray that Helena hadn't taken any notice. The wet trainers would mean he'd definitely have to come clean about what he was doing in the dead of night, and coupled with the wet clothes, Helena would surely start to piece it all together before he had a chance to think of a good cover story. He just hoped she wouldn't.

Chapter 22

Fortunately for Martin, the journey home that day passed without any real incident. They were home within two and a half hours and Helena mostly slept and read her book on the way home. He was always amazed at how she could do either of these things. Reading would make him dizzy, no question. Sleeping? Well he was only capable of doing that in a bed or somewhere comfy due to his lanky and awkward sizing.

As they drew up outside Helena's parents house, it was a cheerful enough departure. Martin exited the car to help her with her luggage and the two kissed and hugged before he set off again. He usually wanted her to invite him in after this sort of drop-off. To prolong the time together a bit. To just relax in each others company, however that was. But today, he was hoping that she wasn't going to invite him in. All he wanted to do was go home and wallow.

'Thanks for such a lovely weekend,' she said.

'Yeah, I'm sorry. I mean… you know, apart from the obvious, I did enjoy it,' he replied.

'Hopefully the next time will be less dramatic!' she joked.

Well, at least she seemed positive about a future then. That was a small crumb of comfort to be taking away from what was otherwise a disastrous couple of days after the mountain climb.

'I know. I'm sorry,' he said. He felt guilty and wanted to reiterate it again.

'Marty, it's okay. Honestly. You don't have to worry, I still had a nice time, these things can't be helped,' she said kindly.

'Thank you. Okay,' he replied, whilst pulling her in for a hug and kissing her gently on the head. He could've forgotten it all in this moment. It seemed everything about the weekend was now a distant memory. The capitulations, the anxieties, the awkwardness. And this is how he had to try and view things – but sadly his troubled mind didn't work in this way. He knew it would all come flooding back once he was left alone with his thoughts.

With her head pressed against his chest in what was a loving embrace, and quite frankly, a relaxing moment for them both, she broke the silence with a single question that had obviously been looming.

'Why were your shoes soaking wet by the way?'

Chapter 23

If their first weekend away as a couple was meant to be their last, then Martin would've probably not had too many arguments. He looked back on that first weekend together in Snowdonia as being a bit of a disaster. But in truth, he clung to the brighter moments of that trip. Scaling the mountain together and having probably one of his favourite times with Helena. He wished he could've bottled that emotion and access it when he needed. When it was just the two of them, the going was good. Really good. That's what fed his appetite for more with her.

So two years later (with at least six or seven more successful weekends away during that time), Martin and Helena were moving into their first home together. A new build on the help to buy scheme, giving them a real taste of what life together forever might look like. They'd made a nice home for themselves in suburbia, living in a quiet cul-de-sac on the edge of a commuter town in their three-bed semi. It was the next step, naturally. A step they both felt confident about taking. Furthermore, it was a step that Martin didn't really need to think twice about. He loved Helena. He didn't see himself with anyone else so why would there be a question over his commitment and long-term future with her? They had managed to muster up the 10% deposit needed for government match funding and were on their way to being homeowners together.

By the time Helena's 30th birthday had arrived, the couple had been in their new home for approximately eighteen months. He had coasted through the first year in the house together. Enjoyed the security of being with someone who had a life plan, someone he could rely on and piggyback off of their direction. Besides being the trailblazer in all things new home, Helena was also training to become a lawyer, alongside her day job in a solicitors firm. This was mentally and physically draining for her, and in most cases, she needed Martin to be there for support. It's not that he wasn't, but he would quite easily slip into a very lazy and (in Helena's words) 'unhelpful' routine. He of course had his own career as an architect which was going from strength to strength. Despite a few disagreements, there weren't really any rows, no huge arguments or anything like that. In truth, the latter may have helped saved their long-term relationship, by releasing some of the tension that was being built up. But generally, Martin would just simply cop it. Take the hits and the gentle bollockings lying down. He didn't really stand up for himself or talk about his feelings. If anything, it made him more steadfast in his stubbornness to not abide by Helena's ways. It was a counter intuitive approach, because it only left him feeling more miserable as a result. He'd almost done a complete three-sixty. From going with the flow and being pretty subservient, to now flat refusing at times to be a support mechanism and becoming increasingly distant.

A constant theme throughout this time was his honesty. He wasn't being honest with Helena, let alone himself. Most nights he would return home earlier than she would from her day at work and typically spend the next two hours lying on their bed. Sometimes just staring into space, sometimes even sobbing and hating himself for containing so much pent-up emotion.

Helena would then breeze in and he'd act like nothing had happened. He'd lie about why he hadn't been able to cook the dinner, or why the bathrooms hadn't been cleaned. It was hard to tell the truth and so easy to lie. It was like going back to the first weekend away and not telling her why he'd returned to their room soaking wet in the dead of night.

All being said, they still got along fine. But perhaps Martin was blind to the fact that he was lying all the time about his poor state of mind or that he was gradually heading into some kind of depression. This was even talked about between them at one point after a bit of back and forth about why he was led on the sofa in the pitch black one evening.

'Martin. Do you think you might be depressed?' Helena had asked, reasonably innocently.

He didn't really know what depression was, he just felt like himself – this was always how he felt?

'I don't know. I'm just… really tired,' he would lie.

Tired. That was the easy way out. She knew his job was stressful like hers and she knew he loved it and had worked hard for it, so she had to accept it as a valid response. But in reality, Martin was rejecting the idea of depression. He couldn't articulate his thoughts. He would process what was in front of him, because on paper he had a nice house, a decent car, a good job, successful girlfriend etc etc. but none of this really delved into the true feelings that he harboured and constantly hurt him. Everything looked fine, so it must be fine.

Helena was a kind soul really. Full on, yes. Fiercely driven and stubborn too? Absolutely. It was these qualities that Martin had fallen in love with, in a way, but they were also the reasons now that as a couple they were probably starting to resent each other. She was highly motivated to be moving on at some pace, to be starting to think about marriage, kids, a bigger house. But Martin seemed to be traipsing through the mud with his progression. He had a good job, yes. But was he really motivated to do anything else? Not really. He didn't have a huge circle of friends to go and see – George was still his closest, but he'd spent a lot of time in Manchester with his recruitment firm over the last year and the two had drifted somewhat. His parents were estranged. Mum was shacked up with some new bloke called Gary over in Gloucester and Dad was now doing contract IT work which could've placed him anywhere in the country. He was distant from the people he needed most, and was becoming increasingly distant from the one person he truly needed. Perhaps he just didn't sense it, but clearly Helena had, because she was about to act with swift brutality.

Martin had booked The Ivy for the two of them to celebrate Helena's thirtieth – they'd be heading up to her parents on the weekend for a proper family celebration and it wasn't uncommon for just the two of them to go out on either one of their birthdays. They had a nice, if not quiet meal together. Martin wasn't one for big gestures so there were no surprises at the dinner table like the lights being turned low and everyone singing 'Happy Birthday.' It wasn't that type of venue anyway, and he did at least manage to get her a glass of Birthday Prosecco on the house. That was probably about as romantic as it got. Helena spent most of the night on her phone, either responding to Birthday texts or plain ignoring Martin. Again, this wasn't too uncommon when the two of them had gone out together, but there was something different about tonight. She seemed irritable, shuffling and huffing in her seat – almost impatiently. She definitely wasn't her happy inquisitive self. The conversation was stilted at best, they made small talk about the weekend and about the general admin of running a house together, like shopping lists and jobs that needed doing. Martin didn't suspect anything at this point. He was still set on making his move later that evening. His judgement was about to be tested to the absolute maximum.

Three days previous, Martin was walking through the centre of town on his lunch break. He had bought some bits for Helena's Birthday – a nice card, some perfume he knew she liked and in addition he was going to add an experience day doing a hot air balloon ride. They were thoughtful gifts and more than appropriate for a thirtieth birthday. But as he walked through the shopping arcade, his eye was caught by a shop ahead. A jewellers. It was almost as if what he had bought and planned wasn't enough, and he felt that an additional gesture had to be made to appease her even more, because he feared that she may be dissatisfied with his crop of gifts. So what he did next was impulsive and quite frankly, bizarre.

He marched into the jewellers knowing absolutely nothing about what he should be doing in there or what he should be asking for. He had clearly lost himself for a moment, because his confidence was seemingly sky high. He even instigated a conversation with a sales assistant.

'Hello, hi. I'm looking to buy an engagement ring?' He said with the utmost assurance.

'Ok Sir, come with me I'll show you our selection of diamonds,' the sales assistant replied with a smile. She beckoned him over to a cabinet towards the front of the shop.

'Is it a diamond ring you're looking for?' she asked.

Martin really had no idea, but he'd gone in there with all the confidence he could muster so to look like he knew what he wanted, he agreed.

'Umm, yes. Yes… a diamond one, of course,' he replied.

He was shown a selection of rings that were within his price range and ten minutes later he was putting down a £200 deposit for a £2,000 diamond ring. He had absolutely no idea of the size required for Helena's finger, but the sales assistant had assured him that this wasn't uncommon. They'd worked it out based on the size of Martin's little finger and perhaps added a bit of leeway. He would never know if the ring was to fit Helena's finger, it didn't even get that far.

With dinner complete, they hailed a taxi and took the short ride back home. The mood was somewhat tense. He had worked himself up into a bit of nervous wreck now so the conversation was even less than usual. What he didn't realise at the time was that Helena would usually be asking questions or engaging with the taxi driver, talking about something or other. But there was nothing tonight. He truly failed in heeding any of these cues for what was about to come next. They stepped out of the taxi and walked quickly to the door. The rain was starting to fall. It had a been a pleasant September evening, but the sky had turned in the time they had eaten their meal. It was like the atmosphere was in perfect sync with the mood of the evening and how the darkened clouds forming in the sky were about to burst with a storm of epic proportions.

'That was a nice meal,' said Martin, trying to play it all cool.

'Yeah, it was. Thanks for dinner,' she replied, almost sullenly. It was like saying those words required effort to come out of her mouth. 'I'm just going to the bathroom. Be two secs,' she added.

This was it. He had a little bit of time to collect himself while she was in the toilet. He quickly went upstairs and picked the ring box out of a pair of shoes he had stowed away at the back of the cupboard. Still there? Yep, all good as he checked the contents of the box. He raced back downstairs and there was Helena sat on their sofa looking like she was waiting for a job interview or something.

She was sat upright, her feet were tucked in together and her hands stationed on her lap.

'Is, uh, everything alright?' he asked, entering the room slowly and suspiciously. This had clearly caught him off guard. He knew she'd been off colour tonight but he didn't expect her to be acting so serious.

'I think you'd better sit down,' she said quietly.

Never has anyone said those words without a negative outcome. It reminded him of the day he came home from school with his parents sat at the kitchen table. His heart was already racing at a hundred miles an hour and now he felt like he could pass out from the thumping in his rib cage. He sat down at the opposite end of the corner sofa, facing her.

'Martin,' she started, 'I'm… I'm really sorry,'

What the hell was going on here, thought Martin. He was totally and utterly speechless. He was frozen stock still, wondering what was to come next. Part of him already knew the answer though. It couldn't come fast enough either, if it was to be that, but time was just standing still as Helena delivered the words slowly and carefully.

'I'm really sorry, but… I just… I can't do this anymore,' she delivered, finally. There was no real emotion in her face, the words felt cold and without remorse. This wasn't the Helena he'd grown to love.

'I know this is bad timing,' she continued, 'but I've just really struggled with you recently. I don't know what you're thinking, what you're doing or even who you are? I've tried to help Martin, I really have, but you just won't help yourself. If I can't be there for you then who can? I just don't think I've got the energy for this anymore. I need my space and you need help, because I am exhausted at trying to find answers when you don't give me anything!' The last bit was said with more emotion as she broke down in tears. Martin just looked on, completely and utterly bewildered. What the fuck was this? It was a total surprise to him, he'd been completely caught out here and the worst thing that could've happened, on tonight of all nights, was happening. He was meant to be proposing, getting them to commit to a long-term future together. But instead, she was getting up off the sofa and leaving the room in floods of tears.

Two minutes later, she was thundering back down the stairs with a rucksack while Martin just sat there, still in shock.

'See! See? You don't even say anything! You don't even come up and stop me from leaving! You don't even ask if I'm okay, or if there's anything you can do?' she exclaimed, 'You've got no fight in you Martin, none at all it would seem, how do you think that makes me feel? You've not fought for me for God knows how long and now this shit is real, you can't even do anything but just sit there and look at me! What the fuck Martin! What the actual fuck is wrong with you!' She was getting hysterical now, but still Martin just stood there, numb. Helena stood in the doorway with her eyes full of tears and rage.

'I… No, Helena. Please. Please don't say that,' it was all he could say now with his head held low. Those words had hit him like a train. What was wrong with him? He really didn't know. He felt defeated.

'Well, that's it. I'm going now, I can't… I can't,' she said, breaking down again. 'I can't do this now. Goodbye Martin,' and with that, she walked out into the hallway and out the front door with her bag before he could react.

The lasting memory of that night for Martin would be the sound of Helena turning over her car engine at the exact same time he was looking down at the small box he had just opened in his hand. She then sped off into the night and out of his life.

Chapter 24

Present day

Martin was able to return to work after a couple of days in bed. He'd not had a fever, that was obvious. He'd had a breakdown. His hand to mouth mental existence was becoming ever more draining on him. At least a return to work would occupy his mind on something else, if he allowed it.

The time at home alone in his 'sick bed,' with just his own thoughts for company, had given him the chance to reflect on the last couple of days, months and even years. He mused over the break-up with Helena and the time he went to her and begged for another chance. The problem was, she was having none of it. He knew that looking back it was sheer desperation. He hadn't had the chance to reflect properly until now, as it felt like he was constantly dealing with the administration of a broken relationship. The fallout had lasted at least eighteen months from the day she walked out. They weren't married, so it wasn't as if they had to divorce or anything like that. But Helena had stood firm on staying in the house, she was making the case over the fact that it was more 'hers' due to the amount of effort she had put in to making it a truly lovely home. Everything was always equal though, so there was no doubt he'd be able to get his deposit money back, and then some.

The worst bit about this time was that he pretty much had nowhere to go apart from back to his Mum's, who was living with her new partner Gary. He was a nice enough guy, very subservient and kindly, and Mum seemed happy so that was all that mattered. He stationed himself in the back bedroom of their house in Gloucester until it was time to get his own place, whether bought or rented. It was a big come down from being a homeowner in a nice new build development to having to move in with a parent, with who the relationship was pretty disillusioned since he left for University nearly ten years ago. If his Dad had more of a fixed abode then he'd have jumped at the opportunity to go there. With him being away lots, it would have been the perfect blend of father and son relationship rekindling, as well as his own time to be alone. Sadly, Dad's rented one bed flat on the edge of Swindon wasn't really adequate for him, let alone Martin.

He would spend most evenings in the back bedroom of his Mum and new partners home, waiting for the moment he could start again on his own. At the time he had no idea what that looked like of course, but fast forwarding a few months and there he was again, just lying in bed and staring into space. This was now very much giving him a sense of what that was like. New surroundings, same outcome. He sat or laid alone most nights in the rented flat just outside the city. Eat, sleep, work, repeat. His life was one monotonous shuttle journey from bed to desk and then back again. He was unhealthy, unsatisfied, and lonely. Looking from the outside in, you could be forgiven for calling Martin lazy. He was lacking a serious amount of verve. He had no direction, no motivation and certainly believed his own mind when it told him he had no prospects. But he wasn't lazy of course. He was just stuck. Stuck in a wave of depression that continued to pull him under in the riptide of life.

Lots of men his age that were plastered over social media liked to coin the phrase 'winning.' 'Winning' at this thing they're doing with their mates. 'Winning' at this big business deal they'd just done. Or '#winning' because they'd bought a new car and were happily splashing it all over Instagram to get likes or kudos. These superficial and sometimes materialistic broadcasts meant they were clearly 'winning at life'. But for Martin, the way he looked at his situation confirmed that he clearly wasn't 'winning' at life. There was no nice girlfriend on his arm. No family home anymore. No decent car (he would later have to sell that to top-up the gambling coffers) and the losses in his personal life seemed to be stacking up day by day. But would you know this by looking at him? He was thin, yes. He didn't look healthy and full of colour, but apart from that he was doing a really plausible act to portray the fact he was 'fine.'

He knew in himself he wasn't fine and he'd have to act quickly otherwise there would be no winning. Perhaps the biggest loss of all. But perhaps losing and letting go was actually the best way to win.

Chapter 25

Back at the architects firm it was pretty much like the outside world had no insight into what had happened to Martin over the last couple of days. He'd lost the last of his money gambling on football matches he knew absolutely nothing about and had dreamt a very real dream about taking his own life.

'Cuppa tea Mart?' said Susannah. 'Or is it coffee first thing. I can never remember!' she giggled.

'Oh yeah, tea would be good thanks, yeah. Cheers Suze,' he replied.

He was doing his best to feel positive and take his mind off of the final gambling episode. So far it was working, if only temporarily of course.

'I'll get my head back into the Hereford project, that should get me focused,' he thought to himself. The office was filling up now with his colleagues, but he forced himself to stay fixed on his screen and not to distract himself or indeed, to attract attention. One of the partners, Steve, was right. He had a lot to be proud of with this project. He'd essentially devised an eco building scheme for the client that would not only save them hundreds in energy costs per annum, but also revolutionise the sustainability agenda at his own practice, meaning they could tender for more innovative and ecologically conscious project work. He had visions of collecting an award from the Architect Weekly annual dinner for best sustainable build, with that bloke off the tele from Grand Designs handing him an award. That would show them. That would be fucking winning.

'Cuppa tea for Marty B!' said Susannah in typically cheery fashion.

'Oh, cheers,' he replied, without taking his gaze from the screen.

'This looks cracking by the way Mart. I think Steve wants to talk to you later about taking some of these ideas forward for other stuff,' she said.

'Oh really?' Martin said as he turned, his attention finally broken.

'Yeah. He was saying about it on Friday in our team huddle. Shame you weren't around! Perhaps he'll grab you today to tell you more,' she concluded.

'Cool, okay. Thanks. Cheers Suze,' he said.

'Don't thank me! Keep up the good work Marty boy!'

He had a sense of buoyancy after hearing this. The affirmation from a colleague was one thing, and to have the recognition from his superiors was even better. He could recognise a glimmer of his own talents momentarily, he could certainly be proud of his work if nothing else. He tended to be very bashful in this sense and would keep pride to himself. He was never going to be someone who would go round shouting their mouth off about how great they were. A line that had always stuck with him from when he was younger was, 'pride always comes before a fall.' He'd read it in Aesop's fables or somewhere like that. They were meant to teach kids good morals and alike. This was one that had stayed with him throughout his life, which is why he was always careful and reserved in his judgements when it came to self-praise or speaking up to have his voice heard.

Steve called Martin into his office during the afternoon, having been out with a client in the morning. 'Mart? Quick word?' he said across the desks, beckoning Martin over to his glass office.

'Oh yeah… sure,' Martin responded, and got to his feet. He picked up a pad and pen then made his way over. It was always best to look like you might have the intention of taking notes even if you were not even planning to, he thought. Besides, he might be getting the lead on some of the next project work if what Susannah had said was true. He was quietly excited, but also nervous. He always was, speaking to one of the partners, even though his relationship with Steve was really good. They could chat about anything while making tea or having lunch, but once it was work related, he suddenly felt that pang of responsibility and nervous energy that this was official business.

'Take a seat Mart,' Steve said, gesturing over the desk. Martin clicked the glass door shut and moved towards the designer chairs that were positioned at angles to Steve's desk.

'Thanks,' replied Martin and sat down, back straight, feet on the floor and pad at the ready in his lap. He didn't feel as if he could come across as overly casual and wanted to exude the manner of being alert, compliant and ready.

The Martin that Steve was looking at though was drained, tired and looking like he lacked focus. Martin was clearly doing his best to appear calm and ready, but to the trained eye, it was quite obviously an act that couldn't fool someone who knew.

'Just wanted to say well done again on the Hereford job. We have a very happy customer and the contractors doing the work have said they want to be using us again, maybe on retainer, so that's great,' Steve started.

'Great. No, that's uh… really great,' replied Martin.

'Yeah, it is. So well done. I will have no problem giving you the lead on more projects like that if you can show the maturity, poise and creativity that you have on this one,' he continued. 'But that's not actually why I've pulled you in here this afternoon – although I did want to give you a praise for your hard work.'

Oh. This was sounding ominous now. What did Steve know about Martin's private life that was making him say something like this? Maybe it wasn't about his private life? Maybe it was something work related? Had he done something recently that he'd forgotten? His mind raced back over the last few weeks to try and put his finger on what this issue could be. On reflection it was blindingly obvious he had noticed something personal, but Martin was determined not to let on. He was worried that the praise that had just been heaped on him was a bit of a 'shit sandwich,' meaning Steve would give him some praise, then a filler of shit news, then top it with an encouraging, 'you're doing great though' to complete this verbal snack. 'Is everything okay Martin?' Steve said. He paused for a moment, waiting for a reply from Martin. Nothing came instantly, so Steve pressed on.

'We take employee health really seriously here at Williamson Crossley Peters. I do sense that you may be feeling some stress at the moment Martin and I wanted you to know you don't have to tackle whatever it is you're stressing over alone. I know how it feels, believe me.'

Martin let the words carry in the room for a moment. He was surprised that the conversation had gone this way and if anything was intrigued as to what would happen next. He felt the right thing to do was to respond.

'I, uh... yes. Thanks Steve. I do feel stress sometimes,' he started, 'But it's not because of work! I like my work. It's a passion and a pursuit,' he quickly added.

Steve eyed him thoughtfully for a moment. He sat back in his chair and let out a sigh. It wasn't a sigh of discontent, it was more a reflection about what was to come next. He was about to reveal something, and probably not something he was proud of.

'That's good to hear Mart, it really is. I know it's easier said than done, but don't feel like it's a burden or a mask from your wellbeing to be working here. There is plenty of support available to you. I knew something was up the other day when you came in. You looked white as a sheet and I know you're not the loudest, but much quieter than normal too.'

'I know the signs, because I've lived with those symptoms. Now I'm not labelling you with any of those type of things Martin, but when I went through times of high stress and ultimately, depression, I had no idea what to do. All I want to say is that I and we are here for you if you need the support.'

There it was. The 'D' word. He'd said it. Probably the first person since Helena to say it to his face, but in quite different circumstances.

'That's… that's very kind. Thanks Steve, I appreciate it,' he replied.

Steve nodded.

'If you ever want to talk, you have my number Martin. Keep up the good work and don't be afraid to ask for help.'

'I won't. Thanks. Thank you Steve,' he replied.

Steve nodded kindly in Martin's direction to acknowledge that the meeting was over. Martin got up to leave and nodded back. As he exited the glass office there was only one thing on his mind. It wasn't considering how he might get help or support, or how he would turn his life around. The thought of getting the tools and strategy in place to recover some kind of consistent mental wellbeing couldn't have been further away. Instead, his thoughts were consumed with something else. That he'd better improve the act he was putting on to mask his innermost insecurities, otherwise there would be more than Steve noticing something was up.

Chapter 26

In the days that followed, Martin was back in work mode. He had mustered enough personal strength to get immersed in his projects again and was largely focused on the tasks he had going on. There was a little bit of catching up to do and just like his time at school or at any time in his academic life, he thrived on the challenge of working things out, hitting deadlines and generally having his head in his work. It had always been his best distraction and his safety net when shit hit the fan. Like when his parents divorced, which was a key time in his academic life.

It was only until around 4.45pm each day that he started to get that sinking feeling in his stomach again. He'd look up at the clock in the corner of his computer monitor and think that in half an hour or so, he'd be getting ready for home time – or in some cases he might already be at home – where the demons would start circling his psyche. It was a vicious cycle that he was caught in. He had no motivation to get out the house and take his mind off things or do something physical like a walk, a run, or God forbid – even try and join a club or team for some human contact. Instead, he wrestled with the double-edged sword that was at one end, staying at home and hurting himself by sitting in misery until work rolled round again, or at the other end, making an effort to be more sociable and meeting people – both of which he feared equally.

Most nights he would just eat something unhealthy (or barely anything at all) and then just go to bed. This is largely how he got through winter, what with the nights drawing in so dark and cold. There was nothing else to do but to pull the covers over himself and try and sleep.

But sleep, equally, was not always the solace he hoped for. He would toss and turn or wake up at stupid o' clock, wide awake and getting into his own head about things. He would be going over old memories and notions of the past and then left feeling completely alone and frustrated at the plight he had got himself into.

There were of course reasons that he was alone. He'd rejected any sort of contact with anyone and had become increasingly distant from his family. Admittedly, he didn't have much family to go to, but with his parents pretty estranged and only one cousin who was 15 years older than him, it wasn't like the support existed naturally in his family dynamic. This was no more apparent than the Christmas that had just passed – another episode he would rather just delete from memory for all eternity.

*

It was Christmas Eve and Martin was back at his Mum's to spend the period with her, Gary and Gary's immediate family. To say he was dreading it was probably an understatement. He didn't have anything against Gary at all, he just couldn't be bothered to make any effort. His Mum was obviously still bitter about his Dad leaving and the sense was that she could never fully move on. She would make comments in front of Martin such as, 'well, it was his choice,' or 'I bet he wishes he hadn't been such an idiot now does he,' – referring to the fact that he was probably sat alone, single and with nobody to see at Christmas.

Why did she care? He thought this to himself regularly when she raised this sort of point. He half wanted to say, 'just fucking leave it Mum for fuck's sake!' but it didn't bother him enough to start an argument over it –yet. She revelled in this sick kind of misery, getting a kick out of his Dad's perceived unhappiness. There was nothing to suggest it and Martin was sure his Dad did have spells of loneliness and solitude, but was he glad he wasn't married to Martin's Mum any longer? Probably.

Whether the comments and jibes bothered Gary or not, who knew? He just got on with his life in a quiet, controlled manner. He wasn't one for huge amounts of fuss. He was largely subservient, but he also had this calm aura when he was around Mum that she put him on a pedestal. He was slightly older than Martin's Mum, so perhaps it was the natural experience of life and general maturity that gave him this. He spent a lot of time out of the way, mostly in the spare room that Martin had once resided, where he tinkered with bits of old computer or doing long haul flights to Australia on his flight simulator game. Mum probably didn't mind this, because a) she knew where he was at all times, and b) he wasn't in the kitchen making mess. It was an arrangement that suited them both now they were in retirement.

Gary's family wouldn't be joining until the late afternoon, so it would be just the three of them and their dog, Fergus.

Fergus was a puffy white bichon frise with a stupid pink tongue that hung needily from his mouth. He was Mum's baby these days. She would've never allowed an animal in the house during Martin's childhood, but Fergus was pruned and pampered to within an inch of his life, and God bless the poor dog, he couldn't move an inch for fear he might make a paw print on the floor. The dog hadn't exactly warmed to Martin on the occasions that he had been in its company, but he did like animals. Perhaps it was Mum's protective nature over Fergus that meant he was not one for new faces.

Martin was yearning for something else. He had no idea what, but it wasn't this. Perhaps he wanted to go back to those years between eighteen and twenty-one, when it was still school mates catching up again, and mainly George, going down The Hilly and stumbling home with the intention of trying not to appear hungover for Christmas dinner the following day. He'd had fond memories of this sort of thing. He had even spent a couple of Christmases with George's family during the time he was still at University. His Mum had been staying with her sister in Norfolk (he couldn't think of anything worse) and Dad was somewhere up North trying to earn as much money as possible to pay off the credit card bills he'd racked up from solicitors fees.

But this year, now in his thirties, he felt he should make some kind of family attempt, even if he didn't really want to. When the invite was extended his way, he was surprised to say the least but thought it was the best thing to do. He thought to himself about how everyone has this obsession over Christmas about seeing each other.

'Oh, we need to make time for so-and-so,' or 'yes, we're having the morning here then we're popping over to see such-and-such.' He really couldn't be bothered with it all. Was it too much to ask that he just wanted to sit around on his own, watch some sport on the television and wallow in some misery? Nope. He had to try and keep up appearances to some extent and once a year wouldn't hurt, or so he thought.

'Martin, you didn't actually tell me what you wanted this year so I haven't got you anything exciting,' announced his Mum, as they sat in front of the television watching some Christmas Eve drama special.

'Yeah, fine,' he said. Not ungratefully by any means, but just how he always communicated with his Mum. There was a pause as she continued to study her phone for a moment. Probably one of those crappy Facebook neighbourhood groups where everyone thinks they're a vigilante or they simply feel they have to report on everything from where the postman parked his van or whether the loud bang just heard was anything to be worried about.

He had absolutely no doubts his Mum was an avid contributor to this sort of trash. She was naturally nosey after all and loved knowing everyone else's business. No wonder Martin was so private. He'd grown up knowing and hearing about such irrelevant and meaningless crap his Mum drove down his and his Dad's throats, they were just completely non-plussed by it, meaning that Martin modelled himself on something quite the opposite to his Mother.

'And Gary's daughters are coming over tomorrow afternoon with their families,' she continued, 'so we're going to have lunch around two-ish.'

He didn't respond to this verbally, just raised his eyebrows and nodded in agreement. Both Gary's daughters were happily married, had kids and partners so a huge entourage would be arriving at some point. He got along fine with them of course, not that he had had much interaction with them in the time his Mum had been with Gary, but he just really couldn't be bothered to stand on ceremony and pretend everything was happy families. It might be for them, but it wasn't for him. He simply hated this sort of thing. Why he hated it, he wasn't sure. At one point, it was everything he wanted while looking into the future with Helena. Now he was just bitter about it all, wallowing in self-pity and a constant loop of shame.

Gary appeared at the doorway.

'Anyone fancy a cuppa? He said in his gentle Northern tones. He was a decent bloke to be fair, his Mum could've chosen a lot worse, so he had to be glad about that.

'Oh, no thank you darling, I think I'll have a drop of sherry in a minute, but thanks anyway,' his Mum replied.

Darling? Martin couldn't recall a time when his Dad had ever been called 'darling.'

'No probs,' said Gary. He turned to the opposite sofa. 'Martin? How about you mate?' He asked.

'Ummm, I... yeah, go on then. Thanks,' Martin replied. 'I was going to go up to bed in a moment to read for a bit so I'll take it up there,'

'I'll bring it up,' he said kindly, 'pop into the back room before you do, I'd like to show you something,' he continued. Martin was intrigued. What could Gary mean by that? He probably wanted to show him something on flight simulator. But it was uncommon for this kind of exchange to take place. It wasn't like he was super close with Gary or anything. If Martin was intrigued then his Mum was probably more so, unless she was in on this new step-dad type vibe that Gary wanted to establish.

'Ooh what's that about darling?' his Mum announced, true to form. She could sniff out suspicion from a mile off.

'I just wanted Martin's ideas for that summer house I was thinking of putting up. He is an architect after all, if you'd forgotten that Jayne?' He replied to her and winked kindly towards Martin.

'Oh of course, yes. I want that up in time for summer remember!' she replied, half realising that her son was actually quite a decent architectural designer. Not that she knew fuck all about it, thought Martin. It was just drawings and bricks to her, as long as it got done and was free of mess she didn't really care about how anyone went about creating a summer house. 'Yeah, sure. I'll be up shortly,' said Martin.

'Grand. Right, two teas and a sherry on the way for the lady of the house!' he said, walking off in jovial fashion. Martin looked over to his Mum, who was beaming towards him.

'That's nice,' she mouthed towards him quietly, with a look that suggested she was happy there was something they might have in common and the start of a bond.

Martin nodded in agreement. He was going to find out shortly if the outcome of his chat with Gary was 'nice' or not.

Chapter 27

'Here ya go Mart,' said Gary, placing down a mug of tea on the desk that Martin was now stood next to.

'Thanks,' he replied.

'I just wanted to run something by you to be honest mate. And yes, we can talk about the summer house but I'm sure that's well below your level of expertise from what I've heard,' Gary continued.

What was this about then? Martin thought to himself. He did think a load of fuss over a bloody summer house you could basically put in a trolley from Homebase wasn't really worth it, but he would've been happy to consult with him on it.

'I'm conscious that what I'm about to say will probably come as a little bit of surprise to you. Or perhaps not, I'm not sure.'

Martin looked at him, slightly confused. He really had no idea what was going on here.

'I'm a believer in doing things by the book, and well, you're probably the closest person to your Mum for asking this type of thing. I know your relationship isn't what it was, but at the end of the day, you're still her son and I'm really respectful of that.'

Okay. Come on then Gary, spit it out. Although he was feeling impatient and uncomfortable, Martin felt respected by way of this conversation actually happening. He had to give Gary his due, he really was a nice bloke.

'Tomorrow,' Gary continued, 'I'm going to give your Mother a gift for us to go away for New Years Eve. I've booked a hotel and flights to Paris for us to celebrate the New Year in style.'

He paused for a moment while this registered with Martin. Okay, great. That's fine. They don't need my permission to go to Paris, he thought.

'…and while we're there, I'm going to ask your Mum to marry me,' he concluded.

Okay, so there it was. Gary was going to marry Mum. There was absolutely no chance in hell she'd say no, so this was it. Gary would officially be his step Dad. He wasn't sure how to feel about this. It wasn't like it would change his life in any way. His Mum was clearly happy, so what difference did it make? Again, Gary was a decent enough chap. He cared for Mum and hadn't shown any signs that he was going to upset her in any way, so that was all good. He should probably say something about now, as the silence was probably getting a bit awkward, almost like he did have a problem with it in some way.

'So… I just wanted you to know mate. What with your Grandad not being around, I can't really ask for her hand in marriage!'

It was true, his Grandparents had passed years ago. It was a nice thing Gary had done here, he didn't have to. Martin was arguably non-plussed though.

'Yeah, sure. Of course. That's… that's lovely. Congratulations,' he answered finally.

Congratulations? Congratulations? They weren't even fucking married yet and you're dishing out the plaudits, he thought to himself.

'Thanks Martin, I appreciate it. I really care for your Mum and it means a lot to have your approval for me to do this, so thank you.'

'No, of course. I really appreciate you telling me,' Martin answered.

He stood there for a moment slightly awkwardly. Both grinning at one another with an air that suggested there was not really anything else to say.

'Well, I uh… better be off to bed now. Goodnight Gary.'

'Goodnight Martin. Sleep well mate,' he answered.

*

Martin actually woke the next morning with a small sense of pride. For once, he actually knew something his Mum didn't, and that was kind of exciting. He had a renewed sense of respect for Gary too, the way he had handled the situation was both mature and sensitive. So his Mum would be getting remarried, so what? It didn't really change anything in his life. The only thing he'd have to do was attend a wedding, if they actually had one. Perhaps a registry office would suffice. Yes, less fuss would be Martin's recommendation. In the first instance, he would have to negotiate a Christmas day with his Mum, Gary, and latterly, his family. It wouldn't be enjoyable, getting questions fired at him from all angles by his Mum about whether he'd managed to get a girlfriend yet, why he hadn't shaved properly or that the t-shirt he was wearing was too creased to wear outside or in front of other people. He knew that she was going to start talking wistfully about Helena again. It happened all the time at these sorts of occasions. That was just what he needed to bring the mood down even more. Perhaps now that Gary was a bit more of an ally, he could rely on him for some support. There was a long day ahead and this would only be the start of it.

The Christmas morning he had woken to was a far cry from mornings in his youth. As an only child, he was probably a bit spoilt, because there was never any fuss about getting what he wanted. His parents were earning and could afford decent presents. And lo and behold, when the bag of presents turned up at the foot of his bed he'd get his hands on new train sets, Scalextrics, bundles of Lego or for a couple of years it was bikes and other big and exciting presents. It was only after his parents split that Christmas started to become a task rather than a celebration. He had checked out from the celebration and the present giving. The joys of tearing off paper and getting stuck into some new toys were a distant memory by the time he was 14. He loved the memories of a quiet Christmas just playing at home with his gifts, or getting Dad to help him construct the latest Lego vehicle. He recalled getting all the good food out and watching heart-warming films on the television. When all that disappeared, Christmas became sad, and bar the odd occasion he wasn't spending it with family, it was a reminder of those difficult years where the festivities were anything but happy. Today he'd have to get into some kind of mindset that it was only one day. He could disappear back to his flat the following morning and enjoy the solitude he was craving right now.

He walked downstairs to find Mum and Gary sat at the kitchen table drinking tea. Fergus was sat in his bed and barked when Martin entered the room.

'Happy Christmas Martin!' his Mum said, getting up to hug him. She was in an unnaturally laid back and jovial mood. Had she had a sherry already?

'Happy Christmas Mum,' Martin replied, hugging her back.

'Here's a tea for you mate,' said Gary, pouring him a mug from the pot. 'Thanks, and Happy Christmas,' he said appreciatively.

'And to you, Martin,' Gary replied with a wink.

'Martin I've had wonderful news already, possibly one of the best presents I've ever had!' his Mum said excitedly. Oh God, had he done it already? Gary was grinning like a Cheshire cat. Maybe he had?

'...We're going to Paris for New Years! Isn't that wonderful? You know I've always wanted to go to Paris!'

Martin actually had no idea whether she had always wanted to go to Paris or not, but went along with it. It wasn't like his Dad would've ever dreamt of taking her somewhere for New Years. It would seem that this new and exciting world for his Mum contained all these opportunities that previous married life had deprived her of.

'Oh wow, that's uh... that's great. A lovely idea,' he responded, knowing full well the intentions for that trip which Gary had laid out last night.

Martin's Mum trotted over to the sink to busy herself with nothing in particular. There seemed to be a real spring in her step. Gary looked across at Martin as he took a seat at the table and shot him a satisfied wink and a grin. So far, so good on the planning front for Gary.

Lunchtime arrived without any drama. The morning was mainly spent lounging around while Mum chatted on the phone to her sister, Aunt Sarah. Gary was prepping the veg and turkey under her watchful eye from the kitchen table. She would no doubt take the lead again once their completely meaningless conversation about Great Uncle Andrew's seventeen-year-old cat Troy was finished.

'Yes, but the poor thing has only got one eye,' he heard her say for about the hundredth time.

The actual food was okay. Gary had done a good job on the turkey and the veg was plentiful. His Mum's cabbage was its usual flavourless green slop that was easy to bypass. Otherwise, it was the probably the best meal Martin had had in a long time. When he was cooking for himself, he could seldom be bothered to do anything interesting or even nutritious. There was a time when he and Helena were into all the latest fads, healthy meals with added protein and more meals containing pulses that you could ever dream of. This was of course a bit of phase. The pair had been doing gym work and their health kick gave them something to do as a couple, what with Helena's strict planning, they were turning into refined athletes and one day looking to run marathons. Those days were long gone. He could hardly find the motivation to walk to the kitchen, let alone a jog round the block.

Martin spent the entire meal more or less in silence, his Mum filled the table with most of the conversation about nothing in particular. Fergus eyed him from the foot of his chair with eyes that suggested what was on Martin's plate was far more attractive than what had been in his bowl. His ridiculous pink tongue dangled from his mouth expectantly.

'Thanks Mum, thanks Gary. That was, uh… really nice,' he said, laying his knife and fork alongside each other on a pretty much empty plate, save for a bit of turkey and a sprout.

'You're welcome,' said Gary, collecting their glasses and some other bits from the table. 'Another sherry dear?' he asked Martin's Mum.

'Oh, yes please darling!' she replied, getting up to start proceedings with the puddings.

Fergus continued to stare at Martin from the floor. Martin eyed him back. He knew exactly what the stupid animal wanted, but he wasn't going to get it. Mum would have a head fit if she saw Martin giving the dog scraps from the table. It wasn't the way she wanted to look after her dog, but clearly this thing was bloody needy. With Martin's Mum's back turned towards the hob as she busily warmed through the custard and Gary with his head in the drinks cupboard,

Martin quickly threw a spare bit of turkey from his plate down onto the stone floor for Fergus.

'Now fuck off you little twit,' he hissed at the dog, not audible enough for anyone to hear as they clanked around in the kitchen around him.

To be fair to Fergus, he did exactly that. He scoffed down the turkey without any protestation and curled himself up in his bed by the door.

'Good boy Fergie,' his Mum said to the dog as she appeared back at the table with a saucepan of hot custard and a piping hot Christmas pudding fresh from the microwave.

They were all seated again and ready to enjoy pudding when from over in the corner a wheezing sort of cough was heard. A pathetic sounding one at that, and seemingly nothing to cause alarm. But given the fact the three of them were already seated round the table, it must've come from Fergus. They all turned to the dog who had his head slumped over the side of his bed, glazed eyes that looked full of fear and that stupid dangling tongue hanging pitifully from his mouth.

'Fergie? Oh Fergie! Is everything okay?' Martin's Mum said. It wasn't like the poor dog was going to respond, he just looked over at the table blankly, wheezing all the while.

Martin felt the guilt begin to drain through his body. Shit. It was the fucking turkey wasn't it. He's choking on a bit of fucking turkey.

'Gary, call the vet!' his Mum said in panic.

'Hang on, what? Call the vet? He's only coughing. He'll be fine,' Gary said calmly, not wishing to be disturbed from his pudding.

'Gary, this is serious. Fergus does NOT cough. He will choke to death if we don't act now,' she replied.

'Okay,' Gary replied, almost grudgingly. Martin could tell he wasn't overly worried but acted subserviently. You've made your bed, he thought to himself cynically.

Martin continued to scoop his pudding into his mouth and try and ignore his dramatic Mother who was getting increasingly worked up by Fergus' breathing which was slowly developing into more than a wheeze and had become more laboured.

Martin could hear Gary in the other room begin talking to the vets.

'Yes… no. Yes… yes. Okay. Yes, we'll bring him in,' he could hear him saying. He re-entered the room with his phone in his hand and addressed Martin's Mum who now had Fergus in her arms. This was still all a bit dramatic, Martin thought to himself. He's only got a bloody cough, or so it seemed. Perhaps it was the turkey? Maybe he had had an allergic reaction? No, it was probably a bone or something. Shit. They were definitely going to find out it was a bone from the turkey. Maybe he could play dumb and just hope they assumed he found a scrap on the floor? It wasn't like Fergus was going to grass on him. He already disliked Martin anyway so if he disappeared it made no odds to him.

'Right, shoes on then Gary,' demanded his Mum.

'But Jayne, we've had a drink. I can't drive, and nor should you. That sherry is lethal,' Gary replied.

They both looked over to the table, where Martin was calmly scraping up the last of his custard from the bowl.

'What?' he said with a knowing air about what was about to come next.

'Would you please take us to the vet Martin?' his Mum said.

Fergus let out another pathetic cough while she waited for his answer. He was about to spend the rest of his Christmas day in a vets.

Chapter 28

Martin sat in the deserted waiting room of the local vets while his Mum took Fergus in for observation. He'd been there once before when he was younger. His first pet rabbit 'Patrick' (not the same rabbit who stopped his Mum attending football tour) needed to be put down in 1996 because of the amount of maggots he had growing out of his anus. It was pretty unsavoury to say the least.

He looked around. This had to be up there with one of the most depressing places on earth right now. Of all the places to spend his Christmas, this was absolutely perfect. He even got a slight kick out of it. In the corner, a sad plastic tree was tilting under the weight of flashy lights and the CD player next to it was spinning some kind of ghoulish rhymes about festive times. There were tacky bits of card and glitz added to walls with pasted messages of joy simply there to cover space it would seem. It really was a shallow scene. Why did people do this? A half-baked effort at some decorations was hardly worth it, it just looked like shit.

Martin's stagnant gaze across the room took him back in time to years gone by. This year would certainly linger in his mind for years to come, if he got there that was. He flicked through his phone, subconsciously. All the social feeds were littered with festive greetings or about how people had 'the best boyfriend/girlfriend' and they were so happy to be 'spending another Xmas together wiv u xxx.'

It was the kind of drivel Martin despised. People living their lives online, broadcasting fabricated messages of contentment in order to 'get' likes from other people they would barely speak to if they passed them in the street. What an absolute load of bollocks. Deep down though, was he jealous? He didn't really know what he was in this particular moment. But that was about to change as his Mum appeared from the consultancy room, ashen faced and dog-less. Holy shit, he thought to himself. Now he was worried. The bloody dog had copped it, hadn't he.

'Fergus is going to have to stay here a while until they work out what's wrong. They think they can see something lodged in his throat so have put him on a ventilator until they've managed to sort it,' she explained.

'Oh. Okay. Hope he's alright,' Martin lied. It wasn't that he didn't have any remorse, he was just completely bereft of emotion towards the animal. Some would say heartless, but Martin would probably describe himself as morally bankrupt, he literally didn't give a toss about anything, especially not the yappy little fucker who Mum seemed to love more than her own son.

'So… what do we do now then?' asked Martin.

His Mum sat down beside him on the row of chairs that filled the waiting area.

'I, I… don't know really. I guess we wait and see,' she said blankly. In a way, Martin felt a little bit sorry for her, given that her mood was verging on joyous not two hours ago. Should he admit that he was the one who offered Fergus the turkey that was now having a bearing on whether the dog would live or not? Christ. He couldn't, could he? His Mum would simply bollock him, regardless of how many sherries she'd had. No. It was best to leave it for now. Let sleeping dogs lie… or sleeping dogs die, he thought cynically. God, I really am sick, he thought to himself. Perhaps he should be comforting his

Mum right now, but instead the pair of them sat – Martin slumped, his Mum upright – staring straight ahead as a Christmas song by Greg Lake drifted across the room again for about the fifth time.

*

'Mrs McKeown?' called the vet from around the door of room number two. It had been at least forty-five minutes to an hour after his Mum had come out of the room she was being called from. Gary's family had probably arrived at the house by now and would be tucking into turkey rolls, crisps and the like. He'd actually rather be back there right now rather than having to sit here and wait for the news on Fergus. This thought actually surprised him. Maybe it was his new-found respect for Gary, because 'family time' and any sort of social interaction with people wasn't usually at the top of his list. Perhaps that said it all about the situation he was in right now. Sitting in a deserted vets surgery waiting for the news about a dog he had potentially murdered. It was absolute purgatory.

His Mum filed over to the consultancy room with a worried look on her face. The vet wasn't exactly giving anything away with his expression. He gave a half smile which could've suggested death and some comfort that was about to follow or that the prognosis was actually okay. Christ. Imagine if Fergus was in there dead right now? He'd be in deep shit if his Mum ever found out, she'd probably disown him immediately. But on the other hand, the guilt might be worse. Once again, he was getting inside his own head and weighing up what the lesser of two evils might be. At the moment, and until he knew Fergus' fate, he'd have to stay quiet. He'd had plenty of moments recently where he felt alone, isolated. And now, given the occasion and the circumstances, he felt more alone than ever. The novelty of all this had now worn off. There was a stark reality about his own life now sinking in very quickly. The only companions he had in this moment were the ghosts of Christmas hits that continued to whir round in the corner, accompanied by the low buzz of bright white lights overhead. It really was anything but festive.

Fifteen minutes later, or what felt like an absolute lifetime given the circumstances, Martin's Mum came out of the consultancy room and took her seat back next to Martin.

'He's okay, for now,' she said glumly.

Martin didn't respond, he was waiting for his Mum to elaborate. There was a pause while she let out a sigh. 'The vets have managed to remove something lodged in Fergus' throat,' she continued.

There was another pause where it felt like she wanted Martin to start filling in the blanks. Did she know? Was this a test of his character right now? Martin could feel himself getting hot. He decided to stay quiet for the foreseeable. If anything, he was getting angry at the slow and seemingly patronising speed his Mum was talking at.

'It looks like he may have swallowed a bit of turkey bone. Goodness knows how he got hold of it,' she said, finally. Martin still didn't know whether to offer anything to this exchange or not, for fear he might reveal some guilt. His silence may have also been construed as guilt, but he was hoping that because his Mum was so wracked with worry right now that she might not notice. He decided to break the quiet.

'So… what happens now? To him… to Fergus, I mean,'

'He's still under general anaesthetic for now, so it's likely he'll be in overnight,' she said.

'And what are we doing then?' replied Martin. He was genuinely interested, because he sure as hell didn't want to sit here all night. It was nearly 7.00pm as it was.

'Don't be so insensitive Martin,' his Mum said, 'My dog is in critical condition right now and you're not showing a jot of sympathy!'

Clearly the sherry had long worn off. He literally couldn't give a toss about the stupid dog and it was probably showing.

'I was only asking,' he said, quietly. This was another instance of his Mother shooting him down into sufferance. It was a theme he'd lived with his whole life, whether delivered aggressively or not. No wonder he struggled with relationships and with his feelings. He'd never been allowed to express himself it would seem. But that was another story. This whole experience today had got him in a bad mood. He hadn't been looking forward to the day as it was, and to be fair, it had shown signs that everything might be alright as Gary was showing him both kindness and sympathy. But this whole debacle with the dog, in the vets on a dreary trading estate during Christmas was just about pushing him to his limits. He could feel an anger rising, a fury towards his Mum. A pent-up rage that had built inside him for years and was now going to take centre stage. He hadn't taken her comment very well, he felt shunned. There was guilt in him too, of course. He knew he was indirectly at fault for them both being here and it was probably that which added to the stew of negative emotions he had swimming in his head.

'Do you know what Mum?' he said suddenly.

'What Martin,' she replied, irritably. She was clearly not in a good place either and Martin's lack of sympathy had wound her up.

'If Fergus hadn't been begging so much at my feet during dinner then we probably wouldn't be here right now,' he said. His Mum looked at him puzzled for a moment.

'What do you…' she began, but Martin cut her off immediately.

'What I mean is, I gave him a bit of turkey from the table because he was doing my head in and wouldn't leave me alone.' He was getting his words out, but there was a slight quivering in his voice which suggested he wasn't entirely confident in taking his Mum on in this way.

'And another thing,' he continued. 'That stupid dog has never liked me anyway. It would seem you like him more than me nowadays too. Would it not hurt to check in with your son once in a while rather than be a serial God botherer and neighbourhood watch wannabe?'

She looked at him incredulously. The resemblance to who she thought her son was right now couldn't have been further apart.

'And to be honest Mum, I couldn't give a fuck about that dog, because nobody gives a fuck about me. And don't pretend like you do, because you literally have no fucking clue. So that's it, I'm done, because I definitely won't be staying here all night like some kind of freak. Happy fucking Christmas Mum,' he concluded.

By this point he was stood up looking straight down on her. Thirty-five years of anger had just poured out of his mouth, with a helpless little dog at the root of it. He turned his back before his Mum could even really react.

'Martin! MARTIN!' she bellowed in disbelief. But he was already out of the door.

Chapter 29

It wasn't the smartest thing to have done by any means. Leaving your own Mother stranded in an out of hours veterinary practice on the afternoon of Christmas Day, but that was exactly what he had just done.

It was probably the first time he had ever shown any bravery in front of his Mum, a combination of years staying quiet and not speaking his mind that then blew up into a tirade of emotions. He felt relieved that he didn't have to carry the guilt of the reason why Fergus had ended up on canine life support, but there was probably ways he could've handled it better. But that's something that can't be controlled sometimes. Emotions have no visible boundaries. Whatever it was in his head had just simply stretched too far and wide for him to cope, a tensioned cord that had powerfully pulled itself to the last thread of reserved silence. It's fair to say that when it went snap, Martin then bungeed out the door with the momentum you'd expect from being catapulted by a giant rubber band snapping in two.

But there he was now, back in his flat sat still, with his heart rate steadied and a head full of regret. The rage had subsided and the remorse had taken hold. But perhaps his head wasn't completely full of regret? If it wasn't, it must've been pretty close. He was a tiny bit proud of himself for finally saying something to his Mum, but in hindsight he wished he could've delivered it with more decorum.

He didn't know what would become of his relationship with her. It would probably take a lot of patching up. He literally didn't know anyone who had ever spoken to their parents like that. It was like something you might see in a TV drama, not in real life. But sadly for him, this was real life. There were consequences. Right now, the consequence was a head full of shame and that guilty feeling that, a) he may well have indirectly killed a dog, and b) he had sabotaged a relationship with his Mother that he saw no way of immediately rectifying.

He would need to go back up to his Mum's house at some point and get the personal belongings and overnight bag he had left up there, but that wasn't really an immediate concern. Perhaps he could sneak in one day while they were away for New Years (providing they still were going away for New Years that was). He had a key from a while ago when he lodged with them after the Helena split, so it was no issue to let himself in.

Sat in the dark, he decided to do what he did most nights when he was alone at home with just his thoughts for company. He put the kettle on, made a decaf tea and went to bed. If there were to be any repercussions with his Mum then they could wait. He walked over to his bedside with tea in hand and placed the mug down on the cabinet. He sat on the side of the bed for a moment running his hands over his face and through his hair. He blew out a large sigh as if to say, 'for fuck's sake,' and then did actually curse himself. Because in that moment he realised he'd left his only phone charger plugged in at the bedside of the spare room at his Mum's house.

'You prick Martin,' he said aloud.

*

Waking up the next day, he had no idea what the time was. It was light, so it must've been beyond 7.00am at least. His phone had since died and he didn't own a watch. He started to think about how he might go about finding out the time. Wait for a church bell to ring out? Ask a neighbour? He imagined the scene in his head.

(Knock knock)

'Oh hello there, it's Martin here from 18A. Hope you had a nice Christmas day. I'm so sorry to disturb you, but you wouldn't happen to have the time would you?'

What a completely ridiculous thought. If he didn't feel insane enough already then the look from a bemused neighbour on Boxing Day, having just been asked what the time was, might well push him firmly into the camp of insanity. It would've surely been easier to ask for a spare phone charger, or at least borrow one for a couple of days.

Thankfully there was a clock on the oven in the kitchen, which he knew was never right, but he could calculate a rough time, despite it being over an hour too slow. He obviously wasn't thinking too clearly because switching on the TV would've done the trick, or even his laptop for that matter. Oh shit. His laptop. He'd taken that with him up to Gloucester as well. This would mean for a few days at least he'd genuinely be 'off grid.' He could easily go out and buy a charger of course, but lying there in peace with the rain gently tapping on the skylight in his room, there was something quite intriguing about the idea of being cut off from the world. He'd have to be disciplined about it, yes. But the reward could be the thing that he had seemingly craved for a while now. Pure anonymity.

The festive anonymity project had started reasonably well. He managed to get himself back to sleep until around 9.00am and casually got himself up to make a tea, feeling almost invincible. Nobody could touch him right now, absolutely nobody. He was completely alone and answerable to no one. He thought about his Mum and Gary scrambling around trying to get hold of him. He hoped and prayed they wouldn't turn up on his doorstep. But if he knew his Mum like he did, she'd be too het up fussing over Fergus, if he was still alive. Even so, if they turned up at his door then he didn't have to answer. He had an intercom that he could see who was at the main door, so he could easily ignore them. Lights off, curtains closed, car safely stowed away in the car port beneath the block. They'd never know if he was there or not. It wasn't going to come to that though, he was sure of it.

With a cup of tea in hand and a moth-eaten dressing gown draped over his bony shoulders, Martin went to go and get comfortable in the lounge. He switched on the TV and savoured the peace he was currently enjoying. He was genuinely content for the moment. Nobody could bother him, nobody could contact him and it almost felt like nobody knew him. It was wonderful.

However, an hour into his solace, an old foe was lurking. Lurking in the metaphorical sense of course, not physically. Martin's flirtation with gambling had not long passed. He'd become an overnight addict, desperate for a thrill and eager to change his fortunes. Losing the thousands of pounds on third-rate football matches and obscure sports around the world was still relatively fresh. It was only a matter of weeks ago in reality. He'd had work to keep him occupied in the short term, so that had become fuel for his brain to run on. But he hadn't foreseen this sudden turn. Being completely alone and cut off from everything else was now a risk, a real danger to what he could do next. The TV was punting out advert after advert about offers on football 'accas' as well as free bets, incentives and more.

He was being invited back in. It could be a way to avenge the losses and then finally call it quits. Draw a line under it all and get back to square one. Could he? Surely not. He only had a credit card with any meaningful funds attached to it. His current account had been run almost dry and the Christmas bonus had already gone on trying to get him back into the black.

The one saving grace was that he had no phone and no laptop to get any bets placed. He didn't even have any money, but he wasn't worried about that. In fact, that was the last thing that had occurred to him. After all, the Christmas period was completely awash with live sport – a plethora of football to choose from, horse racing and the now ever-present festive favourite, the darts. He could recall watching the latter with his Dad over the Christmas period, it was one of the small things he and his father were able to do together in the house. They'd stay up until late watching the drama unfold with his Mum up in bed and out of the way. She didn't care for sports, certainly not darts.

'Oh look at him, so uncouth. Can they not just get on a diet? This is not even sport, it's a pub game. A room full of drunkards watching little pins being thrown into a board? It's stupid. I'm going to bed. And don't stay up late you two. My sister is coming tomorrow,' she would say. Or something along those lines anyway.

All of a sudden he had some renewed vigour to get a phone charger. No, he told himself. That is one of the most stupid ideas you've ever had – and there had been plenty. He fiddled with the tassels on his dressing gown, anxiously. The idea of having a little flutter had quickly taken over his mind.

What if you could win back what you lost?

But what if you lost it all again…

Yeah, but imagine the feeling winning!

Okay, but imagine the losing feeling again…

The odds wouldn't be too bad, surely?

You never know what sort of outcomes might happen. It's too risky…

Well what is reward without the risk?

How would I even fund it…

You have a credit card with a decent limit?

I need that for rainy days…

Today is a rainy day? It could become one of the best days!

I can't…

But just think. You could win back EVERYTHING YOU LOST.

The cycle started over in his head. The last words of the exchange carried heavy, 'you lost.' Yes, it was true. He'd lost big time. This sort of debate he had with himself was tiring and he was caught in the middle again. Emotions were still high after last night and despite the earlier feelings of contentment, now it was jeopardy, anxiety and hatred for himself. The adrenaline of yesterdays bravery had worn off. It was those big three emotions that continued to control him. He had to take his mind off this threat of losing everything again. Well, everything had already been lost in his eyes, so perhaps it wasn't like there was anything else to lose at this point.

He exited the room leaving the TV on in full flow. Sky Sports News was doing its cycle of inane sports news and dreadful, empty punditry from so-called experts. He decided to have a shower. It was disappointing, because the day had started with such promise too. Now it had taken a turn because he'd let his head twist what was a perfectly steady morning into a chaotic and desperate situation. There was a plan afoot in his head. He was going to do something about it this afternoon.

Chapter 30

The rain battered against the windscreen of his car as Martin made his way back up the M5 towards Gloucester. There was a 50mph cautionary limit in place as the light from the day started to fade. Thankfully, it wasn't a busy motorway and he wasn't in any rush so he stuck to the inside lane and ploughed on through the dreary Boxing Day weather. He was headed back up to his Mum's house. He felt desperate to get his charger back, as well as his laptop. Visions of anonymity had been quashed now, he was on a mission to get his stuff and get back home again. There was only a vague plan in his head and a wishful one at that. He was hoping to stake out near his Mum's house and either wait for them to go out (wishful, in this weather on Boxing Day in the late afternoon) or stay in the car until it was night and get into the house while she and Gary were asleep. If he knew his Mum, she would be in bed for 9.30pm sharp. At the very worst, Gary would be in the back room on flight simulator where Martin knew he liked to use the headphones to give a much more realistic experience. There was still a lot left to chance in this scenario, but he felt confident that this would be the case.

He arrived outside at around 5.30pm. The lights were on in the living room and Gary's Ford Mondeo was on the driveway. This of course meant they were in the house. He decided that he would come back later and assess the situation, so he went to the nearest retail park to find a McDonalds, or whatever other fast food outlet was open during this time.

Fifteen minutes later, he had pulled up at the drive-thru at McDonalds. A bored and muffled female voice came through the speaker.

'Hello, McDonalds can I take your order,' it said.

'Hi. Yeah, ummm…' he started to reply indecisively, 'I will have the… Chicken Legend meal with a… diet coke. Please.' He finished.

'Is that a large meal?' the voice replied.

'Umm… I'm not sure, is it a large meal?' Martin said. This wasn't really something he did very often so the question was entirely innocent. There was an audible laugh through the intercom.

'No… I mean… do you want a large meal? It's either medium or large,' said the voice. 'Oh… I see. Umm… yes. I will have the large one,' he said, embarrassed.

For fuck sake Martin, why are you so useless in social situations, he thought to himself.

'Thank you Sir. Please make your way round to the payment window.'

Martin wound his window up and slowly moved his car forward until it reached the little window, where a teenage girl greeted him with a card machine. She was smirking at him, probably because of the comment. It was second nature for her to know the difference between medium and large, but Martin wasn't to know. The innocence had clearly tickled her. She was perfectly pleasant though.

'That will be £7.49 when you're ready please Sir,' she said. Martin tapped the card machine and thanked her.

'Thanks,' he said sheepishly. He was still thinking about the fau pais he dropped earlier. He tucked his wallet back inside the breast pocket of his jacket and waited. The girl was now taking another order on her headset for another customer who was next in line. She gave Martin a confused sideways glance which suggested something like, 'what are you still doing there?' It turned out that's exactly what she was thinking. She muted her microphone for a moment and leant towards Martin's car.

'Sir, you can proceed to window number two now to collect your food,' she said, pointing towards the next window which was clearly marked 'collect here.'

He'd done it again. His lack of awareness in these situations had left him red faced. He felt ridiculously awkward and self-conscious.

'Oh, I see. I thought... never mind,' he said, defeated.

She smiled a sympathetic smile down at him as he prepared to move forward. The girl was pretty, there was no doubt about that, but also seemed quite kindly. Maybe that was why he had got all awkward around her. Martin nodded back and tried to move forward. He'd taken the car out of gear and revved loudly before stalling the engine as he fumbled around with the gearstick. It was almost comical. The girl gave a quiet giggle as Martin looked up at her and mouthed the words, 'sorry.' It was probably the least smooth thing he could ever have done and he was left to rue yet another embarrassment as he sidled up towards the serving hatch to collect his meal.

'Thanks,' he said to the boy at the serving hatch and he reached over to get his meal. This time he carefully put his car into gear and drove out of the drive-thru lane and over to a parking space to wallow in the sadness of what his life was right now.

The reality was that he was probably stuck there for a little while. At least another hour, perhaps, maybe two before he could be sure he could sneak into his Mum's house unnoticed. The rain was continuing to fall on his windscreen, it was damp, cold and dreary. It almost mirrored what his mental wellbeing was right now, with no shine of a brighter day in sight. Eventually he felt it was probably time to get going and continue his stake-out outside the house. He turned on the ignition and navigated his way out of the now deserted car park. The crop of teens who had gathered earlier in what was probably their parents little run-around cars had left, leaving a mass of rubbish in their wake. Martin thought that at least they had each other. They weren't spending Boxing Day alone like he was. He pulled out onto the road and proceeded back towards his Mum's house. Clearly he wasn't concentrating because he had taken a right turn, rather than left.

'Fuck sake,' he said, in frustration. There was nobody around, so he pulled over to the side of the road and got his car in a position to do a U-turn. He had nearly completed the turn when from around the corner a motorcyclist appeared through the drizzle. He witnessed as the rider broke hard and swerved into the raised kerb of the bus stop and proceeded to collide with it until skidding across the road where he was unseated and left a trail of debris in his wake.

'Oh fuck! Fuck fuck fuck,' said Martin in a panic.

He pulled over at the side of the road and put his hazard lights on. He rushed out of the car and over to the motorcyclist who was getting to his feet.

'Shit, I'm sorry, I didn't… are you okay?' he asked.

'Fuck sake, look at my bike. Must be at least two grands worth of damage,' the man replied.

'Are you, are you alright?' Martin said again.

'Yeah. I'm fine. Bike is fucked though. Look at it,'

They both looked over to the bike which was lying at the side of the road looking severely scratched, but not as the rider put it, 'fucked.'

Martin was in shock. He didn't even consider that he wasn't actually at fault, he hadn't hit the motorcyclist or anything and the manoeuvre he was performing was well within the rights of that road.

'Where's a copper when you need one,' said the rider.

'A copp… why would we need the police?' Martin replied.

'Well… it's a road traffic accident mate. You made me crash,'

'I… didn't… I don't think it was me,' Martin stammered.

'Well you've accepted responsibility. The first thing you said was sorry. You need to give me your details sunshine. This is an insurance job now,' the rider told him. The guy was almost trembling. Whether he was in shock or maybe he didn't really believe in what he was saying.

'I, uh… don't understand how this all works. Like, you didn't hit me, it's not an accident?' Martin surmised.

'Well, you can say what you want mate. My bike is fucked and you're to blame,' he said, handing over a piece of paper with his details on which he duly wanted in exchange for Martins.

'What's your number mate,' the rider asked.

Shit. He didn't actually know his number off by heart.

'Umm… I don't know,' Martin said.

'You… what? You don't know?'

'No. I actually don't know and I haven't got my phone on me,' he admitted.

His phone was switched off at home with no battery. If he had to explain the story of why he didn't have his phone then this whole episode could get a whole lot stranger. It would seem like he was lying. Like he was backtracking all of a sudden. It definitely wouldn't do Martin any favours in front of someone who was clearly determined to get their own way.

'You don't have a phone on you?' the rider tutted. 'Okay, well I'll take photos of your car and your license then,' he said, almost confronting. He was taking control of the situation, it was almost like this bit was pre-meditated. The rider seemed to know exactly what he was doing. Martin was left slightly dumbfounded; he had certainly been taken advantage of here.

He was obviously too shocked and naïve about how to deal with this situation so he duly obliged in letting the rider have his details.

The fact he didn't have his phone on him either probably hadn't helped his situation. He had nothing to go on apart from a scrawled name and address on a piece of paper. It could easily be fake. The rider took pictures of Martin's car registration and license which Martin almost willingly provided without question.

'You can go. I'll get myself checked out,' the rider said, not looking up from his phone.

'Are you sure you don't… need a lift… or want me to wait with you?' Martin asked sympathetically. 'Nope. I'll stay here. Bike is fucked but I'll wait for a mate,' he said, taking a cigarette from his pocket.

'Okay… well, uh… good luck,' Martin said.

The rider nodded, while taking a drag on his cigarette. He seemed much calmer now he had what he needed. It felt like a stitch-up.

Martin walked back to his car and set back off into the night, full of regret. What the fuck just happened here?

Chapter 31

After what had just happened, Martin decided that 'breaking' into his Mum's house was probably not the best idea. He felt far too panicky and anxious, the last thing he needed was more stress. The idea of betting and pissing a load more money up the wall had long disappeared. He was now focused on the potential that he may have to shell out some compensation from his insurance and worse still, end up needing to dig into his own pockets to fund the 'damage.' It was an added stress he didn't need to what was already a scrambled mind he was carrying upon his shoulders. He replayed the incident over and over in his head continually as he drove southbound on the M5.

He concluded that he hadn't actually done anything wrong. He hadn't hit the motorcyclist, he hadn't collided with him and there wasn't any visible injury to him either. Nothing like broken bones or anything like that. Another thing that had occurred to him was that there weren't any witnesses around either so it was literally his word against the riders. Was that a good position to be in? He didn't know. Perhaps he should speak to his insurance company. But to-day? Tonight? Surely they wouldn't be around now It was gone eight on Boxing Day after all. He'd have to wait until the morning in that case. Which meant another fitful night in bed wondering whether he was about to be put through more misery. What hadn't occurred to him at this point was how on earth he was going to call them. He still didn't have a working phone.

By the time he reached Michaelwood services just outside Bristol, he was fuming with himself. You don't have a usable fucking phone with you Martin, so how the fuck were you thinking you'd get in touch with anyone? He decided to exit the motorway and pulled into the services to collect himself. What an absolute shitshow this was. The last 24 hours had been a complete mess. He had to think clearly now about what to do next. Could he turn back and stick to the original plan? Would it really matter if calling the insurance company was delayed a day or two? Or should he act quickly to put his mind at rest? The sooner he knew, the better, he thought. He put his forehead on the steering wheel and shut his eyes. He'd catastrophised this as an absolute disaster. Could it get any worse? Right now, he needed the support of someone, anyone. His parents seemed like the obvious choice, but the relationships were strained. Perhaps George could give him some good advice? Christ, George. He hadn't seen him for ages. No, he didn't want to spoil the festive period for George. He knew how much he and his family liked to celebrate and enjoy each other's company. The last thing he needed was for Martin to rock up and fill him up with doom and gloom.

There was a tap on his window.

'What the fu…' said Martin, startled by the stranger who had loomed up against his window. Martin wound the window down.

'Yes?' he said, shortly.

'Just thought you'd like to know… yer rear brake light is out. I saw you pull in and thought you oughta know,' said the man. He was a sturdy individual and spoke with a pretty thick Welsh valleys accent that missed the annunciation of any 'T' sound form the end of his words. Martin just looked back at him, unamused. It was probably the last thing he needed to hear.

'Right, okay. Thanks,' Martin replied irritably, winding the window back up. He wasn't in the mood for chit chat with a stranger. The man looked slightly crestfallen, he'd offered some help if anything, but thankfully it seemed like he hadn't taken too much offence. Martin put his head back against the head rest. There was another tap on the window. Martin wound it down again. This time he didn't even say anything, he just looked at the man with an expression that suggested, 'what the fuck do you want now?'

'I was only sayin, like. I'm a mobile mechanic see. Jus' been up Dursley for a job, thought you migh be needin a han like,' he said. 'Bu no bother, like. 'Appy Christmas.'

Martin ran his hands over his face. This guy was certainly persistent.

'Yes, sorry. No, really I am sorry,' he called after him. 'I didn't mean to be rude. It's been a bit of a shit day.'

'Too righ, mate. It's bloody Boxing Day like, 'n av been driving for 15 hours straigh,' the mechanic replied. He was obviously quite chatty and seemed kindly. Martin thought that he was probably lonely too.

'Tell you wha. I migh have a spare bulb in the van, see,' he continued, 'Lemme hav a look, like.'

He disappeared into the darkness for a moment. The rain had subsided slightly, only spitting now but the spray from cars flashing past in the wet from the main carriageway was still providing the soundtrack to this dismal evening. Martin wasn't sure whether to follow him or not. Two minutes later he reappeared at Martin's door with a bulb.

'I reckon I migh hav it yur. Wan me to hav a look like?'

Martin was confused as to why he was being so helpful. He had become quite cynical recently, no more than today after the incident with the motorcyclist. Martin was wary though, especially with what had just happened a couple of hours ago.

'Pop open the boot mate, 'n al av a look, like,' he said, enthusiastically.

Martin exited the car and walked towards his boot. He unlocked the boot and the mechanic set to work.

'Oh, am Gareth by the way,' he said, extending one of his huge hands towards Martin.

'Martin,' he replied, taking the outstretched hand.

'Righ. Les av a look see,' said Gareth, starting to take apart the off-side rear brake light. He had almost invited himself to help out and Martin had hardly had any time to protest, but this was all very kind.

'Look at im. Absolutely shot like,' he said, holding up the light-bulb.

Martin couldn't really see what he was looking at but nodded his head in agreement.

'Lemme jus pop this one in yur. Won be a minute like,'

'Thanks, that's very…' Martin began, before he was cut off.

'Righ bugger these things mind. Always the way. Where you off to anyway butt?' said Gareth, with his head still buried in the boot of Martin's car. He was making light conversation.

Well, that was the question. Where on earth was he heading right now?

'I uh, I'm on my way home. Had a bit of an issue this evening,' replied Martin.

'Oh ahh, say no more butt. Say no more. Plenty of domestics this time of year like. Did you know Christmas is the worst time of year for family conflict. Mental tha.'

Christ. He didn't know the half of it. He'd potentially (and inadvertently) murdered a family dog and more or less told his Mum to 'fuck off.' Where to start?

Gareth diligently completed the light replacement and surfaced from the depths of Martin's boot.

'Tricky little buggers these, but thas all done for you now mate,' he said, closing up the boot.

'That's really kind of you, thanks. What do I owe you?' asked Martin.

'Ahh don't worry bou' tha,' he said, putting the dead bulb into his tool pouch. 'You still look a bit shook though butt? Yer white as a sheet like! Shall we get a coffee inside? I'm gaspin like,' Gareth offered, but really it was Martin who should probably do the honours.

Martin figured it would do no harm. He certainly owed Gareth something for his kindness. It wasn't something he would've normally done, or ever for that matter. Sitting down with a stranger he'd just met at a motorway services for coffee. Gareth was probably right. He was still reeling from what had happened this evening and had no doubts that he looked pale and in need of a hot drink.

'Yeah, sure. But let me get you one, you've helped me out tonight. I'd like to say thanks,' replied Martin.

'Well if you insist!' cackled Gareth as they made their way over to the entrance.

They opened the doors let the warm air from the inside hit them, it certainly emphasised how miserable it was outside. Though warm and reasonably welcoming, the place was pretty deserted, save for a few families doing the rounds in WH Smiths and a group of older men in scarves and football shirts who were probably travelling back from a Boxing Day match. They were silently tucking into fast food as the pair passed them.

'What can I get you?' asked Martin.

'Oh a black coffee is fine with me butt. Cheers,' answered Gareth. 'I'll be sittin over yur,' he said, pointing towards a table. Martin raised his thumb in agreement and approached the counter.

'Hello. A black coffee and a uh…,' he paused for a moment while studying the extensive line-up of hot drinks.

'A cinnamon latte please,' he said finally. Fuck it. Why not get into the festive spirit a bit he thought. 'Oh, and uh… a couple of those gingerbread men,'

'Yep, sure. And can I take a name for the order?' replied the barista. 'Martin,'

'No problem sir, that will be £11.70 when you're ready,' Martin tapped his card and made his way over to the end of the counter to wait for the drinks. He turned round to see what Gareth was up to. He was looking at his phone. He grinned at Martin and raised his thumb. He was certainly a jolly bloke. It was probably what Martin needed right now. Even though he had no idea who this guy was, where he'd come from or why he was so keen to help out. Martin hoped he wasn't a serial killer or anything. Although, it wouldn't be the worst thing in the world, he thought darkly.

'Marty?' the barista called over. 'Here you go,'

Marty. There was one person who coined the nickname 'Marty' for him and the tone and style this pet name was just called out in sounded much like the original. He felt a sudden pang of sadness. He really was lonely.

'Thanks,' said Martin. Why do they always get the fucking names wrong, he thought to himself. He carried the tray over to where Gareth was seated and placed down the drinks.

'Ahhh cheers butt, thas proper tha,' he said, gleefully.

'I thought I'd treat us to a bit of festive cheer,' said Martin, handing over the Christmas themed gingerbread man. There was of course a tinge of irony to how he said it. It was probably anything but cheerful, but at least he could be grateful for some company, albeit in the most unlikely of circumstances.

'Oh, yer too kind butt. Cheers,'

He unwrapped the biscuit and took a bite.

'Corrr, thas good tha,' he said, holding it up with a mouth full of gingerbread.

'You're welcome,' Martin nodded back.

'So whas the story then butt? You looked pretty shaken up when I seen you,' asked Gareth.

Martin thought he may as well just spill. What was there to lose? It wasn't like Gareth had any other details on him. If things got too weird, he could leave. He'd back himself to out run him to the car if he did turn out to be a serial killer. Besides, this was a relatively safe space. There were people around and staff members at the services. Everything on CCTV too. Christ, give the guy a chance, he thought to himself. It was always like this in his head though. A topsy turvy ride between all scenarios and focusing on the negative ones in particular. He began to recollect his story from earlier in the evening.

'Well. As I said, it's been a bit of a shit one tonight,' Martin started. He wouldn't be going into too much detail but Gareth could have the gist of it for sure.

'I was actually getting a McDonalds in Gloucester and going back to my Mum's there because I left my phone charger at hers on Christmas Day. But then things started to go a bit wrong when this motorcyclist came round the corner as I was pulling out of the retail park and he crashed his bike into the kerb. He then tried to blame me that it was my fault.'

Martin paused. Gareth encouraged him to continue, he could obviously tell that there was more to it.

'I didn't hit him or anything, but the guy was fuming with me that 'I' had wrecked his bike because of the manoeuvre I was doing. He then took all my details and everything. I think I've dropped my foot in it though, because the first thing I said was that I was sorry.'

Gareth took a sip of coffee with a confused frown.

'Hang up. So this fella on a bike comes roun the corner, bangs himself into the kerb and then blames you because he's crashed?' asked Gareth.

'Yeah, pretty much,' said Martin, matter of factly.

'I hate them motorcyclists. I really does. Nothin but trouble see,' he said, darkly. 'So what now then? You gotta pay him off or summet?'

'Well I dunno. Like I said, he took my details and said his insurance company would be in touch. But I don't see how he can do anything. I didn't even hit the prick!' said Martin, with a little bit more angst in his voice now.

'Souns like a fit up to me butt,' he said, gravely. 'But thas the way the world works see, feels like everyone's against you sometimes don it.'

Martin could tell that Gareth was about to open up about something and he was happy to let him. He'd revealed as much as he felt comfortable with for now and had not gone into much detail. It was clear Gareth was lonely and appreciated the company, so any chance to talk would be taken and it duly was moments later when Gareth cleared his throat.

'See, I've ad my fair share'a bad luck like,' he started.

Okay, this was it. Martin wasn't sure what was coming next, but looked at him while nibbling at his gingerbread biscuit.

'Bein alone at Christmas 'as become pretty common like. Certainly since my wife wen tha is. Broke my heart in two she did. Proper set me back tha.'

Martin didn't really know what to say. This could well get quite deep, very quickly. He wasn't expecting him to go straight in. Martin felt out of his depth all of a sudden.

'So I come home from the pub on Christmas Eve see, an she's with another fella in bed like. I couldn do much, was completely frozen like. I walked out of there and drowned my sorrows for the next 3 years. I been on the brink mate. I really have. But I tell you wha, every Christmas I think to myself… the only gift I wan,' he paused for a moment to have a sip of coffee. He looked rueful. Martin was waiting for the conclusion of this anecdote.

'The only gift I wan,' he continued, 'Is the gift I already hav. Because that gift is the gift of life. And no matter how bad things migh be, life is truly precious. So don you forget it butt,' he ended, taking a big swig of coffee.

Martin didn't really want to ask the intricate details. He felt a little bit embarrassed if anything. Listening to Gareth put his own thoughts and feelings into sharp focus. He'd not exactly suffered any trauma to that sort of level. Okay, so he lived through his parents getting divorced and the rows that followed. He'd had Helena walk out on him, but not because of someone else, more so his own fault probably. He'd lost money through betting (again, his fault). But there must've been something in what Gareth was saying that resonated? He didn't know him well enough to ask for any details.

'I'm sorry to hear about all that,' said Martin, 'So what makes life a gift for you? Like, what keeps you going after such a bad time?' It sounded a little bit cynical, and perhaps it was from Martin, but he felt like he needed the justification.

'Well you know wha, it's the people. People I don even know, or maybe people I migh never see again. People who will jus do the unexpected,' he said, then took the last bite of his gingerbread man. 'Much like wha I did for you tonight,' he finished.

'Yeah, but people are pricks. That point was proven earlier tonight. Present company not included of course,' Martin made sure to emphasise the last point.

'Yeah, people are pricks. We're all pricks. Bu lemme tell you a story before I gotta get goin. Need to be in Risca tomorrow mornin like, an it's nearly my bedtime!' he said with a laugh.

'Okay, go on then…' Martin prompted. He was intrigued.

'So don hold nothin against me now butt, I swear to you it was a different time an I was a different person like,' Gareth began.

Martin was ready to hear.

'After my wife left me for another fella, I hit the bottle. I hit it big time ya know. I always been a mechanic, bu not a mobile one like now. That would be carnage with the drinkin at the time! I worked in a garage up Merthyr see. Lovely little place, but somewhere where everyone knows everyone's business. An of course, everyone knew bou this fella an me wife like, so it was like walking down the streets everyday an everyone would be looking thinking, oh the poor guy his missus wen off with tha other fella like. I only ad one form of defence, an tha was booze. If I ad been drinkin I couldn care less if people were lookin at me like some circus act. It was like throwin a blanket over myself to hide from others. I was done with the sympathy vote see, I wanted to move on. So one day, I hav a choice see. Pissed out my 'ead I was and workin late. I would sneak a bit of voddy or a whiskey in everyday like. Course back in those days, a few fags would mask any smell, 'specially the forty I used to smoke a day. I saw myself in a wing mirror as I was workin. I looked like shit. Booze don even touch the sides no more but I'm angry. I'm really fuckin angry. It's in my system an I can feel it. I wanna go an find this fella and tell him how he's ruined my life. I wanna beat the living daylights out of him. Why should he deserve to get away scott free with my missus an ere I am necking cheap voddy from Asdas and getting depressed. It was a vicious cycle that never let up.'

Martin was listening intently, he let Gareth continue and nodded whenever there was a pause to encourage him on.

'So I get a wrench from the back of the garage an lock up the unit. Am fucking wired like. Big ol fucking wrench, like a cast iron cricket bat. Am not even present at this moment, no way. I get to the house they're livin in an knock on the door. She lets me in, like. I say where is he. She says who? I say you fucking well know who, where is he? He's hidin in a cupboard see. So I find him and smack him. I hit im ard, harder than ever before. Not with the wrench, I'd av fucking killed him with tha. So I leave him with a couple of teeth missin like. Bu now I'm cryin. I'm cryin because I don like this. I don wanna be this man no more. I walk outta there an somehow drive up to Cefn Coed. Thas a viaduct in the town. A big fuck off bridge thing. I get out my car with one thought on my mind. The booze aint a factor no more. I'm thinkin clear like. I felt so guilty for wha I jus did and so low, I needed to go. So I walk along the path until I find somewhere, a good spot. I stand there wonderin wha next. This is it like, the end. No more me. Bu you know wha I was sayin bou people? People you don know, or migh never see again. Well tha night someone saved me. Wha they did was offer the gift of life. They talked me down, gave me perspective. They told me that no matter how dark things may seem, believe tha even in yur lowest moments you still have control. Tha was the perspective I needed, right there. I was rushed to hospital and kept on suicide watch for the next week. Bu after rehab an all tha, I can tell you now, people are the reason I'm yur. An don forget it fella. So from tha day on, I said to myself, always help those in need, no matter wha their need,' he finished.

It was really quite profound.

Christ, that really did put things in perspective. 'Even in your lowest moments, you still have control,' that seemed to resonate. Martin was talking to someone who had been on the brink, and then survived. Perhaps this was meant to happen tonight? After all the shit that he'd dealt with in the last twenty-four hours, Gareth's intervention had been timely. Perhaps there was a way to fight your demons, a way to take control from the lowest of ebbs. A way to get perspective and move on from the internal struggles.

'Thank you for sharing,' said Martin. This moment had started to have an impact on him.

'Thas okay butt. Now look after yourself. Here's my card if you ever run into trouble. Keep an eye on those brake lights!' he chortled, as he got up to leave.

'Thanks mate, much appreciated,' replied Martin.

'Ta da, butt. Merry Christmas and thanks for the biscuit like,' he said, then disappeared out the door.

Martin sat there at the table for a little while longer to finish his coffee. It felt like Gareth had just poured out his heart and soul, then happily trotted off into the night. It almost felt quite surreal. How could someone steer themselves through the emotions of what he explained and be at peace with it? Martin felt confused. Because to him, being on the brink would be exactly what it says it is. On the brink of escape from the world and never looking back. There was no sane recovery available to him. He didn't know whether to feel inspired or cynical about Gareth's story and it didn't sit right with him in this moment.

Martin downed the rest of his coffee and made for the exit.

He had work to do.

Chapter 32

Back in the car, he felt like things were a lot more lucid all of a sudden, like he had a clear head. Gareth's recall of his experiences he'd had put things into focus for him. It had given perspective about where he was at right now (which admittedly wasn't a good place) but at least it wasn't terminal, yet. He still had control. It just felt like he was doing dumb things, getting a spate of bad luck even. He couldn't help it, these things just kind of kept happening. But maybe it had always been that way? And what was it that you had to do to create some good luck? He felt that since his teenage years, he'd been riddled with bad luck, and apart from his work and academic achievements there was probably more bad than good. It was high time to make some good luck for himself then, he thought. He exited the services and re-joined the carriageway to go Southbound. But only for a short while. He was planning to go back North towards Gloucester and carry out what had been his original plan for the evening. Getting his phone charger and laptop back was a key part of the work he had to do. The plan would start in earnest tomorrow morning with a call to his insurance company and there wasn't a moment to lose.

He drove to the next exit just a mile or so down the carriageway and immediately re-joined the motorway to head Northbound. It was like the last 5 hours hadn't happened, he was locked in on the original plan again, albeit after a slight hiccup in proceedings. The only difference was that it was darker and later now. The carriageway was almost deserted and the rain was still falling silently onto his windscreen meaning visibility wasn't great. However, he ploughed onwards until he found himself back at the Gloucester junction. He felt like his senses were somewhat livened after what had happened earlier, it had galvanised him into being more aware of himself and anyone on the roads. He was determined not to be blindsided again. Perhaps a lot of this was a fabrication in his mind, a false worry about the fact that there might be some more bad luck on the way. Still, it wasn't the worst thing in the world to be constantly prepared. He would have to have his wits about him shortly as he planned to make it into his Mum's house and rescue his tech belongings.

Ten minutes after exiting the motorway he was back in the cul-de-sac where his Mum lived, ready to get his possessions. He sat stock still in the car for a moment with his eyes locked on the house. There was no sign of life or movement, not even a light in the upstairs room where Gary would usually be housed, tinkering with his computers or playing flight simulator. He also wondered whether Fergus had been discharged from the vets yet. Or worse still, perhaps he was dead? He hadn't really thought through this next part.

What if the yappy little fucker was in the kitchen? That was the only key to the house he had, the key to the back door which led directly into Fergus' line of sight. Oh well, he'd just have to deal with it. Or him, rather. He locked up the car and walked towards the house. All was quiet in the street, save for the usual neighbourhood noises you'd expect. A cat flap clicking open, a dog barking, someone putting their recycling outside the back door. Most people were probably settled down with their families on this Boxing Day night, so it wasn't as if there was anyone watching Martin. In fact, there was no need to act stealthily or suspicious. Most of the neighbours knew his face, he'd lived in this street for a short while in between breaking up with Helena and finding his own place. He probably did look a bit suspicious though; after all, it was the second visit he'd made to the street this evening. But still, that was totally reasonable. He had to block out these thoughts and focus on being natural and calculated.

So, undeterred by the thought of getting caught (while doing something completely innocent) he drew the keys from his pocket and slowly turned it in the lock of the back door.

This was the critical moment. If Fergus was there, he'd probably go batshit crazy which would raise the alarm. He had to hope that he didn't or wouldn't, or better still that his Mum was moddy coddling the poor hound up in her bedroom. It had been known even with him not having any ailments.

He carefully pulled down the handle and entered the kitchen. It was of course spotless, he could tell that even in the darkness. No sign of Fergus in his bed so perhaps he was probably with his Mum either in the bedroom or living room. Or dead. That was still also a possibility. Martin felt guilt all of a sudden. Oh well, there wasn't anything he could do about it now. If he was gone, he was gone. There were no lights visible from downstairs as he peered along the hallway, so he assumed that they'd gone to bed – good. This meant he could sneak around downstairs and get the things he needed without having to go upstairs. He remembered leaving his charger on the sideboard and laptop charging behind the sofa. He just had to hope his Mum hadn't done anything with them. Going upstairs was a huge risk and he'd prefer to not have to. He noticed some medication on the kitchen worktop. Some word he could barely read and the words 'to be taken twice daily.' This must be something for Fergus, meaning he was still alive then. Unless he had snuffed it since of course? Anyway, the good news was that the dog wasn't in the kitchen and Martin had managed to enter safely without him yelping and blowing his cover. He was probably upstairs on his Mum's bed getting the royal sympathy.

Martin edged carefully out of the kitchen and into the hallway, conscious of the staircase next to him and the noise that could travel upstairs. There were no lights visible from down here so it was safe to assume they were all asleep. Martin walked through to the lounge and was able to spot his phone charger over on the side. Good – at least it hadn't moved. As expected, his laptop was also stowed away behind the sofa out of view with its charger. Martin felt relief. Thank fuck for that, this had been pretty straightforward and there was a good chance he could get out of there without any issues. Or so he thought.

With his laptop in his arms and chargers stowed on top, he began to make his way towards the lounge door. But a split second before he was about to exit, he heard a rustling of keys at the back door and muffled voices.

'Yes, yes I've got them,' said a voice. It was Gary. He was with someone too.

Martin was paralysed. He stood silently and waited for the next noise of the door opening that would inevitably follow. All the feeling in his body had disappeared entirely. It was like he had been preserved in stone for an eternity but still had use of his mind. Not even his eyes were blinking in the moments that followed.

'Oh… it was unlocked?' said Gary, confused. Did you not lock it Jayne?' as both Gary, his Mum and Fergus entered through the back door. He could hear the click clack of claws and soft padding of Fergus' paws on the kitchen floor.

'Yes, I did lock it!' his Mum said pointedly.

'Well, it was definitely unlocked just now,' Gary replied calmly, flicking on the light switch.

'It was locked Gary. Definitely locked when we left,' she said back. She was always very certain of herself, his Mum. Historically this would have turned into a full blown argument with his Dad, but Gary possessed far too much prudence to be entering into any arguments. He just shrugged and continued to take his coat off, putting it on the back of one of the chairs. 'Okay, well it will certainly be locked now,' he said, walking over to the door and locking it from the inside.

'Fergie, Fergie, go on boy in your bed,' his Mum said. The dog duly responded and curled up in his bed.

Martin continued to listen carefully. He had to hope and pray they wouldn't come into the lounge, but he also had to move from being in their line of sight if they walked along the hallway and up the stairs. He calmly regained control of himself and tip toed slowly over to the corner of the lounge, out of view.

He had not expected this. In fact, it wasn't something he had anticipated at all. A note to self would be to ensure any future planning to be stealthy would have to be thought through with far more detail and not done on impulse.

'Right, night night Fergie. Good boy,' his Mum called to the dog switching the kitchen light off and plunging the house back into darkness. Good. This meant they were probably heading to bed. Where had they been? A late walk with Fergus? That was usually only something Gary would've done. Either way, it didn't matter. The situation he was in was real. He cowered in the corner ensuring he wouldn't be seen as his Mum and Gary traipsed through the hallway and towards the stairs.

Martin's heart was thundering through his chest. He pictured the scene of being caught. It made him feel sick. The memory of last night and exploding at his Mum was still fresh in the mind for him, so surely it was for her too. As he well knew, his Mum was notorious for holding a grudge. Surely it would be no different for her own son. He didn't want to be having that conversation with his Mum right now. He didn't want to be read the riot act. Though he wouldn't admit it, he was far too fragile for that right now.

Just then someone pulled the lounge door shut. Martin's heart almost stopped. Thankfully, nobody entered. All he could hear from the hallway was his Mum's voice.

'We need to keep that door shut Gary. Otherwise it gets awfully drafty in there,' she said, as they mounted the stairs. Now it was a waiting game. He had to stay in the lounge a long enough period of time so that they went to sleep and then he could start to make his way out of the house. There was also the challenge of not alerting Fergus in the kitchen too. This had become a whole lot harder all of a sudden. He knew from experience that exiting the front door wouldn't be an option, not with the chains and creaks that thing made. He slowly slumped down in the corner of the room with his head in his hands. This was turning into one painful ordeal right now and it was only going to get worse from here on in too. He just didn't know how bad yet.

*

It was indeed, purgatory. He was slumped silently in the corner of his Mum's lounge and listening to the noises that were emanating from the room above. Fucking hell. He knew Gary was around ten years older than his Mum, so didn't really know if he still had it in him. Well, clearly he did because right now Gary was pumping his Mother right above his head. It was literally the worst situation he could ever imagine. He'd never heard his parents do it before (he simply suspected that his Mum wasn't interested), but here she was in her twilight years with her new boyfriend ten years her senior getting a good old Boxing Day rogering. He couldn't tell if she was enjoying it or not. To the untrained ear, it seemed like she was running a very long race, very slowly, but exerting a lot of energy along the way. He cringed hard. So hard that he nearly cried tears of pure anguish. Not only did he have to endure this for another twenty minutes or so, but he probably had to sit there long enough to ensure they'd then fallen asleep. With the time he had available to him, he started to surmise a plan of how to get out of the house without disturbing the dog too much.

The easiest thing to do would be to take his chances and get out of there as quick as possible, no matter how much noise was made. Even if he blundered his way through the kitchen, set Fergus off and scrambled to the back door he could still be out of the house before his Mum or Gary would be able to react. It was probably the best way of dealing with it.

The other option would be to enter the kitchen and try to appease Fergus with some affection. This didn't seem like a very likely option given their previous relationship, although technically, he had treated Fergus on Christmas Day by handing him the turkey from the table. Okay, so it nearly killed him, but all animals were fickle. Perhaps Fergus would recall Martin as the 'meat treat giver' not the accidental attempted dog murderer.

The noises from above his head were becoming faster with the groans and heavy breathing louder. The mattress was withstanding a fair amount of bounce right now with the creaking of the bed reverberating through the floorboards. All of a sudden there seemed to be a climax to the noise. Gary's forceful groan seemed to have brought an end to proceedings. Thank fuck for that. It was barely believable a 67-year old man was capable of such longevity and dynamism, but Martin certainly bore witness to it in the worst possible way. He waited a further ten minutes for everything to go quiet upstairs and began to put his next movements into practice. It was now nearly 11 'o clock. He'd been stuck there well over an hour overall, but now it was time to get going and try his best not to raise the alarm. The plan in his head would be a mix of the two. Act as quickly and as swiftly as possible and offer Fergus some attention if he needed to calm him. He had concluded that it wouldn't be unlikely for a dog to bark in the night, even the best-behaved ones. There could be all sorts of noises in the dead of night, surely. It was just a matter of whether he went completely mental and woke those in the room upstairs. Even while he was ready to move, he continued to toy with the decision in his head. Christ, you're so fucking indecisive Martin, he thought to himself. Just fucking well get on with it.

The small pep talk kicked him into gear and he edged his way towards the lounge door to open it. This was the easy bit – he kept himself together and slowly pulled down the handle of the lounge door. Silently, with the door handle still engaged in his right hand and his belongings tucked into the crook of his left arm, he slid out of the doorway and closed it without anything more than a small click as the mechanism slotted back into place. Phase one was complete without any issues.

Now into the hallway, he faced what would be the toughest of challenges. Another door to negotiate slowly and stealthily but with the added challenge of a very expectant dog on the other side, who historically had not been his biggest fan. The feeling was of course mutual, but Martin did feel a pang of sorrow for the dog with what had happened. He approached the doorway cautiously and repeated the act of a few moments ago to gain entry to the kitchen.

Again, carefully engaging the door handle, he cautiously entered the room. With his eyes adjusted to the darkness he could make out Fergus' black beady eyes. There was a small amount of light in the kitchen, the clock from the oven was glowing brightly and there was a spill from the streetlights in the neighbouring cul-de-sac. Martin locked eyes with Fergus. The dog was sat upright with anticipation. He was wearing one of those ridiculous cones around his neck, no doubt from the fact he'd had to have surgery or something. Or perhaps it was to ensure he couldn't eat anything? Either way, it really didn't matter. In the split seconds that followed, both parties were poised to make their next moves. Martin's strategy was to just get in and out of there as soon as possible, but now, staring down at the small dog in front of him he was unsure whether that would be the case. Fergus was now getting out of his bed and scampering towards Martin at pace. Oh shit, this could be it. All hell was about to break loose. But thankfully for Martin, Fergus seemed to be in quite a sedate mood. He scampered over excitedly and sought some affection. Christ, this was the luck he'd been waiting for, finally. He squatted down to stroke Fergus and spoke quietly to him.

'Hey mate, sorry about the bone thing, it wasn't on purpose,' he said, stroking the dogs back. He'd better not push his luck though, it was time to get out.

'Go on boy, in your bed. Good boy now,' he whispered to Fergus.

Fergus began to trot back to his bed as instructed and Martin made attempts to get back up from crouching down. While getting up, he became unsteady on his feet and in a moment of panic while still trying not to make any noise, he reached out to the nearest chair but could only pull it towards him before hauling it to the floor along with the crash of his laptop on the tiled floor as it escaped his clutches.

Fuck.

Fergus was now going mental at the commotion, sending out large barks after being startled. He had scampered out of his bed again and was barking loudly as Martin lay stricken on the cold floor. He had been so anxious about making any noise that he had become clumsy, over compensating his movements and over thinking the encounter with Fergus. It was quite simply again, the worst luck anyone could have.

He quickly got to his feet, scrambling to get his possessions in his arms and trying to calm down Fergus. He could hear a light flick on in the hallway and footsteps now thundering down the stairs. He sprinted towards the back door and turned the lock. As he grabbed the handle to exit, the kitchen light flicked on behind him. Stood in the doorway, wearing what appeared to be his Mum's dressing gown, was Gary.

'Martin?!' he exclaimed.

Martin looked back at him, wide eyed.

'Sorry,' he called back, after a momentary pause that seemed like an eternity as they locked eyes across the room. He then quickly disappeared out the door slamming it shut behind him.

Then, pelting it up the path back to the car, he tore open the door of his car and flung his laptop onto the passenger seat. Though he wasn't aware of anything around him as he screeched off into the night, during his impulsive getaway a light had flicked on in the bedroom window above. His Mum had watched incredulously through a gap in the curtains as her son sprinted towards his car. At the same time, Gary, with Fergus in his arms barking wildly, stood at the top of the driveway watching Martin disappear up the road.

It was the last time they would see him.

Chapter 33

'So there's no case to be made… because I didn't hit him or anything?' asked Martin.

He had been on the phone to his insurance company for the last half an hour or so. Approximately twenty-eight of those minutes were being on-hold.

'That's right Sir. If there was no collision, then I'm not sure if the claimant will be able to hold you accountable for the damage to his motorcycle,' the agent responded.

Martin paused momentarily. He was in deep thought, because something didn't feel right.

'It's just… he seemed pretty certain it was my fault. Almost like he knew what he was doing?' said Martin.

'Be assured Sir, we will do everything we can to protect you regarding this situation. If anything transpires from this then we will certainly be in touch. But for now, you can rest easy knowing that we will be ensuring any claim against you is going to be rebuffed,' he explained.

'Okay, thank you,' said Martin, still feeling a little bit wary though.

'You're welcome Sir. Is there anything else I can help you with today?' Christ. That was a bloody good question. If only he knew.

'No, I think that will be all thank you,' said Martin.

'Have a good day,' responded the agent and he ended the call.

Well, at least he had heard it from them, he thought. There would hopefully be no case to answer and the insurance company would do all they could to protect him. It was the first thing ticked off his list for the day, a day which would hopefully hold out a little more promise than how the last couple had played out.

In some ways the last 48-hours had felt like a dream. It had been a fabrication of reality and an out of body experience that made him act both impulsively and aggressively. He was also replaying over in his head the words that Gareth had said to him at the services, 'people are the reason I'm here,' he had said. It was confusing for Martin, because people would be the reason he would happily disappear. It was so much easier to get by in his life without other people involved. They were always fucking things up for him. It seemed like people were against him, ready to catch him out and dole out a bit more bad luck for good measure. People were his enemy right now and Martin felt like he could only trust himself. He'd been pushing people away constantly in recent months. When was the last time he saw George? His Dad even? He hadn't exactly wanted to spend time with his Mum, that was clear. Gary had turned out alright to be fair, that was one small positive. He'd done a pretty good job of sabotaging the relationship with his Mum without really intending to though. It was clear there was some deep-set emotion there, with the way it had all blasted out of him in the vet's reception. The more he thought about it, perhaps it was just embedded in him that he was pushing people away without realising

He wanted to be on his own, but didn't want to be lonely. It was like he was happiest in his own space, but equally he was constantly yearning for the human touch and comfort of others. The latter was harder to come by it seemed, so he would regularly default to the former. In a way, it had become a survival mechanism. That was certainly true with Helena, where he withdrew and was constantly conjuring up bizarre scenarios or doing stupid things which meant he could hide behind what was really happening in his head. A deep-rooted depression that cycled round over and over. It only needed the occasional oiling of a daft act to keep it moving along nicely, and that was the status quo as far as Martin was concerned.

A message flashed up on his now working phone. It was pretty rare to get a message from anyone, so he was caught by surprise.

'Hope u had a Happy Xmas Mart I'll be in town this coming weekend if u want to meet up Dad'

There was a lot to unpick here, thought Martin. Firstly, why hadn't he text on Christmas Day? Secondly, it seemed like he wasn't that fussed about meeting up. It's like it wasn't really a question, more of a statement? Perhaps he'd let him off with that though, he never was the best texter with his grammar. Martin felt a pang of disappointment. He'd lost the relationship with his Dad long ago, mainly down to circumstances. His Dad would be travelling round the country with his job and the two could never really align themselves to meet in recent years. They'd done okay for a short while, meeting up for chats at a Nandos or Pizza Express, but slowly this seemed to diminish. It was probably around the time he got a bit more serious with Helena, because inevitably she seemed to take up most of his time and energy. Sure, he could've made it work but he never seemed to possess the enthusiasm to do so. But here, it was a small olive branch of sorts. Maybe an opportunity to rekindle a relationship? He needed at least one parent in his life, right?

It was a strange situation to be in. He couldn't decide whether he felt disappointed or pleased. It was two days after Christmas and by all accounts 'late.' He was too old for presents so didn't expect anything like that, but perhaps a phone call would've sufficed. The retelling of the vets debacle might be interesting though, he was sure his Dad would appreciate that. He tapped out a short message.

'Hi Dad, thanks and you. Hope you had a good one. Shall we meet on Saturday if that works? I'm available all day. You're welcome to pop into mine for a cuppa if easier. Let me know, cheers.'

That should do it. He wasn't expecting him to get in touch very quickly, he could be very flaky since leaving his Mum. His phone buzzed again. Oh shit.

'Hello Martin. We need 2 talk pls. Mum xx'

It was blunt, of course. And what really irked him was the fact she couldn't be bothered to even type out a few more characters to spell things correctly. Urgh. She was such a boomer. He had no intention of speaking to his Mum. She'd have something else to occupy her over the next couple of days with their trip to Paris scheduled for tomorrow. He decided to ignore her, it was probably for the best.

The rest of the day would be spent making plans. A plan to end all this, to finally get away and release himself from the troubles that were ingrained within. It would take time, but he told himself that it was definitely the right thing to do.

Chapter 34

When Saturday arrived, Martin was nervous. He hadn't seen his Dad for a long while and had been building it up in his head. This meeting could be significant. After all, it could well be the last time he saw him if all went according to plan – because the plan had begun in earnest, with the first part of it being to get on good terms with those closest to him and to play a hand that showed him in the best light (or the best possible light that he could muster). It was basically a ploy to show everyone he was absolutely fine so they wouldn't suspect anything. That way, they wouldn't question a disappearance or the like. He knew this would be hard because he wasn't used to showing himself being in good spirits, even if he genuinely was. He just had to keep it together for long enough so that everyone could see that there wasn't anything wrong. And then… poof. He would be gone.

'Would you like something to drink Dad?' he called from the kitchen. 'Umm, yeah what have you got?' his Dad answered.

'Well, no alcohol if that's what you're getting at,' said Martin, astutely. 'Okay, well a coffee will do mate. Black with one please,'

'Yep, no probs,' he chimed back, whilst flicking on the kettle.

He reappeared in the living room with his Dad looking interestedly at the afternoon darts match on the TV.

'Remember this Mart? We used to have a right giggle watching this didn't we!' he said excitedly.

'Yeah and Mum was always telling us off wasn't she, saying it wasn't a sport,' replied Martin.

'Yeah!' he said jokingly, then looked slightly wistful afterwards.

Martin could hear the kettle coming to the boil in the kitchen and disappeared back through the door.

'Have you seen your Mum over Christmas at all Mart?' his Dad called from the lounge.

'Well…' Martin started. 'I've got a story for you.'

'A story? Oh, I do like a story!' his Dad called back.

He then re-entered the lounge a few minutes later with a tray of hot drinks and some mince pies.

'I reckon you will probably want to hear this, but also won't believe it either,' he said, placing the tray down on the coffee table.

'Oh God, go on then, I'm all ears,' his Dad replied inquisitively.

Martin would probably omit a fair chunk of the story, like the breaking into the house to get his stuff and the fact he had bore witness to his Mum and Gary making the beast with two backs, but the vets episode could be recalled in full.

'So…' Martin began. He could tell his Dad was looking for any opportunity to lambast his ex-wife as he sat attentively tearing the foil cup away from the mince pies that Martin had treated them to.

'I went round on Christmas Eve, as planned and it was all going fine really, I kept myself to myself, went to bed, had a decent lie-in, you know. But have you heard about this dog she's got? A bichon frisé?'

'No, what's that?' asked his Dad, finishing off his mince pie and reaching for another.

'It's a ridiculous fluffy little white thing with a stupid pink tongue and it sits on Mum's lap getting pampered. Oh, and it doesn't like me,' explained Martin.

He pulled out a picture of Fergus for his Dad to look at.

'Oh right, okay. Like something from Crufts isn't it?' asked his Dad. 'Exactly,' replied Martin, sipping his tea.

'So, this yappy little thing isn't my biggest fan, but it's Christmas Day and the season of goodwill and all that. The dog, 'Fergus' – his name by the way – is begging me at the dinner table. Now, you know what Mum is like. Wouldn't allow for any of that sort of thing and said as much too. But just to get the bloody thing away from me I slip it a bit of turkey. Well, I didn't realise there was a bone in it and 5 minutes later we're rushing the dog to the vets to dislodge a bone in his throat. It was completely ridiculous,' recalled Martin. He was quite revelling in telling the story. Having an attentive audience for once was actually quite empowering. If anything, he was enjoying it.

'So we're up at the vets, Mum getting all wound up and stuff. She snaps at me about something and then I kind of lose it. I tell her she doesn't care about me and likes the dog more these days. Oh, and I called her a 'serial God botherer and neighbourhood watch wannabe,'

His Dad nearly spat out his coffee. He was laughing heartily, but also slightly incredulously.

'You called her a what?!' he said, roaring with laughter.

'Yep. A God botherer. And then I said, Happy Fucking Christmas and stormed out,' finished Martin. His Dad looked stunned, but strangely, also slightly proud.

'And the dog?' his Dad said, after collecting himself.

'I have reason to believe he is absolutely fine,' said Martin. He wasn't about to explain exactly how he knew that either.

'Okay, well that's good I suppose. Bloody hell Mart, have you spoken to her since?' his Dad asked.

'Umm, well… no. Not exactly. She tried to contact me but she's going away now for New Years so I probably won't for a while and will let things simmer down,' he explained.

'Yeah okay, fair enough. Probably a good move,' his Dad replied. 'God botherer! Brilliant that. Brilliant. The amount of times I wish I could've said something like that. Perhaps I should've, eh?' his Dad said, again, looking wistful.

His relationship with his Dad always seemed to be at its best when it was just the two of them. He thought back to the junior football tour and about how much they had both loved that. His Mum could be quite suffocating and strict. Dad had definitely been on a leash in their marriage and Martin was simply a byproduct of that practice. It was only now that the realisation had come, which was sadly too late for them both.

'Decent little place you've got here by the way mate,' his Dad said, changing subject. 'Work going okay?'

This next part was integral to the plan. He'd have to ham up the details a little bit which he felt uncomfortable doing and quite clearly steer away from the recent episode he had had in the office. Clearly on the surface, everything was fine as far as his Dad was concerned. He hoped that because they didn't talk regularly there would be nothing unusual to pick up on.

'Yeah all good. A few big projects on at the moment which I'm enjoying. Boss seems really happy, so yeah… all good,' replied Martin.

'Pleased to hear it,' his Dad responded.

There was a momentary pause that suggested his Dad might want a bit more detail and Martin sensed this, knowing full well he couldn't keep a façade going much longer. So he just simply nodded in his Dad's direction before he could ask anything else and said, 'Can I get you anything else?'

'Oh no… I'm alright thanks mate. Good cup of coffee that though! I'd better be off within the next hour anyway,' he said. It was kind of a relief to Martin, though he had to admit that he had enjoyed the company. He felt it was important that they had spent time together, limited though it was.

There was so much more he could talk about or say, but he was more comfortable in closing himself off from it all. The last thing he needed, or so he thought, was anyone else's help or advice with the troubles he'd had over the last few days and weeks. Well, it was now months really. Years, even. He would feel embarrassed about opening up and talking like that to his Dad, it just wasn't the done thing. Men were men after all, or so the saying went. Talking about feelings and being sensitive would not only be awkward, but actually just feel a bit bizarre. Some blokes did it, great, good for them. Usually the ones who were getting paid loads of money to do it for an Instagram reel or after some amazing mental health recovery they wanted to talk about on a chat show which would no doubt boost their ego as well as their followers. It was all bollocks as far as Martin could see. And furthermore, there just wasn't the dynamic he could see developing with his Dad where they could talk about stuff like that after their relationship had become so distant.

He'd spent less than half his lifetime without his Dad than with him, and it had just become the way things were. When he was younger and in his teens, they would meet up every other weekend to eat a sad burger with floppy chips at the motorway services or somewhere else dreary. He would also spend time at his Dad's flat after school on a Tuesday waiting for him to come home with a takeaway. Though he was able to look back and see that these weren't exactly the most memorable or exciting times, at least it was their time. But sadly for both of them, it wasn't enough time. It never was. Martin wouldn't have been surprised if his Dad was equally struggling and depressed. He was from a different era, a completely different generation. He wouldn't understand. He'd probably never know either. Time had ticked by and now it had probably run out for good.

The next hour was spent in each others company, doing what they used to do around Christmas time. They watched the darts in relative silence, only occasionally adding their own bits of commentary as and when required.

'I'd better get going now Mart,' his Dad said finally, 'I need to pop in and see Great Uncle Vince, he's not been well lately so I've heard.'

'Yeah not a problem. Thanks for coming over, was good to see you,' Martin replied.

There was a surprisingly tender moment as he got up to leave. His Dad gave him a big hug as if to suggest something. That thing could've been anything from a long list – sympathy, sorrow, regret, relief, love, care, and just generally a shared knowing that they were both alone and probably needed each other more than they realised but were scared of saying. 'Give me a call soon Mart. We'll fix something up,' his Dad said, walking towards the door to get his shoes.

'Yeah of course, I will. Got a, uh… busy start to the year with work but we'll definitely do that,' Martin said. It felt empty. He hoped it hadn't sounded like it.

'Sounds good,' his Dad said, reaching for the latch. 'Oh, and try not to commit attempted murder on that dog again!' he laughed.

Martin smirked.

'See ya Dad,' he said, somewhat sombrely as he disappeared down the stairwell. This had been another box ticked off.

Chapter 35

Martin's phone buzzed unapologetically on the side. He wasn't used to getting many messages from people.

Hello fella, happy new year and all that. Fancy a pint down the hilly soon? Be good to catch-up. Cheers, G

It was the first time he'd heard from George in a little while. He knew his family liked to go all out over the Christmas period so wouldn't have expected to see or hear from him unless he was actually involved or invited to something. The message kind of came out of nowhere, and in reality, it probably did Martin a favour. It meant that he didn't have to instigate anything (as that might seem odd). All he had to do was accept and get through an evening without coming across as too depressed. He typed out a message in response.

Hi mate. Yeah cheers, and you. Sounds good, shall we say the 24th? I've got a bit of work on first couple of weeks back so once that's passed, I'll be free. Let me know if that works. Cheers

Okay, it was a good response. He had planted the seed about working and being busy so that if on the evening they met he appeared tired or irritable then there would be a reason that could be evidenced back to this moment. It wasn't like he had to offer much dialogue to proceedings anyway, George was a good talker and Martin generally liked listening to his stories. George messaged back almost immediately.

Cool. 24th it is. Catch you shortly.

That was in the diary, sorted. He tapped the details into his phone to remind himself. Next on his list of things to think about was his Mum. He'd hardly spared a thought for her since recalling the story of the vets to his Dad, but now his anxiousness had become very real about how he was to negotiate this situation. He'd ignored her message on the day after Boxing Day and he assumed she had gone away shortly after, preoccupied by the romantic advances of her new husband to be. In fact, he actually had no idea if they had ended up going to Paris as planned, or indeed whether Gary popped the question. There was a fairly easy way to find out and that was probably using social media. Surely his Mum would have littered her feed with terribly framed and mostly blurry pictures of the Eiffel Tower or the Champs-Élysées by now? The ones that are zoomed in far too much or have a giant thumb in front of the lens because she doesn't know how to operate a mobile phone camera.

He could just picture the scene now: Gary standing awkwardly in front of a nice tree or something, totally out of focus and completely unusable as a photo for publishing, but 'a lovely picture' to share on Facebook, she would say. He'd have to do the dirty work here and find out. If not, then maybe he'd have to reach out to her. Urgh. He knew he would have to at some point. The suggestion of the latter was the lesser of two evils so he decided to just ignore it and have a look on Facebook, just out of sheer curiosity for now.

Almost grudgingly, he pulled his laptop out and logged onto Facebook. God knows why he was still on this ridiculous site, he hadn't posted anything since his Uni days.

Back then it was all fun and games, trying to get girls that George had introduced him to on nights out to respond to his somewhat haphazard 'pokes' and DM's that made polite comments on their photos, like 'hahaha was fun night ;).' It wasn't exactly the most forward of approaches, he just simply didn't have that in his locker. In hindsight, it probably had come across as a bit creepy. But to an eighteen year old lad, there wasn't much thought about this sort of thing – even Martin had been known to be slightly impulsive in this respect. Needless to say though, this approach had got him absolutely nowhere. He keyed in his username and password, landing on the main newsfeed. He was immediately greeted with the photo of an engagement. The trouble was that it wasn't quite the one he had expected or had come to find.

It was Helena.

Helena was engaged. His heart literally sank about a mile, to what felt like the depths of an already shattered soul. He'd avoided seeing information like this by being on a social media hiatus since their break-up. He'd dip in and out now and again, just to be a bit nosey, (perhaps that was inherited from his Mum) but he had never seen much to force the sort of reaction he was having right now. He felt like every drop of blood in his body had immediately drained itself. He felt hot and anxious. This was real. It felt like the worst of news had finally manifested itself. Up until now he had held some kind of distant hope that he and Helena would end up together. It had felt like destiny, in a way. It was just a shame that only one of them thought this way and God knows why. Helena was all he had been interested in when it came to having relationships. He'd become completely fixated on her, because it was someone and something that he couldn't have. She had drawn the line pretty indefinitely. What Martin couldn't accept though was that anything in life that he had worked hard for usually came to fruition. However, what he didn't realise was that maybe he should've worked harder on himself and realised the kind of person he was turning into and what impact it was having on his relationship with her. In the time that seemed to drift by afterwards, he simply couldn't be bothered to put himself out there and find someone else to be with. He was still convinced that it was meant to be Helena.

Helena was the only person who had provided the security of something that felt like a genuine relationship. He had become confused and upset, completely frozen with anxiety of a relationship with somebody else, and ultimately, in this particular moment he was finally heartbroken.

He had made a number of attempts over the years to try and 'win' Helena back. These advances had ranged from the subtle to the downright stupid. Perhaps the most cumbersome of approaches was during Cameron Stacey's stag do. He knew that Helena still lived in the house they had once owned together and it was only a short journey from the City centre where they were to where she would be. He exited the Saturday night of the stag early and got a taxi to his old address. What was he actually hoping for? He wanted to be noticed. He wanted to do something outrageously romantic, to show her his worth and hope that everything would be fixed again and that all the wrongs of the past would be righted in one fell swoop. It wasn't a good idea. What had seemed kind of goofy and cute at the time of being in a drunken stupor turned into a very, very bad idea really quite quickly. One that ended in the usual embarrassment and hot shame he had become accustomed to.

'Thank you,' he had said, ridiculously loudly and completely lacking in self awareness to the taxi driver who had taken him there. He stepped out onto the kerb and looked up at the house. This was it. This was the moment. It was spontaneous and out of character – she'd like that, he thought.

He walked towards the house and called her name up the pathway. In his head it was like Romeo and Juliet. In reality it was more like something that gets recited on the Jeremy Kyle show.

'Helenaaaaa!' the call echoed around the street, which was draped in darkness and peace and quiet until just now.

What on earth was he doing? There was literally no thought of any kind at this moment. Maybe it was the emotions of seeing someone else get engaged and then ultimately go and get married. Maybe it was the alcohol. Maybe it was the pent-up emotion that had been waiting to escape and flow out of him. Maybe it was all of the above.

'Helenaaaa?' he had called again, a little more desperation in his voice second time around.

A light flicked on in the upstairs bedroom that had once belonged to them both. The profile of someone appeared in the window. It was a man. A man probably a similar age to himself.

'Oi! What the fuck do you want mate? It's twenty past fucking midnight,' he hissed down at Martin.

'Where's Helena,' he had said dumbfounded, albeit in a slightly more controlled manner this time.

'There's nobody here called Helena,' the man had replied, 'now get the fuck out of here because I've got a wife and a newborn here that you're going to wake-up you dozy twat.'

Martin stood there confused. He didn't really understand what was going on. The man closed the window and pulled the curtains shut. The light flicked off and the house was plunged into darkness again.

Martin was sure this was his old house. He was drunk, yes, but he still had his bearings. Helena had moved out then, perhaps he should've known that. Even his drunkenness couldn't mask the embarrassment he felt as he trudged back to the main road. He didn't stop walking until he was back at his hotel for the night, which had taken him nearly two hours. He'd wandered this way and that replaying the scene over in his head, trying to pinpoint where and how it had all collapsed around him again. Thankfully nobody noticed when he returned, indeed George, who he was rooming with, wasn't even there. It had been a stupid idea and another one in the long list of judgement errors he had made.

Other attempts at trying his luck with Helena were of course slightly more subtle. Thankfully nobody would ever know that he had tried to see her on the night of the stag do, but the shame he felt was real and would stick with him. He had tried his best to be noticed by her, to be recognised subtly, from small acts such as changing the course of his drive home from work or being clever about which neighbourhood he did his shopping in. Alas, none of these efforts ever yielded any interaction or even a chance meeting. He was just left yearning again and again, trying to hatch a plan of how he might rekindle some kind of relationship with her. What was strange about this approach was that he had avoided social media to see what she was doing, for fear of seeing something he really didn't want to. What was even stranger was that he didn't really know if he did truly want her, and on what terms. She had irritated him at times and suffocated any personality that he did manage to squeeze out, so why was he so infatuated about getting back with her? Perhaps the ghosts of his parents relationship was having some kind of impact on him.

The fact that it had failed? Perhaps he wanted to rectify that and not succumb to the loneliness his Dad seemed to live with? Although he sometimes appreciated his own space, this thought terrified him.

Furthermore, it was like in his work, he couldn't bear to leave something unfinished and it had only felt like that because of him and his actions. He knew it was he who had fucked up. He still blamed himself for that and struggled to shift the mantra in a more positive direction.

Smiling back at him on the screen was Helena and her new fiancée, 'Tom.' He didn't know who this guy was, but he seemed to fit the archetypal sort of bloke she would go for. He had the same sort of twatish grin that was also worn by her ex-boyfriend Nick. The broad shoulders of a rugby player and the chiselled jaw of a private school boy. Martin had to concede that although he looked like a twat, he was indeed the same twat who had exactly what he had wanted all those years ago. So who the real twat was now was pretty obvious. Not that he quite got round to asking at the time, but he had just wished for Helena to say yes to his own twatish grin and for everything to just work out okay. Things certainly looked okay for these two, the promise of marriage and happiness together. It was the exact opposite of what Martin had right now. He'd had some genuine moments of loneliness recently, but perhaps this one trumped them all. He had never felt more alone seeing Helena with someone else. Although what he was seeing now in the cold light of day was adding fuel to the fire that had been smouldering for some time now.

Perhaps this was the final ignition for it that he didn't realise would set things into a complete blaze over the coming weeks.

Chapter 36

The robotic voice on his phone signalled that there was a new voicemail message.

'You have… one… new voicemail message. Received today… at… seventeen, fifty-two… pm.'

'Martin, it's your Mother here. Please can you call me back when you get the chance, I have some news for you. Thank you.'

'To return the call, key hash. To save it… key two. To delete, key three.'

Martin pressed the key firmly with his finger.

'Message deleted. End of messages.'

He then put the phone back down on the sofa and went to the kitchen to make a cup of tea.

Chapter 37

Present day

It was the morning after meeting George at the Hilly. Martin had mixed feelings as he woke for work. He'd enjoyed spending time with George, albeit rather briefly and he was also slightly buoyed by the fact he had managed to hold a reasonably good conversation with Ruth. The trouble was, he didn't believe in himself much more than he should've. The meeting with Ruth should be leaving him excited to try and meet again. He actually couldn't believe he'd asked her out, as much as it was a hasty and jumbled delivery at the time. It was a strange move, considering the context. Perhaps it just felt like the right thing to do? But it almost went against what he'd been planning over the last three weeks. Oh well, he thought. Life goes on with or without me and this is all part of a wider plan to portray normality.

His Mum had given up trying to contact him now. Why hadn't she just come to his house? She obviously didn't want to speak to him that much. It was hard to get his head round the fact that he didn't want her to speak to him, but did want her to make effort. He was her son after all. It was quite clear what the news was anyway. Gary had proposed in Paris, he'd heard from his Dad of all people. He had texted Martin with what looked like a message that was written by a teenager.

'So ur Mum is getting married then lol good luck 2 the fella!!'

Martin imagined that he'd probably found out through a friend of a friend. Everyone was nosey these days. They all knew one another's business. But not Martin's. His levels of privacy were increasing day by day. He was like a small woodland creature gradually going into hibernation. He was gradually getting his affairs in order and waiting for winter to begin. In Martin's case, winter was the cold dark release from reality and life as he knew it, and a disappearance not just for a season or two, but forever.

He couldn't fully comprehend why he was even doing it. This question had plagued his mind for a while now. All he knew deep down was that being alive was a constant and depressive struggle and a never-ending conflict with himself that never subsided. There were small wins and battles he would win, like last night for example. He'd managed to ask out Ruth and he'd enjoyed George's company. But the narrative he stuck with in his head on reflection was negative. 'Oh, well you only asked her out after a couple of drinks,' he told himself. He wouldn't have done it if he had been completely sober, meaning that in fact, though he was pleased with himself for doing something positive, he couldn't shake the monologue that suggested failure. It was a crippling state of mind to be in, constantly wrestling with his inner voice that accepted defeat and negativity. He knew he was a complex character, unique even. He had told himself on many an occasion that nobody else in human existence suffered like he did and that the only solution to his issues was to solve them himself.

The problem with that was he didn't know how and he was constantly frustrated as a result. His learning behaviour throughout his existence had been to simply work out how to solve something, come at it logically and think it through with a plan. Well, he'd thought this through a number of times now and the best way to solve it was to get out. In his mind he'd exhausted all other options available to him. The final solution was to go for the jugular. To accept that if he wasn't here to feel pain, then there simply wouldn't be any ever again.

There was planning to do still, of course. He'd considered financial assets (of which there was little in his account at present), his car being the main one. That wasn't worth much, so wouldn't be a burden on whoever was unfortunate enough to inherit that. His possessions? Well, phone, laptop and other gadgets like that were material. The flat he was renting was devoid of any character. He'd hardly laid a finger on it by doing anything personal – maybe that's why his Dad said he had liked it, being a true nomad these days as he was. Most of the furnishings were owned by the landlady and everything from the pink emulsion wall in his bedroom to the bowl of potpourri really emphasised the fact he didn't feel very at home here. So all in all, he didn't really have much to offer his next of kin. This made his planning a lot easier. All he had to consider was if there was to be any last communications or a paper trail, so to speak. He'd probably just leave his phone in the property he thought. No point in having that on him where he was headed. He'd need a tiny bit of change for the car parking so would have to go to the bank to get a little bit of cash for that. Everything would largely slot into place when it came to the day, he was sure of it.

He thought again about last night. He had started to think about the wake that was happening in the main bar at The Hilly. He hadn't thought too much about it until now, but it had started to nag him. He could see happy faces there, yes. They were probably reminiscing and thinking of better times. However, they were also depressed and subdued and he could sense the general feeling. Is this the kind of feeling he wanted to inflict on others by his actions? Would he be punishing others? He was certainly punishing himself by being here he thought. He wrestled with the idea that suicide was a selfish idea and didn't know which side of the debate he stood on right now. Yes, he could see how the pain and suffering of others in the aftermath might be, but they'd get over it? It wasn't like he had any dependents, a wife, brothers or sisters. It was just him, seemingly all alone in the world with just himself for company and nobody else on earth would stop if he ceased to exist. He could sympathise in part for those closest to him who would feel sadness, but that was nothing compared to the genuine sadness and unhappiness he felt within himself right now. It was a downward spiral that continued to circle and plummet. The trajectory of his respect for himself was sinking in every act and he couldn't wait to get it over with. Was he being selfish? Perhaps, yes. But he needed to act for himself and this was the only way to do it.

A strange number was calling Martin on his mobile. 'Fuck sake, not again,' he muttered to himself.

He ignored the call and muted his phone while putting it into his desk drawer. It was the second time that day. He generally didn't trust numbers like that, he was very wary of scams and such like.

Moments later he could hear buzzing in the drawer, the vibration of his phone echoing against the metal. 'Fucking hell, fucking leave me alone!' he muttered under his breath.

'Everything alright Mart?' said Susannah, considerately.

'Yeah, yeah fine. Just this number that keeps calling me. That's the third time today,' he replied irritably.

'Why don't you Google it? See if it's a nuisance number. There's websites that have all that kind of stuff,' she said.

'Oh right… is there? Didn't think of that. Yeah, okay… will do. Thanks Suze,'

'No worries. I get it loads. First thing I do is Google it. Once I did answer though and it was some weirdo pretending to be my insurance company. Said I'd hit my car into someone else's. They'll try anything if they can get hold of you,'

Shit. The insurance company. Never mind Suze's scam caller, it could genuinely be his insurance company, he thought to himself.

'I'll have a search,' he said, reaching into his desk drawer to get his phone. He typed out the number into his laptop.

The search results appeared in an instant. Express Line Auto Insurance – his insurers. What did they want with him? He searched further into their website for more details. Yes, it was definitely them, the number matched perfectly. Why the hell couldn't they just leave a message? He wondered what the call might be about. He was hoping that the claim with the motorcyclist had gone away. He hadn't heard anything about it since calling his insurers in the days that preceded the 'accident.' They'd given him their word that there was protection for his case and he had nothing to answer for. Perhaps he should call them back? He sat motionless for a while, panic starting to rise within him. He wasn't great at reassuring himself in these situations and seemed to dwell on what might be damaging news.

'Suze, I'm just going to nip out quickly and call these people back. I think it's legit,' he said.

'Yeah sure. I'll let Steve know that's where you are if he comes looking,' she replied.

He pulled up the number on his phone and rang through. The automated voice at the other end began with a list of options. Martin proceeded to general enquiries, which was of course last on the list.

'They make it so bloody hard,' he said impatiently under his breath. A dial tone was heard on the other end of the line.

'Your call is very important to us, please hold and a member of our team will be with you shortly... we are currently experiencing a very high volume of calls and are doing our utmost to connect you as soon as possible,'

Martin observed this automated message at least twenty times in between the crackling classical music before he got connected to someone. He'd been on the line for nearly fifteen minutes by this point.

'Good morning Express Line Auto Insurance, Mandy speaking, how can I help you today?'

'Yes, hello. I'm just phoning as I've had a number of missed calls from you today, but no message so just wondered if there was some kind of issue with my account?' Martin asked.

'Can I take your name and policy number please?' the agent asked.

'Umm... yes. My name is Martin Baines and uhhh... I don't know what my policy number is. Hang on... sorry. Let me find it,' he responded haphazardly whilst talking into his phone and then attempting to scroll through emails.

'That's okay Mr Baines, take your time,'

'I know it's here somewhere... ahh yes here it is. BA1-0198-BLX,' he called out.

'That's great, thank you,' there was a slight pause while Mandy punched in a few details.

'Yes I can see here that we've tried to get in touch about a vehicle recovery?' she said.

'A recovery? What's that for... my car?' asked Martin, slightly confused.

'Yes. So our accident and recovery team have been in touch to try and get the best time with you to survey the damage to your car which was inflicted on, when was it… the 26th December last year,' she explained.

Martin was even more dumbfounded.

'What… hang on. Damage to my vehicle? There was no damage, I mean, is no damage to my vehicle. I've spoken to somebody about this already, this must be a mistake?' he said, getting slightly exasperated.

'Yes Mr Baines. It says here your vehicle was involved in a road traffic accident and we are obliged to send an agent to you and check the vehicle over in order to survey the damage caused,' the agent explained.

'Yes… but… there is no damage to my vehicle? I didn't have an accident,'

'It says here a claim has been made against you citing that your vehicle was involved in a road traffic accident,' she said again.

'Yes, I know that, you said already.' He was starting to get more and more irritated now, as well as worried. The whole incident and the memories of that night were coming back to haunt him.

'There was no collision with my vehicle, you will find no damage on it. I witnessed an accident caused by a motorcyclist, to himself in fact, but I did not cause one and nor did my car incur any damage upon it,' explained Martin. He was trying to be as forthright as possible.

'And furthermore, I spoke to a colleague of yours on the 28th to clarify whether there would be legitimacy of a claim against me since I had no direct involvement in this 'accident' you're referring to,' he ended on a stern note.

'Well, we need to come and examine your car Mr Baines. It's part of our due diligence. I have no notes here saying about a previous call to us.'

Martin felt hot and anxious.

'Hang on, no record? What? Are you… are you sure? I definitely spoke to someone,' said Martin.

'I'm sorry Mr Baines but I can see anything right now. Would you like to provide me with a suitable time to come and inspect your vehicle?'

Actually, no I fucking wouldn't you bunch of crooks, thought Martin. Yet sadly, he was resigned to obeying the request and duly sorted an inspection of his vehicle for later in the week.

'That's great, thank you Mr Baines. Our accident and recovery consultant will be in touch with you an hour before the appointment to give you an estimated time of arrival. Is there anything else I can help you with today?'

But Martin couldn't speak as he slowly removed the phone from next to his ear. He had seen something not twenty yards away that had grabbed his attention and sent his heart racing with anxiety.

Chapter 38

Once again, it was Helena.

Of course it was fucking Helena. She was showing around some clients at the old paint factory units where Martin's firm was located. There were a host of business and residential units there and her job as a property lawyer must have brought her there. She did a double take towards Martin without so much of a smile and then looked away from him like he wasn't even there. That probably hurt the most. He felt the pain and rejection of the past again, but this time it felt truly real. He'd had her ignore messages and not respond to comments, but that was easy in the digital world. What could he do? A physical snub was so much worse and much more painful.

He trudged back inside. It had been a double whammy. Just when things got bad, they seemed to plummet even further. He really wasn't prepared for seeing Helena again. It wasn't like they'd ever crossed paths (despite his best efforts). Far too much time had elapsed as well, she had moved on and was happily engaged.

He just couldn't understand. What was stopping her from raising a smile? A cursory wave perhaps? It was like she was embarrassed by him. He felt so disappointed with her that it physically hurt. Okay, so he had been the one that was probably the main reason behind their break-up. He just hadn't seen it coming in the circumstances. He didn't know how to articulate his feelings towards her and their relationship. If anything, this frustrated him more. It wasn't like he was ever trying to annoy her or even make any judgments of her. He was just too passive and rather than have it so they could work on something together, she simply phased him out. Martin just hadn't noticed at the time. Now she was just plainly ignoring him. It was childish and petulant really. All he wanted was a bit of an explanation. He knew they would never be together, he probably didn't want that deep down anyway. He knew he wanted someone though, he just hadn't been able to find anyone – or rather, started looking, let alone know how and where.

Still, this encounter had thrown him. He'd always been easily thrown. He was a sensitive soul with a knee jerk reaction to disappear into himself and hide. Despite all the bravado in his head about exit plans and not caring (the exchange at Christmas with his Mum being a good example), he was still dangerously fragile and crumbled quickly at the first sight of emotional trauma. He needed help, and lots of it, but he just didn't know it. He was sticking to his guns and leveraging his own narrative to self-medicate on a cocktail of denial and disappearance.

*

'Is that Mr Baines?' bellowed a brash Brummie voice down the phone. It was 7.27am on Thursday morning and Martin had barely opened his eyes yet.

'Ye...' he started to reply before being interjected before he could even finish the simplest of responses.

'Hello there Mr Baines. It's Simon Dunstable here from Express Line Auto Insurance. I am the Accident and Recovery Consultant who has been assigned to your case,' he continued.

'Oh, hel..' Martin started before getting interrupted again.

'So I'm looking for a convenient time and place to run through the particulars of your vehicle and if that time and place is today then that would be most helpful,'

Martin was half scared to respond. This guy was relentless.

'Yes, any time today would be fine,' replied Martin.

'Well, any time isn't a time Mr Baines,' he scoffed, 'I will need you to specify a time and place as I have a host of appointments that aren't going to organise themselves,' he said, sounding mildly irritated.

Martin thought to respond but was slightly taken aback.

'Oh, umm… okay, shall we say 11.00am?' he said, nervously.

'I can't do 11.00am. Let's say 1.00pm Mr Baines,' said Simon Dunstable.

'Yeah, I guess 1.00pm is alri…' Martin started, but couldn't even finish before he was yet again interrupted.

'Thank you Mr Baines, see you later,' and he was gone.

Martin didn't really know what to make of the exchange, but he was very conscious that the appointment later on with Simon Dunstable might well be a challenging one.

He had been dreading it all morning. The guy had been unbelievably rude on the phone and Martin had been intimidated by that. He was already nervous about what the outcome of this insurance debacle would be and this certainly wasn't helping, especially if he couldn't even get a word in edgeways.

'Are you alright Mart?' said Suze from across the desk.

'Yeah I'm okay,' he answered. Although he obviously wasn't. There was a genuine stress about most things in his life at the moment, right down from the tiny niggling issues, to the wider more blatant things he had in front of him right now, like trying to appease the impatient Simon Dunstable from Express Line Auto Insurance.

'You've got that thing today haven't you mate?' she said, making conversation.

'Yeah. The bloke this morning rang me at half seven. He sounds like he will be a right barrel of laughs,' Martin replied sarcastically.

'Would you like me to come and sweet talk him for you?' giggled Suze.

'I might actually need you to at this rate,' Martin said wryly.

When 1.00pm arrived, the wry comment would've probably been best repositioned into reality.

'Mr Baines, hi. I'm Simon Dunstable. I'll be taking you through this assessment today. Would you care to show me where your vehicle is located please?' he said, assertively.

'Hello. Umm… yes, it's over here,' said Martin, rather timidly.

They walked over to Martin's car which was parked in the staff car park.

'Would you be able to drive it out if possible please? This is so I can get a good look at where the impact was sustained during the accident,' he instructed.

'I'm sorry to waste your time Simon, but there is no damage,' replied Martin, 'I didn't hit anything and nobody hit me. In fact, I don't even know why you're here.' He was starting to find some courage. The subject annoyed him so no wonder he was getting slightly worked up.

'Well I still need to see the vehicle from all angles I'm afraid,' replied Simon Dunstable, taking his digital camera out of his bag. Martin looked at him unamused. Then turned on his feet and got into his car as instructed.

Simon Dunstable had the pompous middle management look of someone who thought they were far more important than they were. Brushed back spikey hair (a bit like the younger of the Chuckle Brothers) and an ill-fitting suit from Primark. He was confrontational without being explicit about it, his demeanour was simply dripping with it. Throw in the phone call that Martin had received this morning which was ridiculously passive aggressive and you literally have the image of a man who just clearly wants to upset people for a living.

Martin got into the drivers seat of his car and turned over the engine. He edged the car out of the space so that Simon Dunstable could start performing his photography duties. Martin looked across at him trying to hide the disgust on his face. Simon Dunstable looked up from his camera and raised his arm as if to say, 'stop there' and then looked down again. Martin got out of the car and turned the engine off, shutting the door behind him. Simon Dunstable just looked plain confused.

Why?

'Can you pull it up a teensy bit closer please, just so I can get a good view of the back without having that other car in view,' he asked, completely deadpan.

Martin just looked at him. This bloke was a complete prick and it was becoming harder by the second not to scream at him. He literally raised his arm to get me to stop, thought Martin. Why did he let me turn the engine off and get out the car before telling me?

He turned on his heels again without a word and climbed back into his car. Martin was cursing under his breath using words that are best not repeated. He proceeded to pull the car not even a foot closer with Simon Dunstable raising his hand again in agreement and could see him mouthing the words, 'perfect.' It was clearly a power move to try and intimidate him. Martin got out of the car with the engine still running to make sure that he was happy with the positioning this time.

'You can turn off the engine Mr Baines. No need to keep it running. I'll be a while,' said Simon Dunstable, without a hint of irony.

Christ, this bloke was an operator. Martin assumed this was his way of gaining some kind of control over him and the situation. Martin didn't really care, the guy had been sent to control the situation regardless but why did he feel the need to be a complete and utter bellend? This was winding Martin up all the while and the guy was only just getting started. He proceeded to turn the engine off and closed the door. Simon Dunstable was peering at some notes on his corporate ring binder whilst holding his camera in the other.

'Right. I'll get to work now shall I?' he said again, in a passive aggressive tone but also trying to appear amusing, if only to himself.

It was like it was Martin's fault that he hadn't managed to take any precious photographs yet. He detested this kind of character but thought it was best to stick around because he simply didn't trust him. So what if he lost his lunch break today? He could eat a sandwich at his desk. He wasn't letting this guy get away with anything if he couldn't help it. Martin simply stood around shadowing Simon Dunstable as he diligently took photographs and made notes in his stupid little pad. Now and again he would make inane little comments like,

'Offside rear… let's just see here,' mumbling to himself.

Martin was getting increasingly irritated and worked up, but he was determined to see this 'appointment' through. Finally, after thirty-five long minutes, Simon Dunstable clicked down his corporate branded biro and folded the cover on his leatherette ring binder.

'So Mr Baines. I've completed my preliminary checks for now. All seems to be in order,' he said, with an air of satisfaction.

'Well, yes. I knew it would be. I told you it would be,' replied Martin shortly.

'I am only performing my duties Mr Baines, I make no judgements or have no pretence about any visit I make,' he said, looking back at the photos he had taken on his camera.

'The next thing I need to do is ask you a few questions Mr Baines.'

Okay, here we go thought Martin.

'What I don't understand is if there was no impact with your vehicle and the claimant, then why would the said claimant be looking to make a claim from you?'

This was surreal, surely he knew the answer.

'Ummm, well… I don't know. But he definitely didn't hit me and nor did I have any…' he started to respond.

'That's not the question I'm asking though is it Mr Baines,' Simon Dunstable interjected, 'So let's move on then for now shall we?'

Martin was feeling bemused. What in the hell was going on here?

'What were the conditions like on the evening of the accident?' He asked.

'Well, it was wet… visibility probably wasn't fantastic. It was dark,' said Martin.

'Okay, okay. So there's a chance you didn't see the motorcyclist coming then?'

'Well, I… uh… only saw him after I turned I suppose,' said Martin, feeling cornered.

'Right okay. Yes, so you're saying you could've avoided him?'

'No, that's not what I'm saying. I didn't hit him, he caused his own accident,' said Martin. Who's side was this guy on? This was ridiculous.

'So, the conditions were poor and you could've avoided him,' said Simon Dunstable.

'Yes the conditions were poor, I said that, but I was performing a perfectly legal manoeuvre. If anything, he should've been avoiding me, given that it was my side of the road I was on,' Martin was getting even more irritated now. Perhaps it was the only way to get Simon Dunstable to listen.

'Right… well, Mr Baines. Our insurance policies generally cover those situations in which drivers have absolutely no liability in the cause of an accident. I have studied your car in detail, and yes, it is clear you haven't made impact at any point with the claimant. However, I must add that this is a very unique situation and I cannot guarantee that we will fully protect you in this instance. It sounds very much like you are culpable here for the cause of an accident and are getting away Scott free unless you have a much stronger case to put forward to me right now,' said Simon Dunstable.

What? What the actual fuck was going on here? Was this guy having a laugh?

'I, I… I don't understand,' stammered Martin, who had lost any ounce of confidence he may have possessed a few minutes ago.

'Well I'm sorry Mr Baines, but that is policy I'm afraid,' said Simon Dunstable, packing his things into his bag. Martin was incredulous, this made absolutely no sense to him. Was this good news or bad news?

'Hang on, what is the policy?' asked Martin pointedly.

'I suggest you call our helpline to follow-up on those details. I will be submitting my report in due…' he began to answer, but his time it was Martin's turn to interject.

'I DON'T WANT TO CALL THE FUCKING HELPLINE,' he roared. 'This whole thing is an absolute fucking farce. Why aren't you protecting me? Why aren't you helping me? I pay for your fucking services and you're being the most difficult cunt I've ever met!'

He'd completely blown his fuse. It had certainly been building up. Simon Dunstable just looked at him, in shock. But he wasn't finished yet either.

'So why don't you and your fucking bog brush haircut just FUCK OFF!' He finished.

Simon Dunstable had already started making his walk away from Martin before the 'bog brush' comment without so much as a look behind him. That was the least of his worries. Simon Dunstable could fuck off, that was fine, because Martin knew deep down that he'd probably get nowhere with him anyway.

However, unfortunately for Martin, he hadn't seen that behind him an audience had appeared. Helena and her clients had just been privy to his foul-mouthed rant. Martin turned just in time to see his ex-girlfriend's shocked and disgusted face looking straight back at him. There was absolutely nothing he could do to reverse what had just happened. His pent up rage had just played out in public in the worst way imaginable. It had felt good for a minute there, to release that aggression, but within seconds, it had gone somewhere the opposite. It was embarrassment and shame that was overwhelming his body right now. He slowly got back into his car and gently reversed it into the parking space it had been occupying previously. With his head bowed in typical self-loathing style, he walked back to the office hoping that he would never have to see Helena, or indeed Simon Dunstable, ever again in his life.

The way things were going, there was probably a good chance he wouldn't see either of them.

When Martin got home that night he went straight to bed. He wrapped himself into his duvet and curled up, weeping to himself and just simply staring into the dark space around him. He was like a hurt little boy. He felt lost, ashamed, anxious and helpless. He was replaying the earlier events in his head, just going over and over the narrative and picturing the face of his ex-girlfriend. He didn't care about Simon Dunstable, although there was a slight pang of guilt about how he had reacted to that. To make matters worse however, Helena had messaged him about an hour after the incident.

Martin, what on earth was that? What I witnessed was completely vile and not something I expect from you. Who even are you? My clients and

I were simply appalled at you!!! If I lose this big deal it will be your fault.

Followed moments later by another short message:

You need help.

Her words were stark and cutting. Martin's first reaction was simply to think, 'wow, it's all about you isn't it? If I lose this deal yada yada, it's all your fault blah blah.' He hated the selfishness of the message. He still had a small ounce of adrenalin running through him despite the shame. That was quickly wearing off as he read the words again from his lonely bed though. He was desperately ashamed. Also, she was right, like she always was. Who even was he? He wasn't even sure he could answer that question. He felt as if his identity had been wiped from his being, he was simply just a body, some kind of vacant shadow that floated through life with no control over his words, his actions or his mind. Of course he needed help, he knew that. But where from? He didn't know. The only way he thought would help himself would be to completely blow away the lingering shadow that he'd become and then suck it up into a vacuum of disappearance for it never to return. He was determined to solve his own problems rather than open up and seek help. It was the only way.

Night had fallen like a blanket over Martin's room. Not that there was much difference in the light to when he had arrived home. This time of year always seemed dark. He typically left and returned from in the dark most days. But this was now heavy darkness, his room full of negative energy and not so much as a glimmer of light. Anyone would think he was just wallowing in self-pity and regret, but while this was true, it was far more serious than that. There was a deep set emotion within him that wasn't allowing him to free himself of shame and anxiety. Though he'd got used to this, the last few weeks or so had been mentally draining and absolutely prime for silly mistakes which he would later hate himself for. The tears continued to silently flow from his eyes, as he clung onto the duvet for security, slowly drifting into a sleep where he could remove consciousness for a while and be safe from the prison that was his own mind.

*

He was back at the spot in the woods which led to the opening in the fence. It was still exactly how it was the last time he was there, though now winter had taken its toll, everything was wet and muddy. The leaves from the trees had disappeared and everything around him had a spiky, stripped back version that only winter was able to portray. It was a metaphor for his own state of mind and demeanour in many ways. The scene he had arrived at wasn't like the last time he was taken there, on that balmy September evening just as Autumn was arriving.

He hadn't pictured himself there for months, but the scenario was eerily familiar. The woods were still, but for a slight rustle of branches behind him and the odd eerie creak of a tree in the breeze. Like last time, he clambered through the hole in the fence and through the undergrowth which had largely died away. They were sharp and thorny, but they made absolutely no impression on him at all. It was like he was already hurt so much that any additional touch or stab wouldn't even have the slightest affect on him. He was now standing on the edge again, looking down at the gorge below. He was familiarising himself with the feeling of standing there, taking in the environment, the smells, the sounds and the touch of his feet on solid ground. He closed his eyes and held his arms out like wings, soaking in everything around him. This was it. This was the position he wanted to be in, he was in control. This was how it was going to be. He switched off completely and floated away into the darkness, falling gently and without consciousness to a new world where no pain existed.

When Martin woke the next morning, he was surprised to find himself still in his bed. Being at the spot again had felt so real, like he was ready to go. The earlier anxiety and adrenaline had long worn off during sleep. His heart beat fast, more in anticipation and excitement than anything else. The visualisation of the final piece of his plan was going to be the hardest to carry out, but the dreams were so real, so natural. They made complete sense to him and now he felt ready to carry it out.

The last step was a big step, a step into the unknown, but he'd convinced himself it was a necessary step to take to rid himself of the negativity that surrounded him. It would release it all in an instant – in fact, he wasn't thinking about this as an ending, but more so creating a fresh start, a clean slate. He wasn't spiritual in any way at all. Of course his Mum was religious but all that was simply bollocks to Martin. This was true enough in his own head though, wiping out something completely was the only way to start afresh and that made complete sense to him. Was he able to start again in some kind of afterlife, who knew? He wasn't as bothered by that point at all. He just fantasised over the wiping out bit. Erasing all memory, all emotion and all consciousness to where he couldn't be harmed. It was a huge undertaking, but as he sat up in bed to go and undress (he'd fallen asleep fully clothed again), he felt more confident than ever about seeing it through. This was the beginning of the end, and he well knew it.

Despite this new mindset, Martin was still feeling severely depressed. It was a feeling that never left him. He dragged himself round the flat and got ready for work slowly, his motivation low for doing pretty much anything right now. When it was time for a shower, he could barely bring himself to stand up, so sitting in the bath tub with the shower head positioned low, he sat for at least half an hour with the warm water flowing down on him, eyes shut, his mind seemingly vacant, but at the same time filled with a thousand thoughts that were jostling for precedence in his head. Each one was screaming for attention, trying to be heard above all others and simply creating a din of nothing to focus on with a void within it that couldn't be filled by logic or reason.

By the time he exited the shower, his hands were wrinkly and he was no doubt going to be late for work. He looked in the mirror. If he didn't know any better, then he would say it was a stranger looking back at him from the reflection. Or indeed, some kind of ghost that he could just see right through. His skin was sallow, sunken and tired. He looked not even half of his former self. How had he managed to hold it together the other night in the company of other people? Perhaps it had been such a gradual decline for him that nobody had noticed. It wasn't the kind of thing his best friend would've brought up anyway and the age old excuse of just being simply 'tired' probably held up for as much as it needed for George. He didn't like looking at himself really, no wonder he didn't recognise the reflection. During the past few months he'd barely made an effort with his hair. He had the patchy attempt at a beard that was mostly unkempt and he just looked weary and beaten. He was thin by nature, but he looked even bonier these days, like he needed a good meal or five.

He'd been beaten by his own self loathing, ground down by the narrative that continued to play out in his head and his life. He brushed his teeth and got ready for work, changing into the same boring polo shirt and chinos he'd always gone to work in.

When he arrived at work, which was not too late in the end, which was good – therefore nobody would really notice his presence. It was perfectly normal to be in a couple of minutes after nine, especially with all the traffic in the area.

Martin sat down and positioned his laptop on the desk, booting up his emails. There was one unread message waiting for him in his inbox that had been forwarded to him and the rest of his colleagues from Steve. It had been sent by someone who worked for the management company for the site. It was the exact type of busy body that thinks everyone's business is their business. It reminded him of his Mum. He hated that sort of character. He noticed that the original message had been sent to the three partners of the architects firm. They were Steve, Karen and Mike.

Fwd: FAO Unit owners - disturbance today FYI
To: steve@wcp-architects.co.uk; karen@wcp-architects.co.uk; mike@wcp-architects.co.uk From: nicola@painthouse-mgmt.co.uk
Sent: Thursday 26th January
Subject: FAO Unit owners - disturbance today

Hi all,

I would just like to bring it to everyone's attention that the disturbance in the car park yesterday was most unwelcome and unacceptable. I have had numerous complaints from other units as well as a property lawyer who operates for us on the site that an individual was heard to be using both aggressive and inflammatory language.

I would like to remind that whoever the culprit is, this is both a commercial and residential site and this type of furore will not be tolerated.

With regards, Nicola

Oh shit. Martin's face went bright red. Someone had witnessed, or at least heard the altercation with Simon Dunstable yesterday. He also assumed that the property lawyer must've been Helena. For fuck's sake. Why did she have to get involved? It obviously meant she missed out on her deal or something then. There was worse to come though as Steve leant his head around the door of his office.

'Mart, a word please mate?' He said.

Well, this was ominous. His complexion was still flushed after reading the email that had landed in his inbox. He slowly got up and trudged over to Steve's office to face the proverbial music.

'Take a seat Martin,' offered Steve from behind his desk. 'How are you this morning?' It seemed like a genuine question. It wasn't intended as loaded thought Martin.

'Umm… well, yeah. I'm alright,' shrugged Martin, which was of course a lie. Steve looked across at him pensively.

'Martin, I'm not going to beat around the bush here. I really don't think you're alright,' he said, after a slight pause. Martin looked up, the challenge had surprised him.

'Look. I know talking about it, or admitting it might be hard, but I've obviously observed some out of character behaviour on your part recently,' he continued. 'You may not feel comfortable to talk about things right now, but I just want to ask… and you don't have to answer now of course.'

Martin bowed his head. It was quite obvious he didn't want to talk about anything. He mustered a, 'I'm fine,' which wasn't all that convincing, but it did lead to the next point which probably confirmed that it wasn't the case at all.

'We had a complaint yesterday from Nicola the site manager, about something that was heard in the car park. Is there anything you know about that Martin?' asked Steve.

This time, it was definitely a loaded question. Surely he knew full well that Martin was the instigator of the commotion. He looked down again, ashamed.

'I'm sorry,' he started, 'I saw the email. Yes, it was me. I snapped at the guy who was doing an assessment on my car for an insurance claim against me. That's a very long story. But yes, I said some things that I probably shouldn't have.'

'Look, it's okay to let off a bit of steam sometimes. We all do it. To family, kids, friends, clients… it's human nature. The reason I've got you in here isn't just because of that, but I think what was observed yesterday is a big factor in a wider issue,' Steve said.

Martin wondered what could be coming next.

'I think it might be best for you take some leave for the next couple of weeks. I can see that the stress of life at the moment is taking its toll,' he continued.

'No, really, I'm fine. I don't need that, really,' Martin was stirred into life from his slump. He knew that he needed to keep working as it was the one thing that kept him going for now. To be at home alone with his own thoughts was quite simply, not an option. If anything, it would speed up what he'd been planning in his head.

'I see your projects have matured nicely and anything new we'll have a hold on as team,' said Steve. 'Please just consider this a way of you hitting the reset button on things and I'm sure you'll come back refreshed in two weeks time. I'm sure it will give you some time to think and reflect. I know you've had a tough couple of years and I'm sensing that it may have caught up with you,' he finished.

Oh good. Some time alone with my own thoughts, he mused to

himself cynically. He had to hand it to Steve though, the guy had this situation worked out to a tee. Perhaps Martin wasn't so good at hiding his demons all the time. He was in work all the time after all and yes, there had been traumas as well as incidents.

'I am grateful for the acknowledgement. I appreciate it, I really do, but my work is probably the only thing that focuses me Steve,' replied Martin.

There was another pause while Steve looked pensively across the desk at him.

'I get that mate, I really do. And the quality of your work has never been in question. You know how much I value you and your talents here. The most important thing for me though, is that we have the best version of Martin Baines here and first and foremost our duty of care is to ensure your wellbeing is looked after. Please accept this offer as a helping hand and not see it as a negative.'

He was good with his words, he had to give it to him. Every single thing that Steve had just said made complete sense. In the real world, this wouldn't have been a problem, but Martin wasn't living in the real world. At the moment, Martin's world was in some defeatist parallel universe that couldn't be reached because it was surrounded by some invisible and impenetrable forcefield that couldn't accept help. Even so, Steve wasn't really giving him a choice here, despite letting him down gently.

'Okay,' said Martin eventually.

'Great. I think it will do you a world of good mate, I really do,' continued Steve.

'So… what happens now then?' Asked Martin.

'Well, you can just tidy up whatever projects you're on right now and if you could just drop me an email with those details, then pop your out of office on and that would be fine.'

'Okay. Will do,' responded Martin. He didn't know how to feel about this. He felt like he was being gently ushered away from view because he had become some grotesque creature that was sucking the life out of everything around him. Though this wasn't true of course, he couldn't help but think it was. The depression had a tendency to do this. To him, he felt like he was exuding or portraying all his emotions on the outside in a physical respect. But emotions were hard to see unless you really dug deep down, but Martin wasn't giving anyone access to a spade. Everyone he knew therefore was scratching around at the surface with their hands and not finding anything, or even looking for that matter.

He left work an hour later and headed back to his flat. 'Well, what the hell happens now?' He thought to himself. There seemed like there was only one thing for it.

Chapter 39

If Martin was writing a diary, then every single day over the course of the next two weeks would probably look the same. There was no real deviation in thought or process over the first few days. He slept or stayed in bed most mornings. If he felt like it he would get in the shower and sit down in there for as much as an hour at a time. He would then walk aimlessly around his flat wondering what to do next. He would barely eat, or at least when he did it was usually a heavily reduced ready meal he'd got from the Tesco Express down the road. This became his ritual, in a way. Step out into the night at round 8.00pm and scan the reduced section. Buy something that could be chucked into the microwave or prepared without fuss.

One night his evening meal consisted of a pork pie and a packet of 'plastic' burger cheese. He really didn't care what was going in him, it was simply means to an end. At the end of the first week he had grown bored of this new routine. It was time to act. The final trigger was when a letter came in the post containing some very bad news indeed. The printed logo on the envelope had set the tone before he'd even opened it.

Express Line Auto Insurance. Private and confidential.

Well, this was it then. Surely a decision about what the hell had gone on with this claim. It could literally go one way or the other. He carefully tore at the envelope, intrigued as to what the contents inside were.

Dear Mr Baines,

I write to you with regard to case number BA1-0198-BLX. We regret to inform you that the claim made against you has been upheld. The claimant and their associated legal team have been able to provide us with an independent eye witness account of the events. This has left us with no alternative but to provide the claimant with a case that we can settle.

The details of which can be found below.

The claimant has been acknowledged to not be at fault with regards to the Road Traffic Collision on 26th December.
The respondent shall sacrifice 3 years no claims guarantee from his insurance premium.
The claimant shall be due a one-off payment of £4,250.00 of which 50% is due by you, the respondent (please find payment details below).
The respondent shall also pay a charge of £300.00 in costs.

And so it went on.

Martin had lost this insurance battle that had seemingly escalated out of nowhere. He was also going to be nearly two and half grand out of pocket because of that scumbag on the bike. Where the fuck had an eye witness come from? Seriously. It was a complete and utter stitch-up. He simply didn't have the money, not for a one-off payment anyway. Though it wasn't astronomical by any means, this sum of money was going to break him, he literally had nothing. His overdraft was maxed out. He already had loans against his name and there was likely no room for more. He wasn't going to ask his Mum for money, the shame of doing so would be unbearable. His Dad didn't have a penny to his name so there was no point in asking him. George? The embarrassment would be of an astronomical scale.

So this was it then. He had nothing. He'd lost every single thing he'd ever had in his life. His job (for now, anyway), his girlfriend, his home, his parents and now on top of that, his dignity, sanity and money that he definitely didn't have either. He was, quite simply, lost.

He'd lost. So therefore, was there anything else left to lose?

It was time to cut his losses.

Chapter 40

This was it. Time to kick his plan into action. The longer time had gone on, the simpler his plan had got. He had written up a short list for whoever would be the first to come into his flat. It might be a police officer of course, but in his head he imagined one of his parents. The list contained all the details of his financials, where to find things of any value (there wasn't much), what keys he had and what they did. It said exactly where he was going to park his car and what he was going to do next. It was almost a will with instructions, of sorts. It didn't feel like a suicide note. He couldn't stand the drama of that. He was never one to draw attention to himself. This was more about the nuts and bolts, the practicalities in the aftermath of taking your own life.

He would switch off his phone, too. There was no need for anyone to contact him in his final moments, or rather, for him to contact anyone else. Again, there was no theatre here. He wasn't doing this for dramatic effect. He just wanted to disappear without a fuss. In Martin's mind, it felt like the most dignified thing to do. He'd leave his work laptop on the side with a post-it containing details of how to login – he'd already provided extensive handover notes of what he was doing when he left work a few days ago. He emptied everything in his wallet apart from his driving license, he figured that this would make it easier for him to be identified by the authorities, if and when they found his body.

Once all these tasks were carried out, he would position everything neat and tidy on the kitchen worktop next to the note, slotted into an envelope with the words 'To whom it may concern' and then, he would leave.

*

At precisely 10.00pm Martin was ready. He'd been ready for hours really, but he'd settled on this particular time as a target for some reason. Although it had been somewhat of an effort to collect himself and accept that this was becoming real, it wasn't a question of whether he was doing it or not. It was very real now. What he'd decided to do was the chosen course of action that kept outweighing all other options. He wanted to die. He only had to think about the time he threw up on Helena or when he'd told his Mum to 'fuck off' to feel the shame of his life wash over him.

In fact, you could've chosen any one of the shameful moments he'd experienced in his thirty-five years on planet Earth, they all seemed to carry some sort of magnitude that collectively brought him unhappiness. The truth of it was simple, his time was up now. No more beating himself up about faux pais or pent up rage. No more hurt from the pain and rejection he'd had. The battle was lost, he had no stomach for the fight and life was simply something he'd failed at in his own eyes. He felt unloved, unapproachable and unkind to others that were living happily.

He'd lined up his possessions on the side in the kitchen as planned, laced up his trainers and slipped on a jacket. The heating was turned down low and the lights were shut off. He'd tidied the flat one final time and had been sat on the sofa waiting for the clock to reach his chosen time. There wasn't a hint of regret or inclination to back track now. His heart beat fast, but in anticipation rather than trepidation. He was rueful, but angry. Angry at himself for ending up this way. He was blaming himself, playing over in his mind what he could've, would've or should've done.

But now it was too late. It was 10.01pm, and now, it was time go.

What Martin had failed to realise was that none of this was ever his fault. Despite the fact he was standing on the edge waiting to take his life wasn't because he deserved to – or even that he really wanted to, he didn't even know what he was doing come to think of it – and in truth it was a completely ridiculous thing to be doing. But in the strangest possible terms, when he thought about it, the whole concept of this just scrambled in his head and then quickly screwed itself up like a piece of paper into a tiny ball which then got thrown into some far away galactic dustbin that could never be reached. The conclusion was always the same: what he was doing right now was the only way.

He festered over the fine details for a moment. The pain of rejection from Helena. The random outbursts of rage that were totally uncalled for. The seemingly uninspired upbringing he had with his parents. The insurance debacle. The gambling phase. The guilt. The humiliations. Getting punched for doing a good deed in Kavos. The pent up self-loathing that continued to consume him. The fact that he felt like he was living in the wrong body and there was no voice that would ever be able to come out of him that justified his inner self.

This long list of things and more stuck with Martin like it was all his fault. They were some, if not all contributing factors to the way he was right now. The build-up in his mind about his constant failures would in truth, read reasonably insignificant to an outsider. People make mistakes, it's human nature. After all, Martin was not a failure. None of these things were really his fault and he wasn't culpable for causing any of the things that had happened. He was involved, of course. After all, it is was life, but the thing with Martin was that he never really felt in control of life until just now, as he stood waiting to take it away from himself.

The realisation was starting to sink in. He could change all this in one single moment, for better or for worse. To release himself from the depression, to take the pain away and to stop living in a bubble of self deprecation. For once, he was fully in control of what was happening, but there was an underlying sense that this control was unfamiliar and wasn't really what he wanted. He had a choice. Remember Gareth's words in the services that night… 'even in our lowest moments, we still have control.'

He could certainly continue with a life that had control – control of his emotions, control of his future by making positive decisions for himself and not putting others before him – and generally leading a life where he would be happy with himself, and within himself to feel like he had succeeded and not failed. Finances could be sorted. Relationships could be fixed. Therapy could be sought. The only person who was telling Martin that he was failing, was of course himself.

Time was standing still, as was he, on the summit of his life. A gentle breeze was softly shaking the leaves and foliage behind him. It was a still and clear night with no noise at all, a chilly one – there would probably be a frost come the morning. This world Martin was in right now was completely silent and without consciousness. He'd heard the saying 'it was like my life was flashing before my eyes' a thousand or so times, but right now life was not flashing by in any sense at all, it had stopped, almost paused momentarily while he collected himself, thinking about memories that kept him stock still on the edge of the gorge. No matter how much he had calculated this exit from his life, the process had halted while he reflected in silence, entranced by the impending euphoria of what was to come next, or so he had visualised. But something was starting to eat away at him ever so gradually. A question of consciousness? A sudden change of heart? He considered the how and the why of what he was doing for a moment. He was hurting inside, another internal debate raging in his head. Mixed emotions that were flooding in and then not draining out. His head was becoming a stew of thoughts, full to the brim and boiling over. He couldn't take the desperation any longer, he wanted to release it, to exonerate himself, to give his troubled mind a break from the pain.

So there was only one thing for it.

He let go.

Chapter 41

Miroslav Piwowar was just coming to the end of a long driving shift that had taken him all the way from Katowice in Poland to Avonmouth, near Bristol. He was driving a 44-tonne lorry full of steel products heading for a warehouse at the docks.

Technically speaking, Miroslav should've been on a break between the hours of midnight and 6.00am, having already been on the road for over 20 hours without a stop since boarding the train at Calais, which took him through the channel tunnel. He had instead decided to push through and get to his destination before dawn. This would make the boss very happy. Miroslav was indeed tired, but determined. He needed to head straight back to Poland the same day and there was not so much as an hour to lose in this respect.

It was a clear night, which was rare for the start of February – Miroslav had been used to driving across the continent at this time of year in the rain and sleet. Given the clear skies above and a chilly bite in the air, frost had fallen with a glazing of ice over the roads meaning he'd had to slow down whilst making his way around the M25 and then onto the M4. The boss would not be very happy if he was late, thought Miroslav. He ploughed on wearily. He was already tired from being up most of the night with his young daughter. His wife, Agata, was at home with their five-month old baby girl Zofia who was struggling badly with her sleep due to colic. He'd had plenty of rough nights in the last week or so but it hadn't affected his driving up until now.

Miroslav was a hardy type, from the village of Mysłów in Southern Poland. He'd had a tough upbringing in what was a relatively impoverished home, but a seemingly happy one. His grandparents and others in the village had been subject to war crimes from Nazi Germany and the scars of those abhorrent acts had certainly left their mark there, making everyone that little bit more wary and subdued about life.

Miroslav however, moved to Katowice when he was barely sixteen to start work in a steel plant just outside the City. Now at thirty-three years old, he was still with the same company, but hauling their products across Europe. He loved driving, it was the one thing he had always set his ambition on, to move out of the village and earn enough money to own a car. He could well remember picking up Agata for their first date at the age of eighteen in a beaten-up old 1995 Opel Astra that he absolutely adored. Now that driving was a living for him, there probably weren't many carriageways or U-bahns in Europe that he didn't know well, but tonight was trickier due to circumstances. He'd never felt this tired in all his life. Nursing Zofia to sleep while his wife managed to get some rest had taken it out of him more than he had realised. He simply accepted that he'd be alright for his next driving shift, it was just his way to carry on. However, this was different. A different kind of tiredness and exhaustion that he'd never felt before. He'd driven long hauls before – perhaps when he shouldn't have – but he'd always been okay. Tonight was just another one of those times and he'd manage to get through it without a stop. He could rest while the guys at the warehouse were unloading and they probably had a decent enough coffee machine in their canteen to help perk him up.

So for now, through bleary eyes he battled on through the night.

He needed to prove to his boss he was worthy of that Christmas bonus they'd recently had. He was planning to take Agata and Zofia away to celebrate being together for fifteen years that summer and was looking at the possibility of warmer climbs such as Spain or Portugal as a destination. He was taken away from the cold night on the M4 momentarily, with thoughts switching to that of summer and somewhere he could treat his family for the hard work he'd been doing.

At 1.20am, Miroslav backed his lorry into the loading bay at the warehouse. He'd made it, but he couldn't really recall the last couple of hours. The thought scared him slightly. Where had that time gone? Well, he was here now and the boss would be happy about that. The warehouse yard was lit up with flood lights that cut through a low mist that had developed. Miroslav made his way into the canteen which was barely warmer than the cab of his truck. The filthy office chairs that were lined up around the perimeter of the room were about the only place he could relax for a moment. He fetched a coffee from the machine and sat down, sipping at the piping hot drink. He retrieved his phone from his pocket and messaged Agata. There was a good chance she'd still be awake.

I have made it here, hope you and Zofia are okay see you soon my sweet xxx

He tapped out the message and put his phone back into his pocket. He put his head back against the cold brick wall behind him and shut his eyes. This was good, a rest that he had deserved. He was dreaming of somewhere warm, with a cold beer or two watching Agata and Zofia play on the golden sand of a sun-drenched beach…

'Has anyone seen the driver for bay 5?' called a voice with a strong Bristolian accent out in the corridor.

'I think he's in there,' replied another voice from inside a nearby office.

'Okay, cheers,' said the first voice.

Moments later, the warehouse manager was in the canteen standing over Miroslav who was fast asleep in his chair, coffee still in hand, albeit now cold. He hadn't moved an inch in the hour or so he'd been asleep.

'Hello mate. You alright?' said the manager.

Miroslav stirred, discombobulated. He was wide eyed, but groggy.

'You okay there mate? Sorry to wake you, we're all done,' the manager said again, 'We've got some paperwork that needs sorting before you can head off. Shall I give you a minute?'

Miroslav was still coming round. He had absolutely no idea where he was for a moment there.

'Yes… Yes, okay. I can do paperworks,' he said, rubbing his bleary eyes.

'Great, thanks mate. We're in the office just through there. I'll give you a minute,' and the manager walked back through the door over to the office.

Miroslav nodded in agreement with the request. He looked at his phone. Shit. It was now 2.30am, how had that happened? He was panicking now. He had wanted to be back on the road nearly an hour ago, if not sooner. This was not good. The boss might be unhappy about this if he knew he had been sleeping.

He pulled himself up from the chair and headed over to the office to complete the paperwork. Twenty minutes later, he was clambering into his truck with a fresh coffee and ready to get going again. He'd completed his checks and locked up the trailer ready to leave. The low mist was completely covering the yard now and visibility wasn't great, which would probably add time to his journey until the sun rose. Miroslav got himself comfortable in his cab and set about getting his route home set up. He was constantly rubbing his eyes. Perhaps he should've prepared a couple of coffees for the journey?

He desperately wanted to get back to his wife and daughter, and if he had a good run, he could be back home by 7.00pm in the evening. That was the plan anyway. He started the engine and pulled out of the bay into the blanket of mist immediately ahead of him. A yard foreman had signalled to him from the small booth by the gate and proceeded to let him through. He gestured a cursory wave at Miroslav and then it was back onto the road again. He knew he'd have to make up for lost time now, falling asleep wasn't the best thing to have done but at least it would help see him through. He felt tuned into the drive ahead now, fully focused on the task in hand. He drove out onto the main road and followed his navigation towards the motorway. The roads were completely clear and he felt as if he could perhaps increase his speed a bit. The trailer was empty so he wouldn't be weighed down by the heavy steel on his route back and was ever more conscious of getting home to his family and a nice warm bed later that evening.

He pulled out onto the dual carriageway and made a head of steam towards the motorway.

'Continue for 250 yards and then, enter roundabout. Take the third exit.' The sat nav advised.

He powered forwards, taking up the majority of space available on the road positioning the lorry across nearly three lanes. He was an experienced driver so he knew how to negotiate the bends in his lorry, in all conditions. Entering the roundabout, he gently swung the lorry to his left side to give himself extra room and forgo the need to slow down. He then pulled the steering wheel back to his right to cruise round towards the third exit. Anyone witnessing this would have probably said this lorry was going too fast, but seeing that the roads were clear there wasn't too much danger.

Except they weren't completely clear and there clearly was danger with the poor visibility and slippery surface. Just ahead at the third exit, a car was emerging. Miroslav hadn't noticed it through the mist initially, but seeing the headlights had dazzled him and he instinctively slammed his foot to the brake, worried that he might hit the car head on. The lorry skidded forwards and then Miroslav wrestled with the steering wheel to keep control, hoping that he wouldn't hit the car that he was now heading straight for. The front wheels of the cab bumped onto the kerb of the roundabout and sent the trailer swaying fiercely in the other direction. The pace of all this was incredible and devastating, but everything was happening in slow motion right now, not least for Miroslav who was trying to get back control of the lorry and stop himself from hitting not just the car, but the railings and lampost that were just beyond the exit. The empty trailer detached from the cab with an earth-shattering jolt, and the sheer velocity it was travelling at, managed to break the mechanism like a rubber band snapping from too much tension. The trailer flipped violently in the direction of the car he had just avoided with his cab and was heading for the stationery vehicle which had nowhere to go and was completely rooted at the junction. The huge trailer slammed into the front of the car and gave a tumultuous thud as both glass and metal came into contact. The sound of an airbag exploding open and the high pitched screech of the horn echoed like a siren around the otherwise deathly quiet scene. Miroslav had managed to stop his cab from careering into the railings ahead and brought it to a stop just beyond where the trailer was resting. It was a scene of pure carnage, with Miroslav's trailer now resting on top of the squashed vehicle. He was unscathed himself, thankfully, but now he feared for the life and welfare of the driver in the car at the junction.

'Fuck fuck fuck,' he said in English, which was unusual. He was full of panic and desperation as he scrambled from the cab and over to the wreckage. His trailer was submerged over the bonnet of the vehicle. How could anyone have survived this collision? Even without the load, his trailer was significantly heavy. Whoever was inside the car was probably crushed to death. Miroslav hurried around the stricken trailer and over towards the drivers door. A million thoughts had entered his head. He'd go to jail. He'd lose his job. He'd lose his family. He'd lose everything. His life was over.

He'd killed someone, he couldn't believe it. He was shaking with fear, this was not meant to happen. He had always been so careful before. In all the journeys he'd made across Europe, through Germany, into Ukraine, the Balkans. He'd negotiated snow, ice, rain, sleet and everything in between. But here, on the deserted roads of Bristol, he'd made a stupid error by losing concentration and pushing things too far.

He approached the car with fear. There was steam and water spilling out, and most probably fuel too, meaning the car could blow up at any second if a small spark was to ignite it. He was petrified of finding a crushed body, most certainly dead, but he had to find out what damage he had done. What must've been a component under the bonnet gave an earth-shattering bang, thankfully stifled by the fact it was submerged by the trailer at the time, but all the same it sent Miroslav cowering backwards. He managed to prize open the battered door to find a man in his thirties sitting back in the driver's seat, seemingly unconscious, blood streaming from a head wound he had sustained. Was he breathing? That was the most important thing, but how could he tell? Should he try and move him?

He scrambled his phone out of his pocket and dialled for the emergency services.

'Hello hello, ambulance, doctor, please now! Now! Car and man, maybe dead!' he screamed into the handset.

'Can you please provide your location?' answered the voice at the other end.

'Location, I know not. I am Polish driver. I need help. I am in Bristol,' he responded as best as he could through the panic.

'Can you please provide us with your name? We are trying to ascertain your location,' they answered.

'My name Miroslav, my English not good,' he said.

'Okay, thank you Miroslav. Please stay calm, we will do the best we can to find you. Can you see any road signs around you?'

'Yes. I see sign. It say M5, number 4 after. I see word I know not. Big roundabout. Lots of road,'

'Okay, thank you Miroslav. Stay calm, we are doing our best,'

Just then another vehicle emerged from behind. It was a van from the fruit market. Miroslav waved his arms desperately as the van pulled over, clearly stunned by what had appeared in front of him through the mist.

'Here come someone, I let them speak! I let them speak!' Miroslav cried desperately into his phone. He handed over his mobile to the man who had hurried out of his van.

'Hello? Yes. We're at the roundabout near Patchway, just down from the Almondsbury interchange. I'd say about a mile or so from the Sainsburys up by the MOD,' the van driver explained.

'I think you'll need an ambulance, police and possibly the fire brigade too,' he continued. There was a pause while he listened to the instructions on the other end of the line. Miroslav had his hands on his head in disbelief. He was staring at the man with blood on his face in the car. This sight would surely haunt him forever and beyond.

'...right, yes. Okay. I will go and see,' said the van driver, walking over to the injured man in the car.

'He's not responsive,' then there was another pause while he listened down the line again. 'Okay yes, we won't try and move him. I will stay here,' he said.

Moments later, a siren was heard in the distance and flashing blue lights started to emerge from the darkness. A police car arrived with an ambulance not far behind from the other direction. They were quickly on the scene.

'We'll take it from here,' said a paramedic calmly, setting to work near the injured man. The fire brigade had also arrived and were cutting away at the frame of the car in order to free its incumbent. Two police officers took Miroslav to one side to calm him down. They wrapped his shoulders in a blanket and sat him in the back seat of their car.

Meanwhile, the paramedics carefully removed the injured man from the car and placed him on a stretcher, covering his body with a blanket. They were working quickly and efficiently, because moments later they had loaded him into the ambulance.

Miroslav was shaking with fear, crying tears of pure shock and regret.

'Have we got an ID on the driver of that vehicle yet?' asked the Sergeant who had arrived on the scene. 'Just having a look if there's a wallet or something Sarge,' another one responded.

There was a short delay while a fire officer carefully unearthed the injured mans wallet from the debris from inside the car and located the identification of the driver. He passed it to the female Sergeant who was standing nearby.

'Martin Baines, Sarge. 35. From Gloucester,' she said.

Chapter 42

He couldn't do it. He just couldn't. He was even beating himself up about this as he clambered back into his car. It was freezing cold. He'd been standing out on the ledge for nearly three hours just gazing into the darkness, not thinking, but also not acting. In the end, some version of a clear thinking head took control. It was the old fight or flight.

In the end, albeit reluctantly perhaps, he chose the fight. He was also cold to his core. It had been a rough night, standing there on the brink. What now? He decided to drive round the deserted streets for a while. He felt stupid going back to his flat where all the prep had been done for his departure. In fact, he felt stupid about the whole thing. It was just another cycle of thoughts that plagued his mind, with seemingly no way out. He had wanted to disappear, he was sure of that. But to die? Perhaps he was less sure about that bit. Disappearing felt easy, but dying was very final. With disappearance, there was a choice. He could easily return. With dying, that was it. There was no coming back. Whatever it was in his head that came to this simple conclusion just now, was quite possibly the thing that had kept him alive.

He began to circle the ring road for a second time. There was nothing else to do but to reflect on what had just happened. Should he tell someone? No, surely that would alarm them. Who 'them' even was he didn't know. He had nobody to really talk to, or so he thought.

He continued this trail of thought as he drove mindlessly around the deserted streets. He was just about to rejoin the dual carriageway when a set of beaming bright lights appeared in front of him, almost from nowhere. The sight shocked him, he'd been in a daze not really paying attention. A huge lorry was careering around the roundabout and had seemingly lost control, its heavy trailer now heading straight for Martin's car, which was rooted to the spot like a sitting duck. It loomed over him like the huge crest of a brutal black wave on an ocean of pure terror. In the seconds that followed, he was in fact, genuinely scared. This was death. Now that he couldn't control it, he now didn't want it.

There was an enormous crash and then any remaining light Martin could see was gone in an instant. His world went dark.

Chapter 43

George was awake. Something had unsettled him about his meeting with Martin recently. He'd hardly spoken to him since and although Martin had told him he'd been fine, there was a nagging sense that he probably wasn't. It was a hard one to work out. Martin had always been quite quiet and withdrawn. It was in his nature and just the way he always had been. Perhaps he should've pressed him more, but that didn't feel comfortable. His own nature was to make light of situations, to tell an anecdote, make people laugh and just generally mask any situation with a bit of bravado. It wasn't like he lacked sensitivity, it was more so that he didn't believe that the tools really existed in his arsenal.

He knew there was something up, he just didn't know how to broach the subject. It was early, but not late enough to really get up for the day, so he decided to go for a run. He sometimes did this on Friday mornings, it was a good way to squeeze in some exercise before the weekend. Especially as most Friday's ended at lunchtime and he'd be pissing it up with the other consultants in the pub all afternoon with the obligatory hangover to follow on Saturday. He looked out the window, it felt slightly eerie. There was a lot mist and the temperature looked pretty close to frozen. His city centre flat in the financial quarter flanked an old industrial estate which had a number of recycling centres, car dealers and a few accident and repair garages. It was typical inner city industry, wedged between gentrified areas that were now host to plush high rise flats and penthouses.

He enjoyed these morning runs, albeit more so in the summer when the weather was good, but this morning he just couldn't relax, so there was only one thing for it. He pulled on his leggings, grabbed a beanie from his drawer and laced up his running shoes. He stuffed his key fob into his shorts and made his way out of the block into the sleeping city. Recycling trucks were getting ready for their early morning pick-ups and council workers clad in full high-vis were chatting at the gates waiting to be let in for work. George nodded as he ran past. Christ, he felt tight this morning. But he really couldn't be bothered to stretch, so he just eased off a little. What was this feeling that was preoccupying him? He felt tense, hoping that the fresh air would help clear his head and loosen his body.

He came to a stop suddenly as a man in high-vis was ushering a recovery truck into a car impound. The bright orange flashing lights and beep-beep-beep of the reversing lorry cut through the early morning quiet. George didn't take any notice to begin with, he'd just stopped outside this particular yard because he had to give way. However now something had caught his eye. The car was mashed on the front drivers side. He took a double take. Something was familiar about the vehicle that was on the back of this recovery truck.

'I think Martin has got that car…' he thought to himself.

The truck continued to reverse and he caught a glimpse of the registration number. Fuck.

This was Martin's car. The pair had joked when he bought it, the last three letters on the plate reading 'BLX' which they used to say stood for 'the bollocks mobile,' because the car, they agreed was, 'the dogs bollocks' – albeit in an ironic way. He knew Martin had sold his other car about a year ago for this one and George never knew the reason why. But this was definitely the bollocks mobile alright. But what the hell was it doing on the back of a recovery truck smashed to bits? George was never one to lack confidence or ask questions so he followed the reversing truck into the impound and asked the driver. 'Excuse me mate. That car… do you know what happened to it?' He asked.

The driver climbed down from his car whilst pulling on some grubby work gloves, ready to operate the tail lift of his truck.

'Accident on the ring road early this morning. Fire brigade had to cut some lad free after a lorry fell on him,' he responded.

'Oh shit. Really? And the driver? Is he alright?' said George, with some panic in his voice.

'Dunno mate,' said the driver, and he looked up ominously at the wreckage he was just about to let off the truck. 'Don't look good, do it.'

George did the same, trying to piece together the situation with such little information to go on.

'Cheers anyway,' he said, and sprinted back to his flat.

*

George had been spooked. What on earth had Martin's car been doing on the back of that recovery truck at 6.00am in the morning? Something didn't feel right. He tapped out a message almost as soon as he flung himself through the door of his home. The sun was beginning to come up over the city and an orange hue filled his apartment, a blinding light that spilled through cracks between the tower blocks and reflected against the glass around him.

Mart, morning mate. Is everything ok? Just saw your car on a tow truck and wondering what's up?! Give me a shout when you can.

He pressed send and waited for the delivery confirmation ticks to appear on his message. Martin's 'last seen' was over 24 hours ago. He knew that his friend had never been the best with responding to messages, but this all seemed to play into the narrative that something was up and even if he were overcooking it in his mind slightly, it was still concerning. He waited and waited for the double ticks to appear, but the only thing that changed was the time. He decided to go and shower, then head to the office early. This was all very strange. After showering he went back to look at his phone again. Still nothing. It was now 7.15am. Was this a respectable enough time to call? He knew Martin wasn't exactly an early riser given the proximity he was to his work but surely it would be okay to check-in? He felt panicked. Had he not seen the car wreckage then this wouldn't be an issue right now, he would be none the wiser, but was he just blowing it all out of proportion? Perhaps. He decided to call and find out.

There was one ring and then it went straight to answer phone. Martin's voice started after a some shuffling and rustling. He spoke slowly and carefully, surprisingly even more measured than his usual self.

'You must be the change you wish to see in the world… And I have tried to change, but I am me. With regret, my world is no longer changeable.'

There was a pause and a large sigh on the recorded message before a final word:

'Goodbye.'

Shit. What was this? Now he could panic with legitimate concern. What had he done? Written his car off on purpose? Caused an accident on purpose to end his life? Christ. This was huge. It was incredibly chilling too. He had to find out more. He felt hot and sick. His freshly ironed white shirt felt restrictive all of a sudden, it was tight around his body as the heat from the shower he had just had poured out of him. He turned on the TV. Surely there would be something on there if there had been a casualty? Stood in the centre of his lounge, phone in one hand and remote control in the other, he waited patiently for the bulletin, if there did happen to be one. It was akin to panic normality. He was panicking massively, but had the sense of purpose to put the TV on and park what he had just heard for the moment.

As he scanned the TV guide, the words he had just heard through the phone continued to whir around his head.

'You must be the change you wish to see in the world…' Where had he heard that before? He zoned out as he flicked through the listings, he was barely concentrating on what he was doing. The words seemed so familiar, so distinctive. Martin was profound, yes, but this hadn't come from him. Perhaps this statement had been planted there, waiting to be found? In essence, this could be Martin's suicide note? An artistic yet understated exit from the world. It pretty much summed him up. He finally settled on BBC1 just in time.

'…And now in the West, a recap on the travel news this morning for the roads and the rails…'

George was back in the room in an instant, the travel news might reveal something if there had been a big accident overnight.

'…There is queuing traffic through Filton and towards the ring road after an accident in the early hours of this morning which involved an overturned lorry. Road users are being warned to allow extra time for

their journey and to take extra care due to the frost and ice out there this morning. On the rails, Great Western Railway trains between Bath Spa and Westbury are being replaced by buses…'

Another piece of the jigsaw for George to piece together. So there had been some kind of accident this morning, but he couldn't find anything online other than traffic disruptions. This perhaps meant that Martin was unharmed? George felt like his head might explode, there was too much information to take in. The message on his phone, had anyone else heard it? The car on the recovery truck. It was surely linked, but he couldn't find out how. He thought about Martin's parents and his work colleagues. Would they be phoning him to find out where he was?

Little did George know that Martin wasn't even working at this time and the row with his Mum over Christmas meant that they weren't in contact. By all accounts, George was the only person right now who had the information that his friend had potentially committed suicide. He went numb at the thought. What should he do? The time was just nearing 7.30am now.

Unbeknownst to him, it was also at this exact moment that Jayne McKeown (formerly Baines) had closed the front door at number 9 Bayhill Gardens where two police officers were stepping back out over the threshold of her home. It had been approximately thirty-seven minutes earlier that they had been knocking at the door wanting to come in.

*

'Who on earth is that at this time in the morning?' said Martin's Mum, tightening the cord on her dressing gown and rushing through the hallway to the front door. She had been in the middle of making her new husband Gary a cup of tea to have in bed. She could make out the silhouettes of two people through the distressed glass in the front door. She proceeded to open the door.

'Mrs Baines?' said one of the police officers, standing on her doorstep.

Martin's Mum was taken aback slightly, but she still made a point to correct them on what was her maiden name. 'Well, it used to be Baines but it's McKeown actually. Is… is everything alright?' she answered nervously.

'I beg your pardon, Mrs McKeown. Yes, it's about your son. This is the last known address we have for him and I take it that you're his Mother?'

'Yes, yes. Martin. What's he done? Is he in trouble?' She asked fervently. 'I think it's best if we came in,' said the police officer.

'Right, yes, okay. Of course,' and she moved aside to let them through.

Gary was making his way down the stairs now, with his own dressing gown on looking worried. He had reached the bottom of the stairs to see the police officers entering the living room with his wife following in down the hallway after them. 'Jayne? Jayne! Is everything okay?' he said in a hushed tone.

'It's Martin,' she replied irritably and made her way into the living room after the police officers. Gary followed. 'Can I get you a cup of tea?' offered Gary, kindly.

'Oh yes please,' said the first police officer, Sergeant Mark Hanley. His colleague, Beth Sharma, agreed to the same. The officers looked subdued and slightly uncomfortable.

'What's the issue here then?' said Martin's Mum, almost flippantly. The officers looked at each other gravely.

'Your son was involved in a serious car accident in the early hours of this morning,' began Sergeant Sharma, 'He is currently receiving emergency and critical care at Bristol Royal Infirmary.'

The officers let the words sit for a moment while they registered with Martin's Mum. The colour visibly drained from her face before it began to crumble.

'No, no. Not my Martin. How? Where? Why?' she started, incredulously.

'Well Mrs Bai… sorry, McKeown, we're not really sure of the why at the moment but we are studying the traffic cameras from near the scene and we have taken a man into custody who has been charged with driving without due care and attention. The how is also a slight anomaly at the moment. By all accounts, he is very lucky to be alive right now,' added Sharma.

There was a slight pause while Martin's Mum collected herself, still seemingly in shock and with a million questions running through her head that would seemingly go unanswered. Sergeant Hanley then took control of the conversation.

'I suggest you make plans to see your son in hospital immediately Mrs McKeown. At the moment, I am not at liberty to say how serious the injuries are that Martin sustained, but he is receiving the best medical care available to him,' he said seriously.

'Bu… but, is he responsive?' Asked Martin's Mum.

'We believe he has been put into an induced coma for his own safety at this stage,' said Hanley.

Gary appeared in the doorway with a tray of teas. He'd been half listening, but it had been difficult to understand what had been said from within the kitchen.

'Is everything alright Jayne…? Jayne?' He said, looking over at his ashen faced wife who was clearly shaken. Tears were now falling silently from her eyes. She was the stoic type, but this would've been a different level of bravery not to show any emotion. He put down the tray of teas on the coffee table and quickly walked over to his wife where he put his arm round her for comfort. She immediately began to let out more emotion, sobbing into Gary's dressing gown. The police officers looked at each other gravely.

'Gary, is it? asked Hanley. 'We've just informed Mrs McKeown here that her son has been involved in a serious car accident and is currently in an induced coma. His condition is critical, but stable,' said Hanley.

'Oh my… oh my Christ,' said Gary, 'It's okay Jayne, it's okay my love, it'll be alright. He'll be alright.'

Hanley reached for his tea. You could tell that this was clearly the part of his job he liked the least. He looked like one of those coppers who just loved to nick bad guys, breaking the sensitive news was part of the territory, but at least he wasn't reporting a death. Well, not just yet anyway.

'Thank you for letting us know officers,' said Gary, who had taken over from his wife who was clearly reeling from the news and unable to speak.

Hanley nodded and then began, 'Would you happen to have any idea as to what Martin was doing on the road at 3.00am this morning? We're trying to piece together the sequence of events. I know this is a personal question, but it seems very strange as to why he would've been out at such a time. I understand he is an architectural designer?'

There was another silence as Gary and Martin's Mum considered the question.

'Did you… did you say 3.00am?' asked Martin's Mum. 'What on earth was he doing out at that time? It was freezing last night,' she managed to say through stifled sobs.

'Well, this is the thing Mrs McKeown. We really don't know. By all accounts, there were very few cars on the road at this time and it seems that he has just been very unfortunate. A delivery driver from the fruit market arrived on the scene and rang through. This is the only information we have at this stage,' answered Hanley.

'I really have no idea what he would have been doing,' said Martin's Mum.

In this moment, it really began to dawn on her how little she knew of her son. The ties had been cut, so to speak. They hadn't spoken since Christmas Day and she had been stewing over his dramatic exit ever since. She suddenly felt guilty for being stubborn and not reaching out. If what the police officers were saying was true, then that may well have been the last time she saw her son conscious, and it had ended incredibly badly. She wept harder into Gary.

'It's okay darling, it's okay,' he said reassuringly. Sharma leant over with a card.

'Look, here's my details should you wish to speak to us. I've written the ward number of where your son is currently. As my colleague here said, I suggest you make arrangements to get to Bristol as soon as you possibly can.'

It all seemed very final to Martin's Mum. She'd lost her son over the last few weeks, but this time it could be permanent. This loss certainly had the feeling of being irreversible. The officers motioned to leave.

'Thank you for your time Mrs McKeown. I really do hope Martin makes a full recovery,' said Sharma.

Of course, there was no guarantee that he would, or rather, whether he would still even be there by the time they had managed to get to Bristol.

Chapter 44

George was still reeling. He had to find out more about this quote that was searching for its owner in his head. He pulled up a chair to the breakfast bar and got out his laptop. He felt like some sort of detective all of a sudden, but not even in a novel way – this was serious. He had to get to the bottom of whatever this mystery was. He dialled Martin's number again and listened to the answerphone message.

> *'You must be the change you wish to see in the world… And I have tried to change, but I am me. With regret, my world is no longer changeable.'*

He said them back aloud to himself, then tapped out the words into Google. The picture of an elderly smiling man came up who was distinctively spectacled.

Ghandi. Of course. He remembered now. He thought back to his Philosophy and Ethics classes that the two of them took for A-Level. It was a subject that neither of them really wanted to do, but Martin had helped George get through it. Martin's Mum had strongly encouraged her son to take it, what with her religious beliefs and well, George just needed a bit of a 'doss' subject to help him along to uni so he could do his course on Sports Marketing. Scraping a 'C' would be absolutely fine to get him onto this, whereas Martin was looking for straight A's across the board, which of course he did achieve.

George stared at the page in front of him for a moment. He was momentarily lost in thought and was taken back to memories of Year 13 Ethics class.

'...Now of course Ghandi is recognised the world over as one of history's most transformative and inspirational figures. He won hearts and minds for his non-violent and dignified approach to peace and spiritualism,' said Mrs Bletchley, at the front of class.

George was too busy peering over his shoulder and making eyes at Carla Biggs to be paying attention, while Martin sat beside him listening intently.

'...Ghandi was considered humble and empathetic, with skills as an incredible listener – which is more than I can say about some people in this room right now George Miller,' she said, with the rising volume and crescendo that only secondary school teachers are able to achieve. George spun around on his chair immediately. It was like being eight years old again. 'Ooops. Sorry Miss,' he said.

'Yes, sorry indeed Mr Miller. Remember, this is further education now so there is no legal obligation for you to be here. If you carry on disrupting other pupils in my lessons then I strongly suggest that you are not,' continued Mrs Bletchley.

George nodded back, sheepishly. She began to address the class again.

'As I was saying, many of Ghandi's philosophical musings made him an international icon, and his quotes continue to inspire countless people across the globe. Let's take this next one for example and discuss in your working groups using the key questions on the sheets in front of you – be sure to understand meaning and context before doing so. The quote you are working with is as follows...,' and she wrote the words upon the whiteboard for the class to see.

'You must be the change you wish to see in the world.'

And there it was. Etched into his mind for eternity. Though not that he knew it at the time. George convinced himself that the answer phone message had been planted there for him to find. This had all moved so quickly, who could he speak to? He had to find out whether his friend was still alive and it was no good sat there on Google looking at Ghandi quotes. He looked up a number to call for the police, which was probably a good place to start. He couldn't exactly just dial 999 and see if someone had died this morning, although it had crossed his mind in the first instance. He found the number online, 101.

'Hello, I was wondering if you might be able to help me. My name is George Miller and I'm just calling to see if you have any information on a friend of mine. I have been trying to get in touch with him but I have only been able to reach his voicemail,' he began.

'Hello Mr Miller, many thanks for you call. I can put you through to the missing persons helpline if that's any better?' The reply came back.

'Well… I don't know if he is actually missing,' said George, thinking about the stricken car on the back of the recovery truck only a couple of hours ago. 'You see… I saw his vehicle being taken into the Council impound in the early hours of this morning… and I just need to know if he's, you know… not dead,' he said. The words didn't even sound real coming out of his mouth. There was some serious gravitas surrounding the word 'dead.' It felt stupid saying it out loud.

'Okay Mr Miller, I will have someone look into this and call you back. Would you be able to give me the name of your friend please?'

'Yes, it's Martin Baines. He's 35 years old. If you've got any information then please let me know. I really am fearing the worst here,' said George, with a slight quiver entering his panicked voice.

'I will find out for you as soon as possible. Can I take your number please?' asked the voice at the other end of the line. George read out his number and was told to wait patiently to be phoned back before he ended the call.

He was not really any further forward, but at least it was a start. It was purgatory. He wondered whether he should reach out to Martin's parents. He didn't have their numbers, but he could go on Facebook. No sooner had he thought about this, he then quashed the idea. Imagine that? He thought about what it would say:

'Oh hi Jayne, it's Martin's friend George here (who you never approved of because of my views on Christianity). Just checking in to see if you've heard from your son? Because I'm worried he might have taken his life last night, cheers.'

He wasn't about to do something like that. Imagine if he was dead? What a way to find out. And furthermore, imagine if he wasn't? He'd scare the wits out of her, or at the very least she might think it was some kind of sick joke. He would just have to sit and wait on a phone call from the police.

Meanwhile, he text his boss to say he would be working from home that day. He didn't say why, yet. Not that he would be working much anyway, there was far more important things to be concerned with. He'd turned into some kind of nervous wreck-come-detective type. He switched on the local radio to see if there was any further reporting. An hour went by with nothing new apart from the usual traffic, which was arguably lighter at the end of the week.

His phone buzzed on the counter-top. Unknown number, it must be the police. This was it. He was nervous, and that was very unlike George Miller to be so. His whole being was prepared for news of his friend. He was white hot and it felt like his heart might explode through his throat as it was beating so heavily.

'Hello?' he said, with trepidation.

'Hello, is that Mr Miller?' said a man on the other end of the line.

'Yes, speaking,' replied George.

'Hi there Mr Miller, this is Sergeant Mark Hanley from Avon and Somerset Police. I understand that you made a call to 101 earlier in order to check on the wellbeing of your friend?'

'That is correct, yes,' said George again. He wasn't sure whether good news or bad news was to follow here. It was hard to tell by the tone of the Sergeant's voice.

'I'm afraid I have some quite upsetting news concerning Mr Baines. I have just returned from his Mother's house in Gloucester,' he went on.

Oh shit. This was it. He'd done it. He'd actually gone through with it. Martin, oh God Martin what have you done? George was silent on the other end of the phone. He was stood up, but he didn't know how, his legs were shaking.

'Mr Baines was involved in a serious car accident in the early hours of this morning. He is currently receiving critical care at Bristol Royal Infirmary,' explained Hanley.

George felt a small weight of relief lift from himself.

'So… so he's alive?' George asked, hopefully.

'Yes. Martin is alive, but he is very lucky. He was put into an induced coma. But don't panic at this – medically, it is the safest thing to do.' Hanley paused for a moment.

'I understand you are a friend of his?' he continued.

'Yes. We've been friends since school… I, uh… I saw him last week actually,' said George.

'I see. Well we are still trying to understand the sequence of events, but as this is an ongoing enquiry with a man in custody, I can't really discuss the particulars at present. His family have been informed and as far as I know, they are at his bedside now,' continued Hanley.

This raised more questions for George. A man in custody? What the hell had happened?

'Thanks for letting me know Sarge,' said George, instantly regretting doing so as it was far too casual given the circumstances.

'I mean, Sergeant. Sergeant Hanley, Sir,' he corrected himself. He probably overcooked it slightly so it came across as even more ironic but didn't seem to phase Hanley.

'Not a problem. I hope that Martin makes a full recovery,' said Hanley.

There was a pause. George thought about the answer phone greeting message. Now would probably be a good time to say something?

'Is there anything else I can be of assistance with Mr Miller?' asked Hanley.

'Uh… Umm… no, I don't think so. Thanks again,' he replied.

'You're welcome. Cheers,' said Hanley casually and ended the call.

So he was alive. George figured that the police already knew about the answer phone thing. They'd have tapped into his phone by now surely? These coppers were all over shit like that. Perhaps for now it was best that he didn't say about it. The immediate goal was to go and see his friend in hospital, if he was allowed to that was.

Chapter 45

Where was he? The details were hazy, at best. Had he jumped into the gorge as planned? He wasn't sure. There was no consciousness, but he knew his body was around him, though he couldn't actually feel it. All he could describe was a blur in his mind, like he'd reached some kind of netherworld. His senses were available to him in glimpses, albeit not particularly strongly. He couldn't feel a thing physically, but it seemed like his brain was still registering something.

Is this what it was like to disappear? To find himself in some unknown land where nothing could be seen or heard? His thoughts then melted away like a cloud drifting through the sky and disappeared again into nothing…

*

Dr. Uhlenbeck entered the room, closely followed by Martin's Mum and Gary.

'We are obviously monitoring Martin very closely Mrs McKeown. He suffered a serious head injury which we understand may lead to some long term traumas, but by placing him into an induced coma means that we are able to protect the brain from any serious damage,' he explained.

Martin's Mum put her hands to her mouth at the sight of her son, all wired up and with an oxygen mask covering his mouth. His head was wrapped in bandages and there was evidence of where some blood was. Gary put his arm around her to offer some comfort as she sobbed quietly.

'Martin is what you would say, unconscious to us, but he will still be registering certain signals around him. It is important during this period that we keep a dialogue with him, as he will no doubt be taking some of this in,' continued Dr Uhlenbeck. 'I will leave you for a moment with him and will come back shortly to answer and questions you may have.'

Martin's Mum sat down beside her son and reached out to touch his arm. She clasped it gently, not wanting to let go. Gary put his hand onto her shoulder and wiped away a tear from his own eyes.

'Oh God Martin. I'm so sorry. I, I… I should've got in touch. I never thought this would happen. I, I… can't believe it. I've been praying for you sweetheart, I really have,' she said solemnly.

'Please be okay. Please, please,' she said finally. Her eyes were filled with tears.

It was probably the first time in Martin's life that she had showed some raw emotion towards him. It was the love and concern that had been missing from his life for so long, and only now it was coming out. Not that Martin knew it of course. They sat in silence with only the metronome style beep of the heart rate monitor to fill the room.

The quiet was broken just minutes later when the door opened and in bustled Martin's Dad. 'Where is he?' He exclaimed.

'Where do you think Alan,' replied Martin's Mum cynically. Despite her sadness, she still had the capacity for a frosty reception with her ex-husband. Martin's Dad eyed her.

'Yes, hello Jayne,' he said, and then extended his hand towards Gary. 'Hi, you must be Gary,' he said genially enough.

'Nice to meet you,' responded Gary shaking the outstretched hand. It was about as well as anyone could've hoped an introduction could've gone, given the circumstances.

'So… I obviously got your message? Any updates, what's going on? Is he alright?' The questions fired out of Martin's Dad in a state of panic but also concern.

'He's stable. The induced coma is to limit any damage to his brain, so the doctor is hopeful he'll come away without too many problems. He's… he's…' and then Martin's Mum broke down.

'He's very lucky to be here,' finished Gary, with nod.

'Do we know what happened yet?' asked Martin's Dad, with the conversation now seemingly taking place between himself and Gary.

'Well the police are still looking at traffic camera footage and conducting an assessment of the road to discern what happened, but as it stands, we still don't really know apart from the fact that a lorry ended up crushing his car,' replied Gary. There was a pause while Martin's Dad reflected. He then asked the question that everyone seemed to be asking.

'What on earth was he doing awake at that time anyway?' he said, 'it seems very out of character for him, don't you think?'

He was right, it was out of character. But perhaps it wasn't as much of a surprise to both Gary and Martin's Mum. After all, he'd got into their house and caused a commotion without giving any context for it. This in itself was out of character, perhaps a pattern was in the making even at that time, but they hadn't had the foresight to acknowledge it.

Dr Uhlenbeck re-entered the room.

'I am sure you are all wondering about what happens next here, so let me reassure you about the steps we have in place to ensure that Martin makes the best possible recovery he can,' he started.

They all looked up at the Doctor, who glanced over at Martin's monitor and took some notes onto his clipboard.

'Martin is doing okay. We are confident he will make a full recovery, but we are all mindful that with all head or brain injuries, there are elements of the trauma that are sometimes, quite literally, black spots. Therefore, we intend to keep Martin in the coma for at least another 72 hours, if not longer. During this time he will obviously not respond, but he will have an element of consciousness, so talking to him and being around him will certainly help. I know it may seem strange, but just your voices and even physical touch can register with him. Some Neurologists believe this is an important part of the healing process and for me, it certainly can't harm to be around him and offer that level of comfort.'

He handed out some information to both Martin's Mum and Dad.

'This will explain a little bit more about the coma and hopefully allay any fears you may have for his safety during this time.'

'Thank you Doctor,' said Martin's Dad.

'Yes, thank you Doctor,' added Martin's Mum.

'I will leave you with your son for now. There will be a nurse monitoring Martin, but I shall also be around should you need me,' finished Doctor Uhlenbeck.

'Would anyone like a tea or coffee?' Said Gary, kindly. He was experienced enough in life to read the situation and understand that Martin's parents might want a little bit of time alone with their son.

'Yes please darling,' said Martin's Mum.

'Oh… uh yes, yes please Gary,' said Martin's Dad, displaying the same sort of apprehensive awkwardness his son would've in this sort of situation. Gary left the room quietly.

Martin's parents sat in silence for a moment at his beside, looking across at their son. It was the first time that the three of them had really been in the same room together since that fateful day around the kitchen table back when Martin was fourteen.

'Congratulations by the way. Gary seems like a decent guy,' said Martin's Dad, breaking the silence.

It was almost like Martin's Mum had to fight her inhibitions not to say something cynical, but even she knew that this moment was not the right time.

'Thank you Alan, I appreciate it,' she said.

There was another pause while they seemingly wondered what else would be a valid form of conversation to break the silence. They had hardly uttered a word to each other in what was nearly 20 years, so it was not exactly easy for either of them. In fact, there wasn't really much else to say as they reflected on the scene in front of them, which was in fact their son currently on something close to life support. Gary returned with the drinks and pulled up a chair next to his wife. Martin's Dad sat opposite them on the other side of the bed looking over ruefully at his son and sipping on the hot tea. Martin's Mum was holding her hands together as if in constant prayer for her son, with the occasional sniffle the only noise heard from her. Though there was silence in the room, it wasn't awkward.

The one sole reason they were there was for their son and him only. The only uncomfortable piece in this situation was the fact they really didn't know how they had ended up here. Okay, yes, there had been an accident and Martin was very lucky to have survived until now, but clearly they were all deep in thought trying to work out how they had got to this point, piecing together a slightly wooly narrative.

All the circumstances were strange. Martin's Mum and Gary had only seen Martin at Christmas, where his behaviour had been normal until the flare up in the vets which was then followed by the encounter in their house. For his Dad, he didn't know any different either. He'd found his son to be in good form when he went around for coffee. It was certainly puzzling. Not one of them there could have anticipated what news was to come, if it was ever to do so.

Because sadly, the one person who would be able to provide answers was currently incapable of doing so and he may never be capable of doing so either. The other, who knew very little too, but perhaps slightly more than those who were sat around Martin right now was desperately trying to find a way to his friend.

George dialled the number again for the hospital. It seemed to ring forever, but he was determined to speak to someone as he had to see his friend. It was no use, he would just have to go there and see if he could get in somehow. Was there a limit on the amount of visitors someone could have? Were there specific times for this sort of thing? Surely it didn't matter, he was in a coma. He knew nothing about any of this, let alone comas. He got changed out of his work clothes and pulled on a hoodie with jogging bottoms. There was absolutely no need to be wearing his smart clothes, not a jot of work was being done today, as he would make his way up to the hospital shortly.

Meanwhile, Martin's bedside party seemed to be getting along just fine. The conversation wasn't exactly flowing, but at least it was genial. In the circumstances, nothing else would do of course, but the fact that Martin's Mum and Dad hadn't spoken a word to each other in the best part of 20 years, it was pretty good progress over the last few hours. After the small talk, it was time to broach the subject of why and how their son had ended up lying motionless in front of them in a hospital bed.

'I did manage to get round and see Mart over Christmas ya'know,' started Martin's Dad, 'He said that you guys had gone to Paris?'

'Yes, that's right,' said Martin's Mum, intrigued.

'Well he told me about an argument he had had with you Jayne. It seemed… slightly out of character I suppose. Don't you think? Perhaps you can tell me more,' asked Martin's Dad.

She looked over at her son, there was even a tinge of guilt in her face.

'Looking back now, I can see that he was probably struggling with something. He seemed irritable, not the Martin I know. Granted, I don't see him too much nowadays either and definitely not much since he lodged with us after his break-up,' she said.

'But perhaps I shouldn't have been so hard on him. It wasn't like I ever asked how he was.'

The last words were said almost mournfully, like a realisation that reaching out to her son could well have gone a long way. Martin would always think that ever since his Mum and Dad split her infatuation had been with trying to spite her ex-husband, trying to put him down at every opportunity. It had made her less approachable as well as increasingly more bitter. It wasn't until later that she softened slightly with Gary (which in turn became a new infatuation) and then becoming overly obsessed with Fergus. She had been there for her son, like when he split with Helena – any parent would be, but Martin certainly felt that he was just simply a reminder of his own father to her, which she just simply couldn't get over. What this meant was that Martin could feel quite unloved and unwanted by her. It had taken until now for her to realise that this was the case, with him lying as close to death as one probably ever could be whilst still being alive.

Martin's Dad was deep in thought. He too hadn't had the closest of relationships with his son over the last few years. In fact, there was only probably one or two people that had. Helena being one and well, she was long gone now. The only other of course, was George.

'His mate, Jayne… George? Where is he nowadays?' asked Martin's Dad.

Little did he know that the man in question was just making his way through the sliding doors at the hospital right that moment.

*

George was a believer that if you entered into any situation with supreme confidence and a general air of looking like you belong somewhere then you could pretty much do anything in life. What he didn't realise was that the security at Bristol Royal Infirmary was quite simply not one of those places where that sort of thing really works. Nevertheless, he approached the reception with enough confidence to suggest that he knew exactly where he was going.

'Good morning, I'm here to visit my friend. His name is Martin Baines,' he said breezily. 'Would you be able to let me know which ward he is on?'

'Are you a family member or close relative?' Came the response from behind the desk. 'Yes. He's my brother,' lied George.

'Okay, let me have a look for you. Can I take your name please?' said the receptionist.

'Yes it's uh, George… Baines,' he lied again. In reality it didn't really matter what surname he provided, it was 2024 after all.

'Okay Mr Baines,' she said, scanning the screen in front of her, 'I can see that your parents have already arrived and are checked in, but we do have a limit on the maximum number of visitors at one time, especially for patients in critical care,' she explained.

'I can send a porter along to let the family know that you're here to visit?' She offered, kindly.

'Oh… that won't be necessary. I will, uh… I will text my Dad now and let him know I'm here,' George said, having been taken off guard slightly.

It dawned on him that he had literally no plan. This was his style, to completely wing it. It was the sort of strategy that had worked up until now, but it had the potential to come unstuck very quickly. Unlike his friend, George had the ability to not dwell on the details much, he would just simply roll with it. It was a knack of his.

'Yes of course,' replied the receptionist. If there's anything else I can do to help then please let me know.'

'Thanks,' said George, with a smile. Then he made his way over to the Costa Coffee shop that was at the front of the hospital. What now? He thought to himself. He wasn't one to waste an opportunity per se, so he ordered a coffee and sat with his eyes on the doors that led to the lifts for the wards.

As luck would have it, out walked Martin's Dad not fifteen minutes later. Well, it certainly looked like Martin's Dad anyway. George studied him as he walked up to the counter to order some drinks. He hadn't seen him in years, perhaps the last time he was stood on the touchline at their junior football team games. Back then he probably had more hair, a few less wrinkles and wasn't wearing glasses – but it was definitely him. George kept his eyes on Alan Baines as he collected the three cups of coffee from the end of the counter.

'Alan!' George called out, unapologetically. He was about 10 yards or so away from him and the shop was busy so it was said with some reasonable volume. Martin's Dad looked over in surprise from where the voice had called.

'George?!' he said, with a look of incredulousness on his face.

'Hello, how're you doing?' said George, extending his hand as Martin's Dad placed the tray of coffees on the table. 'Yeah, yeah… not bad, not bad. Considering,' he replied. The surprise of seeing George here seemed to mask what was otherwise a sombre day indeed. 'I'm guessing you've heard about Martin then?' he added.

'Yeah. I came straight down when I found out,' said George, 'In fact, I've got something that I should probably tell you.' Martin's Dad looked surprised.

'Oh right… what's that then?' He asked, intrigued.

'How about we sit down for a minute and I can tell you what I know,' said George. It was still quite mysterious at this point, but the whole thing was really.

'Okay, let me just take these up to the room and I'll meet you back here in a moment,' said Martin's Dad, then he rushed off through the doors back to the ward.

George was hopeful that between them they could piece together the mystery surrounding his friend. Martin's Dad retuned a few minutes later and sat down at the table opposite George.

'I think we're all wondering what's happened here,' began George, 'because I found out something this morning that I think you ought to know.'

Martin's Dad eyed George over the top of his coffee. He looked concerned.

'Well of course, I think everyone is searching for answers as to why he was out in the middle of the night, and more so, what led to him being involved in a car accident,' said Martin's Dad.

'I think I can help you with the first bit, but the accident, I'm less clued up on what happened there,' said George. He then began to tell Martin's Dad about the smashed up car he had seen this morning on his run around the trading estate.

'…and so I thought, what's happened here? Then I got home and called him to see if he was alright,' he reached into his pocket to get his phone out.

'I think you ought to hear this,' he said, gravely.

Martin's Dad reached over the table and took the phone from George and put it to his ear. He listened to the answerphone greeting and passed the phone back with his hand over his mouth. He looked shocked and emotional.

'I, I… I don't understand? Was he planning something?' asked Martin's Dad.

'Well, I guess so,' answered George. 'As we both know, Mart is a very thoughtful and measured person. It sounds like whatever he was up to, was planned.'

'And… what about this quote? It's very… uh… philosophical?' said Martin's Dad, still trying to take it all in.

'Yes. So I can explain this bit,' said George and he recalled the famous quote and where it had come from.

'Mart was always a deep thinker. I think he held in a lot of what he was feeling you know,' said George.

'Absolutely,' added his Dad, still taken aback, but the words he had just heard from through the phone receiver. 'I hope and pray that he recovers well enough for us to understand what his motivations for all this were, it's absolutely heartbreaking to hear.'

They both sat in deep thought for a moment, wondering what to say next. It was then that Martin's Dad offered his own limited insight on what his son had been like over the last couple few weeks.

'You see, I saw him at Christmas. He seemed well enough to me. We had a bit of a laugh at his Mum's expense, then watched the darts on tele – it was all very genial. I had literally no idea that he had been struggling so badly to want to take his own life. It just goes to show… It's so hard to understand what someone is feeling on the inside. Even your own son. Your best friend even – might not have the slightest understanding of the issues in play,'

They both reflected on this for a moment. It seemed like there was absolutely nothing they could do regarding the fact that Martin was, to all intents and purposes, not conscious.

'Do you think we should tell his Mum?' asked George.

'Well… I suppose we ought to. But perhaps not immediately. She's a bit of wreck as it is,' answered Martin's Dad.

'I tell you what, I'll get you on the ward and you can see Martin, then perhaps we can all have a chat later on,' he continued.

'Yeah okay,' said George, 'but you're gonna have to do me a massive favour…'

'Oh right, what's that?' said Martin's Dad, curiously.

'You're gonna have to say to that receptionist over there that I'm your son, because I told her I was Martin's brother.'

Chapter 46

They just about managed to pass George off as a son of Martin's Dad. It was a good job Martin's Mum had no involvement as her Christian values would've surely meant she wouldn't have been prepared to be in on the rouse. By that time anyway, Gary had gone home so he could tend to Fergus (this was on his wife's orders), but he had also sensed that it was probably time to leave Martin's parents alone with their son for a while. So now it was George who entered the room and sat down on the chair at the foot of the bed. He exchanged pleasantries with Martin's Mum and it was all in good spirits.

'Mrs Baines?' said George, albeit slightly nervously.

'McKeown,' she responded.

'Sorry?' George said, confused.

'It's McKeown, George,' she added, offering a cursory glare over at Martin's Dad.

'Oh, God. Sorry. Force of habit there. Sorry… Mrs, uh, McKeown,' he said, slightly embarrassed and then shot a look across at Martin's Dad, who raised his eyebrows as if to say, 'well don't look at me mate.' She probably hadn't been that keen on the blasphemy either, but there were more important things at hand to be worrying about than that.

'Anyway,' he continued. 'I was speaking to Alan outside the room earlier and there's something which I think you ought to listen to.'

'Oh, what is it? Is it about Martin?' she said.

'Yes. Yes it is. But before you do I need to tell you about what I saw this morning.'

She eyed George with slight suspicion. It was like a school teacher getting ready to hand out a bollocking, it really was that sort of look and one that George had seen many times.

'George Miller, if you are involved in anything that has caused Martin any harm…' she began, until Martin's Dad cut her off – possibly for the first time ever in his life.

'No no Jayne, it's nothing to do with George. He's just got some things that might help us to start building a picture of what Martin was doing out and about in the early hours,' he said, with reassurance.

'Okay, sorry. It's been a very emotional day, for obvious reasons,' she said, apologetically. So then George explained his story about seeing the tow truck and smashed up car.

'As soon as I saw it, I ran back home and called him straight away. It was then that I discovered this…' and he handed the phone over to Martin's Mum to listen to the recording. She almost immediately put her hand to her mouth in shock.

'What… what is this?' she said, handing the phone back. There was silence in the room and George looked across at Martin's Dad.

'I think this might have been Martin's way of saying he doesn't want to be alive anymore,' said George, as sensitively as he could. They all knew that of course, having now all listened to the message.

'I guess he was just unfortunate to be in the car accident… unless of course that was a premeditated wish of his?' Martin's Dad offered.

'Who knows. I'm not 100% sure, but I don't think he would've caused an accident on purpose. Having said that, I didn't really see any of this coming either,' said George. It was Martin's Dad's chance to offer some theory.

'Yes, true. But the police said that they'd taken someone into custody, so that would suggest that Martin wasn't at fault. The part of the puzzle that needs completing is clearly the bit to understand if and why he was out at that time of night to commit the act he alluded to in his message,' he added.

They all looked mournfully down at the person who was absolutely central to all this, but he was of course lying motionless and unresponsive.

Martin's Mum was now staring into space, daydreaming it seemed. 'I have a key,' she said, unprompted.

Martin's Dad and George both looked up, curiously.

'A key? A key to where?' asked Martin's Dad.

'I have a key to his flat. For emergencies. I brought it with me just in case I needed to stay there overnight, but I think I will just stay here,' she said.

It was obvious what they were all thinking, but nobody said it immediately. It was then George who spoke first.

'What are you suggesting Mrs McKeown?' he asked. She was seemingly still transfixed on something, staring into space.

'Perhaps we, well you, should go and see if there's anything in Martin's flat that would provide us with answers?' she said.

'Are we allowed to do that sort of thing?' asked George.

'Well, it's not an investigation. He hasn't died, and the police aren't treating anything as suspicious with the accident so, yes, I don't see why not?' said Martin's Dad.

'I'd like to go and find out,' said Martin's Mum, 'But I don't want to leave him.'

It was obvious that she wanted Martin's Dad and George to go and see what they could find, she simply had to know. This was something that probably overstepped the mark of being nosey, even by her standards. But the justification was of course that he was her son and this was a totally unique situation for all of them.

A nurse entered the room and checked over Martin. She took some readings and noted them down on a sheet. 'How are we all?' she said, kindly.

'Yeah… not bad, considering,' said Martin's Dad. He'd really taken control of some of the speaking today, it had been very unlike him. Perhaps that was because he had the support of George with him. His confidence could be infectious sometimes.

'I'll have to ask a couple of you to leave in the next hour I'm afraid. I'm sorry about that, I know it's hard,' she said.

'That's okay. I think his Mum will stay for as long as possible,' he said, looking over at his ex-wife. 'We'll be getting off shortly anyway,' he added.

'Not a problem Mr Baines,' she said with a smile, and then left the room.

'Right. I guess we're going to go and find some answers then?' said Martin's Dad, tapping his hands on his thighs and motioning to get up. George followed suit.

Martin's Mum shuffled in her seat and retrieved her bag where she dug out the key to Martin's flat.

'The fob is for the main door and the key is for his front door,' she explained, 'please let me know if you find anything unusual. Otherwise, I will see you in the morning Alan. Nice to see you again George.'

'You too… Mrs McKeown,' he said, carefully.

'I'll be in touch,' said Martin's Dad and they left the room giving a small glance back at Martin himself who had of course not moved an inch during the whole day.

*

By the time they'd made their way across the Friday rush hour traffic, the sky had darkened and despite the day being relatively bright, a winter chill had filled the air. Martin's Dad reversed his car carefully into one of the visitor spaces at Martin's building and then he and George walked over to the main entrance. They had been quiet for the majority of the car journey, just small talk about George's parents and some other names from the past. But now they were quiet, since the anticipation of finding something they didn't really want to see was now sinking in.

Martin's Dad held the fob against the entrance and they filed in. Light automatically filled the lobby area and the walked over to where Martin's door was. It felt strange to be doing this. Martin's Dad had been there recently, but for George, it was probably a good six months since he had last come around to see his friend. He felt the guilt of this as Martin's Dad unlocked the door of 18A.

The flat was cold and felt empty, even though it was still being lived in. This gave an eerie feeling to the atmosphere, so they turned on the lights. The place was spotless, but also devoid of any real character. Anything that was on show was neatly aligned, methodically and purposefully. Martin's Dad scanned the living room and walked over to the bedroom. Meanwhile, George entered the kitchen. The fridge gave a hissing noise which drew his attention to it. He looked inside. It was pretty bare, save for a tub of butter, some jars of condiments and a very questionable cucumber. It would seem that Martin hadn't really been eating much recently if the state of his fridge was anything to go by. On the countertop was a pile of papers next to a laptop, a mobile phone and a couple of post-it notes. George flicked through the papers, just as Martin's Dad came into the room.

'All seems pretty normal around the rest of the house,' he said, 'what have you got there?'

There were bank statements, loan agreements and credit card bills. George didn't need to look that carefully and the numbers on the pages to know that Martin had got himself into some serious debt. The card statements were maxed out. The loans were sometimes going unpaid and his current account was pretty much solid at the end of an overdraft.

'Shit,' said George, 'He was always so careful with money,' he said shocked, and passed the papers over to Martin's Dad who started to look in detail at his statements. He immediately noticed a recurring theme.

Money paid in from savings, money out to betting apps. Money in from savings, more money out to betting apps. And then, money in from payday loans, then out to betting apps. In some cases the borrowing was covering rent and other things, but no wonder his fridge was bare, he was spending all the money he earned on paying off debt or feeding an addiction which seemed like in the end was just simply chasing losses.

Martin's Dad stood aghast. He did some quick calculations while scanning over the papers.

'Jesus Christ. Mart must be at least forty grand in debt, maybe more, depending on whether this is all of it and that doesn't take into account the savings he had, which I know was around fifty grand,' he said.

It truly was an eye-watering amount to lose in the space of a couple of years, especially for someone whose annual salary was only around two thirds of the losses he had.

'I wonder why he never said anything?' said George.

'Pride, I suppose,' replied Martin's Dad.

'I didn't even know he liked betting? There was only once he came to Cheltenham with us lads and although he won a bit that day, it was a fucking disaster in the end,' added George.

'Well I guess that's it then. I know our Mart is a private chap, but we never know what some people are concealing until it's too late,' said Martin's Dad.

The pair stood for a moment looking over the bank and credit card statements, wondering what should be the next course of action.

'We should probably let his boss know what's going on,' said George, 'look, there's a number here on that post-it by his laptop. I'm sure he's said before about a guy called Steve.'

Martin's Dad took the post-it note and they decided that they would call his boss over the weekend.

'I don't really want to be here much longer,' said George, 'it's a bit eerie, isn't it.'

'I know what you mean,' responded Martin's Dad, 'I was thinking of staying over here, but it doesn't feel right. Not right now, anyway.'

It was decided that Martin's Dad would stay over in George's spare room overnight and he could therefore get a reasonably good night's sleep and return to the hospital in the morning. It felt strange leaving Martin's flat, like something was very final. Probably because the property didn't feel particularly lived in. It was devoid of colour and had a feeling of emptiness around it. George switched off the hallway light and looked into the darkness. If Martin was to make a full recovery, he vowed to himself that he would just simply not let him move back here on his own.

Chapter 47

He was back in the woods. It was dark, but he could easily feel and trace his way through to the spot. It was a well worn path in his mind, even if he'd only actually ever once followed it physically. He felt his way through the undergrowth, finding himself on the other side staring at what was now quite a familiar sight to him. The foot of the gorge below which he could see past the end of his feet seemed closer somehow, like it had been sucked up closer to him. He felt weightless and dreamlike. The scene was not fully rendered, it felt like it was still building within his mind and filling in the gaps – but it felt real enough to believe that he was there. Maybe he was there? He walked out off of the ledge and into thin air expecting to fall immediately, but he knew he wouldn't. His footsteps carried him far enough until there was an enormous thump as something heavy struck into him.

He didn't know what it was or where it had come from since he had been completely blindsided. But all of a sudden, he was weightless no more. He had crashed down to earth flat on his back looking up at the ink black sky above, which felt like it was about to close down on him and wrap around his body. He could feel an enormous pressure on his head and his chest, yet there was no visible weight upon him. His world was spinning and glitching, getting faster and closer to something he couldn't see. He wanted to reach out, but his limbs were rooted to the ground. He was twitching inside with nervous energy, like an angry hose submerged under water ready to break the serene surface and explode into life. The pain was getting stronger, more real and physically demanding. If only he could break out, release himself and be free from the invisible shackles.

It was then that he woke up.

Chapter 48

Dr Uhlenbeck was standing over a very confused patient right now. His name was Martin Baines and he had been in an induced coma for just over a week.

'Hello Martin,' he said, happily.

Martin looked at him, albeit groggily. His head hurt like mad and his right arm felt like it was stuck to his body.

'You're probably wondering how you got here,' the Doctor continued, 'Well all that can be explained in good time, I'm sure. Right now, what I would like to know is how you are today?'

Martin wasn't really sure what to say. His brain was telling him to say that he was alright, but the words just weren't forming in his mouth so that they could be heard.

'Okay. I understand Martin. It is of course difficult to communicate after such traumas, but just so I know you have understood what I am saying, would you be able to blink twice in reasonably quick succession? Just to acknowledge the fact you are now awake.'

Now awake? What was going on here? Martin was quite obviously very confused, but he understood the Doctors question and proceeded to blink twice as requested.

'Wonderful. Thank you Martin,' said Doctor Uhlenbeck, 'I will allow you to rest for now and a nurse will come in shortly to tend to you.'

This was all very strange. A nurse? Where was he? He didn't recognise the man in front of him at all, but he seemed like a pleasant enough individual. He looked down at his right arm. It was in a cast. Again, he wondered what had happened there. It didn't hurt per se, he was just finding it annoying that he couldn't move it. Even more frustrating was the fact that his head was pounding. It was like a headache that wouldn't shift and he felt a continuous thud-thudding in his temples.

Just then a woman entered the room. He didn't recognise her either, so he assumed that this was what the man had referred to as 'a nurse' just now.

'Hello Martin, I'm nurse Zara. How are you feeling today?' she asked.

Martin simply blinked twice. That seemed to be the way the doctor wanted him to do it?

'Ahh I see. Dr Uhlenbeck has also asked you already today,' she said. 'We will prepare you something to eat shortly, but I am just going to take some readings including heart rate and blood pressure.'

Martin lay there while the nurse went about her duties. He didn't really know what to do, so he just watched, intrigued as to what was going on.

'Excellent,' she said, 'I'll be back shortly to help you with some food and water.'

When she returned ten minutes later, not much had changed. The room was still the same and he couldn't move his right arm. It was really starting to bother him.

'What's this?' He said, motioning his chin towards the arm which was sitting across his chest in the cast.

'Ahh, wonderful to hear you talk Martin,' said Nurse Zara. 'That's a cast. I'm afraid you've had quite a bad accident and broken your arm.'

'Oh. Okay,' he responded. He didn't really have much more to add at that point, so just considered carefully what he'd been told.

'Right, is it time for some food Martin? I'm sure you're hungry,' said Nurse Zara.

Yes, he was hungry, he thought to himself. He'd forgotten what it had felt like to be hungry. Then his mind gradually began to fill in some of the blanks.

Being hungry causes an uncomfortable or painful physical sensation caused by insufficient consumption of dietary energy, i.e. lack of food.

He was relearning the meaning of things as and when he heard about them. He looked up at Zara. She was a happy and industrious type, the sort his Dad might call a 'pocket rocket.' Oh his Dad! How was he? wondered Martin, then forgot about him almost instantly.

Zara helped him eat some food. He had no idea what it was but it tasted okay. In fact, it was probably the most fantastic thing he had tasted in ages, or rather, ever.

'Well done Martin, you've done incredibly well there,' said Zara, 'is there anything else you would like?'

'Umm… no, no I don't think so,' he responded. He wasn't very sure of what else he could really ask for. He was starting to feel a bit better, but his head was still very painful.

'Would you be able to help me with this pain I've got in my head?' asked Martin. At this point, he hadn't seen himself in a mirror, he had no idea what it was he looked like all wrapped up in bandages.

'Certainly Martin. I can prescribe some painkillers for you, but I must warn you that they are quite strong. The strongest we can prescribe at the moment given your state,' answered Zara.

My state? Thought Martin. He wondered again about what she meant by that. His surroundings were very unusual, come to think of it. He'd woken up in a bed that wasn't his and didn't recognise the room or anything or anyone around him. Perhaps his Dad would know something?

'What am I doing here?' he asked, casually.

'I'm afraid you had quite a nasty accident Martin. Dr Uhlenbeck will be able to explain a little bit further about what happened in due course, but most importantly, you are safe and well in a hospital bed here in Bristol,' explained Zara carefully. 'However, before we go on, let me see about those painkillers first.'

Martin blinked and nodded at the same time, just to be sure that Zara had been understood. She smiled a sympathetic smile and left the room.

So he was in a hospital. What on earth had happened? He was using his brain to what felt like its full capacity and it wasn't doing his head any good. It hurt from the pain of whatever had been inflicted on him. And his arm of course. He couldn't really feel that right now, but he knew that he definitely couldn't move it.

*

His mind was forming something. Something very faint and far away. He couldn't reach it but he could see it. He wanted to get closer to it, but his legs wouldn't carry him. In the distance, he could see a figure bend down onto all fours and crawl through a gap in some fencing. Now his body moved forward and he followed to where the figure had disappeared only moments before. He found himself on the other side of the fence looking out into a vast gorge. There in front of him was the figure, seemingly waiting for something, just stood completely still and looking out into the darkness in front of him. It was a man. Average build, fairly slim, dark hair and dark clothes. Martin wanted to get closer to whoever this was but he was stuck where he was, just looking at the back of the man, wondering what was going to happen next. The man in front of him looked familiar, but he couldn't see his face from his own position, down on the ground, just by the clearing on the other side of the fence. There was not a single noise, just a light breeze that tickled at the trees and bushes around him. Everything was calm and serene.

Without any warning, the man in front of him leant forward and let his body fall from the edge of cliff into the darkness below.

'NO!' Screamed Martin and startled himself with a jolt as he woke up again in the hospital bed. When he came to, there were three faces looking down at him from all sides of the bed. They were familiar faces at least, for there at his bedside were his parents and George.

Nurse Zara walked in, having heard the cry from next door.

'It's okay, Martin, I think you may have had a bit of dream,' she said.

She then turned to Martin's parents who in truth looked a little bit shocked, but also slightly relieved that they had witnessed their son say something.

'The sedatives will eventually wear off and agitation or outbursts will become less,' she said quietly to reassure them. She then turned to Martin.

'Are you okay Martin?' she asked.

'I… I think I had a dream,' he said.

'That's okay, totally normal. You have some visitors here now who are excited to see you,' she added.

Martin's Mum's eyes were filled with tears. They looked like the sort of tears of pride that a parent gets when they see their son or daughter collect an award for good behaviour in front of the whole school. In some ways, Martin was collecting his award right now because life itself was the gift and he was a beneficiary of it. His Mum was incredibly proud, if not more relieved than anything else, to see it too. His Dad looked wistful and held out his hand to rest on Martin's leg. It was probably the most tender family moment they had ever had together.

It was a far cry from the staged photos they used to have on family holidays or turning up in a fluster at a family function because Martin's Dad 'couldn't get his act together quick enough.' This was genuine love and respect right there, pride in their son for simply being alive. And of course, there was George. He looked delighted too. It was a bit strange that he was there, but still, he'd been the closest thing to a brother that Martin would ever have.

'Hello?' Martin said, almost nervously.

'Hello darling,' replied his Mum, 'we're so glad you're awake.'

'Good to see you matey,' said his Dad and George added a, 'glad you're okay pal,' to round off greetings from the group.

'I will leave you in peace for now Martin,' said Zara, 'please just use the buzzer if you need me for anything,' she smiled and left the room quietly.

There was a tinge of awkwardness in the room while they all wondered what to say next. It was becoming increasingly obvious that Martin's Mum was bursting to ask about what he was doing out in his car in the dead of night, but even she understood that perhaps this was not the right time. It was unlikely that Martin would even be able to currently answer that question anyway, so it would be completely wasted. Instead, they all just sat there relieved, if not slightly awkwardly. It was Martin himself who broke the silence.

'Why are you all here anyway?' he asked, completely innocently.

They all looked at each other wondering who would field the question. It was his Dad who picked it up.

'Well… it's because we wanted to see you Mart. You had a, uh… quite a nasty accident which you needed to go to hospital for,' he began to explain.

'Oh. I see,' replied Martin thoughtfully, 'And how long do I have to be here for?' he added.

'We don't know yet mate, but the Doctors will make sure you're fit and well before discharging you,' his Dad said reassuringly.

'Oh, okay,' responded Martin, seemingly satisfied with the reasoning.

The next couple of hours were spent with Martin intermittently asking a number of basic questions as he tried to form a narrative in his head. Over the coming days he would begin to realise in his own mind and that there was a very specific reason why he was there in the hospital bed with a nagging doubt that the real reason was indeed hiding under the surface, waiting to be let out.

Chapter 49

Martin was back in the spare room at his Mum's house in Gloucester. Both of his parents and Gary had agreed that this was the best place for him during his recovery given that his Mum and Gary were both retired. George had also mentioned to them what he'd felt about Martin going back to his flat too, as he still felt some kind of eeriness at the thought of him doing that. This would be one for the future and at the time had probably got slightly lost in the immediate plans of Martin leaving hospital.

So for now, it was back to where everything had seemingly started to spin wildly out of control. The memories of Fergus choking on a turkey bone, a foul mouthed rant at his Mum and then the breaking in for his phone charger and laptop. The memories were all still there, but thankfully not a preoccupation for him while he spent most of his days either in bed or on the sofa. He would occasionally accompany Gary on short walks around the block with Fergus for fresh air and thankfully the weather and season was now turning into early spring, so no doubt that was helping his rehabilitation too. He was still depressed, but not in the way he had been. What he felt more than anything was shame. What had happened had been a real shock to the system. A genuine threat to his very existence and a warning that his life could've been over. Was he thankful for life? Perhaps not fully, yet. He had planned to leave it and never look back. He could reflect on how desperate and dramatic it all was, but at the time he didn't see it like that. It just simply felt like it was something he needed to do.

Undoubtedly, the questions still remained over why he was out that night and for now he'd just been able to pass it off with a, 'I don't know,' which was feasible enough, given the sedatives he'd been taking. However, these were wearing off day by day as his medication weaned. Sooner or later he'd have to talk about it and confront it when asked properly, as it was something that couldn't remain hidden for much longer.

It was in bed a few nights prior that he had had a realisation. He'd had another flashback to the gorge and watched from close proximity at the man stood on the edge. It had taken a little while to work it out, but he'd realised the figure on the cliff edge was actually him. The only difference to the actual reality was that he'd walked away from doing what the man was about to do, rather than let himself fall to his death. What followed after with the road accident was not his fault, he was just simply in the wrong place at the wrong time. He knew now what had happened and he knew he had to get himself ready to talk about it, as there would be no escape from it soon. He felt weak though. He felt pathetic and embarrassed. But how long could he hold on for?

He sat on the sofa for most of the hours he spent in the house watching daytime television. As he sat there watching the mid morning lineup of Bargain Hunt and Homes under the Hammer, his phone lit up. It was George.

'How're you doing mate? I'm up in Tewkesbury this afternoon with work and wondered if I could pop in to see you on my way back? No worries if not. G'

This presented itself as a potentially good time to start talking. He knew his Mum and Gary did pilates on a Tuesday evening, so they would be out. Perhaps he could start by giving George some background on what had happened on that fateful night.

'Yeah sure. Would be good to see you, thanks mate'

That was the simple response back, along with his Mum's address. He now had to ready himself for a later conversation, since there would no doubt be questions. There was no immediate pressure of course, but he'd finally realised he had to talk. He felt uncomfortable at the thought of telling his Mum and worried about the judgement from her. His Dad would probably want to get his Mum involved through old habits of his, but George – he was understanding, he wouldn't judge?

What Martin didn't know however, was that George already knew some of the background, having been privy to the bank statements, the voice mailbox greeting and the quiet behaviour his friend had been showing in the lead up to the accident. But Martin didn't remember any of this. He hadn't been to his flat since the crash and his phone had been completely mashed up in the process meaning he had needed a new one. Therefore, these obvious prompts to jog his memory were missing, but thankfully it meant that George already knew most of what Martin might begin to talk about one day, just maybe not the stark details about the planned suicide.

'See you later darling,' his Mum called round the doorframe. She had an exercise mat underneath her arm and was wearing her outfit primed for Pilates class. Gary leant his head round too.

'Send my best to George,' he said, 'although I might see him depending on what time we're back,' he added. They liked to have a drink in the social club after their Pilates, so they wouldn't be back for at least a couple of hours.

'Okay, see you later,' Martin responded.

They left the house leaving Martin in silence. Fergus trotted over to Martin and sat at his feet. The two had become slightly more bonded over the course of the last few weeks and he no longer growled at Martin. Instead, he quite enjoyed the company of someone who didn't try and brush or style his fur every few hours or so like his Mum did. With his right arm still in a cast, Martin used his left arm to lift the dog onto his lap and began to stroke his head. Nobody would've foreseen this a couple of months ago, not least himself. He and Fergus both seemed content, but the equilibrium was broken only moments later when there was a knock at the door. Fergus darted off into the hallway going ballistic.

'Alright, alright, calm it Ferg,' said Martin, getting to his feet to answer the door. It was of course George. Martin opened the door and his friend threw himself upon him giving him a big hug.

'How's it going mate? Good to see you,' George said cheerfully.

'Yeah not bad thanks. Getting there, getting there,' Martin replied. 'Come in… don't worry about him, he won't bite. He's soft as shit really,' he said, speaking of Fergus who was busily sniffing at George's feet.

They walked through to the lounge and Martin resumed his seat on the sofa. George took a seat opposite on the other sofa.

'How many mid-terrace two-beds have you seen renovated in Stoke-on-Trent this week then eh?' George asked jokingly, who knew Martin would've been watching plenty of Homes Under the Hammer.

Martin laughed, 'Oh loads mate, loads, but they always skimp don't they. Magnolia walls and brown carpets. What's that all about?'

There was a pause for a moment, which Martin then followed with, 'not exactly much else to do these days is there,' he said, half cynically and holding his right arm up slightly to show the cast.

'Hey, it's important you recover mate. I know you'd rather be working and doing your thing, but this is the best place for you at the moment,' replied George.

'Your scar is looking better. I can hardly really see it now mate,' he added, pointing towards the place on Martin's head where a metal plate now existed beneath what had been a significantly deep wound.

'Yeah. It's a story to tell at the airport at least, isn't it,' said Martin.

'Not like we'll be off to Kavos anytime soon though eh mate!' laughed George, who well remembered the lads holiday he ended up taking Martin on with him.

'Oh Christ, don't remind me. What a disaster that was,' and he looked wistfully across the room. In many ways, the holiday had been a bit of a watershed moment for Martin. He had learned a lot about himself in those two weeks. Coupled with the panic attacks, the nearly broken nose and meeting Helena. It had pretty much shaped the next ten years of his life.

Martin offered to make drinks to which George took it into his own hands. He was that kind of friend, even in someone else's house he liked to help. Martin could hear him singing cheerfully to himself from the kitchen while clunking around trying to find mugs for the tea. 'Ooops, sorry Mrs Bain… I mean, McKeown,' he said out loud, having fumbled with the sugar leaving crystals scattered over the worktop. 'She'll have me by the bollocks for that one,' Martin could hear him say under his breath from the next room. He couldn't help but smile to himself at that. George emerged a few minutes later with the teas and sat back down opposite his friend. He reached into his pocket.

'Here… got you something,' he said, throwing over a toffee crisp, 'just like…'

'Wednesday afternoons,' they both finished together and smiled.

It was a reference to the Wednesday afternoons the pair used to spend together after sixth form lessons playing PlayStation at George's. They would regularly do this instead of homework or revising – though this was only really to George's detriment – and George's Mum would bring the teas and chocolate bars into the room while they played for hours on end.

'Good times mate,' said Martin, who had nearly forgotten about the fact that the majority of his later teens were actually reasonably happy. It was probably because he spent most of it at George's house in his attic room. It was the perfect bolthole for teenage lads with everything from a PlayStation to a flat screen TV and sofa. George's family had welcomed him with open arms and looked after him well, they never said anything but they must've known his home life was tough after his parents had split. Martin thought that George's parents probably saw him as someone who would keep George in check and focused on his school work, unlike his other friends who were getting paralytic at house parties or getting in trouble with police community support officers. They were right to an extent, his help had managed to secure George a place at University and keep him on the straight and narrow. That was really all that mattered at the time and it was good for them both to bond.

'Bloody good these, aren't they,' said George, through a mouthful of chocolate.

The pair reminisced for a little while and it was nice for Martin to just feel at ease with the company of someone who wasn't his Mum or Gary. To have his mind taken off everything that had had happened over the last few weeks and months was a real blessing, but it wasn't until there was a lull in the conversation that Martin felt it was probably time to open up a bit. He felt as if he couldn't deny George some kind of truth any longer.

'So you're probably wondering what I was doing out in my car on a freezing February night aren't you,' he said unannounced.

It took George by surprise to hear Martin coming out with this all of a sudden, but yes, he had been wondering. A narrative had formed in his mind for sure, but now hopefully his friend might be able to fill in the blanks.

'I'd be lying if I said I hadn't,' responded George sympathetically.

Martin took a deep sigh. Compared with moments ago when they were talking of old times, he looked a different person all of a sudden. He felt embarrassed and ashamed.

'Well, there was a reason,' began Martin and he dropped his head, almost in shame. George could tell that this wasn't easy. 'It's okay mate. Take your time. No judgement here,' George offered. Martin took another deep breath and waited for the words to form again.

'I was out because…' he started, then just tailed off again, this time breathing deeply and putting his head back against the sofa with his eyes shut. George came and sat next to him on the sofa to show support.

'Look, I know this is hard mate. I can tell you want to say something, but maybe I can help,' George offered. He was always Martin's saviour, doing the talking when needed so this suited the situation.

'I have a feeling I know what you were doing out that night, but I guess we all just need to know a bit more as to why,' he continued. Martin sat up again, eyes open now. He nodded slowly.

'When you were, uh… in hospital during the coma, myself and your Dad went over to your flat to see if we could help make sense of things. It was only after seeing the bank statements and post-it notes in your kitchen that it started to click into place. I had heard the voice mailbox audio you left too, which confirmed what I feared. You wanted to kill yourself,' he said. The words were stark and slightly uncomfortable. But they were also true.

Martin stared blankly out into the room in front of himself, saddened and ashamed to hear it now as it was being played back to him. But there was also slight relief in this too.

'Yes,' he said finally, 'I wanted to die… I think.'

George looked across at his friend. It was heartbreaking to hear it. He already knew really, but having heard it, made it real.

'When you say, I think, do you know what you mean by that?' asked George in the most sensitive and quiet voice he could muster. He didn't want to overwhelm Martin, but he felt the need for his friend to talk.

'I don't know. I hated myself… hate, even,' he said, 'I just wanted to disappear. Everything went wrong. It all went to shit. Then I got myself into another load of shit and then that was even deeper shit. So in the end I just wanted to get out my head and have some kind of… release, you know?' he said, with the sadness increasingly more visible on his face.

George nodded sympathetically which also suggested to Martin it was safe to continue talking.

'In the end, I couldn't do it. I looked into the darkness and didn't want it. I don't know why, but I walked away from it,' he continued, 'And even that I hate myself for. I couldn't even do that properly!'

'Walked away from what mate?' asked George.

'I was going to jump into the gorge,' he said, 'I'd had visions in my sleep, in daydreams. It became a fascination for me. I wanted to try it out. Like I said, I wanted a release from life. I was getting so down, so depressed. I was just losing all the time and I hated myself,' he continued.

It was difficult to know what best to say in this situation. George had heard it now, but he was no therapist, so he did what he knew best, and that was to put his arm round his friend.

'It's okay mate, it's okay. Well done for telling me,' he said. The tears began and Martin sobbed quietly in his friends embrace.

'We can get through this Mart, trust me. Everything will be okay. We'll get you the help you need and ensure you're looked after. You're not alone in this,' said George, 'it's my turn to save your life,' he added.

Even in this tender moment of sadness and reflection, it was vintage George to recall a story from when they were younger. It had the right effect too, because it did raise a smirk from Martin.

'Are you ever going to not talk about that?' smiled Martin through a face flushed with tears.

'Not until I know that I can say for certain that I've done the same for you,' said George.

'Cheers mate,' he said.

'Let me get you some kitchen roll or something,' said George, and he disappeared into the kitchen for a moment, while Martin sat up and collected himself.

'Where the fuck is everything in this house?' said George to himself from the kitchen.

'Bottom of the cupboard under the sink,' called Martin from the lounge.

'Got it!,' was the shout that came back, 'I forgot your Mum is like some kind of robot when it comes to worktop clearance. It's mad that,' he laughed, re-entering the room.

'Thanks mate,' said Martin, blowing his nose hard into the towel as best he could with his left arm. George looked at him amused.

'I might be your best mate, but I ain't wiping snot off of you!' he laughed. 'Yeah fair enough,' replied Martin with a grin.

George sat back down on the sofa next to his friend.

'Seriously though mate, I know that was hard to admit all of that, but you've got to keep talking,' he said. 'Look, I ain't no therapist or anything, but there are people out there who are and it definitely helps to use them. I'll help you find the right person, someone who can listen and make sense of it all. Trust me, it will be okay.'

'Thanks mate. I hope so. I can't… I just can't carry on like I was, I know that,' replied Martin.

'Well let this be the moment that things change for the better. We're all here for you and we'll do it together,' said George.

He didn't quite know where all this was coming from, but George was turning into something of an inspiration here. All of a sudden, things seemed clearer, like there might be a glimmer of hope for the future. He was right, talking about it did help. It was hard, yes. Keeping things to yourself and generally just lying was easy. Telling the truth was hard, but it came with big rewards and most importantly, a clearer head.

The keys turned in the door and into the house walked Martin's Mum and Gary. George got to his feet to say hello and gave Martin's Mum a hug as well as shaking Gary by the hand.

'So nice of you to come over,' said Martin's Mum, 'I'm sure it's done him a world of good to see you George.'

'Yeah, we've had a good chat and a catch-up,' replied George. He wasn't about to go into much detail about what they'd talked about, but he was keen to discuss something else with the group that he'd been thinking about.

'So… since we're all here, I wanted to run something by you,' he started. They all took seats with Martin's Mum and Gary sat on the opposite sofa to where George and Martin were.

'When Mart is fit and able enough, I thought it might be a good idea for him to come and flat share with me in town. I can't bear the thought of him going back to that flat I saw him living in. Plus, I think the company would be good for us both and would keep him from being under your feet here too.'

Martin's Mum and Gary looked across at their son, and then at each other. 'Well Martin, what do you think?' asked his Mum.

Martin was a bit surprised, he hadn't seen this coming. He felt a little bit of excitement if truth be told. Away from his flat and no longer being stowed away in Gloucester, perhaps this would be the best thing for him?

'I… I, yeah. I'd love to mate, thanks,' he replied.

'I think it's a great idea,' added Gary, 'thank you George.'

'Look, we'll sort the logistics of all this at a later date, but it would be great to have you mate,' said George.

What he was doing in this moment was becoming the rescuer. He so desperately didn't want to see his friend fall by the wayside again – at least he could keep any eye on him and it was close to work. So close even, Martin could probably walk. There was work to do of course and George knew it would be hard, but looking after his friend with all he knew know was the absolute most important thing.

When it was time for George to leave, he embraced his friend again and told Martin just out of earshot from his Mum and Gary, 'Keep talking mate.'

'I will,' answered Martin.

So now it was out in the open. George knew the truth. Okay, so there was plenty more to pick at, what with all the experiences and low points that contributed to such poor mental health, but the beginnings of a recovery had started in earnest. He didn't know how much yet of course, time would tell, but it certainly felt like a little bit of light was starting to push through the darkness.

Martin sat back down on the sofa and Fergus resumed his position upon his lap. He still felt ashamed of his actions, but there was an element of relief from the admission he'd made to George about his struggles. He gently put his head back against the sofa and shut his eyes for a moment. It was only moments later that from the kitchen that he heard his Mum say, 'You can tell George Miller has been here, there's sugar everywhere on this worktop.'

Chapter 50

It was strange being back in the outside world again. Martin had been in a bubble ever since the accident and for two weeks he'd not even been conscious. His rehabilitation was seemingly on track and his broken arm was now out of the cast.

Physically, he was healing. He just had to make sure that mentally he healed at a similar pace. Though arguably, there was far more of a recovery required in this area. He'd hardly been alone over the course of the last couple of months. His Mum and Gary were always around for company and to essentially keep an eye on him. George would check in regularly too, giving him a boost every now and again which was good for his wellbeing. The challenge that hadn't been tackled just yet was the inevitable therapy that would follow. He'd finally confessed to his parents and Gary about what was happening on that fateful night and though it had come out in a jumbled mix of sorrow and an attempt at justifying his actions, at least it was out in the open. Gary had almost immediately set about contacting an old friend of a friend who he knew had previously trained as a counsellor.

'But how will I pay for it? Aren't these things extortionate?' pleaded Martin, who was not all that comfortable talking to a therapist, or indeed spending money he definitely didn't have.

'We'll get to that later,' said Gary softly, 'don't worry for now.'

There was also a conversation about going to see a doctor.

'I'm already seeing enough doctors, I don't need another one,' he had said irritably to his Mum.

'I don't mean about treatment for your injuries Martin. I'm talking about medication. Perhaps it would be worth a conversation?' his Mum suggested.

Martin sat there looking like a sultry teenager. Since the painkillers and sedatives dosage had been lowered, he was showing moments and outbursts of anger again. Mild they might seem, but enough so to cause concern.

'If I take any more medication I'll start fucking rattling,' he said.

'Martin! Language!,' his Mum responded.

Martin didn't even respond. He just continued to sit there looking glum with his arms folded. After an hours worth of debate it was finally decided that Martin would go and do some counselling. He'd definitely grown stronger over the course of his physical rehabilitation, with hospital visits and cognitive tests all going well. It was clear that he was starting to know his own mind again and although dark thoughts and irritability still consumed him from time to time, at least he knew the outcome of what ending your life might look like, which he wasn't that keen on either.

Where this left him for now was quite literally, in a state of purgatory. He desperately wanted to feel better, but he just couldn't visualise the pathway or access to the tools he would need to make that journey, which resulted in a state of confusion, angst and frustration. He rejected the idea of medication for now. Talking therapy would be the first step. Meeting a counsellor would be that first step and he was about to take it, albeit slightly grudgingly. Little did he know at the time that it would change everything, forever.

*

Bill Milton was a retired pharmacist who had been practicing counselling for nearly ten years. He had the kindness and warmth of someone who had a lot of life experience and knew how to communicate with literally anyone. Of course, Bill had faced much sterner challenges with his clientele. He had met people from all walks of life. Drug addicts, victims of domestic abuse, parents, couples, divorcees, teenagers, children and so many more. Martin was of course a complicated puzzle in his own right. Not one that he couldn't solve, but certainly one that required a little bit more thought. Perhaps Bill saw a bit of his former self in Martin?Someone who was unsure of who they really were. Someone who needed the confidence to communicate and let out a deep rooted angst that he held against himself.

'Martin, lovely to meet you,' said Bill kindly as Martin walked into the small but cosy room. It was filled with books and artwork, some slightly eccentric. It was like walking into somebody's study at their home, but in fact was just a simple office in a block of other commercial units.

Bill extended his hand to which Martin took and shook it back.

'Hello,' replied Martin.

'Please, take a seat. Would you like a drink of anything?' asked Bill.

'No, I'm okay thank you,' said Martin. He felt nervous. Nervous about what Bill was going to extract from his troubled mind. He knew he wouldn't be judged, but it certainly felt like there was the potential for an uncomfortable interrogation. Martin observed the surroundings. There was a jug of water, some house plants and a box of tissues on the side. He thought this was probably for the people who crumbled and burst into tears. He told himself that this wouldn't be necessary and would fight any inclination to break down into tears in front of another man, who at this point was a complete stranger.

'So, tell me Martin. How are you today?' asked Bill.

'I'm... I'm alright,' was the non-committal response. He didn't feel very chatty.

Bill looked typically relaxed, he wasn't phased by the obtuse nature of Martin's words and demeanour. He continued to explain a little bit more about himself and his experience as a counsellor. He generally came across as quite cheerful and understanding. There was a pause. Bill then pulled himself off of the sofa that was opposite to Martin and put a chair out into the middle of the room. Martin was surprised at this change of pace and seemingly completely random act. Bill sat back down on the sofa facing Martin.

'Martin, would you like to go and stand on the chair for a moment please?' asked Bill.

Martin did as he was asked. It seemed odd, but he didn't question it and got up and went to stand on the chair that was now positioned in-between them both. Once upon the chair, he looked down at Bill with a look that seemed to suggest, 'is that okay?'

Bill looked up, 'thank you Martin, you can get down now.' Martin sat back down on the sofa looking puzzled.

'I imagine you are thinking what the point of that exercise was,' started Bill, 'the reason being, is actually two fold. Do you think I asked you or told you?'

'Ummm... I don't know?' replied Martin, 'You told me?'

'Ahhh, so here is the first important thing to note. I asked if you would like to go and stand on the chair, rather than telling you. There is a key difference. This first intervention I made about asking you is to highlight the subtleties in what is truly being communicated and what we are fully hearing,' explained Bill, softly.

Martin looked back at him, feeling slightly embarrassed.

'Secondly, it is to show and I guess prove to me, that you already trust me seeing as you quite willingly stepped up and did it. This was of course secondary, but also very important,' he continued. 'In just that small act, we have come a very long way already Martin. Thank you.'

Martin had never been in a room with anyone like this before. Everything that was being said to him was just making sense. The ice was partly broken and yes, he did feel a little bit more comfortable and was starting to understand what this sort of therapy might be about. Bill had won his trust, not by being smart but by simply proving a theory. The next few questions would not be as easy though.

'So tell me Martin, you're here with me now and I understand you need help. What is the main thing you would like help with?' Bill asked inquisitively. It was his job to challenge and he was doing it in the most sensitive way possible.

'I… I, uh…,' he stammered. He took a deep breath and a sideways glance again at the box of tissues. He could feel himself crumbling already. It was hard to admit. He felt idiotic saying it out loud. Bill simply faced him just looking encouragingly across at him.

'I want… well, wanted… to die. I wanted to die. Well, disappear. I don't know,' said Martin.

'Okay,' answered Bill, 'And can you tell me if there was any specific reason for that?'

Martin just looked down at his lap. He felt defensive. He wanted to get out. He felt nervy and panicky again.

'There are no stupid answers here. No matter how big or small you think they might be. We can break it down bit by bit if we need to,' offered Bill.

There was a longer pause this time while Martin prepared his answer.

'I hate myself,' he said, finally.

'Hate is a very strong word Martin. What is it that you think you hate about yourself?' asked Bill.

Martin compiled a very long list in his head. There were too many to choose from. Too many mistakes, mishaps and stupid decisions by his own standards.

'I'm not sure,' Martin answered.

'What would you say other peoples perception of you is? Would you say they hate you too?' asked Bill. It was a challenging question, but fair nonetheless.

'I don't care what other people think about me,' answered Martin, somewhat defensively.

'Okay,' said Bill. He didn't seem convinced, 'Lets try this.'

He sat back in his seat and mused over an example.

'Do you think you have changed, or change, as a person in order to avoid criticism?' asked Bill.

It was a good question and pretty much cornered Martin.

'I… I don't like criticism, no,' he answered.

'Of course, nobody does. Criticism is often considered to be something negative and we put up barriers or change our attitudes when hearing it,' explained Bill. 'Can you think of a time when you may have done so?'

There were probably far too many. After all, he'd grown up in a house with his Mum and then had a long term relationship where he often kept quiet to keep the peace.

'Yes, lots actually,' he replied. 'There's been plenty of times when I felt I should've said no or not committed to something I didn't want to, but mainly because I didn't want to upset anyone or lose face.'

'Ahh yes, okay. And I'm not trying to catch you out here Martin, but this is a perfect example of you caring about what others opinion of you might be. Of course, it's natural to want others to like and respect us, but worrying too much about the thoughts others have is something that is completely out of our control. For you, now, it is about taking back control of who you are and who you want to be. Not about others – we may as well forget it – because people have their own opinions, as do you. The key thing? We can't control their opinion. So why spend precious energy on worrying about what others think when we have absolutely zero control over it,' explained Bill.

This made sense. It was so simple, but so true. Martin was hanging on every word now, just trying to drink it in.

'Now this isn't something that will just happen overnight. It takes time to understand and control our own minds. But there are ways of course. We need to expect and accept that people will have opinions of us – that's human nature. Focusing your energy on your own goals and values is a good way to start and this is going to be a big part of your learnings away from these sessions where we can then come back and discuss,' said Bill.

It was hard work, but it was progress. Bill was patient and understanding over the course of the hour they had spent in his office. He began to help make sense of the suicide attempt, the self-loathing and the shame Martin felt, but these topics were to be explored in more detail over the coming days, weeks and months.

'Your body language has changed entirely over the course of this session. It is my job to observe and it is something that has been very apparent,' said Bill.

Martin felt surprised, he hadn't even noticed.

'You've done very well today Martin, especially given the fact that it was your first session. I suggest we book in for the same time next week?' asked Bill.

'Yes. Yes, please,' said Martin, raising a smile for the first time during the session.

Martin walked away from the session with a head full of thoughts, as usual, but encouragingly they were clearer thoughts. They were less of a muddle. Even the smallest bits of advice from Bill were starting to build clarity. He knew there was a long road ahead, but at least it had been a positive start to therapy.

Gary was downstairs ready and waiting to take him back to his Mum's house. Martin was out in the world again, no longer confined to the four walls of the house. He had felt like a hopeless little animal coming back after hibernation, afraid and scared of the outside world and weakened by the lack of sunlight and nourishment. It felt strange, but gradually it would start to feel better. It had the feel of a new beginning, a recovery.

'All okay Mart?' asked Gary, opening the passenger door to his car.

'Yeah. Yeah it was, thanks,' replied Martin, probably the most optimistically sounding he had ever been.

'Excellent. Your Mum will be at W.I this evening but she's put us up a sausage dinner. Potatoes, veg and onion gravy. Does that sound alright?'

It was more than alright, thought Martin, because finally he had realised, even after just an hours session with Bill, that despite all the ups and downs, the good and the not so good, he knew he was loved. He just had to start giving himself some love too.

Chapter 51

It was nearly three weeks after the first counselling session and Martin was settling in at George's apartment for his first night living there. There had a been a number of conversations about Martin's continued rehabilitation with his parents and Gary, as well as George himself. In the end, the latter had insisted that if Martin was to return to some kind of normality, then the best place for him was with his friend. He would have a short commute for when he returned to work and the security of living with someone who knew him well enough, but wasn't immediate family.

Living with his Mum had never been a 'normal' experience for Martin anyway and although she had shown herself to be the most caring she had ever been towards him since the accident, it was time to find his feet outside the confines of the sanitised home she had once again established around him.

Martin's counselling was progressing well too. He'd learned a lot in the time he'd spent with Bill. They had hatched a wellbeing strategy for him to use and continued to break down the complexities of Martin's psyche, undoing the tangled circuits piece by piece. They went into a lot of detail about Martin's childhood and upbringing, particularly the details behind the relationship with his parents and their relationship with one another.Martin was talking about his past like never before and Bill was pulling information out of him that he scarcely thought even existed. Or rather, it had been pushed down so low and so far away that it didn't really exist, but it's legacy had left scars and lasting bruises on Martin's mental health.

'I would quite often blame myself… I suppose,' he had confessed, 'It didn't seem like anyone else's fault, so it must've been mine?'

'Yes, I see,' said Bill. 'This is very typical of a child who is caught in the middle of an adult relationship that has broken down. Rest assured, it was not your fault in any way shape or form. You were still developing as a person during that time, so learning behaviours tend to stick,' he explained.

Martin looked reflective. He could cite numerous examples of what Bill was referring to. 'And the rages? What about those?' Martin asked innocently, but also searchingly.

'I suppose this is somewhat similar in terms of a learning behaviour. You were growing up in quite a toxic atmosphere after your father left so it would be surprising if you hadn't picked up on some of the behaviours your Mother was showing.

Certainly some of the examples you have told me about anyway,' said Bill.

Martin had told Bill about the time when his Dad left and his Mum had packed up every single item of clothing his Dad owned and sent it straight to the charity shop. When his Dad returned the following day to pick up his things, there was nothing left and a blazing row had taken place. Martin was already a sensitive soul and these experiences only added to his anxiety when growing up.

Bill had the sensitivity to explore these themes with Martin and to break them down into something that just simply made sense. Perhaps one of the most emotive and striking things he had said to Martin was about being in the moment. To put behind him the past and not worry about the future – both of which cannot be controlled.

'Yesterday is history and tomorrow is a mystery… but today is a gift. That is why it is called the present,' Bill would say. Where the quote came from wasn't too important. It was quiet twee really, but had plenty of meaning as well as a stark reality that this was actually the truth.

'Learn to love the present and be thankful of the gift that it brings,' Bill explained.

Martin was starting to learn it in some respects. He blocked out quite a lot of the noise that surrounded his past – the traumas, the heartache, the self-loathing and more. It was hard to get a complete grip on, but it was a work in progress. As for the future, well, Martin was still taking his recovery and indeed his life one day at a time. Bill had taught him a powerful way to help deal with this aspect of things.

'I would quite often get worried about what was to come. I felt like I had no sense of direction after breaking up with Helena and it's caused me to worry at levels I never thought possible. I guess just worrying in general too,' he admitted.

'You would consider yourself a creative wouldn't Martin? As in, your work. It's a creative pursuit in some ways. It requires a visual aspect that is integral to the output, am I right?' asked Bill.

'Yes. I guess so,' he answered.

'Well think of it like this… because visualisation of the problem can really help us learn about the impact and the affect of things in our mind. If you visualise your work on a daily basis and problem solve through visualisation then consider the thought of this,' and Bill began to roughly draw out the image of a backpack.

'This is a bag. Let's make it in into a backpack. That way we can carry it on our shoulders,' he said, drawing the straps and outline of a simple backpack.

'If we are wearing the backpack everyday of our lives and it is full of things, it will be heavy and become tiring, yes?' he asked.

'I would agree, yes,' answered Martin.

'So in which case, imagine that this backpack is full of worries. It's full of thoughts and fears – it's a big bag of worry that we carry around with us all the time,' explained Bill, 'do you think this would become tiring?' he asked.

'Of course, yes,' said Martin.

'So sometimes we have to consider whether carrying that backpack is always worth it. Indeed, we may need to wear the backpack through life, but it doesn't have to be full to the brim. It is natural to worry, so let's help ourselves and break things down. Imagine removing what we don't need and just carrying a more manageable sized backpack? In fact, it doesn't even have to be a backpack, I'll leave that one to you,' and he drew a smaller looking bag next to the one that had been drawn full to brim with things.

'My question to you is, which one of the bags do you think would be easier to carry?' he smiled willingly over at Martin. 'Don't worry, this is not a trick question.'

'This one,' said Martin, pointing at the smaller of the two bags that Bill had drawn.

'Yes of course, it's simple. The reason we choose this one is because it won't weigh us down as much. It's manageable and easy to carry. This is much like worry itself. We can cope or manage with a finite amount, but when we consider every single worry in our head, or rather, cramming them into that backpack, it becomes unsustainable. It's heavy and it's overwhelming. Therefore, carrying all our worries on our shoulders brings us down. Always think about how we can unload some of those things in that bag to make our journey through life more manageable,' Bill concluded.

Martin looked back and nodded in agreement.

'Here, you can have this. That'll be on display in the Tate one day,' he said, passing Martin the sketch with a grin. Martin smiled back at him.

So many of Martin's sessions with Bill would generally have one of these lightbulb moments where breaking down an issue or a problem was either put into plain English by Bill, or positioned in a clever way that just simply made it make sense.

That was the beauty of his therapy, it wasn't all doom and gloom. There were of course tough sessions spent on that well worn leather sofa. The box of tissues had been used on more than one occasion for the tears that flowed. For Martin though, rather than feel inferior for crying out his emotions, he felt stronger and more capable. He'd learned to be honest with himself by showing emotion, as well as gaining the confidence to talk about how he felt. There had been a huge step change in the way he viewed himself, as well as the way he wanted to be seen by others.

Bill had done his job. Therapy was working.

Chapter 52

18 months later

Martin and George were back at the Hilltop Arms enjoying some pub fare on a Thursday evening after work. It was nearly 18 months since the pair of them had been here, where Martin's mind had been consumed with thoughts of disappearance. They could well remember the evening, with the wake happening in the main lounge bar.

'You know, I had a feeling something was up at the time. But I have to admit, you did a bloody good job to hide it,' said George.

'I know, I know. I'm sorry. You know I've always been quiet so I could probably get away with it… and I guess I did,' Martin replied.

'Well it's taught me a valuable lesson as well to be honest. I could sense something, but I never truly believed that there was anything up. Which breaks my heart to know you were struggling,' George continued.

'I've learned a hell of a lot in the last year. It's certainly been a journey,' said Martin, 'and not one I want to take again!'

'Well, I guess that calls for another drink then,' said George, collecting the glasses.

'Cheers, G,' replied Martin.

He felt that familiar squeeze on the shoulder that George would do, but this time it felt like more. It felt comforting and supportive, because he wasn't hiding anything. For George, he knew now of how he could help his friend if the signs were there.

Martin got out his phone and scrolled through his notifications. He had a couple of work emails (they could wait until the morning), a message from his Mum to see how he was and another which grabbed his attention. Moments later, George was at his shoulder with the drinks and playfully teasing Martin about being on his phone.

'Oooh, who's the lucky lady then?' he laughed.

Martin quickly locked his phone and put it face down on the table.

'Oh, nobody,' he said, with a grin on his face.

'Yeah, yeah whatever!' laughed George.

Martin was clearly a bit bashful, but George let him off with a knowing look and a wink.

'So how's things going then mate? We obviously talk a lot more these days, but I'm just checking in,' asked George.

'Do you know what?' Martin replied, putting down his drink, 'I feel positive. It's the first time in a long time that I can say that. But I really do. For once, I've got things in life and in my mind with how I want them. I'm not wrestling against some kind of inner monster telling me not to do something or saying I'm not good enough. I'm starting to see the future now,' he said.

'That's great to hear mate,' replied George, 'I'm so glad to see you happy and settled. If there was one good thing that has come out of the bad, it's the fact that we've reconnected and spent some great times together. Even if it's just been at home or here at the pub. I really underestimated the significance of that quality time with a friend and I'm so pleased to have that and…well you, back.'

Martin was feeling a bit emotional, George's words were powerful.

'Thanks mate, I truly appreciate everything you've ever done for me,' said Martin. 'Well, what did I say? I think I owed you one from Year 8 Science didn't I!' he laughed.

In many ways, the moment felt a little bit like an ending, but perhaps more so the beginning of a new chapter as they reflected together. The friends had lived with one another for about a year and at one time or another either one of them was going to be looking at a relationship of some sort. George had been going steady with a girl for around 6 months now and although it was hard to say whether that would transpire into anything more serious, it was a small sign that both he and Martin probably wouldn't be living together forever. Martin himself was still recovering, doing therapy and working on ways to improve his financial situation. George had assured him there was no rush to move on and that helped take off the pressure, because although the relationship with his Mum had improved immensely, he was not prepared to move in with her again.

'So how about you and Lauren then, going well?' Martin asked.

'Yeah, all good mate. She's a great girl and I can see this one actually going somewhere,' he said wryly, 'There's been a few false starts over the years hasn't there!'

'Well, it was always going to take the right kind of woman to tame the great George Miller!' joked Martin. The pair laughed and reminisced for a while over George's legendary dating record, the best and the worst of it. 'There's someone for everyone, Mart, I truly believe that,' said George.

'I know, I know. It's just about where to find them,' he said jokingly, if not slightly cynically.

His phone buzzed on the table again and without thinking, he turned it over immediately to see who the message was from. His heart gave a flutter of excitement as he read the message. George peered over the table, but this time Martin wasn't hiding his phone.

'I think you may have found her by the looks of things,' he said.

'Shall we say tomorrow night, 7.00ish at mine? x'

That was the message they both read on the screen in front them.

'I know it's only the start, but I think you might be right mate,' said Martin proudly. He tapped out a message that would then start to define the rest of his days.

'7.00 perfect, looking forward to seeing you again x'

And then it was phone away again.

'Fancy another one?' said Martin, almost triumphantly.

George looked on proudly at his friend who was barely recognisable from the man who had sat in front of him 18 months ago.

'You bet mate,' he said.

Epilogue

5 years later

The sun rained in through the blinds and greeted Martin's face as he rolled over. It was Sunday morning. He'd slept well. He loved his bed these days. Learning to love his sleep and not be afraid of the dark horrors that might escalate in his dreams were a thing of the past and it was now a real sanctuary for his wellbeing. Furthermore, he simply loved these kind of mornings, the Sunday mornings that were bright and full of promise. He never seemed to recognise the potential of a day before, but now, he would revel in the thought of what the day might bring. It was these kind of mornings that could be savoured, where he felt lucky to be alive. He looked over at the bedside table. It was later than he thought, 10.30am in fact. A travel mug full of tea was placed on the side. It was still warm of course. A thoughtful act to greet him for when he woke. He leant over and sipped from the mug and noticed a small note beside it.

'Thought you could do with a lie-in this morning! We'll be back around mid-morning x'

Martin smiled a smile that had become increasingly more familiar on his face in recent times. He sat up in bed with his tea, feeling content. This was a far cry from the lonely mornings in his flat that had become poison for his mental wellbeing. He was in a place now where he felt loved and respected. Better still, he felt capable of giving love and sharing his life with others. He put his head back against the head board and softly closed his eyes, letting the morning sun warm his skin.

Dozing only momentarily, he heard the door downstairs. Seconds later, there were footsteps thundering up the stairs and a cry of 'Daddy! Daddy! Wake up!'

Moments later, Martin's peace and quiet was broken by his four year-old daughter. 'Hello darling,' he said, giving her a big hug as she jumped upon him.

'Daddy, Daddy, we saw a big squirrel get chased by a cat!'

'Oh that's lovely darling, was it the big cat from the house on the corner?' Martin replied. 'Yeah, yeah! And he did a big meow then smiled at me,' said the little girl.

'The cat did a smile at you? That's amazing! I didn't know cats could smile?' asked Martin, playfully.

'Yes, they can! They really can!,' said the little girl excitedly.

'Niamh, your Daddy was having a nice lie-in!' said the woman who had appeared in the doorway.

'It's alright, I've had enough rest. Thanks for the lie-in this morning. Where have you two been?' he asked, inviting her in next to him with open arms.

'Oh just a short walk to the park to make sure Fergus had a little run around,' said Ruth, settling down on the bed in his arms.

'Mummy, Mummy, are we going to keep Fergus?' asked Niamh excitedly.

'Well we'll have to see what Nanny says. I'm sure she'll want him back once her and Grampy are back from holiday,' she explained.

Martin grinned to himself. He could well remember the time when Fergus was nearly not with them at all. He had done well to reach his twilight years as a dog.

The scene Martin found himself in was one of contentment. It was a feeling that had been in very short supply during the height of his depression. However, nearly six years on from the day of his accident, he'd made a recovery that he barely thought possible at the time. He'd achieved a life that was scarcely available to him and was now living in what was probably always his dream of a stable family. He was living with a someone who shared a similar ambition as he did and a beautiful daughter who provided him with the playfulness and innocence of youth he had once felt deprived of. He'd managed to make Partner at his architects firm, a goal he had always set himself, but for all the accolades and pride he felt right now at the situation he found himself in, it had come with a lot of hard work and self reflection. The sitting in front of groups of people to discuss his gambling and financial issues, spending hours sat opposite Bill and talking about feelings, emotions, coping strategies and ways to triage himself for certain situations – Bill had been nothing short of a lifesaver and the two still talked every four to six weeks.

And of course there was Ruth. A friendship had been rekindled (with some encouragement from George, almost immediately after he had found out) and when the pair had moved in together, they never looked back. Martin had spent nearly two years with George paying low rent and getting his life back on track. Although there were a lot of factors in his recovery, perhaps none were more important than that of his friendship with George. His rock and his saviour. The stereotypes of two men in their thirties living together can conjure images of going out, living in a bit of cesspit and generally not changing their bedding couldn't have been further from the truth.

Cooked meals with a balanced diet, early nights, gym and fitness routines and coffee morning conversations about how one another was doing. It was a far cry from the clichés of Men Behaving Badly. In many ways, Martin thought George had put his life on hold to help his friend, but when it was put to him he would wave away that sort of claim.

'It's been the best two years of my life mate,' George would say, with a sense of pride that was almost palpable.

So as he sat there in bed with Ruth (soon to be his wife) and his daughter, he could reflect on the journey that had taken him there, but he didn't have to dwell on it. The demons, the inner torture, the self-deprecating cynicism and a depressive monologue that dragged him through life like he was constantly wading through deep mud – he'd learned to package it all up in a place within his mind that was safe. None of it preoccupied him now. They may appear, but only fleetingly. He was able to manage it, as well as tackle it when he needed to. Life had turned out in a way he could never have predicted. He could finally celebrate this and feel proud to be living life like life was intended to be lived. To experience the ups and the downs, to enjoy the good and learn from the bad. He'd once stared into the abyss, seeing only a ghostly reflection of himself looking back through the black. If there was a tunnel with the smallest shred of light during that time it could barely be seen.

Gradually, day by day and piece by piece, he'd built something of his own design. A life he was enjoying and a life he wanted. Staring into the abyss was no more, he would stare into the mirror now and smile.

He was now standing on the edge of something beautiful that he could look down upon and admire. And that was life itself.

Acknowledgements

I have to say a massive thanks to my family for their constant love and support. I can scarcely imagine life without you, you're my constant inspiration and bed-rock with which I wouldn't have been able to do this without you.

Special thanks to my Father, (and part-time editor) Spence for his editorial advice and giving up his precious time in retirement to do so.

To my closest friends who offered their thoughts, their encouragement and feedback which helped me pursue a true passion.

And special thanks to Phil, I am so very grateful for your counsel.

Last but not least is of course to you, the reader. Thank you.

- Stuart Lee, July 2024

Author's note

If you have experienced any of the mental health and wellbeing themes that have been discussed in this book then please do not hesitate to reach out to the following channels (there are of course many many more).

Please don't suffer in silence, someone will always be there to listen.

www.talkclub.org
Talk Club is a UK male mental health charity helping men to improve their mental health.

www.thecalmzone.net
Every week 125 people in the UK take their own lives. CALM exists to change this - by offering life-saving services, provoking national conversation, and bringing people together to reject living miserably.

www.mind.org.uk
Mind are here to fight for mental health. For support, for respect, for you.

www.samaritans.org
Samaritans are here, day or night, for anyone who's struggling to cope, who needs someone to listen without judgement or pressure.

Printed in Great Britain
by Amazon

56234113R00209